ADVANCE PRAISE FOR **wonderkid**

"Wesley Stace has always been the only genuinely gifted fiction writer who also happens to be a rock star, but *Wonderkid* is the book he was born to write. And if you prefer your novels brazen, poignant and hilarious, as I do, you were born to read it. Like a great show, this will stay with you long after the last cymbal crash and power strum."

—SAM LIPSYTE, **author of *The Ask***

"Wesley Stace has written one of the very few novels about rock bands and the music business that doesn't have a single false note or outsiderwannabe pretensions. It's a relief—and a joy—to read about the weird particularities of the lives of musicians by someone who knows the world so intimately. He deconstructs, with an elegant and sharp eye, the heightened sense of the unreality of fame, the relentless grind of touring, and the Ego and the Id made deliciously manifest in the Wonderkids (my favorite new band). He is both ruthless and compassionate, but never cynical. I thought about these characters even when I wasn't reading the book, and the story will stay with me for a very long time. *Wonderkid* has both enormous entertainment value and serious literary worth, a very hard trick to pull off." —ROSANNE CASH

"Highly pleasurable. And unusual, not least because this is a rock 'n' roll novel written by someone who actually knows what he's talking about." —PETER CAREY, **author of *Parrot and Olivier in America***

"Rock 'n' roll is an infantile business, but never more so than in the hands of the Wonderkids, a group of post-teens, playing music for pre-teens, whilst living chaotic adult lives. In *Wonderkid*, Wesley Stace absolutely captures the band experience: the triumphs, the letdowns, the sell-outs, the success, and the scandal, with an extra helping of absurdity. There were times reading this book that I could actually smell the dank dressing rooms, or feel the bus rolling down the highway to the next gig." —PETER BUCK

"Finally, a sex, drugs and rock 'n' roll book for Dan Zanes fans! *Wonderkid* also happens to be one of the best books about fathers and sons since Turgenev."

—GARY SHTEYNGART, **author of *Super Sad True Love Story***

"I can't believe that this amazing book exists. *Wonderkid* is by far the best music novel I've ever read, and the most unexpectedly wild ride I've ever been on. Every detail is perfect. Do you want to read about the music business? Family dynamics? Children's entertainment? The often uneasy relationship between the US and the UK? The creative process? This book lays it all out with love and wild imagination. *Wonderkid* is uplifting, inspiring, unhinged, and unpredictable, just like rock 'n' roll itself."
                                                    —DAN ZANES

"Wesley Stace's *Wonderkid* is a marvelous satiric mashup of rock 'n' roll and pack 'n' plays. It's sweet and funny and knowing—and this is me, holding up my lighter for more."
            —JOSHUA FERRIS, **author of *The Unnamed***

"At turns illuminating and heartbreaking—but always funny— *Wonderkid* is *A Visit from the Goon Squad* for the kiddie music world. A pitch-perfect excavation into the lighter heart of the music industry."
                                                    —COLIN MELOY

"*Wonderkid* is a gem, a rock 'n' roll novel written from the inside, with an insider's knowledge of music and the music business, and all the exhilaration and indignities that come with the territory. Wesley Stace is a wise and witty guide to the career of Blake Lear and the Wonderkids, a fictional band that becomes so real over the course of the novel that you'll think you heard them on the radio."
            —TOM PERROTTA, **author of *Little Children***

"Wesley Stace writes with verve, pace, and great good humor. *Wonderkid* is a flamboyant novel about rock 'n' roll, sex and drugs, broken dreams, and Brits on tour in America. Buy it at once."
                —PATRICK MCGRATH, **author of *Asylum***

Wonderkid

Wonderkid

A NOVEL

Wesley Stace

THE OVERLOOK PRESS
NEW YORK, NY

For Tilda & Wyn

This edition first published in hardcover in the United States in 2014 by
The Overlook Press, Peter Mayer Publishers, Inc.

141 Wooster Street
New York, NY 10012
www.overlookpress.com

For bulk and special sales, please contact sales@overlookny.com,
or write us at the address above.

Cataloging-in-Publication Data is available from the Library of Congress

Book design and type formatting by Bernard Schleifer
Manufactured in the United States of America
ISBN: 978-1-4683-0801-3

FIRST EDITION
10 9 8 7 6 5 4 3 2 1

"And every one said, 'If we only live,
We too will go to sea in a Sieve,—'"

—EDWARD LEAR

Wonderkid

> "Thank you. If you appreciate the tuning so much,
> I hope you will enjoy the playing more."

BLAKE LEAR KNEW ALL THE GUITAR CHORDS HE'D EVER KNOW by the age of twelve.

He first picked up a tennis racket when he was ten. The Eureka moment: alone in the house, everyone else at church (a sore throat his excuse), listening to his sister's copy of the Beach Boys' *20 Golden Greats*, on the cover of which a ghostly silver surfer danced on sparkling aquamarine waves. Admiring himself in the mirror as he mimed the words to "Surfin' U.S.A.," he spied his father's racket, picked it up, and pretended he was riding that surfboard, miraculously playing the guitar: a Donnay Allwood, the Borg model, black frame and rainbow flag stripes. People said they lip-synced on *Top of the Pops* anyway, so what was the difference? Was it essential to make noise? Did he actually need a real guitar? (This would remain his attitude for much of his professional career.)

As *20 Golden Greats* played on—"Fun Fun Fun," "I Get Around"—Blake became a guitar player. By the stately choral fade-out of "Break Away," the last song on side two, Blake was feeling the vibrations in his ears, the sensations at his fingertips, and . . . he needed a real guitar. Only a fictional sore throat and the absence of any hard cash held him back.

• • •

The next day, he walked home from school via the High Street so he could window-shop G&D Keyboards. There wasn't a dedicated guitar store in town, but G&D, despite its keyboard allegiance, had a whole wall full. On impulse, Blake popped in, ostensibly to leaf through the music books, desperate to model one of the guitars that hung like jackets, ready to try on. But he didn't find himself drawn to the gaudy electrics. He wanted an acoustic, although not one of the ones with elastic strings that you plucked in the lonely corner of a Spanish restaurant.

The owner of G&D, eagle eye trained to spot a fledgling musician, could distinguish a wannabe guitarist; keyboard players never looked that haunted. He first tried to foist an unwanted classical guitar on the boy ("easier on the fingers") but was wholly ignored. An instrument finally negotiated (a beginner's model with tortoiseshell pickguard), it became clear that Blake couldn't actually play at all, He could strum the open strings, head thrown back, and move his fingers nimbly up and down the fret-board, but not both at the same time, and to zero musical effect. Mr. G&D hovered ever closer, coaxing the guitar away after its strings were given a brutal twanging workout.

"Just seeing what it can do," Blake remarked, but what he really wanted was to see how good he looked; unfortunately G&D Keyboards didn't have a full-length mirror. All the guitars were too big, but a scale model was out of the question: Blake wanted the real one that he'd always have. He was looking for something to grow into.

"Maybe you want to bring your mum in some time." Always easier to deal with the parents, given that the kid didn't have fifty quid in his back pocket. Or a checkbook.

"My grandmother or my dad," said Blake.

"And you know we can always fix you up with lessons."

Blake's eyes fell upon a lustrous black Eko twelve-string. He had never heard of a twelve-string, never known that double the strings was an option (though the advantages were obvious), was unaware of Lead Belly and the Byrds, but felt instantaneously drawn to the massive headstock with its glittering silver tuning pegs, all twelve of them: twice what everybody else had. He was in love.

"You don't want that," said Mr. G&D, reluctantly getting it down. He didn't want the kid's fingerprints all over it either. "Very specific, a twelve-string. Not really a good starter guitar."

"How much?" It looked good on Blake. Even Mr. G&D could see that.

"Forty pounds. But you really don't want it."

"Why not?" It was shiny.

"Hard to play. Because of the twelve strings."

"Can't you take six of them off, and then it's like a normal one?"

"Well . . ." Mr. G&D was reluctant. "The necks are somewhat wider so it would still be hard to play."

"Adaptable, though," said the ten-year-old. The guitar was as good as his.

Back home, Blake concocted a story in which he had somehow haggled the man down and the guitar represented the deal of the century: a deal that would disappear unless seized upon immediately. His grandmother gave in and bought it for him, while his father, Barry, moaned about the lack of use of the ancient upright piano; in his imagination, both sons—Blake and his brother, Jack—had shown promise. Now no more than a picture shelf, the piano had hardly been played since their mother had gone.

Blake graduated from air guitar to real guitar, via the Donnay, in a week. Jack, being two years older, also wanted a guitar and got one for his birthday: a cheaper electric, a bright red Canora, with the tiniest, tinniest amplifier in the world.

Blake wasn't Blake then. His name was James, therefore Jimmy, but only Jack and his father called him Jimmy. They never graduated to Blake, even after he changed it. And Jack's name wasn't actually Jack; it was Jeremy, but no one ever called him Jeremy except his father. Jack was short for Ejaculation, a name given to him as a pubert by (of course) Blake.

At school, the brothers kept their distance. They walked there separately; never acknowledged each other on the playground; showed no outward signs of being related. Inasmuch as they behaved fraternally at home, they did so mainly to please their parent and their bedridden grandmother. But the sudden appearance of these two guitars brought them together and led them to discover music, rather than the other way round.

Blake was slight for his age and full of quirks: he was given to bursting into song, making up gibberish, and even, in moments that initially caused his father some worry, exclaiming exuberantly in a manner suggestive of Tourette's. It wasn't. It wasn't even a tic. He was just the oddball who occasionally yelled "Quack!"

One of his favorite pastimes was to conduct, which he did at the top of the grass verge behind the cafeteria during break. The massed ranks of the orchestra waited for him to tap his music stand and raise his hand; they then played extremely beautifully under his direction, as any passerby could judge from the pained facial expressions of their conductor and the exquisitely felt movements of his baton. There was no orchestra, but Blake did carry an actual baton in his top blazer pocket.

More than once, Blake's unconsciously brazen parading of his rich fantasy life caused the baton to be stolen, lobbed beyond his flailing grasp. One morning, Jack stepped in; the talisman and its owner were never parted again. This was shortly after the guitars arrived—as if, by their purchase alone, the brothers had formed a band. And you didn't let outsiders mess with your bandmates. They were brothers-in-arms.

Blake didn't want formal musical lessons, particularly at school. Besides, when he was fronting the band, would he actually need a guitar at all? Wouldn't he just strut around? Swing his microphone? Set his hat on fire? Or wear one covered with mirrors? He'd seen it all on *Top of the Pops*—surely being a lead singer was the best job in the world. He bought songbooks with picture chords, often ineptly transcribed, though the Gs and the Cs, the Ds and the E minors were generally in the right place. Those were the only chords he ever learned, and one of them fit more or less anything, particularly when, under Jack's guidance, he started attempting to annex the neck of his guitar with a capo. And he played a lot of chords he didn't need to know the names for, because he only hit a couple of the strings. When there finally was a band, he left them to work out the details. He brought the words, sometimes the tunes. Jack was in charge of the rest.

Jack, on the other hand, was a natural student, a born side-man. He took lessons with a Mr. Stagg, whose qualification was that he had once been, and may still have been, in a band. Stagg had some outré theories about the connection between scales (what he called "the five-chord cycle") and man's emergence from the slime, which if made public might have earned him a severe reprimand from the headmaster. Though he taught Jack nothing musical whatsoever, he helped him master the fingering of every scale—that was all Jack needed, at least according to Stagg. The rest came from within.

Jack and Blake watched *Top of the Pops* together, but they were seeing two different shows. Blake watched the singer. Jack's eyes were on the guy with the big gear, who could blend into the background for a breather, then dart out at an opportune moment, and, while the front man was otherwise occupied delivering the song, play to the girls in the front row, occasionally singing a harmony to remind them all that it was, in fact, mostly *his* band; that true authority was quiet authority; that, unlike someone else, he didn't need to be front and center all the time. Learning the guitar was easy for Jack: he couldn't do it, he couldn't do it . . . then he could. At which point he'd pick another thing he couldn't do.

As the school year went on, imaginary orchestra was suspended, and the brothers were regularly having "rehearsals" at break in the cricket pavilion (unless Judo kept them out, in which case they'd climb a tree; unless it was raining, in which case they'd stay in the classroom). They didn't really play music, except inasmuch as Jack practiced scales. What they did was make plans. As a result, two became four, and they had a nameless band. Pete and Steven were drafted: neither could play an instrument, but both had access to one—Pete knew "Chopsticks" on the piano and Steven's older brother was a drummer. They all liked the Beatles—everyone liked the Beatles—so they decided on some songs they could introduce into their repertoire. "Lovely Rita" was at the top of the list. Very little music was made, but a name was finally decided upon: the Meetles, whose first album would be called *Beat the Meetles*. A singable manifesto was produced, ratified by the four members: "We will never play sport again / Unless we are coerced / Band practice comes first." Their time was mostly consumed with the design of "In Concert" posters, which, advertising notional rather than actual events, lacked dates and venues. One surviving example simply says "The Meetles In Concert," and boasts an eye-catchingly Russian constructivist design, duplicated on the old machine in the school attic, then hand-colored.

Eventually, music was made. The count-ins sounded authentic and promised much, but things got weird after 1,2,3,4. This was a new band—same members, but all options for the graphic design of the word Meetles having been exhausted, they were now the Brutles, a tribute to their two greatest musical influences: the Beatles, and Beatles parody band, the Rutles. Jack had picked up a copy of the Rutles' soundtrack, *All You Need Is Cash*, at a market, and, though the whole thing was obviously a joke, the songs were in no way inferior to the Beatles' blueprints, and had the distinct advantage of being funnier. The Beatles were odd, in part because (according to Blake's father) they were "druggy," but they weren't actually funny like the Rutles or goofy like the Monkees. The brothers didn't *get* all the Rutles jokes, but at least they knew when to laugh.

And so the Brutles were born. Although there was still no specific repertoire, plans for a concert (involving the school tennis court and some lights from the drama department) were at an advanced stage. The poster for this gig in the sky surpassed even the Meetles' most ambitious promotional campaigns.

The Brutles needed a project. They also needed to learn to play together. Jack was getting good, and Blake had mastered the capo, which no longer flipped off like a tiddlywink, but Pete and Steven were lagging. There was no strife within the Brutles' camp, however—the production of the occasional poster made everything official. It was now unavoidably time for songwriting, so Blake decided to write a modest rock opera. The obvious influences were *Jesus Christ Superstar, Joseph and the Amazing Technicolor Dreamcoat*, and the spate of shorter song cycles (*Holy Moses, Captain Noah and His Floating Zoo*) that were choir practice staples. The recipe was straightforward: first, a biblical story—literally anything would do. Look up the best known, avoid Jesus, Joseph, Moses, and Noah, and you were made; amplify to include colorful extra characters; and then give each a number in the style of a well-loved musical genre. At the tender age of eleven, Blake had cracked the code.

And—hey presto!—*The Prodigal*. Details remain sketchy. Jack remembers a song called "Pistol," Pete can still play one called "With You" (I remember him plunking it out on a piano backstage somewhere) and Blake is convinced he shoehorned "I Know She'd Leave Me," the very first song he ever wrote, in there as well: "Not *I knew*," he always said, "but *I know*." As though this mild temporal confusion had been the secret of its success.

So there was an unperformed rock opera based on a parable, a repertoire of potential cover versions for a nonexistent concert, a series of limited edition posters, and some unoriginal originals. Not bad for a boy just about to turn twelve.

Public school beckoned: common entrance, scholarships, the absence of girls, the advent of masturbation. It was 1977, the dawn of slogans on T-shirts, and while the front pages of the music papers heralded the onslaught of punk, the back still contained advertisements for comical posters (one buzzard says to another "Patience, my ass! I'm gonna kill something!"), Oxford Bags (for the complete David Bowie look), offers of complete sets of live photos from Kiss concerts, and spoof adverts ("guy with quarter-inch prick seeks nasal sex"). Schoolboys everywhere, Blake among them, opened wide, bracing themselves for punk's astringent. Death to Emerson, Lake & Palmer!

But not long after composing *The Prodigal*—a few months into his thirteenth year—Blake happened to see a TV show, *So It Goes*, at which point everything changed. *So It Goes* was the talk of the playground: one of the few shows that let punk bands actually play—national exposure that was often the occasion for newsworthy behavior, the reason Blake was watching in the first place. So, this one episode: Tony Wilson interviewing Jonathan Richman about his music. Wilson says that when he hears Richman accused of simplicity and naivety, his reaction is: "What about William Blake?" And Richman, referring to Blake's poem "The Lamb," which has aired earlier on the show, replies: "You know what? I just started crying. I've been crying for the last five minutes, listening to that thing at the beginning by William Blake. It's so funny that you would mention that right now, because if that makes me simplistic, liking stuff like that, then I'm one, 'cause that little thing 'Little lamb who made thee' that just wet me up."

"In the nineteenth century," continues Tony, approaching peak smarm, "they said Blake was simplistic, that he was an idiot . . ." Then he deadpans: "*And now he's dead popular.*" And when the camera pans back to Jonathan Richman, he's in tears, barely able to respond.

In tears!

In 1977, crying on TV was *out there.* Displaying any overt emotion besides anger, producing any bodily fluid besides snot, phlegm, bile, and piss—particularly in response to a poem about a lamb—was severely antithetical to those unsentimental times. Richman's tears were a formative event in Blake Lear's life.

The young Blake found a used copy of the poems and engravings of William Blake, who reminded him of Lewis Carroll and Edward Lear, both of whom he'd been introduced to by his mother. She'd read him so much Lear in bed—"The Dong with a Luminous Nose," "Calico Pie," "The Jumblies"—that, though Blake understood that Lear was the author, he had been under the mistaken impression that the word *Lear* was itself a synonym for poem, like *ballad* or *verse*: *lear.* And when *Junior Choice*, for which he was now too old, intruded on Radio One on Saturday morning, Blake still sang along to Elton Hayes's sweet version of "The Owl and the Pussycat." He was beginning to put two and two together.

From then on, he lost faith in his religious musical. Indeed, he no longer wanted to make any sense at all. He would write in a state of complete innocence, summon up that little lamb or the elegant foul in verse; he wanted to write about sweet things, to make nonsense. He didn't like the aggression in the air, the kids who'd stolen his baton, their scruffy seven-inch singles, their Xeroxed fanzines, their lapels full of safety pins and badges for bands whose art direction never deviated from the ransom note font. It must have felt like punk was going to go on forever. So he decided that he would be a man out of time, that he would opt out altogether. That was when he wrote his first poetry, and the first lyric that is recognizably Blake-ian, if not Blakeian. It appeared in the school magazine and won a prize. A sample:

> The shiny-coats are coming!
> The Hummingbirds aren't humming.
> They're flittering and anxious, asking why:
> Why, I cry—
> Why, I *cry*—

With the winning book token (also good for records), he zipped down to WH Smith, but instead of the new Siouxsie and the Banshees (he left that to the baton stealers, although Jack made sure he heard it), he bought the *Collected Poetry* of Edward Lear, a reprint of Rackham's illustrations of *Alice in Wonderland*, and a presentation edition of Carroll's verse.

And, at the age of thirteen, before he was even at his senior school, you have, in a nutshell, Blake Lear.

Years later, he still had that Richman clip on VHS. I saw it in the back of the bus enough times to memorize it. He even went to the trouble of having it transferred to American standard, no mean feat in those days. He had some Morecambe and Wise and some Two Ronnies transferred, a Spike Milligan or two, some George Formbys—but not much; only the things he couldn't live without.

2

"Do we have permission to jam?
Then jam we must!"

JACK WENT TO THE LOCAL COMPREHENSIVE, WHERE HE WAS PUSHED into learning a trade: printing. This suited him because it didn't take up much of his brain—his only thought was the guitar—plus he'd always been handy with a Xerox machine. Blake magicked up a scholarship to The Queen's School (partly on the strength of a sensitive essay on "The Tyger") where, to Jack's amusement, he had to ponce about in a gown and mortarboard. Band plans melted away without disappearing entirely.

Blake made a success of Queen's: he cunningly juggled work and play, avoided the school corps under cover of advanced pottery, and learned to smoke; his sense of humor ensured he was never considered for positions of responsibility. When he was a relative newcomer, delivering the crate of mini–milk bottles up to the Head of House's empty study, he found a dartboard on the back of the door, with names instead of numbers, his own just above the double top. What had he done? He asked Jack. "They envy you or they love you," said his older brother, "or they wouldn't bother with you."

Blake was writing lyrics, Jack was exploring undiscovered regions of the fret board and making up tunes. Despite their separation, there was a modicum of collaboration, an unspoken agreement that it would continue. Most pressingly, however, Blake required Jack's newfound expertise as a printer.

The Queen's School had an official school magazine, one per term with embossed crest and official notices. It also allowed the publication of a student magazine called *Fore!*, an outlet for artistic expression with an emphasis on gentle parody. To more forward-thinking pupils, particularly a few of Blake's spikier friends, *Fore!* was quite as much a part of the establishment as the official magazine and thus represented a similar threat to individuality. Gentle parody had no effect; it patted itself on the back and preserved the status quo. So they cooked up an idea for a far more radical journal.

Foreskin!, its name an inevitability, would offend. Blake was asked for a contribution—he offered three of his most recent songs, mostly nonsense, somewhere between druggy Beatles, Monty Python, and Edward Lear. He hand-lettered the lyrics, decorated them with doodles, and drew diagrams of the chords. There was debate as to where they should get the magazine printed, and Blake suggested his brother, who would give them a deal.

"Have you seen what's inside?" asked Jack.

Foreskin! contained the vilest parody, barely humorous at all, thinly disguised streams of vitriol aimed at members of the staff, accusing them variously of having sex with their dogs, sex with one another, and sex with the pupils, or of being sado-masochists, aliens, or insane. Pseudonyms included "Piss" Don Sheets, P. Ennis, and, of course, Mike Hunt. The only vaguely amusing items were Blake's songs, which were also the only attributed contributions.

"But how do the songs look, Jack?" Blake asked. It was all he cared about.

The finished magazines, twenty-four pages per copy, 200 copies, were sent to one of the dayboy's homes. Next morning, the group distributed them around the school corridors. Which was precisely when the fun ended. Within twenty minutes, Blake was hauled out of class and frog-marched to the headmaster, who,

though incandescent with rage, calmly named Blake's conspira-
tors and asked if he was wrong. Blake said nothing.

"I'd throw the lot of them out. They'd be no loss to the
school," the headmaster said frankly, "but then I'd have to throw
you out too." He was rumored to have a glass eye. "And that
would be a shame, because I think you're going to amount to
something. So they get off because of you. Sadly, you can never
tell them. Isn't life funny? Wait here, you fool."

As he heard the head bark instructions at his secretary, Blake
glanced around the inner sanctum: in a barrister's bookcase, the
very same edition of Edward Lear that he owned, right next to
some William Blake.

Soon, all five stood in a line in the study, four fearing the
worst.

"Where is Sheppy Printers?" asked the headmaster, flicking
one of the offending rags.

"My brother works there," said Blake.

"How much did you pay them?"

"Fifty pounds."

"This was worth fifty pounds to you to print this? Who
wrote this bit about Mr. Rostron?"

There was a lengthy silence. "Me," admitted Will, the editor.
"Why?"

"Honestly?" There was a shuffling.

"You saw no problem with being honest in print."

"Because I hate him." It seemed a weak reason now.

"Fair enough," said the headmaster. "I know he's a bully,
and I know he's a bootlicker . . . but you don't have to put it down
in print. I don't. For the record, I've also spared both the public
and the private page my true feelings about you. Even on your re-
ports." They could hardly believe what they'd just heard. The
headmaster peered down bifocals at another page. "Mr. Williams,
your Latin teacher, has carnal relations with his dog. I am struggling, as an animal lover, to see the humor. What have you got
against Mr. Williams's dog? That's one of the sweetest animals on
God's earth. That poor hound is just collateral damage to you,
isn't it? And the songs are yours, are they? Why on earth did you
put your name to them, boy? No one else bothered! They chose

to hide behind the veil of anonymity." He tossed the magazine into the fire, which spat its disgust as the flame caught.

"Well, I'm proud of them, sir."

The headmaster regarded the fire with an icy stare. It was true: one of the eyes just didn't seem to move. "I shouldn't think anyone else is proud of anything in here, are they?" They shrewdly recognized this question as rhetorical. "If you ever pull a stunt like this again, you will be expelled. All of you. I will refund you the fifty pounds you spent and you will collect every last copy of the magazine and bring them here where they will be burnt. And that means every last copy. If there is so much as one missing, I will expel you anyway. And you will have no one's sympathy. Not signing your work is cowardly."

Blake left the office feeling much better than when he had entered it. One copy of the magazine mysteriously survives; it contains Blake's first three published songs.

Jack didn't go to university; Blake won a place at Angels College, Cambridge.

There, avoiding an unseemly amount of work, he began to tinker in bands, briefly gigging as keyboard player for Replicants, who were for the worker's revolution, for Gary Numan, and against definite articles. Humping the keyboard was bad enough, the ironing board stand was worse. Blake could hardly play the synth, but Replicants music required only one finger, either depressed on the Casio or raised to society; more important were high hair and stark lighting. The lead singer was less concerned with the quality of the lyrics. Blake's suggestions were laughed out of the union bar. He knew his tenancy was up. But in the unlikely event that Replicants ever made it, he'd unavoidably end up a twig on a Pete Frame Rock Family Tree: a step in the right direction.

Blake read English literature and made it his business to find out how to pass exams; this useful knowledge was wholly unrelated to any study of the subject itself. It involved the thorough analysis of old exam papers to discern the frequency with which certain questions turned up, and then the learning-by-heart of the appropriate essays. With regards to practical criticism, almost

every essay was successfully handled by making a lengthy case
that the poem was about writing a poem, or, failing that, that the
poem was about the condition of art itself. He sailed through his
Part Ones and took a job at the Arts Cinema, for which he wrote
the occasional précis for the calendar (always of films he'd never
seen, always in a last minute rush) and where he ushered, nip-
ping down to the toilets for crafty cigarettes when he'd had one
too many appointments with Dr. Caligari.

He still had his four or five guitar chords and was putting
them to good effect on basic protest songs, mostly written by more
famous, more American, and older practitioners, for whose songs
he'd change the name of, say, Richard Nixon to, say, Margaret
Thatcher. And Bob's Your Uncle! This edified the student masses
in a way Replicants could only dream of. It felt a little punky,
true, but it was Blake's way in. He directed some plays, acted in
a few others, taking none of it very seriously but never forgetting
his lines. A girlfriend called Caroline introduced him to the more
whimsical end of English progressive rock. He'd always hated
that scene, not to mention the attendant literature, mostly because
of the hairy crowd who'd been into it at school, masturbating on
their electric guitars as they broadcast only into their own headphones, extolling the virtues of harmonics and tricky time signatures. But in Caroline's musical world, there were no elves, no
RogerDeanscapes, no *Lord of the Rings*, just solid English
whimsy: Caravan sipping tea with a Golf Girl in their *Land of
Grey and Pink*, Stackridge and their indifferent hedgehogs, and
best of all Robert Wyatt's *Rock Bottom*. Caroline and he shared
their first kiss watching fireworks from his window, and Wyatt
sang words that made perfect sense and none at all: "Burly bunch
the water mole . . ." He had never met a girl who didn't want to
use tongues before—it seemed like some bizarre backwards step
beyond pre-puberty: ". . . Heli plop and finger hole."

The license to specialize for the first time—to zero in on something of actual interest—suited Blake, and he decided to write a
dissertation on Nonsense Poetry, surveying his favorites from Lear
and Carroll onwards. He was supervised for this by a thrilled

Bishop from Caius, dusted off especially for their tutorials, who bandied about words like *mythopoesis* and *glossolalia*. Monsignor Arbuthnot Slade had written lengthily on the subject himself, with particular reference to Edward Lear, *The Ingoldsby Legends* and *The Bab Ballads*, and was delighted to find a student willing to look forward to more contemporary poetry. For this had been the Bishop's problem for many years: after the Victorians, what?

Blake, to the Bishop's frustration, was prepared to stretch the definition of nonsense to the breaking point, happy to include poets and poems from which other minds derived perfect sense.

Blake preferred not to understand them—neither the poets, nor the minds. In many regards, the Bishop and Blake were an imperfect match, an owl and a pussycat, a nutcracker and sugar tongs, yet they happily danced by the light of the moon every Tuesday for two terms. The Bishop had no grounds on which to argue whether Bob Dylan wrote nonsense, not having heard the music of Bob Dylan, or indeed any popular music since Gilbert & (rather than Gilbert O') Sullivan, but he introduced Blake to the following verse of Lewis Carroll written in 1889:

> He thought he saw a Buffalo
> Upon the chimney-piece:
> He looked again, and found it was
> His Sister's Husband's Niece.
> "Unless you leave this house," he said,
> "I'll send for the Police!"

Blake was delighted, and when he told his fellow musos that this was the lost lyric from a *Blonde on Blonde* out-take, particularly when he delivered it in septum-quivering Dylanese, they believed him. Who wouldn't? And how different really was it from the sky being chicken, and saddling up a goose, and the key being Frank, and all that gibberish? "We think so then and we thought so still," wrote Edward Lear, of which Dylan's version was about being younger then and older than that now: why was one nonsense and the other profound? Blake laughed at those who extracted deep meaning from Dylan's lyrics. Agreed, the man was a genius, but only inasmuch as he was the greatest nonsense writer of the late twentieth century. When you added it up—and people often tried (there were plenty of professors waxing lyrical)—the only line connecting Dylan's work (after his brief flirtation with sense, the folky protest period) was nonsense. He was capable of writing either great nonsense (*Bringing It All Back Home*, *Highway 61 Revisited*, *Blonde on Blonde*, most of *John Wesley Harding*) or sense composed entirely of atrocious clichés (the rest of *John Wesley Harding* onwards). It was as if Dylan, it seemed to Blake, was only successful when he wrote rubbish. *Of course* the man didn't want to explain his lyrics: he couldn't. Even the best of his *narratives* were completely nonsensical.

And while everybody else was trying to make sense of texts by deconstructing them and decoding signs, Blake was on the lookout for things that tried to mean nothing, that *stopped* making sense, as David Byrne was currently advising at the Arts Cinema. Blake started to gravitate towards poetry that barely coalesced into words, while simultaneously arguing that T. S. Eliot was essentially a nonsense poet. Yes, "The Hippopotamus" and "Mr. Mistoffelees" and all that, but what about *The Four Quartets*? Weren't these best heard and appreciated as gobbledygook, as pure sound, rather than teased and tickled for meaning that might or might not be there, upon which, anyway, no one could agree? Didn't Eliot himself make fun of all that with his own fake notes?

The Bishop, while full of admiration for his pupil's gusto, was happiest wading in the shallows. Slade's nonsense was literary, a construct in opposition to sense, always on the threshold of knowledge. Blake's church was broader, more catholic even than the Monsignor's. He viewed all poetry, all literature, through this prism. Auden, Bishop (Elizabeth), Empson, Smith (Alexander)—failed nonsense poets all. They didn't have the nerve for it. What a waste! Beckett was the honorable exception: even his *prose* was nonsense poetry. And Joyce had it in him; he could throw a little nonsense around with the best of them. Bits of *Finnegan's Wake* read like Lear's letters. He thought of a name for the dissertation: *'king Lear*.

Nonsense was for adults, but children got it. It was pure pleasure, an embarrassment to academia. It put the id in kids' literature. Children dream without restraint, as Dr. Seuss once said, and Nonsense made kids of adults. Into the fold came John Lennon, *In His Own Write*, and the works of Spike Milligan, the true heir to Blake and Lear; and, though Blake was somewhat reluctant, Hilaire Belloc, anti-Semitism and all. The Bishop was thrilled, despite feeling himself dragged into slightly deeper waters of Dylanology and Lennonism than he had imagined, and began to speak at head table of a dissertation "with potential" by a "most promising" student. He imported into his smoky rooms a visiting Oxford don, desperately hard-of-hearing, to elucidate the links between Lear and Carroll and the works of John Taylor, the water poet. "Sit down, both of you," chortled the Oxford don, "and don't speak a word till I've finished." When tea and scones were served, it was like they were acting out the Mad Hatter's tea party with Blake as the sleepy dormouse.

He was, it goes without saying, not always at his most alert during these tutorials. Blake allotted a portion of his student grant to the various herbs and chemicals that might enhance his enjoyment of, and enlighten his attitude towards, nonsense, music, and anything else he fell over. He was not alone: such beneficial substances were the currency of the college bars, freely available to anyone with money. Thus it was during an acid trip, after a late-night horror film at the arts cinema, that he came up with his most inevitably bad idea. The first bad idea had been to watch it on acid: a slasher movie, the true bloody-humored brutality of which had been severely misrepresented in the program précis (that he himself had written). It had been around the time that a decapitated corpse held its own severed head above the body of a screaming woman, tied to a hospital operating table, and attempted cunnilingus with her, that Blake wondered whether the acid had been prudent. As he walked home across the green, watching (to his satisfaction) the earth shift underfoot like a million squiggling worms, it dawned on him: the real lack of nerve was his own. When he got home, he smoked a joint, put aside a Beckett essay (due the next morning) and began to write the dissertation that would win him his first.

The fateful idea—formally interesting, philosophically unique, academically suicidal—was to write his dissertation about nonsense in the form of nonsense. The Bishop pleaded with him, prayed: all that research, all those modern ideas—what a waste, what a waste. The Bishop would help if only a compromise could be reached: perhaps some illustrative nonsense passages, representing the subconscious resurfacing, weaving in and out of a dissertation, structured around the four monoliths of nonsense: Lear, Carroll, Milligan, and Dylan. Blake, however, had convinced himself: "Take care of the sounds, and the sense will take care of itself," he quoted Carroll (though in fact Carroll had said the precise opposite.)

All was lost. The Bishop, with a rueful smile, wished Blake well, reiterated what a pleasure it had been meeting with him so regularly, and assured him that he should reconsider or regret it the rest of his life. Blake left wondering whether all the Bishop required was an "ideal child-friend" to take him by the hand, row him out on to the lake, and then wave goodbye.

Blake left Cambridge without a degree: the dissertation was, unusually, ruled "unmarkable," thus nullifying other fairly good results across his exams. He hadn't completed the course. Neither his advisor nor his father could prevail upon him to take a substitute exam, and so, rather than becoming an academic or a top man at the BBC, he came home and, after a sufficiency of lolling around, took twin jobs as a primary school teacher by day and cinema usher by night.

That was when the band got going.

While Blake had been paddling on the shore of academia, Jack had become a printer and a part-time carpenter.

Carpentry was a ridiculous day job for a musician, proximity-of-sharp-blade-to-finger-wise. Mind you, it stood you in good stead for making guitars, and, if you lost your fingers, as you almost certainly would, you had Black Sabbath's Tony Iommi as the Satanic Patron Saint of your recovery. On his last day working at a sheet metal factory, Iommi, aged seventeen, lost the tips of two or three fingers on his right hand, before discovering that via the canny deployment of thimbles, he could play again. And he didn't sound too bad, did he? And what about Django Reinhardt?

Didn't half of his fingers get melted, so that he played those crazy solos with just two? He only used the burned ones for barre chords. And Mark Knopfler only ever used a finger and a thumb for his guitar solos: he could have done the decent thing and cut the other three off, out of solidarity. He didn't need them. Who'd have noticed?

Blake had grown a foolhardy (though fundamentally ironic) goatee with a curlicue moustache. Thus, their first post-Brutles lineup was a duo called The Walrus and the Carpenter—the band name still preceded the music. Jack had many tunes, all surprisingly simple given his sometimes proggy taste in virtuosic solos, and Blake had lyrics and a few melodies. They jammed these ingredients into the mixer and found that somehow, despite their vastly differing influences, Jack's riffage and Blake's verbal noodling blended nicely, if fluffed up with a bouncy tune. It was as though this was precisely what they'd been planning throughout their separation. But they were never going to be a duo. They needed bass and drums.

Watch With Mother was the next project, the name taken from the BBC afternoon kids' show that had aired stop-motion classics since the dawn of the Radio Times: *Andy Pandy*, *Flower Pot Men*, and *The Woodentops*, all in themselves perfectly operable band names, and the last of which was already taken by an operative band. Ads were duly posted in the *NME* and other papers of record to attract the attention of an "ill-humored and naughty rhythm section. Must hate the Beatles, Bob Dylan, and all good music."

And, wonder of wonders, the twins materialized. Jack and Blake liked them before they'd even played a note, at their very first drink, though they could never tell them apart. "When did you guys first meet?" someone had once asked them in all innocence. "In the fucking womb!" shouted the slightly noisier of the two. The twins weren't that good, but it looked like they were. Any rhythm section seems tight if the bassist and the drummer are identical. They absolutely wouldn't dress the same, though—that was out of question. And they didn't like the name Watch With Mother either. On this, as far as Blake and Jack were concerned, there was the possibility of negotiation. So with their first gig looming, they sat in the pub and proposed fifty different names, all rejected.

"Okay, then," said Blake in pique, "What name do you two *wunderkinds* want?"

"Eh!" said Tweedletim. "What about Wunderkinds?"

"Yeah!" said Tweedletom. "What about Wunderkinds?"

"It's great," said Jack.

"It's so great that there's probably another Wunderkinds. There are probably twenty other Wunderkinds," said Blake.

"Yeah," said Jack, "but that doesn't matter, we'll just throw an umlaut in somewhere. Is there an umlaut in Wunderkinds?" No one had the faintest idea. "It doesn't really matter. Dad'll know."

"Well, it's an interesting legal issue: how different does a band name have to be? Could we call ourselves the Rolling Stonés with just an acute on the final e?" No one was that interested except Blake. "How about the Direcritics?" But everyone was sold on Wunderkinds.

"Well, let's put an umlaut over the i . . ." said Jack.

"And another over the U?" said a twin.

"And if there's one of those," said Blake. "We'll just call ourselves *Der* Wunderkinds and have done with it."

As if by miracle, everyone was in agreement. They toasted the new name.

"Wunderful," said Jack.

"I always wanted to be in a band called *the* Something-or-others," said Tom. Blake thought back to Replicants. You had to have an article, and it had to be definite. Not having one was pretentious and spelled trouble. Look at Talking Heads; they were so pissed off that they went to the trouble of calling an album *The Name of this Band is Talking Heads*, like they were telling you off for getting it wrong.

The Wunderkinds

The Wunderkïnds

The Wüñdêrkïnds

Der Wunderkinds

They'd finesse it later. Point was: they had a name. With all those accents, an eye-popping logo couldn't be far behind.

And the Wunderkinds needed a singer with a great name too. Not James Lewis. Or Jimmy Lewis. He'd work on it.

Their future manager, Greg, saw them playing bottom of the bill at a Miner's Strike benefit in Shepherd's Bush. Blake couldn't care less about politics, but you could always get on a Miner's Strike benefit. He made a joke, which went over badly (because no one understood it and then he tried to explain it) about how he'd thought it was a Minor's Strike. But they played well.

One might have supposed Greg liked their unfocused raw energy, their songs, or even their trousers (like Leggy Mountbatten in the Rutles movie), but what appealed to him was the concept of a rhythm section composed of twins. He had himself been a bass player, and it made him nostalgic for a twin brother he had never known. He ended up rubbing shoulders with a woman, and as they talked through the band's brief set, he noticed that his pretended vulture-like circling of this potential "baby act" (as though he had far larger, more successful clients on his roster) was proving somewhat lubricious to her. You could always tell a band by the average age and sexual appetites of the females they attracted. (This was a judgment he had to radically reevaluate after the Wunderkinds' first flush of success.) He'd always be grateful to the band for that night's leg-over.

So at first it was the twins, and then foreplay, but Greg woke the next morning with one of the songs on repeat in his head and a scratch on his back, a wincing reminder of the pleasures of the previous evening. And there she was, even now, dressing in silhouette against his white curtains. He didn't have white curtains. Oh yeah, they were in a hotel. He winced again, trying to remember if he'd put his credit card down. Maybe she was paying.

Greg had a history working for some of the more eccentric labels in the distant 1970s, and many good stories to match. It's fair to say he was on his last go round. He was decent, music was turning cutthroat, and he didn't want much to do with it. But he saw something in the Wunderkinds, and as he listened to the Primary

School teaching university graduate telling him about the band at the pub the next night, he fell for the whole thing: Blake, the band, the virtuoso brother, the vision, even the name.

"Wunderkinds. What's that then, German?"

"Yeah."

"Brilliant, man."

Greg liked to stand at a bar, sipping a pint, talking to whomever would listen, listening to anyone who'd talk. He was a man without a man's skin, hair thinning now, once a pretty boy. His skin was so soft, he said, because he'd never told a lie—and this you believed, though it was the first of many exaggerations. Part of his charm was his boyishness—he was scared stiff of foreign words, or long English ones, and their pronunciation eluded him. He'd plump for his own, stick with it, and, bizarrely, people around him would adopt it, too.

Blake loved everything about Greg: his good vibe, his imperturbability, his default mode of friendship towards all, his "bring 'em all in" attitude. He represented something real, something unironic, something beyond the pained political correctness of the union bar. There was nothing evil about the way Greg referred to a woman bending over as "a nice place to park your bike." He was a bit like the monsignor: there were eternal verities; nothing was relative. You had to believe in things, and do what you believed in—that was the only way. Greg hadn't quite grasped that no one else was doing it that way anymore. Blake also loved Greg's mime show—everything came with a visual reference. Ironing, writing, talking on the phone, drying your hair—one hand was always showing you what he meant. Jack used to do a mean impression of Greg ironing and then answering the phone and burning his ear. Best were Greg's Malapropisms, his catchphrases. Blake used more than one of them in a song, and kept a notebook called *Sugar on Everything: Thoughts of Our Manager*.

With Greg in charge, the band was well represented. Blake vowed that they'd always be represented by people who effortlessly understood, from the core of their very being, what the Wunderkinds stood for. That vow lasted all of a year.

• • •

And so, with a manager, and some very basic recordings under their belt (muffled home demos collected on a cassette called *In Wunderland*, the Tenniel Tweedledum and Tweedledee illustration central on each one-of-a-kind decoupaged cover, their fat faces replaced by Jack's and Blake's), the Wunderkinds started to play clubs, to pay their dues, a part of the process that was of paramount importance to Greg, mainly because it excused every setback, as though someone somewhere was keeping score and the dues would finally be paid off.

They were on their way up, without moving terribly quickly, or, for that matter, up. Greg kept spirits high, another of his talents. Jobs permitting—Jack was only able to take so much time off—they worked as they could. The goal was a support act for someone with their own audience, though bands were curiously unwilling to let you open unless you already had an audience of your own.

The arrival of an agent seemed to push things in the right direction. All agents were Irish, and Fintan was no exception. He got them a tour of England supporting a band called the Trevors, whose show, all spiky post-punk posturing, wasn't bad (though you felt for the microphones). The tour, however, was hell. The Trevors themselves were okay; it was the road crew, unleashed hounds of hell, pit bulls defending their masters and their territory.

There was no chance, of course, of the Trevors striking their gear after soundcheck or sharing their equipment, so the Wunderkinds played their show nightly in a portion of stage roughly equivalent to a parking space, in front of an audience who, whether they wanted to pay attention or not, hardly could—the Trevors' crew had been careful to use all the channels on the house board and the monitor desk. Not that the Wunderkinds could have soundchecked anyway, since their uberlords, through no great sense of malice on their part, would soundcheck for the maximum amount of time, until doors if necessary, endlessly running the same songs, and then, as they were slightly drunk, attempting turgid covers that always went unplayed, because forgotten, during the show. If one of their crew had thought to say: "Hey, don't forget the support band, boys. They've come a long way," the Trevors would have been offstage before you could say Smokey Robinson. The one night the Wunderkinds got a soundcheck, Blake said he couldn't hear his voice in the monitor. The soundman laughed at him through the foldback, his own voice ringing clear as a bell: "Well, fucking sing louder then!"

Backstage was just the same. There was no one to get the Wunderkinds their beer, or their drink tickets, or secure them a dressing room. The Trevors' crew arrived earlier (mostly traveling overnight to do so, which perhaps accounted for their foul mood) and cordoned off areas rightfully theirs, generally amounting to the whole expanse of backstage. Dressing rooms varied in squalor, some no more than glorified storage rooms, appliance bone yards, others complete with a sofa and a mirror, everything beneath a thin covering of what Jack called "punk dust." Once, the Wunderkinds were, literally, billeted a broom cupboard.

"It's a broom cupboard!" said Blake in a rare moment of public complaint. Harder men than he laughed. "We can't even all fit at the same time."

They opted to use their van as a dressing room, which remained policy for the rest of the tour, so that they passed through the actual backstage only on their way to play. Whenever they bumped into the Trevors, it was all "Hey man! How are you doing?" very friendly and northern, as though they were all going to head out and get chips with brown sauce afterwards. The headliners were quite unaware that their road crew treated everything as a pissing contest.

"They're like Nazi fucking bureaucrats," said Jack. "Get someone else to do the dirty work and pretend everything's fine."

He rang Greg, who hadn't been able to make the whole trip (partly for reasons of group finance, but also because he didn't care to be away from home): "Man, we need a representative; we need a road manager or something; this is insane. We're not getting our proper bite of the cherry here; we need our own pit bull."

"Just to pick up a hundred quid at the end of the night?"

"Have you any idea what's happening out here? Are you our manager?"

"Yeah."

"Then fucking manage!"

"Look, Jack, I'll get it done," Greg said with exasperation. "Trust me."

"You promise?" Jack pushed. Greg had a habit of letting things slide.

"Spoken word." As so often with Greg, you knew what he meant. "There's a live review coming in *Sounds*," he added in mitigation, though he knew there was every chance they wouldn't be mentioned.

Greg went to the trouble of ringing up Fintan the agent, who was also the Trevors' agent, who rang up the Trevors' manager, who said he'd mention it to the Trevors' road manager. And, blow me down, the next day, the guitar roadie, previously the most aggressive of the aggressors, asked Jack if his guitar was set up right: "Want me to have a look at it?"

Jack's first reaction was: "Of course!" Green though he was, he knew this would mean a debt he would later have to pay, but he simply couldn't resist the thought of this horrible hellhound having to grapple with his touchy Strat, so he said "yeah, thanks mate." That night they got an actual dressing room and an actual soundcheck, and their actual gig actually went better. Jack and Blake had learned a lesson: "Always complain and always get your manager to do it for you."

The good life lasted two nights until the Trevors were spectacularly late for a show, and word came that the Wunderkinds should play longer, a lot longer, to keep the audience drinking. This was impossible; their repertoire was about four and a half minutes greater than their set. Jack decided they should stop before they really embarrassed themselves and the Trevors' guitar tech went ballistic: "I fucking set up your guitar, you arsehole," snarled the roadie, at which point Jack pulled a scrap of paper from his back pocket, scribbled in the certain knowledge that it would later be required, and handed it to the roadie. It read: "I was wondering how long you'd take to call that favor in." The roadie threw a punch, which would have hurt had it landed, and that was that as far as backstage détente.

The band got paid, it was a mostly terrible experience, and everyone was relieved when it was finally over. Except the Trevors, who, on the final night, emerged from the billowing smoke of their dressing room to say how sorry they were the Wunderkids were off and what a good time they'd had hanging. Nazis.

• • •

The tour might have seemed worthwhile if there had been a triumphant return but the band never played a local show that felt remotely like a hometown event. London, where Jack and Blake said they were from (though they lived just off the edge of the Tube map), didn't offer that.

They had ceased to hand out copies of *In Wunderland* with any enthusiasm after a fanzine described it as being of "bewilderingly unlistenable quality": a lack of proper demos represented an insurmountable obstacle to a record deal. The producer, the studio, the engineer: every step of this process became strategically important, the subject of endless debate. Greg had many historical anecdotes at his fingertips to illuminate each decision.

Everything arranged at tedious length, they found themselves in distant Twickenham at the Greenhouse, a bucolic sounding studio that turned out to be a lock-up in a gray Stalinist edifice that may or may not have once been the location of, or had some connection to, a greenhouse. In its grubby control room, acoustic foam baffling peeling from every wall, they were badly patronized by an aged engineer. They were attempting to record and mix five songs in two days, having no idea whether they should all play at the same time, or record just the drums and bass, and then overdub. Everyone suddenly knew all about it and had a different point of view.

"Well, let's see how tight you are," said the engineer, before concluding: "You're what I call live-tight, which isn't really tight-tight."

"Is he going to use the expression 'just a cunt hair'?" whispered Blake. "If he actually says 'just a cunt hair,' I'm walking out."

"He'll do that just before he puts all those brightly colored patch cables on his head and pretends to be a Rasta," said a twin, who had been in studios with another of his bands.

In fact neither happened, but even the calming influence of Greg couldn't ease the tension.

"Could you turn the bass up?" asked the bassist.

"The drums seem a little quiet," said the drummer.

"Guys," said Jack. "Even though we're all, in a way, spending our money on this demo tape equally, that doesn't mean that we have to be equally loud in the mix."

"I just wondered if I could hear a little more of me," said the bassist.

"Who's producing this record?" demanded the grumpy engineer, brandishing a revolting pipe of Balkan Sobranie. It seemed impossible that he'd heard any rock music, let alone made any, yet he'd come highly recommended.

"Jack is," shouted Blake.

"I thought I was," said the engineer.

Everyone looked at everyone else, and Greg said: "Well, yes, you are."

Jack threw up his hands and left for the cigarette that he should have smoked in the control room, if only to combat the Balkan Sobranie. That was the end of the first day.

Only Blake and Jack returned. The five tracks were delivered mixed, and the engineer was paid a little more than they had intended. The credit read "Produced by the Wunderkinds at Greenhouse Studios, assisted by Bob Buddha Bryant." Yet, despite the friction, everyone was happy, except the twins, who felt sonically underrepresented. The songs had the bounce that Blake wanted ("They've got the ginger!"); the guitars rang clearly without getting in the way of the words, which pleased Jack because "it wasn't like a fucking poetry reading"; and the tracks sounded like they'd been recorded with the use of professional equipment, so Greg was over the moon. "Rock Around the Bed," in particular, was a real success: angular and jerky, but infectious and straightforward too, all beneath a waterfall of bubbling Blakeisms. At Greg's listening party, after the ritual toast of "Let's run it up the flagpole and see who salutes!," it was the sheer exuberance of the new recordings that made everyone smile—even the twins; Blake quacked repeatedly.

Handcrafted cover art negotiated, Blake's elaborate ideas finally acceded to (despite his manager's assurance that there was no better way to present demos than in a generic cassette cover with nothing but the band's name and a phone number scrawled on it), the tape was immediately sent to the minuscule Wanted record label, old penniless comrades-in-arms who released practically anything Greg remembered to pass on.

• • •

The five new songs were recent experiments, rather than road-tested favorites. At the primary school, Blake liked nothing more than making up songs with the kids. He'd suggest a melody, write a line, and then let them make the rest up, waiting until they got stuck, listening for their loopy attempts at rhyme. He'd then transcribe it all, sculpt a little here and there and, bingo! A song! Most songwriters get accused of plagiarism once or twice (some notably more often), but there are a few school-kids out there who could have their day in court with Blake Lear. Tough to prove, but he loved to take the words right out of their mouths:

> I like it when we're going
> I don't like it when we stop
> And you look like you have a new haircut on
> There's a bonus point for knowing
> When the firefly lights up
> You get a fresh shirt with a pink button
> I was bored, but I perked up
> I was bored, but I perked up
> I was bored, but now I'm all worked up
> I'm not bored anymore
> I got some new fresh air for my nose!

It's Blake, for sure; Blake and the children of James Lewis's class at Arundale Primary School.

"What song is it you wanna hear?"

CHILDREN AND CARS ARE A HORRIFIC COMBINATION—THE CONFINED space, the boredom, the ease with which vomit seeps down a leather seam to the unknowable shadow beneath. Nowadays it's more child-friendly: one kid's playing *Sushi Cat* on your iPad and the other's watching *Baby Einstein* on a decommissioned phone. There's always a CD you can slide into the stereo, or maybe a satellite radio channel that specializes in "Family Music," if things get really desperate.

The "nightmare car journey" is a genre unto itself, but it has a particularly outsized role in the Wonderkids' origin myth. I heard this one many times, mostly told by the driver, but once by the passenger. He's the real star of the show.

Nick Hedges is driving his son down to the West Country from the Baker Street offices of Endymion Records. Laurie, aged six, had spent a relentless Friday kicking his heels waiting for the head of Endymion to drag himself away from his work and spirit the boy down to their holiday cottage to rendezvous with his mother and brother for the weekend.

"We'll be outta here shortly," was Nick's unpersuasive mantra. They weren't.

The day fidgeted on. It didn't take long for Laurie to tire of his father's determined chair swiveling and phone flaunting, his commanding use of the intercom. Provided with no alternative, the boy dreamed up a game where he carried messages between his father and the secretary, but neither played along. His eyes lit on a pile of cassette cases on the bookshelf by the door, a Babel of C-60s, an Elephant's Graveyard of demos that his father had been meaning to clear away. Nick had warned the cleaners off: it might not withstand even the lightest dusting. To his bored son, this tottering tower seemed full of dangerous potential. Unmonitored, ignored, he started to extricate the most obviously loose and structurally superfluous of the cassettes. This kept him occupied for a few blessed minutes, until his father, noticing, screamed: "LAURIE!" and Laurie started to cry.

"Sorry, Norm, sorry," Nick told America. "My boy's in the office, causing mayhem . . . I know, I know . . . animals and children, animals and children . . ."

Endymion had never been a Virgin or a Charisma or Harvest, nor was their logo as iconic as any of those, but the label had broken a number of household names, even if those bands had invariably moved on as soon as their initial contracts were up. In fact, in the case of their largest act, Endymion had simply forgotten to pick up the option. The first Nick had known about it was a letter from the band's lawyer pointing this out and saying goodbye.

Even if these were no longer the glory years, the label had had real top-ten success, the evidence of which still glinted in the sunlight on the walls. These days, however, Nick was completely at the mercy of Norm Bloch ("The Unmerciful"), head of WBA, Endymion's parent company. It sometimes seemed that the only thing he could do without Norm's written consent was score Norm drugs.

Nick's workday finally fizzled: London had given up for the weekend, New York was in Los Angeles, and Los Angeles was having a "Funky Friday" to entertain New York. On his reluctant way, two folders clamped beneath his chin as he shepherded Laurie out of the door, Nick took a last cursory glance at his office and, in an inspired gesture at spring-cleaning, decided to dump the entire collection of cassettes into a large Sainsbury's bag. His execution was poor (a fair percentage fell to the floor, many shattering at the hinge), but obscured spines were visible for the first time in two years.

"About time. Let's chuck this lot."

His son, however, felt sentimental about the source of his brief distraction. He saw the possibility of a number of distinct structures to be built and then torn down noisily at his leisure, and he insisted his father bring the tapes. Nick, who just wanted his son to shut up, did.

The trip was a disaster. For the few moments Laurie wasn't whining about the window being up, it rained. Nick's back spasmed whenever he reached behind him to pick up something Laurie had dropped (often) or tried to foist upon him something he didn't want. Suddenly it was blazing sun. Nick opened the sunroof, enjoying a moment's silence until he looked in the rearview mirror as they sat immobile in traffic, to see his son squinting in the glare, sweating implausibly.

"Whose stupid idea was this?" he thought. He should have just stayed in town all weekend with his girlfriend.

When they finally hit the motorway, Laurie immediately wanted to stop, but Nick wanted to drive because they'd finally hit the motorway. He was soon met with a damp surprise, so they had to stop anyway. Laurie, pants and underwear removed, was reseated on a throne of Rolling Stones T-shirts Nick found in the boot, stuffed between boxes of promotional Converse. (He liked to impress people by casually asking their shoe size, then lobbing a pair of sneakers at them.) Nick had the presence of mind to dry the offending pieces of clothing outside, closing the window on them to keep them from flying away.

Back on the road, Laurie decided to recite a poem. His father, making mental notes on a deal memo, feigned interest, then found himself genuinely impressed by the sheer mental effort Laurie was putting into his performance.

"Great, mate," he said.

"Well, it took eight miles, that's something," said Laurie woefully, eye on the odometer. "Know any poems, Dad?"

Nick did, but said he didn't. Laurie retaliated by fiddling with the automatic window, which sent his clothes flying off onto the hard shoulder. They couldn't very well reverse up the motorway. The alternative was for Nick to lose his temper, which he did, to which Laurie reacted with his most impressive bout of sobbing yet. Millie was going to be fucking thrilled when her son arrived, shivering, naked from the waist down. Nick tried to imagine every shop between their present location and their cottage, the Sirens. Nothing at this time of night. Wait! Rolling Stones tracksuit bottoms in the boot. The wrong size but they'd do.

"Why don't we put on some of *your* music, Laurie?" asked Nick in desperation. There were tapes that he occasionally allowed his children to play: Sesame Street crap, some bloke who sang "clap your hands, here comes Charlie"-type Christian songs, and a few Disney cassettes rewound so often that parts sounded like they'd been recorded underwater. It was difficult to know which was worse, but there was no choice.

"No," said Laurie, his misery definitive. "Mum took them in the car with Darren."

"Well, I've got some music," said his father unappealingly, before slapping himself on the forehead: "You fucking idiot!" His whole weekend had just gone up the spout: he'd put the CDs down on his desk when he was cleaning those stupid cassettes away. "Sorry, son. I forgot something."

"Why don't we listen to one of these tapes?" asked Laurie. There was one at the top of the Sainsbury's bag with a picture of an old TV with some kids' show on.

"What tapes? Oh, Christ. No. We're not listening to that shit."

God, he wanted a drink. He *deserved* a drink. Enough to leave Laurie sitting in the car with a bag of cheese'n'onion in the sure knowledge that the boy would then unavoidably mention this desertion to his mother? Yes. There was a little pub Nick had noticed many times just off the main road. He fantasized that it seemed welcoming.

"How do you fancy a Coke, Laurie?" he asked, as if out of the blue.

"Are you going to leave me in the car while you're in a pub?" Laurie wasn't a mind reader. It happened all the time.

"Would you like me to sit with you in the garden?" It might be worth it.

Laurie sighed. "Can I listen to the tapes?"

"Yeah, course you can, mate." Suddenly his father was unusually cheerful. "And I've got some spare bottoms in the back you can wear."

In the parking lot, Laurie scrabbled through the cassettes. The one he'd had his eye on had somehow sifted from the top of the heap, so he decided to lay them out on the tarmac as though he was having a car boot sale. His father emerged with Coke and crisps.

"You're gonna have to pick those all up, you know. All of them."

It was a sorry collection, but Laurie finally found the one he was looking for. Its cover, craftily handmade, distinguished it from the others, all beige inserts and typewriter font: someone had actually gone to the trouble of cutting out the front of the TV so, depending on how you folded the paper behind, it could broadcast different "channels," one of which, bizarrely, was a naked woman and her private pieces. Laurie slotted it into the stereo.

He didn't have the vocabulary, nor would he have felt the need to explain, but the herky-jerky simplicity sang to him in a way that his dad's cassettes rarely did. The chorus of the first song seemed to be "I've got a song stuck in my head, I'm gonna rock around the bed" over and over and over, and when his father reemerged, mood two pints less bitter, Laurie was three or four songs in, one called "Lucky Duck." Nick liked nothing more than being able to leave somewhere the moment he wanted, a freedom his family had severely restricted, and when he saw that the tapes were already cleared away, that his son was sitting in the front with a seat belt on, Nick felt benign enough to let him stay there despite the safety hazard and dubious legality. And though there were at least two hours to go—they were about to be funneled off into the infinite twists and turns of country lanes, where the taking of a bend at over ten miles an hour without honking represented a calculated risk about which Nick felt considerably less anxious than usual—he let Laurie leave the cassette in.

"Oh, wind it back to the beginning, Dad."

"Wouldn't you rather . . .?"

"Wind it back!"

When they pulled into the Sirens's driveway, the tape was still playing—they'd been through all five songs about ten times, even had something approaching a discussion, as Nick tried to understand what it was precisely that Laurie liked about it, and what it was precisely that he himself liked about it. Laurie was punching the air with abandon and even Nick was singing along:

> I'm gonna rock around the bed
> I'm gonna rock around the bed
> I got a song stuck in my head
> I'm gonna rock around the bed
> And you can keep your peanut butter
> And your whole wheat bread
> I've got a song stuck in my head
> I'm gonna rock around the bed.

Nick had his weekend's work cut out for him—a terrific relief—and Rock Music for Kids, maybe even Kindie Music (though he did not yet know it as either of those things) was born.

There was a phone number on the cassette and, first thing Monday morning, that number would be receiving a surprise call from the head of Endymion Records, yes, the very one, no this isn't a prank call. The future of the Wunderkinds, the band, rolled out before Nick like a Persian rug from which is delivered, at the end, a beautiful woman—or perhaps, in this case, a Grammy or an MTV award.

And as they walked into the Sirens, he ruffled Laurie's hair and shouted: "Millie, Millie, love! We're here! I've got some amazing news. I'm the man who discovered the Beatles!"

I've heard Nick say: "Whatever inspiration made me bundle all those dusty old demos into that plastic bag that day, we'll never know. Call it luck. Call it fate." He wouldn't say "Call it genius," but he'd let it linger. Who wouldn't?

But he was kind of a genius, Nick, and it made him, briefly, very rich. He had an idea, inspired by the Wunderkinds, and apparently no one had had it before. He heard a band and he saw a niche—Rock Music for Kids—and he wanted that band to fill that niche, and he didn't for a moment consider that there were fairly obvious reasons why they couldn't, or wouldn't want to.

Rock Music had always been for Kids. It was the spirit of Rock Music. That was what Nick Hedges understood when he heard "Rock Around the Bed." But then there was that weird bit about the girl pushing the singer down on the kitchen table and how he nearly fainted as they "got acquainted." Kids didn't want to hear that; or maybe they did, but their parents certainly didn't want them to.

But so what? That's what an edit is for. That's what A&R men do. Or they get the band to sing another song entirely. Because if Nick had learned one thing in his years at Endymion, including when he himself had bent over and let WBA fuck him royally up the ass for a few million, it was this: if you wave the readies, there is nothing people won't do. His three favorite sayings were: "Treat me like a whore; I have the 'integrity' bit covered"; in second place: "The further Monkey climbs up the tree, the more you can see his ass." And favorite of all: "Everyone's a whore. You just need to find out what their price is." There was a theme.

Nick Hedges and the Wunderkinds were a match made in Heaven and Hell.

"I hope we've passed the audition."

GREG'S POTTERING ABOUT, AND THE PHONE GOES.

"Hello?" he says, rather than, for example, "Sugarpill Management: can you hold please?," as he puts his hand over the mouthpiece, rushes over to the stereo, throws on his band's cassette, holds the phone up for a bit and *sees if he can find Mr. Sugar.* Just "Hello?"

"Endymion Records here. Nick Hedges."

Many would have expected Greg to be fazed by this unexpected call from on high: far from it. He chuckled, started to laugh, fell back on the lumpy sofa and kicked his leg into the air.

"Nick, me old mate, how are you? What do you want, man?"

"Who is this?"

"Who do you think? It's Greg, mate. Greg Sugar."

Many would also have expected that Nick, so relatively high up the ladder, might not remember Greg, so relatively low down, but they had passed in their different directions, even shared a rung for a while.

"Greg!" This was going to be easy. Nick hadn't even thought Greg was still in music, let alone management. "It's been a while! How are you?" They hadn't seen each other since the funeral of a mutual friend, a character from the halcyon days.

"Well, my mum's been ill, you know. Double hernia, which

isn't fantastic at her age but, you know, Chelsea keep winning. I don't get to go that often, it's hard to get tickets now, and the weather's nice so I've been riding my bike. Actually, Peachy gave me his wife's old Raleigh, and I've been riding that." It was instructive that Greg thought Nick had rung up for a bit of a yarn. But that had always been Greg's technique: disarming friendliness. "So, yeah, you know, skating away on the thin ice of a new day. How are you?"

"Fine. Look, I'm ringing to see what you can tell me about this band the Wunderkinds."

"The Wunderkinds?" Greg knew he'd betrayed surprise. He had at present only one client, whom he happily, if, by all known professional standards, half-heartedly, managed from his two-bedroom in Archway, and though he'd sent the demos out six months previously he'd received only polite rejections (with the exception of his old muckers at Wanted), clearly written out of respect for Greg's tenured position around the backstages and VIP lounges of London rather than for the music itself. "We really like the record," began one of the few he had been happy to show Blake and Jack, "but it's just not the right time for a label like us to be getting back into this indie market. Some catchy songs, though! And give my love to Pam." (Greg hadn't seen Pam in three years.)

"Yes. I'm just ringing the number on the demo. You."

"Oh, right!" Greg wasn't worried for a moment that it wasn't a friendly catch-up call. His mind was racing. "Yeah, hold on a mo then, I've got something on the stove." He located the demo and the Wanted contract that had arrived only the previous morning. "Back."

"So, we're really liking what we're hearing up here at Endymion Mansions," said Nick. "Love it. And my kid does too."

"How old's he now then, Nick?" Greg pictured a sixteen-year-old in his school blazer, a miniature Nick Hedges with similarly big nose and receding hairline.

"Oh, he's six. He loves it too. We listen to it in the car."

"Well, there you go—six to sixty. Doesn't get any better than that. Perfect democratic."

"Same old Greg. Anyway, we love the tape. Love it. Just love it."

"You love it. Great. That's great," said Greg, and after a wistful pause (his timing perfect): "I only wish you'd got in touch sooner." Nick knew what was coming next. He was nearly right. Greg reached for an antique RAK Records ballpoint pen and a Neil Young promotional notepad. He had an amazing collection of tchotchkes: he parted his hair courtesy of Haircut 100, thought of the band Ace only when he played cards, and surprised numerous women with his sponsored underwear. "Thing is, we've had some other interest."

"Interest from who?"

"Well . . . an indie . . ."

"Rip up the contract, Greg! You're coming back to the big leagues. It's you and me, Greg: the old team. Rip it up! Then *we're* gonna rip it up."

"I can't rip it up. We gave them our word."

"You haven't even *signed* it yet?" Incredulous. Greg looked at the few empty inches that, in about five hours, Blake and Jack's signatures would fill. He said nothing. "Well," Nick continued, "minor sigh of relief. So, no problem. Tell me about the band."

"Well, don't you want a look at them or something? They're a little raw."

"I like raw."

"They're *very* raw."

"What is this, the cheese-shop sketch? It doesn't actually matter how fucking raw they are. Look, can you get in here? I think we should speak first, man-to-man. The thing is: I've had a vision."

A vision. Greg held the phone at arm's distance and puffed out his cheeks. This had money and trouble written all over it. He had to buy himself time to think, an activity that involved better-informed friends. He was never afraid to ask advice.

"Well, I've got my squash lesson in a couple of hours and then I'm pushing my old mum round the gardens . . . hernia, you know."

"I really think we should meet before you break the news to the band."

"Well, I'm dangling another label on a string. And you're only *interested*. You haven't even seen them play."

"Come in tomorrow morning."

"Sure, yeah. Tomorrow morning. Camden?"

"Wakey, wakey. We're on *Baker Street*."

Oh, fuck, yeah. He'd forgotten. It wasn't just Endymion money anymore, it was WBA money. American money. Greg looked at a threadbare patch on the rug and scratched his head. *Endymion*. Poem by Keats. He knew weird facts like that from the general knowledge crossword.

"Right, Baker Street. Gerry Rafferty. I'll be there. Do you have a real door or one of those see-through ones where everyone can see what you're doing?" Humor was Greg's way back in.

"See-through."

"Where do you go for a wank?"

"I have the secretary take care of it for me."

"Great, man, great," Greg chuckled. Old Nick Hedges, last seen taking a huge toot off the cistern at that wake. Greg had once had him shut out of a Junkies' gig at The King's Head because the Junkies' junkie manager claimed that Nick had written an abusive review of the band for *Melody Maker*. "He didn't do it," said Greg, who felt sorry for Nick. "No, I know he didn't do it," the manager yelled in Greg's face, "I wrote the fucking review, but it mustn't fucking look like I did! So get that fucker out." Greg often found himself the pawn.

"Which label is going to be very disappointed?" asked the fucker.

"Oh, er, well you might not have heard of them."

"Name?"

"Wanted."

"Is my silence speaking volumes?"

It was Greg's silence that had the desired effect.

"Well, I'm sure they're very able," said Nick in apology. "But, Mr. Sugar, you tell Whatnot we're very sorry, we're having this band. And you can also tell them that we'll buy Whatnot, if they like, and then we'll have the band anyway."

Greg winced and put the phone down. He couldn't stand big timing. He never again spoke to one particular colleague who, after Greg had left the man thirty urgent messages, finally gave him a reply, which was, in its entirety, "With Joni." Fucker. Fucking Joni who? Joni Baez? Rickie Lee Joni? He knew it was Joni Mitchell—that was what made it was so annoying.

Greg put his head in his hands. He made three phone calls in quick succession. The first was to his oldest friend, Callum.

"Right," he said as he was told what to do. "Yep. Okay. Right. Okay. I know. Nothing signed. Yes, but you can't . . . Yes, I'm a decent man. Put it to the band. Right. It's their decision, not mine. Don't talk to the other label. Wanna go for a drink tonight, mate? Alright. On me."

He next rang William at Wanted, despite the fact that Callum had specifically told him not to. Greg was a sweet and caring man; Callum was the president of a record company for a reason. "William, old mate, yeah, Greg. Yeah, right here on my desk, yeah, looking at it. Yep. Not yet. Nope. Look, I'm meeting with the band tonight. We'll have some news in the morning . . . no, not *news*, I mean, I'll talk to you tomorrow morning. Or afternoon. Maybe afternoon. Yeah, anyway, I've got to pop out for my squash lesson. Backhand's coming along."

He wished he hadn't made the call. But, for what remained of his managerial career, Greg was more likely to be dodging bullets in the trenches with William at Wanted than pushing toy soldiers around a table with Nick upstairs at Endymion Mansions, so he really didn't want William to hate him when this went exactly the way Greg knew it was going to go.

And, in that knowledge, he allowed himself to fall into a reverie. When this went the way he knew it was going to go, if, just *if*, everything went right, despite the unlikelihood of things ever going right at cowardly record companies who ruled by committee, lived in thrall to the bean-counters, and spent their entire time playing catch-up . . . despite all that . . . perhaps just once it *would* go right. And perhaps, just once, he'd fallen over an act around whom everyone would gather like flies on sherbet and he'd be at the center of that sticky cluster-fuck. And perhaps therefore, he'd find another and then another . . .

But this unspooling fantasy of managerial Risk only served to depress him: what he wanted was to play squash and wheel his old mum round the gardens. He was cozy in Archway with his cat and his *Evening Standard*, happy with his place on the ladder. He liked going to Los Angeles but the sun burned his freckled skin before long. He preferred his pub where he could tell stories about the old days, which had been good, when labels were run by a lone lunatic who led by example and took brave decisions for which he alone took the praise or blame, a man who threw a lot of spaghetti at the wall in the hope that some would stick. There were approximately three of those lunatics left, he remembered: *and one was in charge of WBA. Norm Bloch.*

He picked up the phone with renewed vigor and left Blake a message. "It's Greg. Give us a tinkle. Actually, there's news. Quite big news. Band meeting tonight. Maybe 6 p.m. at the Coachy? See you there."

At the Coach & Horses, the entire band had come prepared for their signing photo. Blake, wearing a crown, was brandishing a large peacock feather as a fake quill and a photographer friend was ready to capture the historic moment. Greg waved, raised his eyebrows, mimed a pint, then rubbed his fingers together for money, and pointed to the bar with his hitching thumb. Everyone was spoken for.

"Got the contract, Greg?" Blake didn't care much for business, but he was always up for having his picture taken wearing fancy dress. Greg was constitutionally unable to get straight down to it. He liked a lengthy preamble, a lot of banter. The entire band knew something was up when he launched right in.

"No contract. Look . . ." And then, as if remembering himself: "Alright, everyone? Nice to see you . . ."

"Don't they want to sign us anymore?" asked Jack gloomily; most of the hard talk fell to him.

"The contract is waiting on my desk. We can sign it now if you like. There's news."

"Is it *good* news?" asked Blake cautiously. The feather was now behind his ear. "*News*, though." He weighed the word. "It's just good that there's news. News is good news."

"*No* news is good news," said Jack.

"No," said Blake firmly, ready to riff: "*news* is good news. We don't normally get news. The last time we had news was . . ."

"Well," said Greg, "there's nothing *bad* about it. It might put us in a temporarily awkward situation, but it might be the best thing that's ever happened. I got a call today from an old friend called Nick Hedges; we were at Clarion together way back under Carey-Jones"—Greg hadn't been to public school, but, his tales of seniority and double-barreled surnames made a seventies record label seem a little like Eton—"and in fact I used to date his mum then, but I don't know if he ever knew that." Usually this would have been the blast off to a lengthy anecdotal orbit round the planet of Greg's sexual escapades, but even he now stayed *on message.* "Anyway, he runs Endymion, who've just been sold to WBA, and . . . well, he wants to make an offer for the record."

"What record?" asked Jack.

"What record do you think?" asked Greg. "Yours."

"Quack! But what about Wanted?" asked Blake, exactly as Greg himself had, exactly as Greg had known it would be the first question out of Blake's mouth. Because Greg had taught him all he knew.

"Well, I'm meeting with Nick tomorrow, and let's assume nothing's going to come of it, but let's not sign the Wanted contract just yet. That's all I'm saying. It'll be your decision, after you meet up with Nick. But for one night in our lives, let's play hard to get."

"What *exactly* did he say?" asked Jack. And Greg told them exactly as much as he wanted them to know of exactly what Nick had said.

"So this was in the pipeline and you didn't tell us?" asked Jack. One of the twins was playing imaginary drums, using a pint glass with a beer mat on top as his snare. The other twin poked him in the ribs. They didn't usually contribute much to the decision-making process.

Greg laughed. "Well, I sent him the tape, didn't I? It just took him a little time to get to it." He would never claim credit where it wasn't due.

"Did you make a follow-up call after you sent out the cassette?" asked Jack.

Greg was just about to answer, slightly defensively, when

Blake said, with a big smile on his face, "Boys, can we just bask in the moment for a second? Greg, it's wonderful. It's amazing. We have another offer for the record."

"Bidding war!" chorused the twins.

Every glass raised in Greg's direction.

"I mean, I'm not gonna sit here and tell you it was a managerial masterstroke," he said. "He had the tape from me months ago, and I was sitting at home and the phone goes and it's him—that's how rock 'n' roll happens—and I'm going to meet him tomorrow morning and then he'll want to meet you."

"Is he gonna want to see us play?" asks Jack.

"As sure as ferrets is ferrets!" said Blake.

"Probably," said Greg, "but he said that wasn't strictly necessary. They just love the demo."

"Well, we should tell Wanted," said Blake.

"No," said Jack, ever the older brother. "They're offering us tuppence and friendship. Endymion is the real thing. That's payday. This is my job and to do it, I need a salary. Let's hear what they have to say."

"Well," said Greg, "I'll go meet with Nick tomorrow, but he sounded very enthusiastic. More than enthusiastic."

"Why don't me and Blake come with you?" asked Jack.

"Well, we can't have everyone, can we? Nick and I are old friends, perhaps he wants to have a private chat, you know. There shouldn't be a hitch," said Greg, knowing there was always a hitch, that the whole thing would be full of hitches.

"There's always a hitch," said Jack.

Nothing pissed Greg off except gloominess. Very often he was heard to describe people he didn't much like as "the most miserable man in the world": they had it all on a plate and they couldn't appreciate it. Why were bands always at their most miserable when things were looking up? A little thank you would go a long way as well.

"Cheer up, mate," said Greg. "It might never happen."

"Sorry," said Jack. "It's how I cope with good news. You should meet our old man."

"To own his each," said Greg gnomically.

• • •

There was a hitch.

Nick explained his vision—Rock Music FOR KIDS!—to Greg who nodded sagely, wondering how on earth he was going to get this by the band, trying to imagine the construction of even the most basic explanatory sentence that he could complete without them running in terror.

As Nick went on to outline the budget that was at his disposal, Greg had the uncharacteristically violent urge to reach for the phone, ring his lawyer, and scream "HELP!" Ten percent meant he could retire. And it was at that moment, with that realization, that he inked a date to resign as the Wunderkinds' manager, a date about six months after the contract was signed. His job was simply to shepherd the deal through. He would be quite content to be the one who got the band signed, then walked away. He could live with that. And when the band was sitting at some award ceremony, all those years in the future, they'd invite him to sit with them, because it was his award too, even though in another sense it had nothing to do with him.

"Well," said Greg, throwing up his hands with a smile. "It's all wonderful. The only thing is, I just can't tell you how the band's going to react to that. I just can't say."

"Greg. I'm going to put my money where my mouth is, because I believe this can work. I've spoken to Norm, and Norm thinks this can work too. He says hi by the way; asked how Pam was. First, our lawyer is going to talk to your lawyer. And then your lawyer is going to talk to you. And then the band is going to come and talk to me. And that's exactly what's going to happen. And by the time they leave that door . . ."

". . . you'll be able to do a quick line right here."

"Those days are gone, my friend. And good riddance."

"Shame," said Greg wistfully, though he never did drugs, never had: none. But the *characters* had, lots, and those had been the best days of all, because drugs made men bold. The characters had signed a band simply because they liked them or their manager. And then they had worked the band and given that band at least three chances: no one minded if the first one wasn't a smash, you were just setting up the second, good reviews were nice; and the second album, well, you wanted to see something happening, but maybe it wouldn't happen until the third. And then the third, and maybe curtains . . . but you had room to develop, to grow, and if you didn't have a career by the end of the third, or at the very least a live following, then you were in the wrong line of work. And then that band was dropped, and either everything was groovy or blame was apportioned and grudges held. But both had been fine. Nowadays, you got one shot. And you never made any money on the back-end, so you might as well spend as much as you possibly could at the beginning. It wasn't how business should be done.

Greg was wrestling with that introductory sentence to the band, but perhaps he didn't even have to come up with one. Perhaps Nick would do the dirty work for him. All he had to do was get them in this office; then catch the eye of various members and raise his eyebrow in either amusement, horror, or consideration, whichever seemed most appropriate.

The whole band was in Nick's office the next day.

Greg had been advised on the best lawyer (by his own lawyer, who knew he was out of his league), that lawyer had received and recounted Endymion's first offer, which was sensational and offered substantial "wiggle room," which meant, essentially, that it was beyond sensational. The band was overjoyed: Endymion was serious. Wanted would be told. Greg would do it, of course he would, and everyone would come out of it fine. Wanted would understand. And they *would* understand. No one worried about that now. This was a different playing field. Or, rather, it was a whole new ball game on a different playing field, as Greg put it.

And in Nick's office, Greg sat in the very chair where less than a week before Laurie had seen the pile of crappy tapes, and watched Nick give a master class in A&R. Nick got to his point, so subtly and so charmingly, making it seem that success with the children's demographic would never, *could* never, overtake the band's success with adults, and would indeed be a tribute to their songwriting—"universal popularity" was the phrase he kept using. And hadn't rock always been for children?

Of course, there would be certain stipulations about brand and image in the contract, but Nick downplayed these until they seemed piffling considerations, and Greg found that he was not fielding the expected quizzical or shocked looks from his wards; rather they stared at Nick, mouths open, divvying the money in their heads. Far from worrying whether an appearance on Multi-Coloured Swap Shop represented a prostitution of their talent or a potential blow to their credibility, they were wondering only when they could buy the gear they'd always wanted, get into a proper studio, and start recording.

Nick loved the songs. He loved them so much: he thought "Lucky Duck" might be the first single, but he loved "Rock Around the Bed," too, and he told the band that wonderful story of his son punching his fist in the air, before he happened to mention that there might have to be an edit, perhaps the song was a little too long as it was, and if they were going to make a snip perhaps it should be the stuff about the girl in the last verse, which seemed the obvious edit, really.

"A bit long maybe," murmured Blake, lost in a dream.

And Greg knew only too well what was happening; it was as if the band were hypnotized. Nick couldn't wait to hear more songs: had they thought about a producer? He had a couple of ideas. Yes, the obvious names. But those songs, he could hear them speaking to everyone, not kids particularly, everyone, and that was how you had hit singles. That was when Blake said the magic words: "Well, I do kind of write with children in mind."

And it was true. And it was all over.

The Wunderkinds were dead: long live the Wunderkinds.

In the pub afterwards, they ordered round upon round.

"Whoa! Whoa," said Greg. "Don't spend your advance all at once!" Suddenly Greg was the voice of reason. "Now you know . . . and it's great, and I love you all for being so open to it . . . but you know what he's basically asking you to be right?" Why he was trying to dissuade them *now* he couldn't fathom. Perhaps it was the last vestige of his managerly duty. Perhaps he was only doing it because he knew they couldn't be dissuaded. His 10 percent was safe.

"We're not fools," said Jack, sipping a Jack Daniels, an un-usual celebratory foray beyond beer. "I'm not. This is my shot," he said, lifting his glass with a smile, "and I'm going to take it." He downed it in one and slammed the glass on the table.

"Okay. Devil's advocate," said Greg. Best to get the home truths out of the way. "Can you think of another band that has been marketed specifically at kids?"

The Chipmunks. Pinky and Perky. Rolf Harris. The Partridge Family. They couldn't really think of one.

"The Monkees!" said Tom Twin triumphantly. Everyone drank to that.

"Look. Good music will win out!" said Jack. "Nick said . . ."

"Ooh, I know," said Blake, "let's call him Mr. Hedges. Wing Commander Hedges. No, Mr. Hedges."

". . . Mr. Hedges said we could play our songs, in our way, and that nothing was going to change."

"He suggested edits. You have yet to make the album," Greg reminded them. "He's an A&R man. He's going to A&R. He'll A&R you within an inch of your life. You're gonna be A&Red up the A&Arse. It's gonna be one long A&Rgument." He was pulling out all the stops.

"Jack's right. We want to be heard," said Blake.

"You could be on Wanted and sell 500 copies," said Greg, making it sound as somewhat great as possible.

"I think Mr. Hedges has seen something about us," Blake continued, "and I think he might be right. It always felt a bit like we were raiding the costume box and performing at the grown-up party, didn't it?"

"Then, great," said Greg. He couldn't believe his luck, their luck, everyone's luck. "But when you sign that dotted line, and I'd say this whoever you were signing for, I want you to have no illusions that this is going to go the best way possible. Think of the worst possible way it can go and double it. And that's your future."

"Fucking hell," said Jack. "Why are you at your most miserable when you should be happiest? You've just got us an amazing record deal. We've all made some money. Cheer up, mate. It might never happen."

"I'm managing," said Greg. "This is what I do."

"Besides, you'll be with us," said Blake. "Fighting our corner; good times and bad times; down in the foxhole; making sure we get what we want?"

"Course I will."

But, in Greg's mind, he had already resigned. The fight would be too great; the band would be too disappointed; the retreat too tragic.

He never had to work another day in his life.

"Man, I just work here."

IN OUR SALAD DAYS, THE WONDERFAMILY DID A LOT OF TRAVELING, always by bus. Kids were never buckled, never clunked or clicked; they roamed freely. There was a full refrigerator, a twenty-four-hour deli tray, Twizzlers waving like a bouquet of dead-headed flowers. Even the bunks—the "coffins"—didn't feel lonely; they just promised hide and seek, and the corridor made an excellent gauntlet. There were only three rules: sleep with your feet towards the driver, no bowel movements in the toilet, and, most importantly, don't get left behind.

I remember holidays with my foster parents: holding it in on the long, long drive; "Are we there yet?"; "First to see the sea!"; the inevitable attempt at reading followed by the equally inevitable bout of car sickness and "Look out the window" or "Rub mint on your hands." They actually brought a little plastic bag of fresh mint on car journeys, which never once worked. Just as a menthol cigarette is no less disgusting than a regular one, minty vomit wasn't tastier than standard. There wasn't even a cassette player in the car, just a radio, which my foster father, Terry, didn't like to turn on: the stated reason being that it impeded conversation, giving the impression there was conversation to impede. The truth is he didn't like music of any variety—or conversation for that matter. The major project of his life was to ensure that everybody lived in tomb-like silence. There wasn't a volume knob in the world he couldn't lower.

"How can you do your homework with that racket on?" he'd yell from the hall, much louder than whatever music was playing. Then he'd march in, turn the racket down with a theatrical gesture much at odds with the rest of his dour personality, and leave, breathing the sigh of relief of a man about whose throat a garrote has recently been loosened. Irony being, I could concentrate better with it on.

So, no radio; and reading was out, and conversation never got going, despite the dead air. Terry once went so far as to claim that a radio sapped a car's battery. He was equally passive-aggressive about the heating. Cold silence: that was the goal.

If I have kids, should I have kids, we shall talk in the car; we shall play I Spy, Number Plates, and all the other WonderBus favorites. Blake knew every parlor game that didn't require either a board or a pen and paper to keep score. He'd improvise surreal new rules for the Laughter Game and the Yes and No Game, stretching them out to absurd, distance-busting lengths. He knew every lateral thinking exercise and made up new ones at the drop of a hat. A man arrives at a hotel and immediately finds out he has no money, why? (He's playing Monopoly). A man takes an elevator to the fourth floor and then walks to his apartment on the ninth, why? (He's a dwarf and can't reach a higher button.) The surgeon is a woman; the snowman has melted; the parachute hadn't opened—he knew them all. A rite of passage for newcomers was to sit in a circle as we passed a pair of scissors around and declared them either crossed or uncrossed: the right answer depended on your legs rather than the scissors, but first-timers were slow to cotton on. Wink Murder evolved into something called Mafia. Once, I was killed, went to my coffin, and woke the next morning, three states later, to find them still at it. And Blake taught us how to take an amaretto wrapper, smooth it into a tube, and set fire to it: just when you think it's going to burn the carpet, the vacuum sends it flying angel-like back into the air. The Terrys would have had a conniption! That was the thing: Blake behaved like one of the kids. Terry could hardly bear to hear anything *once*; Blake had the ability to listen to a piece of music or watch a video over and over again. "It's great," he'd say, "you just get more out of it each time." Blake was a kid's dream come true, straight out of one of his own crazy songs.

No meal was complete without the demonstration of some bizarre trick from his repertoire involving, say, a match and the balancing of an interlocked fork and spoon on the top edge of a glass. They weren't technically magic tricks, though he knew those as well—he always carried a fake thumb tip and a hankie in his back pocket—just crap his mind had never thrown away. He left a trail of origami behind him like the guy in *Blade Runner*. (It was how he cured himself of biting his nails.) Best of all, though I was always terrible at it, was the game where you had to reply to the previous person completely irrelevantly. He called it the Nonsense Game. It was hard. It's hard not to make sense when that's all you know how to do.

And if I do have kids, about which (after years of superstitious pessimism) I have become increasingly optimistic, there will be more than one of them. Because being an only child, in the back of your foster parents' car, when you can't read a book because you'll vomit, and when the radio can't be played because it impedes conversation, and when the elderly couple in the front bicker all the time (except for the occasional smirk), and it feels like everything is just about to boil over but, worst of all, endlessly simmers . . . Because being an only child is not a great thing to be.

I always wanted a brother or a sister (I probably had one all along, but this was the era before Facebook weakened the hermetic quality of life as a foster child), someone to wrestle with and argue with, play music with, steal from, tease. At the orphanage, before I was fostered, it was like you had too many brothers and sisters, but none you really trusted, and none specifically yours. Then with the Terrys (he was Terry and she was Teri) it was worse. They had their own son, of course, Ian, much older, out in the world. I was their charity case, a distraction in retirement; they "had the money," wanted to "give something back." They weren't bad people, but they were too old—something they realized soon but not soon enough. There was never a suggestion of their formally adopting me, and every sign that they'd give me up at the drop of a hat. I was the antithesis of all the things they liked: cold silence and no sugar.

Life with the Terrys was trying for all parties involved, so I signed up for any number of after-school classes purely to delay my return to their welcome mat. My eventual route took me past the orphanage (officially a "child care centre" called The Clement Bagley, or Clements), where I'd inevitably see a couple of the kids playing Ping-Pong on that same warped table in the front window; you couldn't help feel a pang of nostalgia for the racket.

The goal had always been to leave Clements: we called it "The Great Escape," but I couldn't say—I still can't—that I preferred life with my foster parents. With the Terrys, nothing was up to me. At Clements, so recently, I'd finally been made a monitor: it wasn't much, but I liked the responsibility. I got to read bedtime stories, which inspired me to organize a pre-bedtime Olympiad to tire the little kids out (so I didn't have to read so long). At thirteen, I was a natural organizer. I even did some of the supervisors' work for them, which they didn't mind one bit. Once I made a chart for a table-tennis competition, with name tabs you could slot into the appropriate position in the league table. On the strength of this, Harmon, the "director" (the previous guy hadn't had a title), asked me to draw up the duty roster, presumably because no one else could be bothered. It wasn't slave labor, though Blake later cited it as evidence of my supposedly lost childhood; I just liked doing that stuff. For example, there was this profoundly antiquated behavior rating system for the kids. I designed the chart they still use, redrawn every year but still to my blueprint, on which the good order marks (red) and bad order marks (black) are stuck next to each student's name. Woe betide the kid with five bad order marks. (Luckily, I was both the only person who knew precisely where the stickers were sold, and the only one with the knack of unpeeling them cleanly, so I could surreptitiously remove bad, or supplement good, at will. Harmon was none the wiser. Both the staff and my peers thought I'd found my true calling.)

For years I'd been made to feel "unfosterable," yet all of a sudden I found myself paraded in the director's office like Little Lord Fauntleroy. Perhaps I never had been "unfosterable"; perhaps I was just *never fostered*. I always wondered whether Harmon had palmed me to the bottom of the deck. We hadn't got on from the beginning. When he took over, I was summoned, as we all were in turn, to his office. I was ten and happened to be barefoot. He asked me where my shoes were, and I said "Cobblers, sir." Bad order mark. The very next day, he saw me with my tennis racket and said all friendly: "I didn't know you had a Head," and I said: "It's what I talk out of." He gave me a look like I'd spat in his porridge.

And there he was, still in his office, oblivious to the Ping-Pong on the other side of the wall, marking up my duty roster.

At home, after the briefest dinner, usually eaten to the riveting soundtrack of the Terrys' evaluation of my table manners, I'd turn on the music and do my homework until the music was turned off and I could no longer concentrate. For Christmas, the Terrys bought me a pair of headphones, largely for their own benefit.

At fourteen, I was a loner. The Terrys had just sent me on my first ever sleepover with Brian, a boy I liked only in their imagination. For whatever reason, our forced friendship was desirable. I like to think that I was shipped off to accommodate the Terrys' annual coupling, but it was probably so they could have *a little peace and quiet* or, in the wildest scenario, play bridge.

Brian was a little prig. We sat down to dinner and he said: "I think you'll find the home-cooking here a little better than at your house." Which I couldn't dispute, of course, but who says that? Later on, in our bunk beds, he told me about his best friend Simon. "He's very nice, but he's a liar like you. You said you were on page 123 of your book, but I looked inside and your bookmark was on page 45."

In fact, a worse lie had already been told. We'd been about to brush our teeth but I'd forgotten my toothbrush, and I couldn't stand the fuss Brian's mother was making looking for a spare, so I told a story (which had its basis in medical truth because I'd seen it on *Tomorrow's World*) about how I didn't ever use a toothbrush;

I squirted toothpaste on my finger and worked it round my mouth. I may have been getting muddled with people who didn't bother with toothpaste, just used a brush, but anyway, that's what I said. No big deal. I had said it only to put a stop to her dramatic search.

Next morning, the Terrys came to pick me up at some idiotic school rugby tournament (in which neither I nor Brian was participating—we were manning the half-time oranges). As I watched them greet Brian's mother and the headmaster, I felt unusually glad to see them, probably because staying at Brian's had felt even less like home than "home." As I cantered up behind, somewhat enthusiastically, even willing to ask them if they'd had a good night, I heard Brian's mother say: "And so he said that, at home, he brushes his teeth with his finger and doesn't use a toothbrush at all," and everybody burst out laughing. And Teri said: "Heaven knows what they taught them at the Clement Bagley!" They hadn't seen me, and so, not wanting to make anyone feel awkward, or even wanting them to know that I had heard, let alone cared, I turned around and walked away.

It wasn't that life was bad; it's just that I didn't feel at home anywhere. I had optimistically expected to become part of the family, part of Team Terry—I thought that was the point—but I was no more part of their team than I was in the rugby fifteen: I was just doing the oranges at half-time, and when cricket season came, I'd be asked to put the numbers up on the scoreboard, but that would be as far as it would go. Their ham-fisted attempts to socialize me made me treasure my own company; my world became my headphones.

So, naturally, I turned to shoplifting.

It was all pretty run of the mill stuff: I'd started off with the penny items at the local sweetshop—Blackjacks were the gateway drug—then moved on paperbacks at WH Smiths, one of which I gave to Terry for Christmas, a historical novel about Caligula. My greatest haul had been twenty birthday cards from Timothy Whites, all very pink. I didn't get my thrills where other kids got them: cheap beer, drugs, glue. All I had was sugar-based products, and every now and then, I wanted a different rush.

But one day, I raised the stakes. I was hanging around at Our Price. When I was little, it was the Gramophone Record Store, or something similarly Edwardian, with a big eye logo, lots of dusty classical records, and a few singles; then it became Small Al's, its greatest iteration; but Small Al, who was enormous, died, and, after hanging on as Stylus for a few months, the shop was transformed into an Our Price, with those gaudy round stickers taking up half the LP cover. CDs were taking over and the racks contracted. It briefly reigned as the world's tiniest Virgin Megastore, at which point LPs disappeared entirely, and then it was called Cut-price or Cheapdeal or something, and for a while it was an HMV, then maybe a Xavvi, which sold mostly computer games, DVDs, mugs, and mobile phones, and then it vanished, entirely eaten up by the theme pub next door, and, what with Amazon and eBay, there hasn't been a record store there since.

It was 6 p.m., I was officially on my way home, and the last thing I wanted was a 45 of the Hollies' reissue of "He Ain't Heavy, He's My Brother," currently charging up the charts, but the store was deserted apart from me in my burgundy school blazer and two bored guys behind the counter debating the merits of Wet Wet Wet. There was a central rack down the middle, and, against the wall, a collection of pristine singles practically begging to be liberated. Front and center: the Hollies. A single, awkwardly sized as it was, represented a challenge, but I was determined to leave the store with one stuffed up my blazer.

I took two or three 45s, turned away, pretending to peruse the back covers, slipped the Hollies inside my blazer, put the others back in the rack and sauntered through the store browsing so as not to provoke suspicion, lingering by the counter, which was at the back of the store, to flip through a box of picture discs. I knew exactly how to proceed.

It would have been the perfect crime had I not reached for the furthest of the picture discs, and thereby pushed the Hollies single up so it just—and really *just*—poked out from the top of my blazer. I was blissfully unaware of its protrusion, but the man behind the counter eyeballed it at once. He had me, and, since I had no idea, he began to tease. He continued talking to the other bloke about some reorder: "I think there's one left. Let me have a look in the database . . . yeah, just the one. It should be in the racks. Could you check it out?" It seemed a lot of tedious shoptalk, and the first sign of distress was when his dimmer mate asked: "Which single?"

"Hollies. 'He Ain't Heavy.'"

I glanced at my blazer—giveaway!—and though I at least had the presence of mind not to catch Mr. Database's eye, I had to think quick because by the time his colleague was down at the other end of the store—and he was already halfway there—I'd have no exit. I picked out one of the picture discs (by that band Boston, their lurid logo underneath a spaceship) and handed it nonchalantly to the guy behind the counter: "Could you play this for me please?"

By now he knew I knew, but he was happy to let his little charade reach its natural climax. The moment he turned, I sprinted down the other aisle from the singles. The dopey one saw me go but couldn't grab me over the central rack, the one behind the counter cottoned on late, and I was gone, out the door, to a cry of "After him!" I felt a bit like the Artful Dodger, which was really the kind of rush I was after: nearly being caught. Maybe *being* caught would be the biggest rush of all; taken back to the Terrys, in shame and disgrace, their rueful looks of disappointment, earnest conversations with the foster agency, and then SENT BACK TO THE CLEMENTS! No, that would all be too much.

I looked over my shoulder as I ran. The guy was coming for me, pointing, yelling "I know you!" I thought of hurling the record in the air so he'd be torn between me and his property, but instead I passed the baton to a surprised passerby with the breathless instruction: "Give it to that bloke, please!" and ran on. This ploy didn't distract my pursuer even momentarily, which was when I realized, for the first time, that he was gaining on me, that he would catch me, that I was in trouble, and that all those fantasies that had seemed so humorous when unlikely, were now imminent events, sharp and painful. So I ducked down the first street I could, hoping he wouldn't see. There was a slightly open basement window, about shin height, and I was either about to force my way inside or die trying, so I reached in, opened it as wide as I could and pushed myself in head first, wriggling like a worm.

"Jesus!" shouted someone inside.

I found myself much further from the floor than I'd expected, but I knew I had to keep delivering myself through this mailbox, however unhappy the landing, before I felt the hand on my ankle. I started to topple in as someone in the room swore, ran over and caught me, or most of me, anyway. I flopped into his arms, just inches from the floor. "Close the window," I shouted, which was when my head hit something.

Someone sang, "She came in through the bathroom window!"

"Sh!" said the man holding me. He winked and everything slowed down. "You alright?"

"Hit my head." I was groggy.

"We saw." He was stroking my forehead as though I was about to die. I felt the goose egg throb. I squinted; there seemed to be tears in his eyes, though there weren't any in mine.

"Do you want anything, son? Glass of water"

"Coke?" I asked.

"Hold your horses there, mate!" said someone else. "The full rider hasn't arrived yet!"

Had I dropped in on an unexpectedly good-natured basement drug deal? I heard the groan-chink-fizz of a Coke can.

At which point I passed out.

When I resurfaced a few minutes later, someone was telling a story about how he'd gone to see the Beatles, one of their early gigs. There were no tickets left so he'd tried to sneak in the back way, and found an open window that he'd tentatively climbed through. Someone helped him in—and who do you think it was? John Lennon! The narrator had landed in the Beatles' dressing room! Lennon guided the kid through the backstage and asked the usher to let him watch the whole show. It was the only time he'd met a Beatle.

"Beat the Meetles!" Someone laughed.

It was the first story of Greg's I ever heard. The story was true, unlikely though it seems, the catch being that it didn't happen to Greg but to Al Stewart, the *Year of the Cat* man. Greg thought stories lost something if you didn't tell them in the first person.

"Ooh!" He said, noticing movement. "Look who's come round!"

I was lying on a sofa with my head on a man's lap; he was stroking my hair. My instant reaction was to pull away, but he seemed harmless, so I lay back again. He had beautiful bright green eyes and a nose like a satsuma—rindy, not deformed, just wider than usual. It was the compulsive jiggling of his right leg that brought me round.

"You were in a bit of a rush, weren't you?" asked my nurse. "Running away from someone?" I couldn't see any point in making up stories, so I nodded. He handed me the can of Coke, encouraging me to sip from it, but I couldn't lying down and I didn't like being a wounded bird, so I sat up, struggling with the buttons of my blazer. We seemed to be in a back room somewhere or other; there were more people in the room than before.

"The fuzz?" asked Greg empathetically. He'd had a partially misspent youth (vastly over-amplified) and fancied himself on speaking terms with the underworld.

"Actually," I said, "I was shoplifting. Records."

Greg burst out laughing, a messy smile all over his face. "Alright! I don't mind him at all! How old are you?"

"Fourteen."

"Where's the record, then?" asked the fidgety man with the nose next to me on the sofa. His leg was quivering like it was being administered its own course of electroshock therapy.

"I ditched it."

"Well, you shouldn't shoplift," he said, as though doing an impression of someone in a position of authority. "Why do you want to go around stealing things? What's your name?"

"Edward," I said.

"Well," he said, "that's a perfectly good name. Edward. Edward Lear. But I can't call you that. It doesn't suit you."

"How do you know?" I asked. "You've only just met me."

"You're not thinking straight. Would you like something to

eat? A sandwich? Some cheese? Pheasant? Slice of quince? Country pie? Lark's tongues in aspic?"

"Got a Mars Bar?"

"No."

"Any chocolate?"

He eyed my can of Coke. "Do you only eat sweets?"

I nodded. "And pizza."

"Maybe I'll call you Sweet."

It was like a magic trick, though I couldn't work out how he had done it. "That's my name! Edward Sweet!" (He'd read it on the nametag on the inside of my blazer.)

"Well, there you go then! But I'm not calling you Sweet like your surname; I'm calling you Sweet because of your sweet tooth. It's completely different; a new name entirely."

"Okay," I said, nonplussed by this supposed rebaptism. He had a name for everyone: Goldfinch, the Ghost, Mum, the Compromise, Ripley, the Damager, the Gee-gee-gee. Each with its own complicated genesis.

"I'm Blake," he said, "and this is Greg, and that's my brother Jack, and those are Timothy and Thomas, the twins, Tweedledum and Tweedledee. We're all mad here. I'm mad. You're mad." He actually didn't seem at all mad. I liked everything about him. "We're a band. The Wunderkinds." He said it in a thick German accent.

"The who?" I asked.

"Wrong again. The Wunderkinds."

"Where are yer instruments then?" I asked suspiciously, a little more myself again.

"On stage."

"So this is your dressing room?"

"He's learning," said Greg. I surveyed the room: a little food, some drinks, and a suitcase that one of the twins was unzipping. There was a rap on the door, through which appeared an employee: "Maybe fifteen minutes, lads? Just trying to get the last of the chairs out so we can squeeze a few more warm bodies in. Hey, what's he doing in here?"

"Fan," said Jack. "Overcome with emotion."

"He's with us," said Blake.

"No, no, no," shushed Greg. "Merch. Merch Boy. Does our merch."

"We can sell it for you in-house," suggested the representative. "Fifteen percent."

"And what are we getting for fifteen percent?" asked Greg. "Placement? Lighting? A table? Back display? No, no: we've got our own lad. Set up a table, and we'll send him out."

"Fourteen minutes now; don't want to keep this lot waiting. Could turn very nasty." The door closed behind him.

"All you know about me," I said, "is that I steal records. That's your sum knowledge. And now you want me to sell yours."

"Catch a thief to get a thief!" said Greg.

"Sweet genius!" said Blake. "You'll know if anyone nicks 'em."

"And we'll give you ten percent," said Blake.

"Five," said Greg. "Or a flat fee. No need to cut you in."

"Seven and a half," I said. That was the way we talked right from the start, haggling, barter without rancor: banter. It was an enormous relief, especially after the grim dirge at the Terrys.

"Done," said Blake. "But be careful out there—this is a new kind of adventure." He winked again. "You're through the looking glass."

The moment I emerged from the cocoon of backstage, it did all get a little *Alice in Wonderland*.

To start with, there was the piercing sonic onslaught, just shy of that pitch only dogs can hear. That, and I was unnaturally taller than almost everybody else in the room, like Alice after a slice of cake. I'd have no more expected a room full of munchkins or midgets than this: hundreds of kids. Where on earth were the parents? I was in the large back room of the local library, and the place was absolutely heaving.

I pushed my way through the seething scrum, avoiding abandoned prams as best I could while drinks spilled and crisps crunched like eggshells under foot. Halfway across the room and I'd seen it all: laughter and tears, nudity, even a full-on fight. And the band hadn't even gone on yet. I suppose it was just like any general admission show, really, except amplified, more extreme, more insane. The noise never abated. Perhaps this was how it felt to see the Beatles live, all that screaming, except that this scream-ing wasn't specifically aimed at, or caused by, the band; it was just the endless screaming that echoes around a swimming pool or a playground, times approximately a thousand. What was I going to see? I had no idea. What band could entertain, much less pacify, this rabble? It'd be like the Christians and the lions. No music ever conceived could shut this lot up.

Per Greg's instructions, I made my way to the back, where the parents loitered, a half-hearted eye on their sugar-hopped off-spring. Relishing my quick ascent from record-stealer to record-seller, I located the table set aside for commerce. There was only one title on offer: The Wunderkinds' first album, *JabberRock*, on CD and vinyl. The cover was a shockingly bright cartoon, recog-nizably the band, with the twins completely identical, dressed like the Thompsons from Tintin, except that one was wearing a white suit and the other a black suit, and Blake, in bright red, and the other one who hadn't said very much and whose name I couldn't remember, in bright blue. Before I'd had a chance to draw any conclusions, the stage lights went up, and on bounced the band, in greatly rumpled versions of those very same suits.

In the years that followed, there is nothing I didn't see at one of the band's shows—breastfeeding, projectile vomiting, grown women in catfights, blood, broken bones, flying food, hysterical tantrums, body-surfing, near-riots—and even though this version, in a small library on our local high street, was relatively tame, the chaos to come was already implicit. Blake hadn't yet worked out how to control all those tiny minds, and the band still played way too long. (All bands play too long. The Beatles had it right at Can-dlestick: thirty-three minutes and off. No encore. Doesn't matter how old the audience is.) But I was fourteen and I got it. It didn't even take getting. They were playing catchy songs about ducks and drakes, and singing riddles about the sun and the sky, and knock-knock jokes, and the parents along the back wall were tap-ping their toes, occasionally darting forward to separate antago-nists in the ruck and maul. It was mayhem. These were the cowboy years before Health & Safety ruined everything.

Then a great moment: some lost lone two-year-old toddles

towards the lead singer, who pretends to be terrified as the kid shuffles incrementally towards him. "Security," Blake calmly requests. Good gag. And then he—Blake that is, not the two-year-old—goes back to bouncing around, an exuberant new-wave twist that's simultaneously hazardous and restrained; I'd never seen anything less self-conscious. He had to anchor himself to the mic between numbers, just to stop himself from jiggling and twitching off again.

I watched in amazement—awe, really—from the strange perspective of the merch booth, where all was calm. Indeed, business-wise, things were slow. No one had even bothered to browse my wares. Greg sauntered back, swaying like a Weeble that wobbles but won't fall down. With him was another bloke.

"How's it going?" Greg asked. "Units?" I shook my head. "Well, where's your sign?"

"Sign?"

"You've got to have a sign. Prices. What's for sale! A sign! Use your noggin! Count it in! Count it out! You're a vital part of the operation. I'll help out with the rush at the end. This is Mister Hedges. This is, er . . ."

"Sweet," I said. It seemed vastly preferable to Edward. It didn't even feel like being called by my surname.

"Yeah, Sweet," confirmed Greg. "He's given up a life of crime to join the circus." I had? No one could possibly have described me so glamorously until very recently: my life had been transformed in the span of an hour. I'd been unexpectedly promoted, improved, a black-and-white movie colorized and made 3-D.

Mr. Hedges ignored me, struggling to make himself heard over the music. "So how's the great experiment?"

"Well," said Greg, scratching his head: "Your guess is as good as mine. They've let two entire classes come in from the local kindergarten and some older kids from the comprehensive; the band are doing their bit; be nice to see some music moving; be nice if you got behind them on the radio, you know; the usual."

"Well, they sound good . . . when you can hear them."

"Yeah," said Greg, throwing me a look behind Mr. Hedges's back.

Mr. Hedges turned to me: "How old are you? Seventeen?"

"Fourteen," I shouted.

"What do you think of them?"

"Honestly?" No one ever asked my opinion. "I like 'em. I thought it was going to be for children, when I saw all the kids, but it looks like the adults are into it as well." How the Terrys would have hated it! "It's a bit like punk for kids."

Mr. Hedges stood back and beamed: "Yeah. Punk for kids. Punk for kids whose parents like punk. Music for kids with cool parents. *Top of the Pops* for Tots. I like it." He turned back to Greg. "Well, tell the boys to keep doing what they're doing, and we'll keep doing what we're doing. We'll get there. I believe in this. And we're gonna join the dots. We're not letting go."

After he'd gone, Greg turned to me with a smile: "*Punk for kids*? You're doing his work for him."

The parents unavoidably passed my table as they exited but very few actually stopped; they had their hands full with their kids and their snacks and their sippy cups. Just when it seemed a total washout, up Blake bounded like a circus ringmaster, standing on a chair and shouting "Roll up! Roll up! Get your music here! Wunderkinds unite!" And the kids surrounded him, clambering on to and over him: it was like he was going to get dragged into the ground by African killer ants. Blake sat the kids on his knee one by one, let them have the prized photo, told a knock-knock joke, asked what they had for breakfast, and offered an autograph. Sales went through the roof. I had never held so much money in my life. I didn't have change, and had no idea how to get any. Greg mouthed and mimed: "Make everything a fiver." Up on the stage, the other three members of the band were breaking down gear, packing it into cases. That was why Blake spent so much time with the kids, Jack said: anything to avoid load-out.

Greg stood back and basked in the moment, watching in admiration; I handed him the fivers as they rolled in. We sold out of everything, but Blake just kept going. No kid ever felt he was shaking and faking. When you were with Blake Lear, he was with you, and only you. There was no one else around. He wasn't some disappointingly thin, dubiously bearded Santa Claus at the end of a long line: he was the man himself, the Spirit of Christmas.

The last kid bailed reluctantly; the infant meet-and-greet had lasted almost as long as the gig. Greg riffled fivers in front of my face and said "I always said we needed a merch boy. Pizza's on the band, Sweet," as he kicked empty CD boxes across the room in celebration: "Blimey, I wouldn't want to clean up this lot." The floor was a scene of terrible devastation, wrappers floating in sticky spillage and oily slick: an environmental disaster in miniature.

Blake breathed a sigh, either relief or exhaustion; perhaps simply pleasure at a job well done. "I'm starving. Can we feed you, Sweet? You want your just desserts? Or just dessert?"

"Don't you have a home to go to?" asked Greg.

"Yeah. I live with my foster parents. Not far."

"Foster parents?" asked Blake. "What are they like?"

"Slightly less fun than the children's home, where I was before."

"Which one?"

"Clements."

"I know that place. They wouldn't have us play there. Shall we see if it's okay for you to come and get pizza?"

"No," I said. "I can just come."

"No, no," said Blake, as he led me back to the dressing room. The band had magicked the cases into a van. "Got to ask permission. Don't want them to think you been kidnapped. Parents worry."

"Foster parents," I said. "They don't worry."

"All parents worry."

"Vol-au-vent," said Greg with a shrug, before rubbing money fingers together, going in search of a check. "I'll do the necessary," he announced, the floorboards a trampoline beneath his bouncing stride.

"Vol-au-vent?" I asked Blake, thinking this might be a less desirable dinner suggestion.

"Yeah. He means 'whatever you like,' 'it's up to you,' or 'comme il vaut' or something . . . but it gets a bit muddled in his head." I nodded. "Come on," he said, "let's ask these foster parents face-to-face. And when they say yes, we'll buy you pizza."

"Vol-au-vent."

• • •

80

It seemed a kind of miracle that Teri agreed, but when I smiled and waved to her out of the van window, just to reassure her that I wasn't being kidnapped, she waved back and made a "shoo" gesture, which I took to mean that she didn't much care one way or the other, though I did notice that she was talking to Blake in an unusually twittery, almost giggly, way. Perhaps she fancied Blake; she certainly never behaved that way with her husband or any other male. Our most regular form of communication was the rap of her knuckles on the kitchen window when she saw me doing something wrong in the back garden. At least, that's how I remember it. (In extreme situations, she would take off her shoe and use that; once when I was "misbehaving" in the car, she put her heel right through the window of a phone box.) Perhaps Blake told her precisely what had happened (with any luck omitting all reference to my spectacular entrance), that I had very kindly helped them out and that they wanted to reward me; perhaps he mentioned that he taught at the local primary school; heaven knows what credentials he offered. But there she was, sending me on my way with a little wave. Bye.

It was the band's last date for a month or so: disappointing. Just as things had seemed like they were getting going. Real life notwithstanding, I'd pictured myself thumbing a ride on the WunderVan, leaving the home counties for dead and lighting out for the territories, eating pizza, drinking Coke, selling merch. That was not to be—at least not for now. In fact I had no immediate excuse to see them for some time. Blake himself was off on holiday: "and all you'll get is a lousy postcard."

Life went back to normal, but normal was now more monotone than ever, completely substandard. Blake's card finally came. On the front, a picture of a sandy beach with CORFU in bright red letters, and on the back: "Sun, sea, and hand in hand by the edge of the sand! I am in a state of *knownothingatallaboutwhatoneisgoingtodoness*! It's perfection! Any son of mine would be here. You would be here. Blake. P.S. Urgent non-band business to sort out on return. A QUEST! Meet me at the Regal, next Friday night, 11.15. By the exit."

• • •

A quest. Scrub that: A QUEST!

In the middle of the night!

The whole thing, although I didn't know it at the time, was typical. Blake's cautious approach to Teri that first evening had been entirely out of character, but it had worked. How could he now expect me simply to waltz out of the house after dinner? That was up to me, none of his concern. I'd better come up with something. A late night screening of *Rocky Horror*? Hmmm. Another sleepover with dreaded Brian? The Terrys' lack of curiosity was easily exploited.

The Regal was on the High Street, just down from the library; Blake worked there part time, a job he scored due to the Cambridge Arts Cinema's prominent position on his CV. It had once been a grand one-screen cinema—double features, Wurlitzer—that at some point was split into five different screens, four of which were only marginally larger than the television in your front room. There was still one big screen, where the hits played, but the others were like pinhole cameras.

Blake ushered me in through the exit, ruffling my hair.

"You're not wearing your blazer: smart." He surveyed the street shiftily. "I'm going to try to turn as few lights on as possible. We're not strictly meant to be here." He handed me a torch. I'd never been in a cinema after hours; it was eerie, echoing, strewn with popcorn and drinking straws; our flashlights made it even spookier. We were evidently quite alone; I felt like one of the meddling kids in *Scooby Doo*.

"The cleaners don't come in until 6 a.m.," he said.

"What?"

"We've got until dawn."

I laughed. "What are we going to do until dawn?"

"We're going to begin at the beginning, go on until we come to the end, then stop. Alice in Wonderland." He led me through a warren of corridors that connected projection rooms, foyers, bathrooms, and screens. Just like the first time we'd met, I found myself presented with weird new perspectives, from the other side of the counter, within the mechanism, behind the scenes, the wrong side of the screen, backstage—places off-limits to mere punters. I was on the inside, and I liked it. "I'll tell you every-thing," he continued, "but we might as well work while I do. Come with me. I have a hunch." Once in the basement, among the pipes, he opened every door, as if he expected to find any-thing but cleaning equipment.

"What are you looking for?"

"*We*"—who were apparently in it together; a thrilling first per-son plural—"are looking for treasure. Open Sesame!" he proclaimed, turning the handle of the final door and throwing on the lights in a much larger room, full to bursting with old cinema seats. He laughed and turned off his torch. "Well, at least we can see what we're doing down here. They ripped all these seats out, but someone was too mean to throw them away. See that door down there?" At the far end of the room, glimpsed just above the piles of seats, there was a door, a door that couldn't have been opened in years, at least since the seats staged their occupation. I nodded, fearing, already knowing that he expected us to move them all to get to it. "Well, that's the goal. Where there's a door, there's a beyond. And I want to get there."

"Why?"

"Doesn't every bone in your body yearn to open that door, that *portal*?"

"This'll take hours."

"We've got until 6 a.m."

"I will not start moving any of these seats unless you give me a good reason."

And, as he rolled up his sleeves, Blake said: "Well, listen to this."

There was an elderly usher at the Regal called Ernie. He'd been there for years, all through the various architectural downsizings, and, though he was famous for sleeping on the job, and seemed mysteriously to disappear from time to time, reappearing smelling of cigar and whisky, Ernie was a fixture; more of a fix-ture, in fact, than the fixtures—the Egyptian fittings that had glit-tered when he took the job, since pulled down to make way for featureless little screening rooms. Ernie kept himself to himself, but enjoyed a cuppa with Blake, along with the opportunity to rattle on about Leyton Orient, the horses, and old films. Right to the end, and quite unnecessarily, Ernie prided himself on his old-fashioned usher's overcoat, gray with epaulets and gold buttons; the dress code had changed in about 1970.

One day, Ernie didn't come in to work: that was that. But a month or so later, his widow appeared—Ernie had never mentioned family—and proceeded to waste the general manager's time with some tall tale about taking delivery of her husband's collection of cinema posters. On his deathbed, Ernie had told her about them; it'd be a nice little pension. She was extremely insistent, the only problem being that no one at the Regal knew anything about such a collection. The general manager dismissed the possibility—he knew the building like the back of his hand; besides it wasn't a museum and any posters were surely the property of the cinema, and Ernie would have had no business using the premises as his own personal store room. He pawned her off on Blake, but Blake, remembering Ernie's quiet resolve, the sly smile that seemed to imply he knew something you didn't, suspected that Ernie wouldn't, couldn't, have made this up, that the posters were there somewhere. Where? And how to get them without arousing suspicion? The widow's mistake had been going to the general manager rather than Blake.

To understand Blake, you have to know that, armed with this suspicion, this *knowledge*, there was no way he could not now try to locate, and succeed in locating, those posters, this secret collection, now amplified in his imagination into an invaluable trove of Rare Cinema History; that was Blake.

"Could you crawl underneath the rest of them?" sighed Blake. We were already tired out. Most of the seats were in multiples of three and shifting them at all was difficult. We'd moved as many as possible into the corridor, now impassable, yet we didn't seem to have made much headway towards the door.

But on we went, stopping briefly for a Coke. Exhausted, I took a breather at about 2. It was fatal. The first time my head lolled forward, I caught myself; the second time, I was a goner. Next thing I knew, Blake was tapping me on the shoulder.

"Well," he said, smiling, happy, buzzed, sweaty. "Do you want to know what was in there?"

God knows how long I'd been out. I looked towards the far end of the room. Blake had parted the remaining cinema seats like the Red Sea, and had been able to slide the door just wide enough to squeeze through.

"What?"

"Nothing!" He said, as though this were quite as good as finding Aladdin's cave. "Nothing! Two brooms and a few buckets." He started to laugh.

"We moved all these for nothing?"

"Absolutely not. We've now *ruled out* this room. The posters are not there. That's one *less* place that the posters are. Besides, there was real excitement and satisfaction while we were moving the seats, wasn't there, a real feeling of potential?" He was nodding his head, eyebrows raised, begging for agreement.

"Yes," I said, shaking my head. "No."

"Much more excitement and satisfaction, and a much greater feeling of potential, for example, than the sinking feeling we're now going to have as we put 'em all back." He laughed. I groaned. "At least, clear the corridor."

The quest was ours, how we started spending time together.

The setback with the broom closet (terminal, I would have called it) was simply amusing to Blake; that's what you got for dreaming. He loved Sod's Law; he laughed at it. In no way would he let it deflect him from his course. The posters were as good as his. And his enthusiasm was infectious. I mean, I was more circumspect, and the battle against the chairs would have put me off entirely, but I happily followed along because, whether he found the holy grail or not, every step of the way was an adventure, even the hard work. I might have drawn the line at another roomful of seats. My arms ache just remembering that absurd evening, the moment he said "Put 'em all back." I kept nodding off at the merch booth the next afternoon.

He took me back to the Regal two other nights, neither of which yielded much as we poked around with our flashlights. I wasn't disheartened because it wasn't my dream, but I worried about him. He set such store by their discovery. And increasingly it looked like he was living in la-la land.

"Wait here a second," he said one night, letting himself into an office. He emerged with two rolled up cinema posters; I assumed them to be posters. "Treasure maps!" he said. First it had been *Alice in Wonderland*, then *Aladdin*, and now it was *Treasure Island*. "Well, blueprints." And he unrolled them on the floor in the main foyer. Someone peered in through the front door at the goofy burglars with their giveaway torches. Blake waved and shouted through a big smile, blinding them with his beam: "We're done for the night! Eff off please!" He turned his attention back to me. "Now, look at these; what do you see?"

"I have no idea what I'm looking at." One was older than the other.

"This is the cinema as it was when there was one screen." I could more or less make that out. "And this is the cinema as it is, now that there are five screens."

"Right."

"If you split one screen into five, what do you get?"

"A lot of very small cinemas?"

"Look at the blueprint." I could still see nothing. "Look at the gray bits," he said. "The gaps between. If you make four small cinemas and one big one, you have to create little rooms, and that means gaps *between* the rooms . . . spaces that could *easily* hide Ernie's little secret. You have to turn your mind inside out a bit."

We knew the screening rooms, the basement, the projection booths, the foyers, the cupboards, but there it was, plain as day on the blueprints: the spaces between. Blake knew he was on to something, but he needed an assistant to get to the places he couldn't reach on his own, someone to wriggle and climb, a little monkey.

It was three months after the first trip, on the fourth foray, still by torchlight, that Blake insisted I crawl under the screen in Cinema B. I wouldn't have chosen to, even in the middle of the day with the lights on: it looked disgusting.

"It's the most obvious big space," said Blake, flapping the blueprint in mitigation.

"Look, how do you think an elderly gentleman got in and out? Crawling under this screen? I don't think so."

"Well, I'll go then. It's the best bet." Of course, he wouldn't have fit either.

"Okay. I'll go. But under protest."

"Would I steer you wrong?"

"What about those chairs?"

"That wasn't wrong. That was right. Besides, that was one of the greatest nights of your life. You tell me that wasn't better than being home in bed."

I ate a mouthful of caramel popcorn, on the house. "You're turning me into a criminal."

"When I met you, you were a criminal. I'm reforming you. Look, are you getting under there or not? Just confirm there's nothing, I'll shine a torch, and then we'll pack it in for the night."

I sighed; it was utterly ridiculous. He lifted the foot-high curtain and ushered me beyond with a sweep of his hand.

"Life is all just one big *Alice in Wonderland* sketch to you, isn't it?" I said.

"Just have a poke around," he said. His last word. He winked.

I found myself crawling through a collection of dingy flotsam, cigarette butts that commemorated a time when smoking was acceptable, pebbles of chewing gum so fossilized they dug into my elbows; the dust got up my nose, in my eyes. It's the only time in my life I ever longed for a pith helmet.

"Anything?" asked Blake, squinting through the curtain.

"Yes, yes," I said as I tunneled forward. "I've found the posters; I just didn't bother to mention it yet."

"Oh, very good. Well done." He shone the torch around more haphazardly than was useful.

"Hold on, actually," I said, feeling myself on a slight downwards slope. The stage in front of the screen was still above me, but not so close to my back; everything was opening up. I got out my torch and turned it on, but as I put it down, it rolled away. I followed its spinning light until it fell a few feet. I crawled forward—I no longer had to slither—and peered where it had fallen. It was casting a little light around a small room, a very little light, but enough.

"Jesus! Blake!" I hissed. "You've got to come, no matter how much of a squeeze it is."

By the time he arrived—and it *was* a squeeze—I had lowered myself down into the small room with the help of a foot ladder, and turned on the little lamp at the single table where I now sat, trying to look casual, feeling unearthly pleased with myself. I looked up and asked in as suave a manner as I could manage: "Is this what you were looking for?"

His mouth fell open, but nothing came out. Tears filled his eyes. On the table next to me was a circular metal ashtray in which sat half a cigar, extinguished neatly for future enjoyment, a miniature brandy, and a chipped green mug. The room was musty, dusty, but not damp. You could imagine, during cinema hours, a soundscape of all the various movies on all the screens playing at once, as Ernie puffed on his cheroot.

"Are you okay?" I asked. Blake still hadn't said a word.

"Yeah," he gulped. "Oh my God!"

He, who had believed in it so much, couldn't believe it; I, who had hardly believed in it at all, found it all quite natural—of course it was here. And at that moment, I thought: "It's a serious thing, to be the way Blake is." Exactly that funny phrase: "it's a serious thing."

"Posters?" he asked, looking around the room upside down.

"And more," I said.

Finally, he lowered himself. There was hardly room for two around the table. Why would there have been? Ernie's was a party of one. Against the wall, a bookshelf with piles of neatly ordered magazines; resting against one another, the cinema posters, mostly old and folded, some rolled in large tubes. And opposite, a little door more like a coalhole. Blake opened it, peered through, his voice echoing beyond: "The staff toilet! That's how he got in. Why didn't we check the staff toilet?" He popped his head back in and exhaled. "Ernie, Ernie, Ernie. The room's just as he left it." I nodded. "And there are the posters. And here, by the looks of it . . ." he burst out laughing: "Oh, Ernie. It's his pornography collection! Men Only!" His eyes filled with tears again. "Ernie's little kingdom; his private life." He flicked through the magazines: "*Parade, Mayfair*: January, February . . . all neatly stacked. And, look, posters, lobby cards. Pick one at random."

There was one poster on its own at the end, folded neatly in a Perspex envelope: it seemed like it might be something special.

"Jesus Christ!" said Blake. "It's a *Wizard of Oz* one-sheet. Be careful!" It had "The Regal" stamped on the back of it.

"I suppose they're all stolen from the cinema," I said.

"Well, they've never missed them, and we're certainly not giving them back."

"Widow's going to have a nice surprise, I guess."

"Yeah," said Blake, as he sat on the floor. He was too tired to explain; besides he rarely explained anything. I put my feet up. "Now we've got to get all this out of here." He tired at the thought. "Give us that brandy," he said.

"We could leave the pornography."

"Jack might want it. Add it to his collection."

There was silence. He sighed.

"What's the next adventure?" he asked himself, already contemplating future missions. "However are we going to beat this?" His eyes were closed. He was a husk: it was as if adrenaline was all he'd had. He began to recite poetry, reading himself to sleep. He always had a poem or a lyric up his sleeve, and he'd recite willy-nilly, occasionally burst into song, sometimes throw out a "Quack." If I could condense all our early meetings into one memory, all the gigs we did on our first travels, it would be that moment, that night, and then that early morning, as we sat in Ernie's time capsule, flushed with our success; Blake started to recite Edward Lear's "The Jumblies" to himself—I kinda knew it, like you do—and he got to that bit at the end:

> And in twenty years they all came back,
> In twenty years or more,
> And every one said, "How tall they've grown!
> For they've been to the Lakes, and the Torrible Zone,
> And the hills of the Chankly Bore!"
> And they drank their health, and gave them a feast
> Of dumplings made of beautiful yeast;

And every one said, "If we only live,
We too will go to sea in a Sieve,—
To the hills of the Chankly Bore!"

And I thought: "That's what people will say about him: 'Well, it seemed a stupid idea, but it was great and I wish I'd thought of it. But I didn't have the guts.'"

Besides, going to sea in a sieve: isn't that *exactly* what we did?

This time I was the one awake, and he was sleepy. He needed a right-hand man, a Tonto, a Robin. I, shortly to be fifteen, was ready for the role, and apparently I'd already passed the audition. He obviously thought of me as a son, and those two things (accomplice, son) go together, right, more or less?

And what I knew then was this: that I'd get in a van with him, go to sea with him, get in a sieve with him, go with him wherever he wanted, to the hills of the Chankly Bore, and that we'd dance by the light of the moon.

And thus began my education, my life as a Wunderkind.

"Where's the money, Clive?"

NO ONE, BY WHICH I MEAN PEOPLE OUTSIDE THE INNER CIRCLE, understood how Mr. Hedges persuaded Norm Bloch, head of WBA, to put his considerable weight behind the move that would catapult the Wunderkinds like *Angry Birds* over the Atlantic Ocean in their assault upon America. Fraught conference calls? Face-to-face negotiation? A series of complicated push-me-pull-you maneuverings with only one possible conclusion? Of course not.

Norm Bloch: equal parts family viewing, X-rated horror movie, public service announcement, and music history documentary—one of Greg's sacred *characters*. His survival instincts—when so many of his species, so long endangered, were teetering on the verge of extinction—were legendary. He worked only by the seat of his pants (his brain too addled to make plans) and had always been shrewd enough to surround himself with capable business people whose entire purpose was to make him look astute. This left him free to indulge his passions, live out his fantasies, attend award shows and sign new acts that nobody else at the label liked or understood. He was a man of fierce loyalty and equally fierce disloyalty. If you messed with him, which of course we did, he turned in a second. After that, there was no way back.

Nick Hedges, he liked. Hedges never considered himself— nor would have described himself as—either drug dealer or pimp, but this was precisely how Norm saw him. Nick's quick ascent up the greasy pole had coincided with one of the great weekends of Norm's life.

Everyone knew Nick was made when he escaped punishment for a promotional stunt that went horribly wrong. I can't actually name the rock star, because I would surely find myself a victim of murder-by-publicist, but it was Nick's bright idea for a fan, a "lucky winner," to meet his idol backstage at a London concert. Nick played chaperone and, unexpectedly, the fan and the star got on famously, and the star, deploying a generosity that far exceeded the modest terms of his original arrangement with the label vis-à-vis the promotion, offered the fan his stash. The lucky winner accepted eagerly, despite his unfamiliarity with rock-star-grade drugs: who wouldn't want to turn on with his idol? And anyway who would be so uncool as to refuse? Nick left them backstage for a few minutes after the show, returning to find a corpse and a horrified idol. "Iggy Pop"—it *wasn't* Iggy Pop, I want to make that very clear. I'd just like you to imagine someone of that stature—didn't want to have administered a drug overdose to a lucky winner, and besides couldn't believe that it had taken that small a quantity for the guy to turn blue. The star himself required a far stronger dosage to notice he'd partaken at all. Civilians!

Nick panicked; called Norm. Norm, remembering that wonderful Nick-arranged weekend in London a month before, made further calls; the cleaners were sent in; and everything was tidied away or brushed under the carpet. The widow had no idea where her husband had procured the drugs, let alone that he had such a crippling secret addiction. The fiasco had no repercussions for Nick, who more or less got away with manslaughter, and it was then that people began to pay attention. Hedges's hold over them was exactly proportional to Norm's hold over him, and Nick turned provider, enabler. Occasionally, in recognition, Norm did him favors. The Wunderkinds were just such a favor.

The accountants, looking only at incoming and outgoing, the bottom line, brass tacks, saw the Wunderkinds as "Hedges's Folly." The British market had not panned out as Nick had hoped, yielding neither a hit single nor any great profit besides tour income, of which the label was not entitled to a percentage. But

Britain was only the fifty-first state. The real money was made in the other fifty. Norm acquiesced to Plan B, gave the word, whining at meetings (as though his word wasn't final, or it was someone else's idea to which he was reluctantly giving in), and the curtain rose on America, the new theater of war.

Norm met Blake in a London dressing room—I wasn't there—and asked him how he'd feel about having his songs in a cigarette ad. It was a test, and Blake knew he'd asked this a thousand times of a thousand new bands. He didn't feel like playing along: "We're a kids' band, right? No one's going to want to put our music in cigarette commercials."

"Hmm," snorted Norm. "Coca-Cola, then."

"Only if we get to do the jingle," said Blake.

"Good answer," said Norm, skin crying sweat though the room was perfectly cool. "There's nothing wrong with liking to teach the world to sing. Let's have some fun. But think about the name. It's foreign." His other two pieces of advice were breathtakingly simple: 1) Get a hot girl in the band and 2) Start the songs with the chorus.

The gigs, though plentiful, were a struggle; even I, passionate convert that I was, could see that. The band was trying to entertain kids by day and adults by night, all with the same material. It was a little ludicrous, and the twins, who lacked investment in the band, writing none of the material, making few of the decisions, walked prior to the American mission. They were bored of the din, sick of kids flicking ice cream at their precious equipment. It didn't ultimately matter whether or not it was intentional: the amp was still stained. Had the twins known where the band would lead, would they have grinned and borne it? No. They had made a chunk of change and left, as they'd joined, as one. There were no hard feelings. The fact is: things weren't that much fun before America, although to me it seemed more fun than not from the playpen of the merch booth.

Jack queued for his visa without excitement. Was it better to have a band and no record deal or a record deal and no band? Blake tried to persuade him that a rhythm section was the least of their worries. They'd pick up another and move on. They included me on these conversations, taking my opinion seriously as though I knew anything about it.

Greg's time had come too. He was trying to effect the ideal exit strategy, but felt it would be disloyal to let them lurch across that ocean rudderless. Time to dust off the passport. Besides, it was a chance to wheel out his astonishing repertoire of anecdotes for people who hadn't recently heard them, not to mention sport a modest fedora, a Borsalino, that Blake said made him look like Bowie.

I was going to stay at home. They'd be back in a few days. There were gigs on the calendar. Greg asked if I'd advance them; save him the bother. He gave me some sketchy advice on how this might be done. I probably arsed it up, but the gigs would never be played anyway.

They left for the west coast two months to the day after the poster haul: August 1989. The idea was that the record would be released on the first Tuesday of the new decade. There was a constant flow of postcards from Blake (all magical: La Brea Tar Pits; Grauman's Chinese; fifteen of the Hollywood sign, at least), full of newsy detail. I heard it all again from Jack when I eventually joined them.

Even their journey to the hotel from LAX had been surreal: the road went on forever.

It wasn't like England, where when you got to someone's street, you were more-or-less at his house. They'd exited the freeway at the appropriate boulevard, but found themselves at number 22002 when they were looking for 1010. Surely some mistake: theirs, compounded by a decision to stay on the boulevard—they must be nearly there after all—instead of merging back onto the freeway.

On eventual arrival, the Sahara Motor Lodge had seemed an oasis of palms and spring water, but this soon revealed itself to be a mirage. The sun beat down relentlessly, the pool was closed, and the air conditioning pummeled you as you walked in. None of them had ever experienced a climate like it—they could deal with blazing heat, they could deal with perishing cold, but they couldn't deal with both of them competing for their attention si-multaneously. From the moment they landed, they were always either overdressed or underdressed—freezing, boiling, sweating, squinting; none of them was prepared to go native, to wear shorts and sandals. Everything went wrong. They tried to walk to the other side of the road, when they should have driven, and to drive to the other side of the hotel, when they should have walked. That first morning, they were eating overly crisp bacon and eggs-any-style, including ones they didn't know, at the Bob's Big Boy at 6:30 a.m. By the time they arrived at WBA for the meeting anx-iously early, they all wanted to go back to sleep, particularly Jack, who, on his first trip to America, chose to lug around a cumber-some video camera in a shoulder bag.

The women in the conference room were strikingly good-looking; the men either notably handsome or obese. Norm Bloch was nowhere to be seen. He often excused himself from strategy meet-ings: the damage was done, and he could do more elsewhere. Mr. Hedges was present on a speakerphone from London, his disem-bodied voice in surround-sound, broadcasting not only from the phone, but also hidden speakers in the table itself.

"Hi! London calling! How's everyone doing?"

Greg, assuming that he himself was everyone, embarked on an inappropriately lengthy and irrelevant anecdote. Everyone paid polite attention as iced water chinked its way around the table, puddling mercurially on the highly polished veneer. Jack considered the gold records on the wall; the gaps seemed to invite the contemplation of your own gold record between them. He wanted to get a shot of them, but didn't want anyone to know he was secretly taping the meeting. He had set his video camera to "record," but left it in his bag slung off the side of the chair. Greg's story finally ground to a halt. There was dutiful laughter.

"Nice gold records," said Jack.

"A lot of them are Platinum, actually," said Craig at the head of the table.

"Well never mind," said Greg. "We'll get you some more gold ones." Craig smiled slowly.

"Exciting times," said Nick, as if rubbing his hands. "A tale of two continents! You've met everyone there and now they're going to tell you what they're going to do. But the most important thing is this: they've got some people they want you to meet, some people who can solve some problems, now that the twins have toddled off. Let's go with the headline. John."

John had been first to greet them, which made him look hands on, a worker bee. He clapped once, put both thumbs up, and said: "You're on *Simeon's House* next Saturday." He delivered this news with misplaced confidence. Britain had never heard of Simeon or his house, though it sounded a bit like *Sesame Street*.

"That's great news," said Greg, hoping it was.

"We haven't got our instruments," said Jack.

"No worries," Nick piped in. "You're in the new world. There's a Guitar Center in every mall and a member of WBA with a company credit card."

"We only have two members of a four piece band," said Jack. Seemed worth pointing out.

"Right," said Nick from inside the table. "I'm coming to that. Sylvie, tell them about it."

If you were used to the girls at your local bus stop, Sylvie could persuade you of almost anything. She radiated health; her teeth out-Osmonded the competition; she wore white linen like a nymphet Jesus, her lack of tan lines suggesting that she usually wore less, often, at beaches. Jack, looking on in awe, would have happily heard her tell him that he had contracted a sexually transmitted disease from her. However, even this dusty beach creature could have chosen her words better: the label had "cast" some replacements.

"What?" said Jack. "I thought we were only out here to have meetings."

"Look, we know you're not Menudo," said Sylvie, glittering. They had no idea what she was talking about.

"Things are happening," said Craig, the fat guru who, by dint of having said very little, seemed in charge. He held his hands together in a way that seemed very considered, only the thumbs and fingertips touching. His accent was so specifically transatlantic that you couldn't tell which side he was betraying. "*Simeon's House*—that's a big deal. That's every kid in America. That's you in the big time." His smile was one of mutual, but mostly self-, congratulation.

Sylvie laughed: "It has a 3.4 share. We'll show you tapes. Guys, it's a big deal."

"Wow," said Blake; the water was waking him up and he needed to pee. "How did that happen?"

"Well, how it happened is *great songs*, my friend," said Craig, leading the table in polite, courtly applause. "We're very excited about the album. Very excited."

"It's a great album," said Greg. He knew how to enthuse about an album.

"It is. It's full of great songs."

"It's a *Tour de France*," said Greg.

"You're right," said Craig, smiling beatifically again. "It's a *Tour de France*. I like that. And how *did Simeon's House* happen . . . Jim?" This was clearly the pre-game, but it was tough to predict what was actually going to happen when the whistle blew, what the game might actually be when it kicked off. It wasn't like any meeting Greg had ever attended. It was a business meeting.

"Yeah," said Jim. "We played "Rock Around the Bed" to the powers that be. They loved it. And they had a cancellation for next Saturday—it actually tapes on Thursday, which is, obviously, in three days' time—and . . . was it Prince that canceled?"

"Prince," confirmed Sylvie.

"Prince!" enthused Blake, conveniently ignoring "three days' time."

"Do you remember that Prince story about the guitar tech who was dressed as Prince and got locked out of the gig?" asked Greg, seeing an open window.

"As Craig says, *great songs*," said Jim, with renewed focus. "And it's going to be you guys instead."

"The Wunderkinds instead of Prince," said Blake, pinching himself.

"Just run the name by me one more time?" asked Craig as though thinking aloud. He couldn't quite bring himself to say it.

"The Wunderkinds," said Blake.

"With a *V*, right?" asked Craig. "Vunderkints?" He shook his head: the wine was corked. "That's the problem."

"It's German," said Blake.

"Exactly. A lot of Americans don't speak German."

"A lot of Americans don't *like* Germans," confirmed Jim.

Blake narrowed his eyes: a lot of Americans *are* German.

"We've come up with an option," said Craig. "An alternative. The Wunderkinds is a great name, but, perhaps, just perhaps, it's been something of an obstacle to your success in England. Perhaps it's . . . *to blame*." He certainly knew where to put the emphasis in a sentence.

"Because people don't like Germans?" asked Blake.

"Because people don't like a word they're not totally confident they can pronounce. It might make them think twice about buying the record. It might make a DJ think twice about playing a record."

"We say: '*When you play it, say it*!' said John by way of explanation. "But if they can't say it . . ."

"We've come up with a plan," continued Craig, "where . . . Heidi?"

And Heidi, with her long brown hair, stood up, smiled, and unveiled a whiteboard they hadn't noticed before, on which was a splendid new logo with, underneath it, in bold letters: YOUR CHILD'S FIRST ROCK BAND. At first, neither Blake, Jack nor Greg noticed that the logo didn't say Wunderkinds at all. It said WONDERKIDS.

There was silence. Glances were exchanged: nervous, flirtatious, hopeful. Bands are a democracy, supposedly, and no one wanted to commit himself to saying something that would greatly annoy his brother or his manager. But the silence had to be broken.

"Wow," said Blake. "*Your child's first rock band*. That's fucking heavy. Sorry." The name-change hadn't registered.

"What do you think?" asked Craig. He focused solely on the logo. "Heidi designed it."

"It's great," said Jack. "Well done, Heidi."

"Yeah," said Greg, nodding like a bobblehead. It was so obvious which of them would be fighting over Heidi. She seemed more realistically attainable than the mythical Sylvie.

"And the name, the Wonderkids," said Craig. "It rings true." The handsome men and strikingly good-looking women nodded. "It's a name this record company can get behind. Now about the album," said Craig, that decision apparently taken. "John, you had some thoughts." It was like a party game where Craig threw a ball out and the rest of the team had to keep it in the air as long as possible.

"Well, yes. We think we should change the title, if you like any of the ones that we've come up with."

"I don't mind Wonderkids, but what's wrong with *Jabber-Rock*?" asked Jack.

"We think *JabberRock* is great. We think it's perfect for England. We think we can go one better for America," said John. "That's our aspiration: one better."

"How about *One Better*?" asked Blake. They did not understand that it wasn't a non sequitur. "That's a good title for a debut album." He paused for a response that was never going to be forthcoming. "Okay. What have you got?"

Greg sighed. The band had been able to go with the flow at Endymion, float along as the label made their tidy edits and their tweaks to the album's cover art. That had been the deal with the devil, this was the pay-off, the pound of flesh: a new name for the band (though even he knew it was better—Wunderkinds had never tripped off his tongue) and now a new name for the album. You had to pick your battles in rock 'n' roll, but the miracle was that Blake and Jack hadn't lost it yet. Greg couldn't take his eyes off Heidi, the logo lady. Was it she who took out the little blade and actually extracted the flesh? Maybe she had a pair of scales on her. How much was a pound anyway? Greg's thoughts were muddled. He was getting itchy.

John consulted his notes, his list of titles: "*The Kids Are Alright*."

Jack was about to say "It's a Who record," but Greg pre-empted him with a gentle hand on his arm.

"There are quite a few. *This One's for the Babies. I'll Be Your Baby Tonight*."

"*Bring that Baby Bottle Over Here*?" suggested Blake. John

reeled off about twenty more: "You see, it's all part of our rebranding of the Wonderkids."

"We're not content for you to have hit singles," said Craig. "We're not content for you to sell out shows everywhere; we're not content with that."

"Anyone can do that," said John.

"Brilliant," said Greg, whose eyes seemed to be experiencing a kind of misty rapture. Wonderkids. Wonderkids.

"We see something new here," said Craig. "You know, I'll be frank. We could go to central casting right now and create a band to meet our needs. Like they did with the Monkees. Like Milli Vanilli. But with you, we see—*Norm sees*—the real thing: we think the kids are going to love you. No one's ever tried to do what we're going to do. And if we want to do this together, we're ready to go all the way."

"All the way," said Nick from England, still hiding just underneath the table. "All the way!"

"But I'm not going to dick around." Suddenly Craig was speed talking. "We have ideas. And we'll help you. We need you to grow two new members by the TV show, because we want to present you as a band; we have some people we want you to see; we need to make some tough decisions on the album, on its title, on the cover, on the edits we want to do . . ."

"They already did edits in England," said Jack, more-or-less firmly.

"That's why they're tough decisions. Also, we're worried about some of the language, specifically the vocabulary; we need to talk about image. We've done some market research. We've talked to *educators*. We're thinking of perhaps replacing a few of the songs with a couple of new ones. For example, we're wondering whether we should replace the song about old people . . ."

"Old Persons?" said Blake.

"Our research tells us that kids don't want to hear about old people."

"Well," said Blake. "You're wrong. Sorry. Your research is wrong. Kids love old people because they're weird and wrinkly and they smell unique. They give you presents. They squeeze money into your hand when you're saying goodbye. They say funny things you weren't expecting, just like kids. And also because they're old, because age involves a lot of counting and kids love to count. Kids *love* old people. You're parents, right?" Nobody either side of the table had children.

Craig looked perplexed at this moment of discord—it hadn't been on the agenda—but otherwise ignored it: "We're wondering if we could get you into the studio real fast, like this week. Do you have any songs ready to go? Repetitive? Simple?"

"Chorus at the top?" suggested Blake, his knee pinging up and down.

"Chorus at the top. We're talking the same language. We're *boldly going*, you know what I mean, Greg?"

"*Star Trek*," Greg replied automatically, as though his function was to gloss every reference. In fact, he felt like he was watching a game of tennis with his neck in a brace.

"And is Andy there?" asked Nick from his office in England. Andy?

"Ah yes," said Craig. "We've got someone else we want you to meet: he's someone we think can help *you* specifically, Greg, navigate these hallowed halls."

"Show me where the toilets are, kinda thing?" Greg had been writing this script for years.

"More than that; help you with the wild world beyond. Andy has a company, which, if you'd like, is at your disposal. They work for us, and they work for you. They'll put up posters; they'll set up meetings; they'll *take* the meetings if you can't be bothered."

"What actually are they, this company?" asked Jack.

Craig stabbed at the intercom: "Could you send Andy in?"

And in walked Andy Light, at which point the whistle blew and the game began.

"Let there be Light!" said Craig, a joke around which he mimed inverted commas in recognition of the fact that it was old.

"And there *was* light!" answered Andy, shaking manly hands, reserving special bird-like pecks for female cheeks. It was almost possible to believe that he hadn't decided the exact timing of his materialization himself. "Andy Light: Light Speed Management. It's so great to meet you both," he said, ignoring Greg.

"And this is Greg Sugar," said Craig.

"Greg! Greg! Your reputation precedes you," said Andy, fixing Greg with laser-like focus. In that moment, Greg saw his exit strategy. He couldn't have planned it better; he had sunburn on the back of his neck and he wanted to go home. The record company saw him as a weak link, and a weak link he was willing to be. He'd heard of acts wooed away from their management while they were on the road, when someone had a chance to work on them away from home, but he'd never seen it done in such brazen fashion before. He was overjoyed. The truth is that if he hadn't wanted to be replaced, he wouldn't have even have figured out what exactly was happening. Did the boys know what was happening?

"So Wonderkids? *Wonderkids*?" Andy scanned the room, eyes full of suggestion. Craig nodded once. "Wonderkids it is! Yes! The Big Bang!" It seemed this might have been his idea. "We're here to help in any which way we can. Craig?"

"Yes, Andy is here to help you in any which way he can."

"Like what?" said Jack. "I'm sure we need help with everything, but what in particular?"

"I can be your eyes, your ears." Both options seemed unnecessary, slightly paranoid. "We need to find you an agent. Greg, any ideas?"

"Well, actually, old Nicksy at Renaissance Artists; he's expressed an interest and we were going to have a chat."

"Old friend of yours?" asked Andy.

"Yeah."

"Great. Perfect. I think we can maybe even shoot a little higher."

"Go one better," said John.

"*One better*!" said Blake. "It's not bad."

"I think we can go to the top," Andy continued. "The gigs are going to make this thing work. Let me say one word: merchandise."

"Go on," said Jack.

"Well, you're selling T-shirts and CDs, right?" Jack nodded. "No one's ever really thought of this before, because no one has tried to sell this sort of music before, in this way. We've been talking, we've been thinking: the point is that the merchandise is not really for the kids, is it? It's for the parents."

"Yeah," said Jack. Greg seemed to have zoned out, but Jack felt that perhaps someone from their team should be paying attention.

"Kids have no money. They have pocket money, small change, and short attention spans. Parents have money. They've already bought the concert ticket; they've already seen you on TV; they want a memento for their children; they want something with educational value; and we're going to sell them what they want. Kids like activities, right? Kids like to have something to do. Busy hands are happy hands, right?" Everyone in the room, except Jack, Blake, and Greg, was enraptured as Andy explained how the world works. "We see Wonderkid educational toys. Because everything, *everything*, is an opportunity to learn. And wherever there is an opportunity to learn, there is an opportunity to make money."

"Good old Andy," said Craig, in avuncular fashion, giving Blake and Jack that friendly grin: "Boys, if you're squeamish about money, block your ears now. If you want to pretend all this isn't happening, then you might wanna pop out and grab a Sprite right about now and we'll give you the lowdown in thirty minutes."

"We're not squeamish," said Jack.

"Well," Andy continued, warming to the task. "There's a whole world of direct sales that can play into everyone's notion of tasteful merchandise. Don't assume the music makes the most profit. It is the most important thing, of course; but it's only one way to make money; it's one slice of the pie. And above all, the joy of teaching these kids things; educating them; showing them the world; being that child's *first rock band*."

"Quack!" said Blake in interruption, his leg now jiggling violently. Noticing this, he placed his right hand on it, stopped it still, then looked up and smiled, like he'd calmed a wild beast. "I'm sure that's all true, but I like kids, and I know what *they* like. We have this thing where we don't care about it making sense so much. We don't want to preach at them. Does it all have to mean something? In a few years time, all they're going to be getting is songs about the environment going to hell and how there aren't any more animals. Let other people be teachers." He started to talk faster just as Craig had. *No one*, even Jack, had ever heard him enunciate it all so clearly; it was as though he had an entire coherent and binding philosophy he'd never bothered to share. "And the adults are the same: what they like at our shows is that they get back that childish sense of wonder for just a little while; it's like a dream for them, and they catch a little of the mayhem with the kids. So the parents are like the kids—except they want a little bit of the awe *back*, because they lost it, because they're not kids anymore.

"And with our nonsense, we're sending out a little challenge. Children like to be horrified, and scandalized, and made to laugh, and scared. Just like adults. I mean, just think of *Struwwelpeter*. It's for children *and* adults. That's why we as a band don't distinguish between the two."

No one was thinking of *Struwwelpeter*, unless Heidi was wondering whether they were the label's new German heavy metal signing. In which case, they'd have to change *their* name too.

"Adults enjoy the shows as well?" asked John, shocked by this left-field revelation.

"Well, yeah, obviously," said Blake. "We didn't really start out as a kids' band."

"You didn't?" said Craig. "That's *fantastic*!"

"Yeah, we don't really see it as kids' music . . ."

"That was my idea," said Nick from a speaker.

". . . We see it more as everyone music. We see rock 'n' roll as everyone music."

"YES!" whooped Andy. "It is Everyone Music!" The phrase, in his mouth, sprouted capital letters. "We're gonna help the kids grow up and we're gonna turn the parents back into kids again. We don't have to make sense!" Plan A had just flown out the window. He was fast-tracking Plan B. "Who needs sense and education? Let's have fun. Let's mean nothing. We're the id, not the ego. Who needs the ego? The ego's for idiots! It's Everyone Music!"

"Then I've got an album title for you," said Blake, caught up in the moment, impressed that Andy had heard him and made a wide turn, particularly impressed with his "ego idiots" line: "*Everyone Music*."

"That's why you're the man!" said Craig. "That's why you're Blake Lear. That's why you wrote "Rock Around the Bed." Now *that's* an album title!"

"And," said Greg unexpectedly, "when Woody Guthrie sang a song, he didn't say "Gather round me, people" or "comrades," he said "Gather round me, children," and that's what you're doing too; talking to your children—everyone." It seemed, to Blake, one of the wisest things Greg had ever said.

Andy laid out his vision, developed over a series of consultations with a multiplicity of PR companies. At meeting's end, he had emerged as the major strategist. By lunchtime, Blake and Jack were happy to have him drive them to Hamburger Hamlet as Greg stayed at the office to catch up with a couple of old acquaintances.

"I don't think Greg's in this for the long haul," said Andy sympathetically. It was as good a way to break the ice as any. He looked like he knew how to break ice. "He'd be at lunch with us if he was."

Jack nodded. Sometimes he winced at the thought of Greg. "It's no bad thing. He's perhaps been a little out of his depth for a while."

"I think . . . he's blinked," said Andy, victor in the staring contest that had started the moment they met. "But he's your guy. He's you."

"It doesn't matter," said Blake, what he always said when it mattered most of all. He knew Andy and Jack were right. As they'd left the office, he'd heard Greg telling Heidi a story Blake had heard many times, and he knew the story ended with Heidi offering to drive Greg out to Malibu to show him where Dylan lived, or a trip to the Farmer's Market, or up into the hills to meet her "boyfriend," which would turn out to be a horse, and Greg saying: "Yeah, yeah. Be great to see some of the sights before I head home. I'll buy you dinner," knowing that she'd buy him dinner.

Greg could get almost anything he wanted in America on charm and accent alone. But he couldn't manage this juggernaut. Andy, on the other hand, was charmless. He could manage the Wonderkids standing on his head—and he'd have to, on occasion, if he wanted to see Blake the right way up.

• • •

Greg's mum had a timely relapse and he had no choice but to go back to England. It was a blessed release. He'd thought he'd have to stay around longer, but he barely made it the few days to the *Simeon's House* taping.

Jack was sightseeing, video camera at the ready (though now he got to leave it in the town car when he didn't need it), so Blake and Greg had a few drinks together the last night before he left. Both were aware, yet unable to verbalize, that this was good-bye. Blake felt disloyal to Greg; Greg knew he was being disloyal to Blake.

"Well, seems like you've got it made," said Greg quietly rolling over, just as he had intended.

"You mean *we've* got it made."

"Well, I think *you've* maybe got it made."

"I only hope they haven't got the wrong end of the . . ."

"Wrong end of the shtick," said Greg. They laughed. It was perfect Greg. "Did I ever tell you the official reason why the band Sailor broke up?"

"Sailor? 'Glass of Champagne.' That was one of the first singles I ever bought at Small Al's. Maybe the first I ever bought with my own money."

"They didn't break up due to 'musical differences.'"

"'To pursue a solo career'?"

"No, it wasn't even 'outside influences' . . ."

"Does that always mean drugs?"

"No, no, I think sometimes it means boilers. *Cherchez la femme.* Yoko kinda thing. It wasn't even 'irreconcilable differences.'"

"So why did they break up?"

"It was in the official press release: *lack of talent.* All bands break up," said Greg. "The only bands who haven't broken up should have broken up years ago. But do you know how a band stays together?"

"Luck? Success?"

"Money. Split the money equally. It's the only way."

And then Greg embarked upon a very long story, which Blake actually hadn't heard before, about how one of his heroes had been drinking next to him at a bar in Newcastle, and they'd got to talking, and they'd actually been getting on really well, but Greg had got distracted by a bit of skirt, and headed off into the night, curtailing the conversation with his hero, who had died unexpectedly a few weeks later.

Greg flew home the next morning.

Things were different with Andy. He wasn't yet officially their manager, merely heir apparent to an empty throne.

Andy didn't tell stories.

"Greg was there for us," said Blake to Andy, during one of their frank early meetings. "Whenever we needed him. In the fox-hole. Are you in the foxhole for us, Andy?"

"I am. I'm totally in the foxhole for you guys. What I'm say-ing is: let's not go there . . ." He saw distress in Blake's eyes. "But if we need to go to the foxhole, I'm there."

"Well, sometimes you can't help the foxhole. You don't want to be there; it's not somewhere you need to be."

"I'm there," said Andy, unconvincingly.

But he was no bullshitter. Within two weeks, they had an agent and the heaviest lawyer in town. From the get-go, Jack liked being managed by Andy, though he pronounced his name with heavily drawn-out emphasis on the first syllable, as if he was sa-voring a conjunction rather than about to say "Andy," which only became clear when he added a helpful little "y" on the end. This was Jack's little power play. Blake missed Greg, but felt momen-tum. He'd never experienced momentum before. It was as if Greg's anecdotes had been slowing everything down.

A little while after his return home, Greg called me. I assumed he was calling from America until he explained about his mum.

"Yeah, man, it's all going great. Come over and have a . . . I'll get in some Coca-Cola. Now, look, I been talking to Blake, and he wants to get you out there."

My heart started to thud like I was hearing it through a stethoscope. "I can't go. I'm at school. The Terrys. It's okay doing the gigs and stuff, but . . ."

"Well, yeah. But here's the thing: if he adopts you, you can do whatever you like." I literally put my hands over the two pieces of the phone so that no one could hear or be heard: pure reflex. "Are you there, Sweet?"

"He wants to adopt me." I was whispering.

"Yeah."

"Shouldn't I talk to him about it?"

"He's gonna come back here, and you can talk then. It's all about if you want him to."

"Is he old enough to adopt me?"

"Yeah. Well, I don't know. Do you wanna be adopted? You're fifteen now. Seems like you can probably do whatever you like next year, right? But he's got some advice from one of the lawyers out there, who's been talking to someone back here, and if you want to do it, then he can, you know, take you out there."

"And I can do merch."

"Yeah."

"What about school?"

"University of life, right? What an opportunity! Wish I'd had it."

"What about the Terrys?"

"They're cool." The Terrys weren't cool. Only Greg could possibly refer to the Terrys as cool.

"When's he coming back?"

"Next week. It's all happening real fast over there."

"Yeah, he sends me postcards."

"Oh, nice. New band members. New name."

"Yeah. I've had a postcard every day."

"I know. I bought him the stamps at the desk . . . Well, so you know, then."

"But he never mentioned this."

"It's a surprise. And I'm not gonna be around anymore, so, y'know, there's another."

"This next one is the first song on our new album . . ."

S IMEON (REAL NAME, SIMON FONSECA)—UNKNOWN OUTSIDE
America, a legend in his own country—had been a modestly
successful folksinger in the early seventies during the bust, rather
than the boom. Too square for the hippies, he'd managed to carve
a niche for himself on Public Broadcasting, singing cheery, empowering songs for children about friendship, cooperation, generosity,
and other similarly uncontroversial behaviors. Favorites included
"You Are Your Own Best Friend," "Today's a Brand New Day (All
Over the World)," and "Giving Is Better Than Getting." He held a
guru-like sway over his constituency. Once you heard his name,
and none of the Wonderkids ever had, he was everywhere: in the
TV Guide in the motel lobby, on the billboards that faced you
down on the highway, in the record stores smiling smugly from
the children's rack, which nuzzled up to the folk section and
numbered very few artists.

Simeon gave up in the mid-nineties. After he had milked the
cow dry, he decided that much of his money had been made
immorally. From then on, he appeared only at events that promoted World Peace, particularly those that publicized, or donated
to, his nebulous Empowering the Child campaign. He was against
everything: television, the Internet, the future, fast food. Only kids

counted, and he didn't like singing for them anymore.

But in 1991, Simeon was the shit, le poop, and the band was to be on his show. Soon. But given that only two of them remained, the appearance came with strings.

One of the strings was Becca, Simeon's daughter from his second marriage.

The first meeting took place the day after the WBA summit at a practice space on Gower. Blake and Jack had never been in a rehearsal studio like it: perfectly soundproofed, spick and span with drinks machines, an un-tattooed receptionist who radiated welcome, and a boutique that sold strings, capos, tuners, and everything else they'd forgotten. The abiding memory of its Brixton equivalent, the Dump, was the hellish noise of twelve different bands playing twelve different musics simultaneously. The first time the brothers booked a room at the Dump, a proto-crustie in war-against-the-man uniform walked by, vicious-looking pit bull on a chain lead. He opened the door to one of the spaces, inflicting the mind-blowing racket upon the corridor, at which the dog whimpered in terror, refusing to pass inside. Blake and Jack heard terrified howls as the door closed; they could only imagine what other medieval tortures lay beyond.

At the practice space on Gower, a house cat purred contentedly by the front desk. The buzz was that Boz Scaggs was in the building. All was heavenly. Becca walked in precisely on time, bass slung over her shoulder, waved hi, smiled a wide smile that deepened the Sigourney Weaver creases around her mouth, and improved on all the parts she'd copped from the first album. Jack had initially been suspicious—"a bassist in exchange for a TV spot?"—but, according to Blake, Jack fell into a reverie almost the moment he saw her: the female, the earth, the seat of rhythm, there was something primal about it. Becca's appearance seemed to change almost by the hour as she tossed her unruly blonde hair this way and that. She made no reference to her father. If one thinks of the Wonderkids as the Beatles for a second (humor me) Becca was the Quiet one, the Dark Horse, the one who did yoga in the corner—as opposed to the mouthy one (Blake), the one who wore all the rings (Blake), or the one without shoes on the Zebra crossing who might be dead (Blake).

It was she who had suggested Curtis, who wasn't her boyfriend, to WBA. Curtis "O" (it was a leftover punk name—he'd once been Kurt Zero) was straight from Central Casting, literally. In other words, WBA, in their attempts to find a band member, put out a call for an actor who could drum: the Monkees Method. And Becca's friend Curtis "O" could drum. His long, smooth dreads also added a certain something that the band had previously lacked. Again, Jack was the one impressed: Curtis "O" had drummed briefly for a legendary LA punk band. Jack loved a good CV, plus he'd never played with a black bloke before. Blake was against tokenism of all kinds—a legacy of the Student Union Bar—but this was "diversity" and he liked the balance. Now they really were *Everyone*. And the proof was in the pudding: they sounded good.

Drinks that night sealed the deal. Blake rechristened Becca "Mum" when he spilled some of his beer and she immediately mopped it up with a wet wipe from her bag: that's just the way she was. That bag contained almost everything you required of a mother: band aids, safety pins, chewing gum, Advil, herbal remedies, a needle and thread. Whatever you wanted, it was all in there: just in case. She made the band feel like a family, which Blake had never even known he wanted, and everyone called her Mum after that. As for Curtis, Jack couldn't believe he'd been in the city's punk scene at all: it must have been quite different from British punk. Curtis was always smiling, always friendly, never spat at you, and greatly admired Sting. Maybe he'd just grown up.

"I like him," said Jack back at the Sahara Motor Lodge, "his playing; everything. But Sting? *Nasty*. And I *love* her but I wouldn't want to see her apartment. I bet all the mugs would be in order of size. Anyway, see how it goes on the TV. Nothing permanent yet, is it?" Band dynamics were Jack's special subject; Blake just liked a nice mix of people who let him do what he wanted.

In rehearsal, Blake had a knack for getting the most out of people while having as much fun as possible, so no one ever felt overworked. Jack quietly got on with his own thing, tinkering with sounds, twiddling knobs, and daisy-chaining pedals. Blake never second-guessed Jack ("Oh, let him fiddle!") and Jack never questioned Blake's lyrics. Curtis was the first drummer they'd ever met who wanted a copy of the words. He liked to sing along. "Do you want a microphone?" Blake asked casually. He did. And they were a band: four singers, one acoustic guitar, one electric guitar, bubbly bass, and the beat of the traps. Making music was easier in America. It was like the whole country was trying to help you.

At first they were only booked for two days until the taping, but the rehearsal studio was to become their second home, more comfortable than the Sahara Motor Lodge. During breaks, they glimpsed passing stars who nodded with musicianly recognition. One day, Ray Davies turned up. Blake observed in awe, determined not to be a bother. Later that day, he went to the unattended front desk, where Ray had left a handwritten instruction for the receptionist—something about a delivery of tapes, in pencil, with a little frame around the note and some underlinings in red Sharpie. Without thinking, Blake (a thoughtful thief) took the note, photocopied it, put the copy back on the desk and pocketed the original.

On the set of *Simeon's House*, the great man himself approached, ignored the rest of the band, and kissed his daughter on the lips.

"Hi, honey. Glad your new band could be on the show. Write, huh?"

She introduced him as her father but called him Simeon. He immediately proved himself to be the dick you suspected him of being: one side of his collar was up and Blake, concerned that no one would spot it before cameras rolled, told him. "Oh yeah? Thanks," said Simeon, in the least possibly grateful way: whereupon he pointedly didn't adjust the collar and walked away. Becca shook her head in embarrassment, excusing her father with a "pressures of show business" shrug, and Blake laughed in polite astonishment.

"Get *her*!" said Jack, in his camp pantomime dame voice.

"He'll have sorted it by the time the red light goes on," said Blake. And he had.

"Big chip; no salsa," Becca whispered in Blake's ear as they watched from behind a camera. "He's my father, but only technically."

The Wonderkids were to play "Rock Around the Bed," minus the verse with the "offensive" lyric ("She pushed me back on the kitchen table / And I nearly fainted / As we got acquainted"): two verses, chorus, and a bridge were quite enough. They rehearsed the song five times for camera after which they were escorted to wardrobe for styling and make up.

"Just a little to take off the glare," said Jack in his best Ringo. It was from *A Hard Day's Night*.

"I love your accent," said the stylist. "You sound just like a Beatle."

Jack looked the most dashing with his hair slicked back. The record company provided the clothes. One trip down Melrose was all it took: lightweight suits in primary colors—red for Blake, blue for Jack, yellow for Mum and white for Curtis. There's a photo of the four of them, waving like a flag, unaware that it is their last moment of obscurity.

If Simeon was Andrew Gold, Randy VanWarmer, Stephen Bishop, and all the other modestly bearded lonely boys of the seventies, the Wonderkids were the Sex Pistols. And he'd let them into his house, invited the vampires in. I have the clip on my laptop. Simeon's intro is like Ed Sullivan's for the Beatles: "They're over from England, with a song that I know you're going to take to your hearts, housemates, called 'Rock Around the Bed.'" Simeon had sounded the death-knell of his own career; it was the first time he'd ever uttered the word "Rock" on the show, and he had no clue how much trouble the band was going to cause him or his family. They were quite unlike anything that had ever appeared on *Simeon's House*: the previous musical guest, in a merino ski sweater, had crooned "Bingo Was His Name-O" to the strains of his classical guitar, foot perched on a knee-high stool.

Blake performed like never before, pogoing like a jack-in-the-box, smiling like a loon. Even Jack looked a little taken aback by his antics. In the control room, the producers reached for their pink pills; it was the first time they'd had drums and bass, and they'd got cold feet at the last minute, knowing their hands were tied—Becca was after all his daughter. Blake had a video sent back to England (though I couldn't even get it in the Terrys' VCR—it was the wrong everything: format, region, standard, shape) with another postcard of the Hollywood sign: "We're going on tour and you're coming!"

Simeon's House aired the following Saturday at 9 a.m. Switchboards jammed, and the single, rush-released to radio, started its ascent up some very specific chart. A tour was planned immediately. The album was pushed forward and released within a month, songs edited to their perfect Platonic lengths, new title—*Everyone Music*—emblazoned on the revamped cover; a video for "Rock Around the Bed" was in production on a triangular sound-stage off Mulholland. For this masterpiece, the band mimed on a set that almost precisely captured the eerie *Little House on the Prairie* vibe of *Simeon's House*, a performance interspersed with footage of the Wonderfamily having a pillow fight around a mas-sive feather bed. By the end of the shoot, there were feathers every-where: in Blake's mouth, Jack's guitar, Curtis's bass drum, and Becca's hair. MTV took note. WBA, however, had a strict path for the Wonderkids from which they would not deviate. Andy agreed, which was his job: "Guys, we have a path. If we follow that path, we will be rewarded. If we get waylaid, we'll get in trouble."

"It's all a bit *Pilgrim's Progress*," said Blake.

By the time I arrived in America almost three months later, it had all happened, and the tour was about to start. Blake hadn't had a moment to get home, but Greg and the lawyers had sorted every-thing. "You should go, Sweet," Greg told me on the phone, as though my arm needed twisting. "Not just for the merch. You're gonna travel around and have some fun. One big happy family. Have you heard of the Allman Brothers?" I hadn't. "Well, it'll be a little like that but less heavy."

There was hardly a moment to stand back and reflect on the evident strangeness of the situation: being adopted by a man not strictly old enough to be my father (let alone speculating on the reasons for this adoption), then following this chubby Pied Piper across the Atlantic. Like an artist who doesn't really understand how they do what they do, I felt as if any analysis might jinx the gift, as though it might disappear into thin air. And this was not a time for second thoughts. It was like I was getting one over on the world for the first time in my life.

I thought I knew how we'd be riding, and I wasn't complaining. In England it had been trains that shouldn't legally have been as full as they were; minivans that reeked of petrol, sweat, and pee; a caravan of old bangers whose boots held surprisingly little. So I was ready for some hard traveling in a grubby van. I was a thrilled fifteen-year-old heading to the new world, and it felt like I'd been given the keys to the Magic Kingdom.

The Terrys deposited me at Heathrow, where I stood in the regular queue for half an hour until an airline official, with a glance at my ticket, coaxed me into a much shorter line that marked the beginning of my magic carpet ride. In this alternative reality, I was suddenly Mr. Sweet and *what was my choice for dinner*. I could smell the difference. I'd known I was traveling First Class but, never having flown, had no firm idea how superior this was: one trip ruined me for life. (I thought they were joking when they offered me a manicure.)

At LAX, after a brief conversation with immigration (my script: I was "spending some time with my father, who's touring in a band"), I picked up my bag, stuffed with various of Blake and Jack's requests (everything from *Private Eye* and *NME* to Euthymol toothpaste), and was met by a white stretch limo with SWEET written on a sign in block capitals. Inside was every soft drink known to man, a Wonderkids t-shirt and yet another postcard of the Hollywood sign: "See you at the band house!"

The band house: every band's fantasy. At least, to start with. During the slow fade, they'd rather live as far away from one another as possible—one in his salmon fishery on Mull, the other near the drugs in Camden—but at the beginning, the band house is the dream in bricks and mortar. Because we've all seen *Help!* and we all want those four adjacent, semi-detached front doors that open on one big house full of comfortable sofas and mate-y companionship.

48002 Lookout Drive wasn't that, but it was a variation on the same dream. There were balloons festooned on the gate as though announcing a children's party and a big sign above the door—WELCOME SWEET! LOOK OUT!—but it was evident nobody was home. I took in the view, not knowing whether to be more impressed by the swimming pool (I'd never seen the kind where the water laps right to the edge) or the Pacific (I'd never seen the kind where a blue sea laps at a sandy shore).

I must have been jetlagged, but I merely felt slightly shitty as I tried to get my head around how it was that a cool breeze was blowing through the house when it was so brutally hot outside. I lay back on the white sofa and surveyed the alien environment, a page ripped from an architectural magazine in the dentist's office. But there'd be no painful injection before a filling. Besides, I was already woozy, growing numb. I was in a dream. And then I *was* in a dream, an attractive Asian stewardess painting my nails, rubbing my shoulders, squeezing my neck, my back, then delving further down.

I came to with a start, then fell back asleep, lulled by the perpetual hum of the ceiling fan. An inflatable plastic bed floated absentmindedly across the pool.

Blake woke me, immediately regaling me with stories; what they'd done, whom they'd met, about Curtis and Becca who'd be here shortly, which room was mine, how great the house was. Even Jack was atypically enthusiastic.

"Look out! It's another looking-glass altogether," said Blake. And when Becca walked in the door, he called to her: "Hey, come and meet my son." And, primed, she hugged me.

Blake said: "Sweet, this is Mum."

I imagined that my real mum had looked like Becca. You only had to take one look at her to know how ideally suited she was to the task. And now here she was, "Mum" to three motherless kids: Blake, Jack, and me. She and Blake would fall in love, have their own kids and forget about me: that was my immediate thought. I didn't have time to tease it out—it was pure, stupid instinct.

The first thing she said was: "Poor boy, I know what you need." She went straight to the kitchen, boiled a whistling kettle and made me a cup of some herbal tea called "Gentle Awakening" that she happened to carry in her bag.

I couldn't figure out time on Lookout Drive. I woke absurdly early the next morning and found myself sleepwalking around the house trying not to wake anyone, looking for things you can never find in somebody else's house.

I fell back asleep, opening my eyes to find everyone in the midst of a business meeting around me. I was allowed, no, *expected*, to sit in. Andy found nothing out of the ordinary in this: if Blake wanted me there, Blake wanted me there. At one point, Jack said: "Well, Sweet has been doing our merch in the UK, and I know we've got a company working for us now, but I'm sure they'll be happy to hear how it's worked before. And maybe they can take him under their wing and show him how it works here. It's a good trade."

"Well he doesn't have to work the whole time," said Blake. "He can just have fun."

"No, I'd like to," I said through a yawn.

"Well, either way," said Blake. "He'll be traveling with us, Andy. All access."

And Andy, to my surprise, addressed the issue with some seriousness: "Great idea. Good to see the youthful face of the Wonderkid family. Absolutely." And then turning to me: "Merchandise: thoughts?" I told him everything I'd learned from Greg, as he nodded vigorously. "I'll put you in touch with Vern. You can iron it out with him. But if you want to keep it in the family, you should. That's the right generational feel; you buy a CD from the singer's own son." I was more than happy to be a handy marketing opportunity.

Mitchell, the new road manager, joined us via conference call. His waspy voice sounded nothing like that of our only other road manager, Knobby ("with a K"), a notable failure whom Greg had had to ship back to his job at an abattoir on the Isle of Man.

"Ladies and Gentlemen, I am honored to be your road manager. *Your* job is to play music, fulfill your promotional obligations, and have fun; *my* job is to strive, to seek, to find, and not to yield. Please open your itineraries."

Itineraries? On cue, Andy handed out ring-bound plastic-covered booklets, each emblazoned with the new Wonderkids logo, their contents a *Rain Man* wonderland of load-in times, hotel confirmation codes, and backstage office fax numbers. With each, like the free gift with a box of cereal, came a similarly-designed laminated backstage pass.

Jack and Blake could have died happily right at that moment.

In my depleted state, up unnaturally early every morning, I auditioned music from the huge piles of CDs that Blake and Jack had been glad-handed by WBA (and apparently every other label in Los Angeles—they were in that honeymoon period when you get anything you want for free). Jack's eagle eye always landed on any label guy's possibly spare stack of promo CDs: "Oh, may I? I haven't heard that." He wanted one of everything.

At home, I'd been strictly a Top 40 boy, a devoted listener to the countdown every Sunday evening, and quite a few of the bands were familiar to me: Erasure, Depeche Mode, the Smiths, the Pretenders—so many of the acts were British; it was that time. But reissues were pouring out too—Hendrix, the Grateful Dead, Crosby, Stills, Nash & Young (you could get everything free except the Beatles: Jack was peeved that Capitol drew the line at Fab Four freebies—everyone wanted the Beatles catalog, so there was no need to give it away)—and they were all there, many still sealed in those shrink-wrapped and stickered plastic cases, so hard to prise open, so easy to shatter.

"Don't listen to that shit," Jack would invariably say when he was making his morning coffee. "You should be listening to this." He'd pick out something recent: "It's called Alternative Music over here, Modern Rock. There's a chart for it." There was a chart for everything.

And when Blake finally got up, he'd hear ten seconds of Lush or Ride or whatever it was, grimace and say: "Sounds very *serious*," and that was that. Not his sort of thing—he didn't listen to anything new. "Keeping up" was Jack's job.

• • •

First Class airfare, stretch limo, and then, to cap it all, not a grubby touring van at all: a tour bus. A streamlined tour bus called "Flame" (airbrushed on both sides in all the shades of autumn), designed for our extended stay. Nothing like a caravan. I'd never really seen anything like it. You could live in it forever, travel anywhere. I felt like I was boarding Apollo 7. A mustached bus driver, introducing himself as Randy, greeted us.

"Last crew I had on here were . . ." He said a name I didn't recognize, the *Something* Boys. "So what's this going to be?" he asked, casting a complicit eye. "*Animal House* or *The Sound of Music*?"

"Mad Hatter's Tea Party!" said Blake.

"Alright!" said Randy. "I can roll with that." He was thin as a rake, had a *Dukes of Hazzard* accent, and flashed a wide smile as we boarded his spaceship.

Blake rechristened Randy and all was well with the world: "Hey, Good Buddy, can we get *WonderBus* put on the sign above the windshield?"

"Ten-four," said Randy, clicking his fingers and pointing at the same time. "*WonderBus* it is."

And there we were in our own WonderBus in Wonderland, tooling down some highway to Six Somethings Over Somewhere-or-other. California was the ideal state for this tour: theme parks littered the countryside. They weren't even to be full shows, just five-song showcases at peak hours.

On arrival, though we'd only traveled three hours, we rather dribbled out onto the tarmac, blinking in the sun, newborn. It was my first encounter with the disorientating effect of a tour bus and its tinted windows: however short the trip, without pee stops or snack breaks, you wind up outside the world, beyond time. Which is why it's a hothouse for drink and drugs. Overnighters and day rooms only make things weirder. I have a photo of a snowcapped mountain, somewhere or other: everyone is outside the bus, in a pristine and beautiful landscape, and every single person is rubbing his eyes with his hands, or has his eyes shut, or covered in some way, except Blake, who is pissing on the emergency pull-off sign.

As we reentered Earth's atmosphere that first afternoon, we met Mitchell for the first time. We couldn't believe his clothes, his *attire*. He was in the wrong line of work. Unusually for an American, he looked ready for a game of village cricket. He was collegiate, smooth, urbane: all qualities quite unnecessary in a road manager. A pager on his belt chirped interruption. He tutted its impudence. He was so calm.

"Ladies and gentlemen," he said, shaking hands, naming everyone (even me) with utter confidence. "My answer to everything is: *it's in the itinerary*. Normally we'd let you relax on the bus until we had you set up backstage, and we're not quite ready for you yet, but if you'll take us as you find us, just for today, we'll get on famously." Blake rechristened him Ripley.

Our own crew numbered two, dapper Mitchell—soundman and road manager—and a roadie type, Joe, with tattoos, a nose-piercing, and a Whitesnake T-shirt. He was the politest man in the world, never traveled with us, and never complained: apparently, he'd been driving a van behind with some of the larger gear. This wasn't our concern.

I expected we'd be led through the interior of the park, where the sun always shines, where everything is sponsored, and paths never fork so as to minimize unnecessary familial debate, but instead, a large freight elevator took us down a floor or two to a conveyor belt, which efficiently bussed the gear a little way, where, to my surprise was waiting an entire stage: amps, drums, instruments, all set up according to the stage plot, tuned and ready to play. We were underground.

I asked Mitchell where the crowd would be, and he laughed: "Dear boy"—there was a touch of the theater about him—"Up there!" He pointed. The roof sixty feet above us was going to open up like the crater at the climax of that James Bond movie.

"Should I do merch up there then?" I asked, keen to stake my claim to that end of business, though Blake had been gently trying to dissuade me.

"Well, for today, why not let the merch company earn their keep, and you stay with the band, get on that stage, and when they go up, you go up. I think you'll get a kick out of that."

Blake was buzzing. "What do you think, Sweet? Five songs and then home!"

Mitchell settled himself into a small office, from which he proceeded to fire off instructions at a military clip: how clothes should be pressed, where hung, when the meal should be served, and to whom the check should be made out. None of these issues seemed more important than any other: he was just ticking off a checklist. I could have stayed all day in the womb of that pleasure palace, with its luxuriously upholstered dressing rooms, all-you-can-eat (and no-one's-checking-*what*-you-eat) buffet, free video games, and mysterious inner mechanisms: yet another new perspective.

"Oy!" shouted Blake, "Give these to Mitchell and get him to Xerox them and throw them round the stage." It was the Wonderkids' first American setlist:

Lucky Duck
The Dog Mustn't Speak!
They Never Came Back
Fresh Air for My Nose
Rock Around the Bed

With the band in place, and me tucked behind an amp on the right, the ceiling parted, and the stage rose like that Boston Spaceship, pivoting slightly as we emerged into the sunlight.

I could hear the crowd, high-pitched, expectant, and when we crested, arriving slightly above them, stage locking into position with a jolt, I was amazed by the throng of kids, the mass of ant-like activity. We were the ones who'd arrived like extraterrestrials, but they were the alien beings. Blake turned around, his suit a red smear on the sea blue sky, and welcomed me to Wonderland with a smile. Curtis counted off "Lucky Duck," and when the new rhythm section came in, it was obvious the band had never sounded better. Perhaps a bird and a black bloke trumps even twins. Jack was trying some genuine guitar moves, a little twist from his hips, and then a duck downwards to the floor. A duck! Then, a duckwalk! He was actually doing duck moves for Blake's duck song. He would *never* have done that in England. Mind you, he didn't smile while he was doing it.

■■■

The crowd went wild. I know that's a cliché, but it's exactly what they did. Actually, they went wildly wild, feral, running around and pogoing, leaping and twisting, doing their fake rock star poses, their antic air guitar strum, as parents tapped their feet and smiled. How many people were watching? Maybe a thousand. Were they even here to see the Wonderkids, or would they have happily watched anything delivered from the underworld? Who cares? We were the focus of all the attention. And then I saw the first of what I realized were hundreds of Wonderkids T-shirts and baseball caps. And they weren't languishing on the merch table, they were proudly worn, along with onesies and twosies with cartoons of Blake's face and the other members of the band popping out from behind him.

At the end of "Lucky Duck," the audience let out an ear-splitting cheer. Parents whooped their appreciation. They were sick of Simeon and "Cumbayá"—they wanted this as much as their kids did—and when they bought the merchandise, they bought it for themselves. Andy's plans had coalesced in a heartbeat.

Before the crowd could die down, Blake wandered over to the most recent addition to the show: a "dressing-up box," which lived at the front of the stage, and in which he kept an ever-accumulating collection of props, costumes, and doo-dads. You had no idea what rabbit he'd pull out next. As he rummaged around, he seemed surprised to find a mad hatter's hat, and put it on as the band unleashed "The Dog Mustn't Speak," prime Blakeian nonsense:

> The dog mustn't speak!
> Not out of his filthy nozzle
> Or his toothy smiling beak,
> The dog mustn't speak!
> His sweet slobber can clobber
> As he spits out his
> Sugared word-barks
> The dog mustn't speak!

And the audience sang along. It was baffling. How did they know the words? Did they know what they were singing? Did they think it meant anything at all? And for that matter, did it?

The show ended too soon. The new Wonderkids never out-stayed their welcome. They'd quickly realized that a kids' gig has its own duration, that the kids tire, that they're easily bored, that they're more interested in themselves than the band. And that the merch table is as good a place for an encore as any. So the band always hit hard and quick. Out the window went all notions of the flow of a show. It was just bang-bang-bang-bang-bang-bye.

The autograph session went on for over an hour. Record companies have a thousand names for it, none very respectful, but to Blake it was always just "saying hi": "I gotta go say hi." I followed the band out, but although Jack (never at ease in this situation), Becca and Curtis were on hand, it was Blake the kids were drawn to, and their magnet had infinite patience. There were a few lines he always used (some gently surreal, some unexpected—he'd learned them as a teacher) to calm overexcitement, to put them off their guards, to draw them into conversation.

And though the plan had been to cordon Blake off from the line, he'd invariably move his chair and invite a free-for-all: kids crawling up on his lap, smiling for the camera, a look of pride in their parents' eyes. Sometimes the mothers seemed as interested in Blake as their children were; in some cases, more interested in Blake than in their own kids. The registers never stopped ringing, and Blake never ran out of conversation.

"Do you study Ancient Greek?" A shake of the child's head. "Shall I teach you some?" He'd wheel out some silliness—have them repeat the component parts of "Awa Tafoo Lie Am" and then make them say it altogether "Oh! What a fool I am!"—or give them some old routine, a tongue-twister ("does this shop stock shot socks with spots?") or even just play a trick on them: "Say 'joke' five times!" ("joke, joke, joke, joke, joke"); "what do you call the white of an egg?" The kids couldn't help but say "yolk"; and if that didn't get a big laugh, he'd have them "Say 'boast' five times!" When then asked "What do you put into a toaster?" no kid *ever* said "bread." Blake's bag of tricks was bottomless.

And the parents waved their credit cards once more. It wasn't until Mitchell came to pry Blake from the melee that there was any sign that it would ever end.

• • •

In the WonderBus on our trip back to Lookout, everyone was tipsy on success. Becca was in awe—she'd known from the rehearsal room and *Simeon's House* that Blake had *something*, but it was the first time she'd found out what it was actually was.

"How on earth do you do it?" She asked, her hands and arms moving smoothly through some kind of seated yoga. She even did it when the bus was moving.

"He's like the Pied Piper!" I said.

"God, I hope not," said Blake, peeling the label from a beer, strip by agonizing strip, as he gave his standard demonstration of restless leg syndrome. "He takes all the kids into a hillside, doesn't he? All except a lame boy. It's not that he took the other kids—that's okay—why leave the lame boy?"

"I don't know how you have the patience," said Curtis.

"My patience for other people's kids is infinite," Blake replied, and then he fixed his eyes on Becca. "All you have to do is look them in the eyes: *never* take your eyes off them. Kids are only interested in themselves."

"Well, you're born to it," said Becca, squeezing his hand. "You're gonna have trouble with the real Mums. They like you."

"Oh, tell *that* story," said Jack.

"No!" said Blake, laughing. "No. Not now. Late, late, another night." He retired to the back lounge, but as he passed the coffins, he looked over his shoulder.

"Sweet, come on. Let's watch some Marx Brothers!"

On the way home, we pulled into a diner, more as a stop on my tourist itinerary than anything else. The waitress put a glass in front of each of us.

"What's that?" I asked.

"Iced water," said Blake. "They always give it to you."

"Am I going to have to have a salad as well?"

"No," said Jack. "Order off the breakfast menu. Syrup on everything."

When our food was in front of us, Blake dabbed at the slick on my plate. "You've found your spiritual home, Sweet. America.

Dr. Seuss! Did you ever read Dr. Seuss? *Cat in the Hat?* Wonderful. Wordy. Fake words. *Green Eggs and Ham?* Weird."

"Doesn't seem any weirder than bacon and syrup," I said, considering my plate. Even I was dubious.

"Oh, Seuss is great stuff. All ages. Our dad wouldn't allow it in the house. Too American."

I had my first bite.

Syrup and bacon. Waffles and strawberries. Pancakes. Peanut butter and jelly. French toast. English muffins. Belgian waffles. Dutch cocoa. German pancakes. Swedish fish.

America!

Jack was too cool to be wowed by it, the weird new continent. He was here to do a job, make some music, amass some CDs. As we traveled, and this is what we now did, if I so much as glanced out of the window at an approaching skyline, he'd sarcastically say: "Ooh! Look at the big buildings!" But he couldn't keep the façade up forever, and even he was impressed as we drove through a lunar landscape of pockmarked desert one night, all of us glued to the windows.

"Hey guys!" Randy shouted from the front. "WNOK, right now! They're playing 'Rock Around the Bed'!"

"Turn it up!" shouted Blake.

The moment was complete. We were over the moon.

And when the song was done, Blake shouted: "Got a riff, Jack? Let's write a swimming pool." Apparently, that's what Lennon and McCartney used to say when they sat down to write a new hit. And it's what Blake *always* said.

"It just so happens that I *do*," was Jack's unfailing reply. They'd head to the back of the bus and there'd be a new song at soundcheck the next day. That night's was called "Noon in June":

Spring, she will come back this way
One day in May, one day in May
Spring, she will come back this way
No matter what your parents say

Summer will return so soon
One noon in June, one noon in June
Summer will return so soon
One noon in June.

In England, you run out of road before it begins, or you're caught in traffic and can't leave the motorway soon enough. In America, you drive forever and it never ends: we were mobile, on the wagon train, young men going east (frequently, and then west back home again). We sampled our first hotels, each a world apart from the grimy B&Bs of Great Britain with their confrontational landladies and sandpaper toilet rolls. Each room, in fact, had its own bathroom, which was a complete novelty; and in that bathroom, a shower that delivered the right water temperature, unlike the showers at home, which were finicky as shortwave radios and needed just as much fine tuning to avoid scalding or freezing. (Blake always bathed for this reason: he traveled with a rubber duck called Lucky.) The service stations, the travel plazas by the side of the highway, were the size of large English villages.

Blake assumed the role of teacher—simple things: how to eat (not just sugar); how to read (not actually how to read words, but how to read books, without music on, to concentrate, and God knows we had enough time); how to buy books (I'd never been in secondhand bookstores before; he loved to be on his hands and knees, the more disordered the stock, the better the browse); how not to steal (from shops—hotels were fine); how to watch movies more than once; how to listen to music—the idea was you didn't just have it on in the background! You listened to it, bathed in it, which had simply never occurred to me. Everything he did, I did, if possible in the precise way that he did it, just as any child might copy his father.

And it was easy to absorb all this because no one had ever taught me anything useful before, let alone with enthusiasm. But it wasn't even just that: it was the first time anyone had paid attention only to me. It's what good parents do. Being singled out in front of the rest of your class is hardly the same; sitting round at the Terrys in a silence punctuated only by a pointedly cleared throat that represented the apex of debate was no substitute.

Later, I'd pick and choose what was really important to me, but for now I just sponged it all up: books, music, films, diet, wardrobe—check. If this was Greg's beloved university of life, I liked the uniform. And the hours.

One evening we drew into a truck stop to stretch our legs, buy "candy," and raid the bargain cassette bin, while Randy "gassed up." I was starting to get the hang of it all.

A trucker approached; he walked like he thought he was hard: shaved head, mirror shades, bushy moustache, and leather jacket, all at odds with the cut-off denim shorts that revealed his hairy legs. We were dressed scruffy, hair perhaps slightly long. As we passed, he muttered under his breath: "Fags."

"Keep walking," whispered Blake, taking Jack and me by the arm.

When we were out of earshot, Jack said, like he might actually do something about it: "Did he call me a fag?" Given the chance, some might have wanted to teach the trucker a lesson in political correctness, but Jack just didn't want to be called a poof.

"Let it go, Jackie," said Blake. "See, what he doesn't realize is that he looks like all the Village People rolled into one." I watched the trucker strut off in his short shorts.

This was the life I'd always wanted.

I wasn't holding a plate of oranges at half-time, caught between the athletes and the parents.

I had my own team now.

Quack!

"Hey, if you think really hard, maybe we can stop this rain."

AFTER THE EXPERIMENTAL FIRST LEG OF GIGS, THERE WAS A BREAK before the real slog began. Blake unexpectedly announced that he and I were heading home for a fortnight to tie up some loose ends. The Terrys had boxed up my stuff, which we'd store at Blake's, where we'd stay. Just as well. I didn't want to spend one more night in the anechoic chamber of their house, even for old time's sake.

Blake had meetings with Mr. Hedges and a valedictory summit with Greg, much to the satisfaction of both.

"Greg's right," Blake said, as he surveyed the rainy London afternoon from the window of his apartment. "They're gonna hate us here now. Unless they forget we're from here. He said: *You can't make a profit in your own parish.*"

"Is that right?"

"It's rightish," said Blake, laughing. "It might even be *more* right." That, in a nutshell, was what he'd miss about Greg

"Well," I said, "be grateful for what you have elsewhere, I suppose."

His grin became a broad smile: "I hate London. I hate the rain. I hate everything."

• • •

We went to visit his father and took tea in a conservatory. It was as if the whole event had been stage-managed to convey the strongest possible antidote to America: a dizzying choice of teapots, carpeting that clashed violently with the William Morris wallpaper, and a vast array of lace doilies on every chair to prevent the spoiling of the fabric by . . . what? Edwardian pomade?

There wasn't a single picture of Blake and Jack's mother, Edie. She was dead, yes, but not one photo? Even hiding in the dusted frames on the piano? This wasn't just *dead*. This was, *and buried.*

"Well, James," said Barry firmly, "it should be *Wunderkinder.*" It was a surprise to hear Blake called anything but Blake. No one called him Jimmy except Jack, and I'd *never* heard him called James. "Wunderkinds doesn't mean anything."

"It doesn't matter anymore, Dad, and I'm not really sure it ever did." They talked on the phone very occasionally, conversations that focused almost exclusively on the quality of their phone connection. The afternoon had begun with a detailed interrogation on the subject of our flight over and how there could possibly be an airline called Virgin.

"*Wunderkinder* is the plural. *Die Wunderkinder.* And no umlaut, you know that, right? You don't use one, do you? I suppose that's some kind of relief."

"Germany as a nation is probably very relieved."

"There's no need for sarcasm." To tell him they'd occasionally thrown an umlaut over the "I" would have been a low blow.

"But you know that we're not called the Wunderkinds or *Die Wunderkinder* any more, right, Dad? We're called the Wonderkids."

"Ah yes," said Barry. "Is that further evidence of what they now call *dumbing down*?"

In Barry Lewis's mind, America and Britain were on two sides of an uneven scale, the balance of which he checked at every opportunity: "I suppose it's mostly that Budweiser rubbish over there, is it? Served ice cold to disguise the lack of taste?"

"Oh, there's good beer. We drink something called Anchor Steam in the bus." Blake seemed awkward; unable either to let the man have it all his own way or to disagree with him.

"*Anchor Steam*!" snorted Barry, as though this name was any more ridiculous than Old Speckled Hen.

"We went to the brewery," I piped up.

"Did you, by Jove?" He turned an enquiring eye on me as though I was expected to provide a full report on the operation and maintenance of the Anchor Steam brewery based on my tour of inspection. That shut me up.

"And what do you eat over there? I expect Anchor Steam beer complements, comp*le*ments . . ."—he repeated it to show he was aware that he wasn't using the word *compliment* and that he knew how *complement* was spelled—". . . your hamburger and fries quite nicely." He pronounced *hamburger* as though the word were freshly minted, a crazy new experience for all of us. At the drop of a hat, I thought, he might conjugate a verb, or start putting the date of publication in parenthesis when a novel was mentioned. There was almost certainly going to be an exam. "A lot of '*have a nice day*' is there, James?"

"Well, everyone is friendly, easy to deal with; everyone's very polite."

"Oh, *customer service*," said Barry dismissively. "Second to none, of course. They've always been good at that. They know how to *keep the customer satisfied*." This seemed to carry some extra implication over and above its (surely accidental) quotation of a Simon and Garfunkel song, as though customer service always masked a sinister ulterior motive. "That's how they *get* you."

"Well, it's quite nice to have people be polite for a change."

"It must be," said his father wistfully, as though no one had ever been polite to him, or that he vaguely remembered a time when someone had been polite to him, since when he'd only known rudeness. "It must be. You must be happy to get a good cuppa inside you back in old Blighty. Bet you miss that. We've still got *some* things going for us."

"They do actually have tea out there, Dad."

"*Iced* tea," said his father. "*Iced* coffee. I see it on the cop shows. *Iced* this and that." It was like a sparring match, but only one person was sparring. I would have enjoyed this kind of thing back at the Terrys. It was combative and relentless but quite funny.

"Well, it's warm out there," said Blake. "The weather is better on the west coast. We haven't seen anything but bright sunshine the whole time, have we, Sweet?"

Barry sniffed at my name suspiciously. "And it's going okay, is it? Die Wunderkinder? My two sons, the fruits of my loins, my progeny: the Wonderkids. Will we see evidence of your success on these fair shores?"

"Soon, I hope."

"But they've taken you to their hearts, the Yanks," said his father, not without pride at the idea of a mini-British invasion. "They've worn their hearts to a nubbin trying to nuzzle up to you. Robert Benchley. Or Perelman. I can't remember which. Now there's an American, every bit the equal of Wodehouse."

"They love them," I confirmed.

"And you're traveling around with them, are you, young man?" He couldn't actually bear to say my name, which made me all the more determined not to reveal that it was really Edward.

"Yes," interrupted Blake. "He's having fun."

"I'm in charge of merchandising," I said.

"And what do your parents, your *foster* parents, have to say about that?"

I wanted to point out that Blake was now my legal guardian, but I thought better of it. Perhaps Barry didn't know. I decided to answer as though his question was: *And how do the Terrys feel about your being taken off their hands?* The answer was the same either way. "I think it's a relief to them actually," I said.

Barry harrumphed. "And how about your education, young man?"

Blake came to my rescue: "It's a once in a lifetime opportunity, a unique education: he's learning every day and we'll sort out the qualifications when we get back. What he needs is a little more childhood before life begins." I wasn't sure I liked Blake's implication, but perhaps this was mostly for his father. He was right, though: I'd read more, heard more, learned more.

"Another cuppa," concluded Barry.

When he was gone, Blake winced and swatted an imaginary fly. "Never changes," said Blake, "but, y'know, family." He felt claustrophobic in the conservatory, clicking his fingers repeatedly in a way that announced an imminent exit. "I'm glad we're out of all this."

"What?"

"England. I hate the way you hear something on *Start the Week* on Monday morning, some tiny silly thing, and then at the pub that lunch people are talking about it, and then it's become a minor controversy by the Nine O'Clock News that night, and then the next day it's on the cover of the *Sun* looking this way and the cover of the *Guardian* looking that. And then someone responds to it, and the next day it's a national scandal, and it's on Question Time on Thursday. It's so small."

"You've only been in America a few months!" I said. I could see his father pottering about in the kitchen, inspecting the leather elbows of his cardigan as he waited for the kettle to boil.

"Well, it feels liberating. I always felt a little gauche over here; over there I realize I'm just normal. Not being the most enthusiastic person in the room anymore: that's good. Do you know what I mean? This place does me in. It's so barbaric."

"Barbaric?"

"Everything. The way you have to put your underground ticket in at the beginning of the trip and then again at the end of the trip. The bayonet lightbulbs," he said pointing above him, then turning his attention to the wall: "those massive plugs with three prongs; that stupid little switch."

"You're as bad as your father."

The kitchen light extinguished before Barry emerged carrying a tray clinking with crockery. His relationship to electricity was very much the same as the Terrys' to volume and heat: off was preferable. "Now . . . Garibaldis, do they have those or equivalent? Or Custard Creams? What were you two Wunderkinder chatting about?"

"How much I dislike America," said Blake, quick as a flash.

"Obsessed with their teeth, aren't they?" Barry mused absentmindedly. "I remember your sister liked the Osmonds. Miles and miles of teeth, gleaming Mormon teeth, rows of huge white gravestones. She had posters of them all over her wall: may still do for all I know." Danielle and Barry didn't talk, though she lived only three streets away. When they saw each other in the post office, they nodded. Barry didn't like her "friend" Michelle. "You'll probably be getting your teeth fixed. But not on the National Health you won't. Not on the National Health."

"They don't have a National Health over there, Dad."

"No, that's right. Because they're deathly afraid of Communism."

"You've never really been that keen on Communism yourself, have you?"

"Are you going to have more of the jam, Sweet? If not, would you mind putting the top back on?"

And on it went.

As we left, Barry threw a copy of *American Notes* by Charles Dickens at me. "It'll be useful. Pay attention."

"So what's the story with your mum?" I asked Blake in the cab. He was scrutinizing the meter.

"I'm sorry to go on about it, but why does the meter keep going up even when you're not moving? That would never happen in America. I'd never even noticed that before. What did you say?"

"Your mum. What happened?"

"She died when I was eight. You know that, right? Why?" He wasn't avoiding the question, just intent on getting to the bottom of the meter mystery.

"I didn't actually. Your dad never married again?"

"No. Once was enough. Put him off for life. Look at that! We're sitting completely still, going nowhere, doing nothing, and the meter's rising. We're paying for this."

"I just noticed there weren't a lot of pictures of her in your father's place."

"Oh yeah. She died, but not until after she'd left him for another man. We never saw her after she left. If I told you it was a Yank, would you believe me?"

"Yes, I would. Sorry."

"Old news." He couldn't help laughing. "He hated America long before that though. That just confirmed his every prejudice. Jack and I both look a lot like her."

"What was she like?"

"She sang; she loved poetry; she had me recite "The Jumblies"; she had long brown hair and she smelled of cloves; and then she abandoned us; and then she died. And I have fought against considering that her punishment, as certain other family members have implied, ever since. So what she's like is an absence, a double absence." He looked at me. "But you'd know all about that, right?" I nodded, but I didn't really feel that double absence. "And I've got my dad," he said, winking.

"And I've got you." I imitated his wink. We didn't speak.

He went back to watching the meter. "But no mums then."

"Well, there's Becca." He put his arm around my shoulder. "Fuck this place. Let's go back to the land of chocolate milk and tupelo honey."

After leaky London, Los Angeles was even lovelier than I remembered. The band had been rehearsing; the record label had been strategizing; Mitchell was in bureaucratic nirvana; the bus was ready to roll; Randy had grown his moustache in preparation.

The front of the WonderBus, the parlor, was where we chatted and browsed magazines; Jack always had some gear porn handy. He'd flick through guitar catalogs with the same kind of rapt attention other men reserve for the top shelf, giving the occasional throaty growl of appreciation. Once in a while, he'd hold a page up, asking only that we join in for a moment before he returned to his private pleasure. And while he read, as if to complete the picture, he'd relentlessly exercise his left hand with one of those little plastic finger-strengthening gizmos. He was scared stiff of carpal tunnel, but, well . . . it looked like he was wanking.

The rest of the time he read the music papers; he didn't care which one. He never lost the need to keep up: "Don't like the sound of this lot," he'd say out loud to no one in particular, as though we were in direct competition with Jane's Addiction anywhere but in his mind: "They're going to make us sound very old-fashioned." Or, "New Primal Scream sounds like it's going to be good. They got Jimmy Miller working on it." These conversations never went anywhere, but he liked to keep us updated with his oral Random Notes.

Becca always sat front left beneath the television, listening privately to headphones—always droney trance music with her, sometimes German, nothing with lyrics: Jack called it "music for people who do yoga." "Tai chi," she once pertly corrected him during one of the few breaks between songs.

Curtis, meanwhile, sat on the other side of Mitchell's desk, never once complaining about what was on the big speakers. In every area but music, he'd done away with punkish things. He read only paperback-thick magazines—*Esquire*, *Vogue*, *Vanity Fair*. He liked the ads, designer watches and fountain pens, the photo spreads, as much as the articles: that was all he showed us anyway, often with a little laugh and shake of his head at the insane luxury of it all. Then he'd toss the book-priced magazine away like it was garbage and buy another, but not before he'd detached all the little perfume samples and the bus smelled like a Body Shop. Finally Jack told him: "knock it off with the frou frou juice"; Curtis responded: "think of it as secondhand perfume." When Jack looked at him uncomprehendingly, he explained: "to combat the secondhand smoke." That was the end of that.

Blake staked his claim to the back of the bus; it became his undisputed domain, home to a growing library of secondhand books, repository for various pieces of purloined hotel paraphernalia. Smoking was always allowed there, more or less insisted upon, and out of consideration for Becca and Curtis, Jack used to head back for his cigarette. It got very hazy. I've never actually had a cigarette myself, but I'm surely one of the most addicted secondhand smokers of all time.

The gigs themselves settled down into a comfortable routine over the next month. We never played actual rock venues, but there were libraries, performing arts centers, Unitarian churches; they treated us well.

"This is where you want to be," said Mitchell. "Where they've cut you a check before you even play. That is class."

The tour was sprinkled with various TV and radio appearances—Blake was often required to mime on the former; but never (his joke) on the latter—all simultaneously unique and repetitive: "Where did you get the name from?" "What's it like being in a band with your brother?" "Do you have a message for the kids out here?" It's like that bit in *Teletubbies* when they show the same movie twice: you think it's going to be pointless the second time, and then you realize how much you missed, almost as though you hadn't seen it at all.

We were very lucky to have Mitchell. Road manager is an easy position to abuse, but Mitchell had style.

He had warned us about a promoter in the Midwest: "He's a real character. A dick. I've got great stories about this guy." At the venue, this same promoter had left a copy of our rider, the various backstage requirements that the agency forwards to the venue, in the dressing room. Every page had one solid *Sharpie* line of erasure through it. He'd nullified the entire thing: no rider at all. Mitchell picked it up and fanned himself.

"Pawn to King *Four*!" he said with admiration. "A brilliant opening gambit, because it's Sunday and we can't ring the agent." He perused the redacted rider and consulted the contract. "Aha!" It was all a little Hercule Poirot. "His Achilles heel. It's petty but it'll do." Mitchell stuck his head out the door and yelled for the promoter. I was wondering whether there'd be a confrontation, but that wasn't Mitchell's M.O.

"Hey! Welcome to the Recreation Room," said the incoming bearded dick. "There's tea and coffee."

"Great. I see the rider no longer applies—no problem about that at all—but I note that, here, the line doesn't reach the bottom of the page, look, so it appears that we're missing 14 9-volt batteries. Could you pick them up?"

The bearded dick looked at the offending line, considering his options before concluding: "Sure. I'll send someone out. If there's anything else you guys need, give a shout."

When he'd left, Mitchell said: "That's the thing about the real dicks of America. They respect you for treating them like a dick back. But it must be done in their language, because they speak no other."

And when the batteries came, Mitchell lined them up on the mantelpiece like Stonehenge, and they were still standing when we left the dressing room after a victorious show. Perhaps they're still standing now. Stonehenge is.

• • •

There was more to Mitchell than met the eye. Back in a theme park one sunny afternoon, I walked into his day office to ask him about set-lists. The door was closed, but I didn't think anything of it.

"Sweet, old chap," he said, looking round at me with un-flustered charm. "Don't they knock where you come from? No matter." He turned back to his business with the promoter. "Meet Mr. Ray Rosenbloom; his boss has these parks sewn up. He'll be paying us. Mr. Ray Rosenbloom, meet Sweet. Sit down, young man. Here," he added firmly. I admired his decisiveness, his fairness.

Mr. Rosenbloom, glasses propped on forehead, was otherwise occupied in the strenuous reading of fine print and did not offer me a greeting. Mitchell opened his attaché briefcase, its entire contents (seen only by the two of us) a gun—a gun!—and a single piece of paper in a see-through folder. He removed the gun and placed it on the desk, barrel towards Mr. Rosenbloom, then took out the sole piece of paper, placing the gun back in the briefcase, which he closed.

"Here's the contract, Ray, and . . . let me check . . . I do believe . . ." he scanned the page, actually going to the trouble of assuming a studied pose of concentration . . . "Yes, yes, I thought so: *cash*."

Mr. Rosenbloom was flustered. "Well, I have a check. I have *most* of the cash."

"Well, that's fine, Ray. But are you seriously telling me that in the entirety of this thriving, money-making family complex, there isn't enough cash to pay my charges their due for the hard work they're going to do for you and your patrons?"

"Five songs," said Rosenbloom ill-advisedly.

"Whose signature is this?"

"Mine," said a weakened Rosenbloom.

"Okay. Okay. *Ray*, this problem doesn't seem insurmountable. See you back here in fifteen minutes?"

"Sure," said Rosenbloom, who left to locate the cash.

Mitchell turned to me with a broad smile. "I love this bit."

"What bit is it?"

"The nightly drama. Do you like David Mamet?

"I don't really know."

"I think of Mamet a lot during these transactions. The pauses. I love them."

"Is the gun loaded?"

"That *question* is loaded. The gun is purely a precaution." He hadn't answered the question.

"Have you ever had to use it?"

"No. Its very presence ensures that it will not be required."

"It's a deterrent?"

"What's your real name?" I told him. He continued: "I think you're going to do this job one day."

"Why?"

"I can tell." He was a dapper gypsy reading my fortune. "I have wisdom for you; wisdom I have earned."

"Did Blake put you up to this?"

"No. He doesn't even want you to do the merch. He just wants you on the bus, on his side, number one son."

"Okay. Well . . . wisdom . . . sure. Can I touch the gun?"

"No. What did you want?"

"Oh, Blake wanted some copies for the stage."

"Ah, second only in importance to getting paid: the setlist. There's the machine. There's the paper. There's the on/off switch. There's the pass code. There's your finger to prod the keypad with. And, next time, please, don't *ever* walk into my room when I'm in the middle of a settlement. It's a pleasure to work with you."

So, preppy Mitchell was slightly eccentric, perhaps a little murderous. "Ripley" was perfect: Blake had known the moment they met. And you kept finding out about him, his life a slow reveal. One foul rainy day, there was some inadequately or wrongly advertised gig to which no one came. As we drove up, Curtis pointed out that a *P* had dropped from the sign outside, which now announced J PRODUCTIONS PROUDLY RESENTS THE WONDERKIDS! I mean, I've done gigs with bands where *no one* came; so let's say that there were ten people at this gig, of which 60 percent were under three feet tall. It was likely to be a bit depressing—Jack was grousing, Curtis was arguing against unpacking the entire drum kit, even Blake seemed a bit put out—but, before the band went on, Mitchell gave a speech, the rock 'n' roll equivalent of the big moment in the Kenneth Branagh Shakespeare movie, the gist of which was this—

I'll never forget it, and I've recreated it in similar situations:

"My friends, there is no one here. There is little point in playing. You could go out there right now, have a bad attitude, phone it in, and that would be that: we'd get paid and leave. You could complain about the size of the audience; you could complain about the sound. But here's why you're not going to do that: because by complaining you are saying 'sorry,' and apologizing is the least rock 'n' roll thing in the world. 'Sorry' doesn't only seem to be, it *is* the hardest word. Audiences don't want to hear 'sorry.' Rise above it, and when you make a mistake, smile. Because audiences love mistakes; they love it when you screw up, because it makes them feel special. 'That was the night Blake ended up with only two strings!' 'That was the night Jack fell over, continued playing and laughed through the whole thing. I was there!' A mistake made with confidence isn't a mistake at all: it's a gift from the Gods. It's the moment they see the real you.

"And forget the size of the crowd: it doesn't matter to *them* how many of them there are, because they have eyes only for you, and you are playing just for them, individually. They actually like the fact that nobody's there, because it means that, for one night only, you're their little secret. You are theirs alone. And what they'll tell their friends is this: 'there were only a few people there, but they did an amazing show, because they really just love what they do.' Bingo! But if you point out how few of them there are, if you make them self-conscious, then all they'll think is 'assholes,' because you're treading on their dreams. That cannot end well for anyone. And they'll never come to see you again. So, don't cheat them. Play your greatest show!"

There was more. His battle cry had been reaching a Shakespearean climax, but he abruptly dropped his voice for the final twist.

"Because, ladies and gentlemen, in a few years' time that little girl out there will be fifteen, and she'll come up to you at an in-store or at the gate of your flight, and she'll say: "I'm sorry to bother you, but that time I saw you at the Whatever, Wherever in Sonoma, California, that was so incredible, it changed my life. I'll never forget it." She won't remember how few people were there; she'll just remember how great you were. And you, remembering that that was the gig you were so pissed about, because there was nobody there, and you didn't give it your all, you, at that moment, will feel *small*. Because you conned her. You didn't bother. And she loved it anyway. And, ladies and gentlemen, that *will* happen. So . . . there's a show to do. Don't play for the people who aren't here; play for the people who are. We didn't drive all this way for the scenery. C'MON! DO IT!'"

He was so great; a magician. You wanted him to teach you all his tricks, but there was nothing to learn, no sleight of hand. It was all above board, in plain sight; the guy was just good at his job. In this instance, the Wonderkids filed past onto the stage and played a very mediocre show to ten people. But that's not the point—at least they went on. In fact, I think Mitchell was playing an even longer game; he was encouraging Blake and the band to dig a little deeper. That was part of his job too.

Things did get deeper one afternoon in Northern California. We were playing an arts center at four one Sunday—"just between nap and bedtime" said Blake, talking about the kids, though he might as well have been talking about himself. He generally dozed in his clothes in the afternoon in the back of the bus, which was starting to look like a Bedouin tent. I loved hanging out back there among the amassed bric-a-brac, the nomad's possessions, but I was more or less the only one who did, apart from its indigenous person. Even Jack was smoking less.

We'd arrived in good time, but were hobbled by the fact that we were soundchecking after a Sacramento rock band doing the evening show. Their roadies somewhat reluctantly shifted their gear back to give us more room.

The rock band, which looked like an MTV recreation of the Velvet Underground, disappeared, and we were left to do our show. The kids filed in, and the mayhem began. Blake's dressing-up box was bulging with little doodads he'd picked up at truck stops—a small hand puppet of the devil, red-faced and horned in a black cape, which he used for a silly ventriloquist routine during a break-down in one of the songs; random T-shirts that he'd throw out to the audience.

It was the first time I'd seen so much breastfeeding at a show. It was hard not to stare. There were boobs everywhere: the mothers nursed babies while the slightly older kids—*playgroupies* was the backstage term—dived into the mosh pit. It wasn't as violent as a punk concert—more drool, less spit—but the noise was immense and the energy ferocious. The stage was high, a rare blessing, in that it prevented otherwise unmonitored children from clambering up to dance where the action was. This saved Blake from taking time out in the middle of a song to get down to eye level, sending a tot toddling off in the direction of waving parents.

Breasts, tots, loud music—all the makings of a Bacchanalian frenzy, and it was in that little performing arts center that the show hit warp speed for the first time. The dads and mums (though it was mostly lactating mums, unself-consciously nursing, boobs akimbo) chatted at the back as the kids ate it up at the front. Blake was in a crazy playful mood. Before the climax, "Rock Around the Bed," he announced "you know what, I'm hungry. It's snack time!" and scampered off stage. I thought for a horrible moment that he was going to reappear with the entire deli tray and initiate a food-fight. Instead, he returned with a loaf of sliced bread, some plastic utensils, and a couple of jars, which he placed on top of the dressing-up box: "Are you guys hungry?" The kids were already standing on a sawdust of crumbled tortilla and shredded graham cracker. "You know what I like most of all? A peanut butter and jelly sandwich. Who likes PB&J?" The band were looking on, amused, knowing this was going to escalate, getting ready to count off "Rock Around the Bed." The kids cheered. As a matter of fact, they *loved* PB&J! He took two slices of bread and opened the peanut butter tin, spreading its contents with a bendy white knife.

"Who wants a bite of this?" Everyone! This was likely to be a disaster. "Now who's fussy about their crusts? I hope no one's fussy about crusts. You don't want to be one of those kids with parents, like: *Oh yes she'll eat anything—oh sure! But no jelly . . . and cut off the crusts . . . on the diagonal . . . make one a circle.*" He cut the sandwich into quarters and passed them to beseeching hands in the front row. "Alright! Now, no mess. But it's going to get kinda messy up here!" He jabbed his finger into the jar and pulled out a big scoop. "And, you guys, and your moms, while we're talking peanut butter, it's okay to put a little butter on your toast and spread the peanut butter on the actual butter like we do in England. It's just *called* "peanut butter"; it isn't really butter at all. Anyway, trouble is peanut butter is so dry. If I ate this scoop, I wouldn't be able to talk for ages."

"Eat it! Eat it!"

So Blake ate it and everyone cheered. Then he took another scoop and placed half down each side of his face like Red Indian war paint. More cheering. And then he took off his red suit jacket, and started to rub the peanut butter all over his face, sipping from a bottle of water. The kids went nuts. Even the parents were laughing.

"What do you guys want to hear?"

"'Rock Around the Bed'!"

"I said what do you guys want to hear?"

"'Rock Around the Bed'!"

"I can't hear you!"

"'Rock Around the Bed'!"

Blake flung the peanut butter up into the air, somehow splattering its contents along a wall of amplifiers—it was that oily, gooey, healthy kind that separates in the fridge, the kind you need to stir just to reconstitute it. Jack looked askance (they weren't his amps, but equipment was equipment and not to be messed on or with), but Blake didn't notice.

"Then let's *Rock Around the Bed*!"

Curtis counted it off, and the audience—what with the flying peanut butter and the teasing frenzy and the mucky lead singer— went completely berserk. Mothers halted their feeding sessions to wade into the maelstrom; the most charitable explanation was that they were keeping a closer eye on their offspring, but it seemed to me that they just wanted to be nearer the fun. At the side of the stage, the other rock band, looking like the four horsemen of the apocalypse, was in fraught consultation with their own crew over the peanut butter situation. The Wonderkids' show ended with a climactic chord that seemed to go on for about thirty seconds and then the band was off and the lights went up. House music piped, in and the audience tried to reunite with the other members of their families, before converging on me like a swarm of bees.

Blake was collared by one of the rock band's crew: "Who do you think you are? Iggy Pop?"

"Iggy Poop!" said Blake triumphantly, scuttling by, leaving Mitchell in charge. By the time Blake materialized at the merch booth, he was all cleaned up, back in his red suit, smiling. We shifted more units (I was getting down with the jargon) than ever. Blake was beside himself, a gleam in his eye: "Wonderkids Peanut Butter! Sell it in a jar with a Wonderkids label." He was joking, but you knew someone in management would take that idea very seriously, and that I and the merch company would be left to organize the lugging of crates of Wonderkids brand peanut butter across the mezzanines of America.

While Blake greeted his peanut buttered child army, Mitchell worked his charm, and the other band calmed down. Becca came out as the line was finally thinning: "Quite a party back there."

When we eventually made it backstage, the party was still in full swing. The other lot had started boozing early, as if to show the kids' band how it was done, while the Wonderkids could do as they pleased; they were finished for the day. Jack was in conversation with the other band's guitar player; Curtis was talking to a young man of unknown provenance; even Mitchell—who had completed the day's business—was relaxing, though he still sat upright as if taking a class in deportment. A couple of mothers nervously decorated the room, obstacles wherever they stood. It was the first time backstage had been breached.

A whiff of pot—it was my first encounter, but I knew from Jack's conspiratorial wink—wafted from the other dressing room. Blake disappeared within for a little while: his intention probably an apology, doubtless best achieved by the sharing of marijuana. I was drinking an ice-cold Coke out of the bottle: it was nice to have contributed my own quirky demand to the rider. Blake stumbled back into the room—eyes a little bloodshot, smile a little broader—and crashed onto the sofa.

"Now that, my friends, was a show."

"We may have to take it easy on the flinging of condiments," remarked Mitchell casually, ushering non-bandmembers away like an apologetic high society host who simply *has* to go to bed.

"Yeah, my mistake. But did you see those kids go! We're showing them real rock 'n' roll. We can recreate it all for them: forget Iggy Pop, though I could easily wear a horsetail. Rod Stewart always used to kick footballs into the crowd."

"Until they started kicking them back," said Mitchell, the voice of reason. "It's all very funny till someone gets hurt." Blake was hardly paying attention. There was a fantastical look in his eyes. He had seen the future.

"How about," said Becca, entering into the spirit, "biting the head off a chicken?"

"Bit of Alice Cooper," said Mitchell. "Nice."

They were joking, but Blake wasn't, and he went off on a riff: rubber chickens, cuddly chickens, organizing them so candy poured out of them: "They don't mind beating the crap out of a piñata when the feeling takes them." He sounded a bit like his father.

Beers were opened. Even Curtis, who was always the last to join in, cracked one. Blake had started a list in his ubiquitous notebook; he was mapping out the Wonderkids' live show for the next two years. Every now and then he'd pipe up: "How about the ELO spaceship! Fog machines, lasers, but not a spaceship, obviously. Maybe a massive pram, stroller, whatever."

"Pricey," said Mitchell.

"Or how about that idiot who used to play the keyboards upside down?"

"Keith Emerson," said Jack. "And didn't he used to stick knives in his Hammond organ as well?"

"No KNIVES!" shouted Mitchell, over everyone's laughter. "Are you all insane? How did we get from peanut butter to knives?"

"Plastic knives? Sporks? Runcible Spoons? We're just chatting," said Blake. "Sweet, tomorrow. You and me, back of the bus—we're going to work this one out together."

"I've got to deal with the new onesies tomorrow. But I can do both. No problem."

"Okay. Let's check into the hotel, and then see this band. And I'll tell you something." Blake's head bowed in a stage whisper. "However good they are. I'll bet they don't whip it up like we did."

They were surprisingly good, and of course they didn't.

• • •

Jack didn't make it to the gig. We found him back at our hotel fern bar, deep in conversation with a woman. I took one look at her and wondered whether I'd seen her breasts that afternoon at the show: weird. But what would she be doing here if I had? Who was looking after the baby? Her husband? Her mother? Jack gave us a casual wave that seemed to invite us to keep our distance or, if we approached, our conversation to a minimum, so we headed back to our rooms.

The next morning, we mustered, waiting for the bus to leave. (Barry had once taken Blake and Jack on a cruise ship, the legacy of which was a surprising amount of nautical language: it was always "mustering" and using "the head," occasionally known as the "poop deck.") Jack made a brief appearance in the lobby, then headed back upstairs with two cups of coffee. I exchanged a look with Blake, but he surprised me: "I bet there's no one up there at all. He's a proud man, our Jack."

"Two cups of coffee?"

"Well, *exactly*," said Blake, making me feel very young.

Jack was always the last to get to the bus. It was a matter of pride: *an elder brother thing*, Blake said. Jack hated waiting around for people, but didn't mind people waiting around for him. Blake would sometimes lay a trap, and we'd look up at the precise moment that Jack opened up his curtain to check if we were ready to roll.

"Bastard," said Blake, smiling and waving up at him. "We've mustered! We're mustard!"

A few months goes by in a blur: we were in our stride now. You only really remember the days you have off and the days you go home. You're in a bubble, and you try to make it resemble real life as much as possible. But it's easy to see how some people turn that into their actual existence—always on the run with cash in your pocket and no bills, a road manager who sorts out everything that you don't want to—because decompression can give you the bends.

Celebrities came to visit us after the show. Kids are kids, and regardless how famous their parents, they want to do the things that other kids want to do, and if these famous parents have the juice, their kids get extra treats. "The cheese," Mitchell called it. "They're getting the cheese." One famous comedian came onto the bus with his gawky daughter. A tall man, he stooped and sat awkwardly, his long legs seeming to take up the width of the bus. He'd never seemed so tall on TV. He told us stories of this and that, congratulating the band on the show, shaking Jack's hand and saying "crack band!" (which Jack, it later turned out, misheard as "crap band"). As he was leaving, Blake said: "Hey, put *this* on for a photo!" pinning a Wonderkids badge on his suit. It was all smiles, but the moment the photo was taken, the comedian looked down at the button and said: "What does it say? 'Asshole'?" After that he was, indeed, forever known as Asshole.

All good merch tables are the same (the only difference: how much lighting is available to you), but bad merch tables are infinite in their crapness. So we took to carrying our own. It was me and Vern from the merch company who did all the ordering and reordering, much to Blake's disapproval. He said I should be having a good time, and I was. Vern didn't travel with us—just popped in from time to time to check in. We got on well. He showed me the ropes, told me stories. His party piece was the one about the eighties power ballad band. He was just a lowly guy at the company, and every night the lonely ladies who loved that band, and in particular their unavoidable classic "Can't Stop Lovin' You Forever," would, at the beginning of the show, buy single roses to throw onstage at their idols' feet. And every night those same roses would be swept up and thrown away. It was Vern who did the math and made the inspired suggestion: "*Plastic* roses!" And ever after, they sold those lonely ladies plastic roses, which were thrown on stage in exactly the same way; but at the end of the night they weren't thrown away; they were harvested, carefully washed, sprayed with fake rose aroma, and sold at the next show.

"That," said Vern, "is how you make a career in this business."

Genius. I told the unflappable Mitchell, and even he was impressed.

All of life was at the merch table. Some people refused change, as though I personally needed the money; other people came to the table with no money at all, as though that was going to do them any good. Some people looked at everything, slowly, and bought nothing; other people just stepped up and bought the whole lot. I saw it all: people trying to bust open the shrink-wrap with their incisors; people who bought their own little shrink-wrap openers, perhaps stolen from a previous merchandise booth—I mean, who carries those?; people who asked for autographs for daughters who skulked in the background; people who asked for autographs for daughters who didn't exist; people who brought those rattling gold paint markers that they had to shake before they exploded over the page, leaving Blake to make a design out of the glut of ink; people who just wanted your name without a dedication because, presumably, they wanted to sell the autograph to the highest bidder; people who bought two or three of a certain item and wanted different names on every one; people who insisted on a very wordy and specific dedication; people who just wanted to show Blake pictures of their collection of Thomas the Tank Engines. And the same names came up but spelled differently: Cathryn, Catherine, Katherine, Kathryn, Katrine—and then, when you thought you knew them all, some weird Irish version with Gs and Hs. Blake knew when to ask.

One night, Vern and I were at the booth and, about two songs into the set, a guy came to buy some CDs, prior to what I thought an oddly premature departure. I asked why he was leaving, while also wondering why he appeared to be wearing headphones, and he said: "I have to, before it gets too loud." Then he added: "I have tinnitus," which he pronounced *tinny-tus*.

And I said: "Tinnitus?," pronounced *tin-eye-tus*, which is how I thought you said it.

He looked a little put out and, as he turned towards the exit, clasping his Wonderkids CDs, he explained in frustration: "NO! ALL THE TIME!"

"Has anyone got a little Irish in them?
Are there any girls who'd like a
little more Irish in them?"

BROTHERS. BLOOD IS THICKER THAN WATER. (GREG USED TO USE THE phrase to mean someone was *really* stupid: "He's thicker than water, that one.")

With Blake and Jack, there wasn't any Kinks action: Ray and Dave Davies scrapping onstage, low-flying cymbals, etc. Nor, at the other extreme, was there any Everly Brothers "nothing sounds sweeter than brothers in harmony." (Mind you, all fraternal harmony got the Everlys was a Gibson smashed live onstage, a public row, and ten years of silence.) Blake and Jack *were* the Wonderkids, everyone knew that. They were quick to argue, quick to make up. The absolute worst you ever heard from Jack was "Fuck you!" That was it. Done. They didn't fall into the trap of flaunting the brother thing. That was the trouble with the other brother bands—they bought into the whole *Brothers in Arms* thing. Dire Straits even called an album that, though Mark Knopfler's own brother had had actually ditched the band a few years earlier.

Blake never suggested I call him "Dad"; I called Becca "Mum" but I never called my dad "Dad." He referred to himself that way, but was always Blake to me. I once tried out "Uncle" on Jack: he didn't like it at all. Blake was a man of whims, and

Jack assumed me to be one of those: he knew that the genius lay somewhere in the whims, he just had no idea precisely where. Though he didn't disapprove of the adoption, the position of "uncle" implicated him too greatly. He liked to think of Blake as "childish"—which he knew was at once the best and worst thing about his brother: the fount of all his creativity and the reason things occasionally went haywire—though he never used the actual word. But the fact was: Jack was the more childish of the two, despite his being the businessman in the band. He was the one who needed looking after.

When Jack's guitar broke that spring, he was heartbroken. It was an old electric from the Watch With Mother days that he'd had shipped from the UK, not at all valuable but his favorite. During a show, a speaker crashed onto his guitar rack, snapping its neck. "That'll never be played again" was Mitchell's frank verdict as he leafed through the contract for the venue's insurance policy. It was "one of those things," and the policy excluded any of those things. "Act of God," concluded Mitchell. "You'll need a new neck." Jack wouldn't stand for it. Wouldn't be the same instrument. It seemed the ideal opportunity to pore over those guitar catalogs or visit one of the guitar emporia whose business cards he amassed as we traveled. Instead, Jack went into weird mourning. He literally wore black for a week.

"I dunno." Jack shook his head as if in a daze.

"It's just like a goldfish dying," said Blake to cheer him up. "You have to replace it without telling the kids."

In the bus at about ten the following morning, Jack poured himself a glass of whisky, on a Benadryl chaser, and went to sleep, whisky glass perched on his right shoulder. I took a photo. He was dreaming of his old guitar, his fingers dancing across the fret board. Blake's sitting next to him, making sure the whisky doesn't fall.

It was a strange trail the Wonderkids were blazing and their success led to copycat signings. America was opening its arms to life beyond *Simeon's House* and *Sesame Street*. There were contenders, but no one—*no one*—like the Wonderkids. The band wasn't inimitable, but their ascent had been quick, and no one had yet worked out how to do a good impression. Part of the initial success was that they were characters, like the Beatles were characters, like that loony from Jethro Tull was a character, like Cheap Trick—with the two heartthrobs and the two nerds—were characters. The Wonderkids recalled the madcap glory days of rock 'n' roll, the unabashed celebration of id that predated the anger of punk and the seriousness of indie and shoegazing; perfect for kids, but easy for the adults to love too. And of course, no one was doing anything to dispel the myth that they'd been *huge* at home—too big, really, for Britain to handle.

We were now on a perpetual tour: it didn't matter precisely where we were, but it was nice to know. Sometimes it was raining on the short walk backstage from the bus and sometimes it wasn't. Itineraries, if they weren't lost, were traded in, the same way you'd return a library book and check out a new one. The novelty had worn off.

In Seattle, Jack—who listened to everything Sub Pop had to offer—insisted we go and see Nirvana, which was sweaty but nothing like that video for "Smells Like Teen Spirit," which would unleash itself upon America—from sea to shining Walmart—later that year. Blake left after two songs, but I stayed out as Jack mingled with flannel-shirted Seattleites, some of whom came to our show the next afternoon, keen to genuflect before Curtis. That morning Blake had taken me to see a fish ladder, but we were both depressed by the reality of the gray, skanky-looking salmon, scales peeling from their ravaged bodies. I'd been expecting more of an Edward Lear drawing: an elegant fish in a top hat climbing up some steps with his flipper. And that's what I remember of Seattle. I can't recall the show at all.

Somewhere in Ohio—I think Dayton—Blake secretly took me out to see Jonathan Richman playing solo to about eighty people. It was around the time Richman was trying to make albums without the use of electricity. Blake was thrilled by every song, whether it was about eating with gusto, the Fender Stratocaster, the city of Paris, or Richman's gossipy neighbors. Blake stood on a chair and yelled repeatedly for an extra encore. At the end, Jonathan was signing copies of his CD at a merch table: I surveyed this badly lit, haphazardly presented set-up with a professional eye. Blake was hovering, hopping from foot to foot like he was cold.

"Go up and say hi," I said.

"It doesn't matter," he said. Then, as we left: "we have to be better."

I remember one of our gigs at some kind of Dr. Seuss, or Children's Art, museum in Massachusetts, though. They played in the main gallery space, surrounded by epic canvases of art from the books. I was out in the lobby (the worst place to do merch) at a remove from the action, and I started to feel distinctly queasy. We were set up opposite an enormous, vertiginous Seuss print in which some cat-human hybrid was anxiously walking through an infinite gothic cellar: that wasn't helping either. Vern told me to go lie down backstage. A few minutes later, I looked into the main room, where they were cleaning up some kid's vomit right by the front door, and the smell sent me scurrying backstage as fast as I could, my hand actually covering my mouth. Becca saw me as I passed, and literally the next thing I remember I'm leaning over the toilet, throwing up, and she's stroking my hair. The band, meanwhile, seemed to have stopped.

"What's . . .?" I asked between bouts of coughing and hurling, eyes watering, the stench of sick in my nostrils.

"Shhh!" She said. "Blake's doing one solo. Don't worry. I'm here."

She handed me tissues from her bag, left me lying on the backstage sofa with a cold wet flannel on my forehead, and hopped back up to finish the set. Food poisoning was the consensus, but I can never see one of those Seuss vortexes without feeling a little rough.

The worst is when you have a show in your hometown (which is how we thought of LA), but the schedule doesn't allow you to go to, let alone sleep at, home because you're pulling an overnighter after the show: they actually sent a runner to get us clean clothes. And the tour rolled on: north by northeast, south by southwest. Even Canada! You remember Canada: they have Marks & Spencer and sometimes talk French.

Arguments ensued about whether the band should travel with their own support. Blake thought it would unnaturally extend a show that was the perfect length, thirty-five minutes: "it looks like rock music, but it isn't, and we can't have it be like an imitation of a rock show—it wouldn't work."

Whenever Andy the Damager materialized, the atmosphere in the bus changed noticeably. People huddled together as if there was a draft. "Here comes The Compromise," Jack would whisper when Andy turned up with this or that instruction from the record company. The good news always came first. "Rock Around the Bed" was climbing another, more important, chart. "Lucky Duck" was going to be used in the bumper for some new TV show. Fender was giving Jack a bunch of equipment. A film director wanted to talk to Blake about a song for a movie. And, best of all, some lunatic had the idea of turning the band and their shenanigans into a cartoon TV series. The mere fact that people were even entertaining such out-to-lunch notions was thrilling.

And then came the bad news, whatever it was; there was always some. Andy considered one particular piece of news so dire that he didn't even bother to soften the blow with good.

In the front parlor, we registered only stern, worried faces heading past to the back of the bus. After a few minutes' ominous silence, there was an explosion of hysterical laughter, and everyone emerged smiling. Andy disappeared after a couple of high fives.

"Well, that was a classic," said Jack, plonking himself down at the front table. "Andy at his very finest." Curtis looked up from his *Times*, and Becca interrupted her seated yoga.

"He delivered the bad news at such great length and so thoughtfully," said Blake. "And then he couldn't understand why we cracked up. A paternity suit. Against me!"

"A paternity suit against Jimmy," confirmed Jack, chuckling.

"There's a bit of a backstory," said Blake. "It's that story I was going to tell you before. Are you sitting comfortably? Then we'll begin. When I was teaching, one of the mothers got kind of obsessed with me. Honestly, I did nothing wrong. But it was weird: every friendly smile, every teacherly observation about her child, she misread them all and the first thing I know, she's announced to her husband, who's presumably as shocked as me, that she's leaving him, and she and I are running off together. And he confronts me. I mean, it wasn't funny at the time. I was, to put it mildly, surprised, and the upshot was I had to get an actual restraining order, against her not him. He was fine. Anyway, the absolute low point, just after that, was when she waited for me outside the school gate, chucked a large birthday cake at me and screamed: 'Happy Birthday, Motherfucker!'"

"And it wasn't even his birthday!" said Jack, with throaty glee.

"Anyway, we thought that was long past, but now she's got wind of all *this*, and she's filed a paternity suit against me."

"But she's mad," I said.

"Did you sleep with her?" asked Becca.

"We didn't even have a cup of milky tea!"

"Well," said Becca, "going to court will be a drag, but at least you know it isn't yours."

"Well, that's the funny thing," said Blake. Jack started to laugh again. "I know it isn't mine, because the one thing for certain about me is that I can't have children."

This unexpected admission sat there. I felt, as I sometimes felt with Blake, that everything had tumbled out in the wrong order. I didn't feel put out, exactly, but it wasn't hard to see where I fit in. I was a readymade, prepared before the show even began, like on a kids' TV show: *here's one I made earlier*. Like any adopted kid, I guess. And then I'd been born, like whichever Greek God it was, fully grown, to the greatest father of all time. Becca instinctively reached for my hand.

"That's a pregnant pause," said Blake drily, and told the story of a girlfriend, her name coincidentally Rebecca, gym teacher at the same primary school. She got pregnant and, after blood tests and so on, it turned out that the child wasn't his. And a biopsy revealed that he'd never have any of his own. That was when he stopped being a teacher and when the band started playing for real.

"Kids' bands and paternity suits don't go together," said Blake. "Andy was a very relieved man. I never knew how useful my medical condition would be one day."

"We've arrived!" said Jack. "A paternity suit!" He toasted it with a sip of bourbon and popped another Benadryl.

Another piece of bad news—less easily brushed off—was that the label wanted to foist a lackey on us, a man who, in olden tymes, would have stayed out of the way, scored you drugs, and made sure you made the in-store on time, shaking the right hands during the walkthrough. But we knew they simply wanted a spy in our midst, someone to keep an eye on their investment. We didn't like it, and we didn't need it. The Wonderkids were a family, and our jokes were at the expense of outsiders. We didn't want spies. We had Mitchell. He made himself hard to find; you could do that in those days. I watched him fade from the record company radar, ignoring pages, unplugging fax machines, leaving messages only at lunchtime when he knew everyone was at Hamburger Hamlet. Mitchell's was such quiet theater, requiring no audience, though I analyzed his every move from the wings.

The other news, apart from my upcoming sixteenth-birthday celebration at Disneyland, was a potential—and then suddenly very real—appearance at a televised music awards ceremony in Los Angeles. "Rock Around the Bed" was nominated, but (Andy seemed to know) wouldn't win—the main thing was to give the greatest ever performance of the song.

Television was again to be our friend: it was where we did our greatest damage. There wasn't much for me to do at such an event, so I became Blake's personal assistant, making sure he did all the relevant interviews, including our first color cover of a weekly: a little landmark, something to send Barry—evidence.

"I've got something special planned for the TV," Blake told me. Peanut butter was now the standard climax. It was time to ratchet it up a notch or two. "I popped out to the store." Apparently, he couldn't achieve the desired effect (whatever it was) with just a guitar, like Richman could, but perhaps a few props would point him in the right direction.

"Shouldn't you tell Mitchell?" I asked, all Jiminy Cricket good conscience. If you told Mitchell, nothing went wrong. Mitchell didn't like surprises.

"Yeah, good idea. I'll tell Mitchell. Could you get me a knife, maybe some scissors?"

I went to Mitchell's office.

"What are the scissors for?" he asked offhandedly.

"Nothing," I said, and went about my business.

By the time of the performance, perfectly rehearsed for camera, Blake had that gleam in his eye. The production team had shipped some kids to the front of the stage, good-looking little child actors ready to play the part of regular punters. There didn't seem to be any accompanying parents; perhaps they'd also hired dwarf chaperones.

"Peanut butter? Tick. Balloons? Tick. Mad hat? Tick." Mitchell was meticulously checking the contents of the dressing-up box. Often as he did this, he hummed "Santa Claus Is Coming to Town," his theme song: "making a list, checking it twice." It was either that, or when things were on song: "everything's coming up roses."

"And, band!" said Blake on the spur of the moment. "Give me the extra third verse for some spice."

"Blake," said Mitchell. "That's not how they rehearsed it: camera angles . . . timings . . ."

"Extra third verse. Let's do it."

No time to argue. They were on.

Mitchell shook his head, but smiled.

The jam (rather than the peanut butter) emerged unusually soon, Blake smearing his face in sticky stripes. Also in the dressing-up box, it transpired, was a pillow, which Blake brandished in the first chorus, recreating the video. Feathers immediately started to fly—he'd sliced it—and when he brought the pillow down on the body of Becca's bass, they billowed everywhere. I was transfixed as I watched the monitor. It looked absolutely amazing, like some crazy visual effect the producers had been planning for ages.

And still the band played. A little plumage wasn't going to put them off. From the dressing-up box came another pillow, which Blake threw into the audience, and another that he immediately started to disembowel. And despite the feathers stuck to his face on the jam, he kept singing, and by the time they got to the third verse—the "controversial" one—there were feathers everywhere, floating up towards the chandelier in the pavilion, tickling Jack's nose, bouncing off Curtis's snare. And the kids in the front were going apeshit.

I looked down at the monitor. Though the band was hurtling headlong into the last chorus, I found myself watching an ad for hairspray. Fair enough, I thought, they ran out of time as Mitchell had predicted: roll credits.

Blake was ecstatic—a pillow fight and jam and the audience had gone nuts—but there was no hero's welcome offstage. In fact, a melee developed in which I could clearly see Mitchell restraining, then blocking, an angry TV employee wielding a violent clipboard from collaring Blake. Mitchell hurriedly ushered the band into the dressing room. It looked like there'd been a party at the slaughterhouse.

"What's up?" asked Jack, but Mitchell had already left. Jack tried the door. We were locked in.

"What a performance!" said Blake, oblivious. WBA had left a celebratory bottle of pop that he shook up, Formula One style. He snorted fizz back out of his nose, then immediately rolled a joint.

"Blake!" said Becca. "Not backstage!"

"Give us a break, Mum!"

"I hope they didn't notice my clam," said Jack, still trying to figure out why the door was locked. "I had a real senior moment there when those effin' feathers started flying. Couldn't even remember what song we were playing!"

"Forget it, man," said Blake. "They love mistakes. Or they don't notice them at all."

Spirits were high until Andy and Mitchell, looking as grave as I had ever seen him, returned. Beads of sweat circled the manager's brow; my head begin to itch.

"Party poopers!" said Blake, taking a toke. "Did we ruffle some feathers?" It wasn't the moment.

In the silence, Mitchell said simply: "Altamont."

No one spoke. We'd just seen the movie on the bus.

"It's not *Altamont*," said Andy angrily. "It's not that bad. No one's died."

"What the fuck's happened?" asked Jack. "Why'd you lock us in?"

"Two kids collided, slipped on the jam. One got his front teeth smashed out and the other has a big gash in his head."

"And tooth marks," said Mitchell.

"Is that why they cut to the ads?" I asked.

"They cut to ads?" asked Blake in surprise. "*What*?" He extinguished his joint in a paper cup, realized what he'd done and grimaced. "When?"

"Last forty-five seconds," said Mitchell. "They had to. An arc of blood actually sprayed across the camera lens."

"You're shitting me," said Jack, laughing despite himself.

"Look, gentlemen and lady," said Mitchell. "In the future, you have to tell me what you're going to do, or I walk. We're all in this together: one for all and all for one. But it's me and Andy who have to go deal with this now."

All eyes turned to Blake. How could anyone else know what was going to happen? Blake never told anyone.

"I'll go and apologize," he said.

"You'll stay where you are," said Andy firmly. "And this dressing room *stinks*."

Mitchell continued. "The pillows, the feathers were *one* thing it would have been nice to know about. But they didn't mind the feathers, despite the fact that Luther Vandross's band aren't going to get their line check because Sweeper's Union 3056 has to get to work on the stage. It would have been nice to tell them about the jam, but they didn't mind the jam. And it would have been nice for me to know that you were going to sing the third verse more than twenty seconds before you went onstage; but they didn't even mind that. What they mind is a *lawsuit*. They are scared stiff of a *lawsuit*. And, in their eyes, you have just incited a crowd of under-eights to violence, put them in harm's way. And if that lawsuit comes to them, then that lawsuit will come to you."

"How are the kids?" asked Blake.

"We will find out," said Andy. "Sit tight. Do not allow anyone in or out of this dressing room. Speak to no one. Do nothing. Give me the weed. And open a window."

"What if I want to go to the bathroom?" asked Jack.

"Piss in the sink."

The five of us sat in our holding tank, picking feathers from each other like monkeys and fleas. Blake couldn't help giggling, which started Jack off, and soon we were all laughing helplessly, trying not to laugh helplessly, which made us laugh helplessly, even though we didn't want to seem like a dressing room of callous performers yukking it up through a crisis, which made us laugh even more. The moment the door opened, everybody stopped. But Mitchell's mood had lightened.

"Great TV, guys," he said, miming looking behind him in case Andy might be listening. "That will never be forgotten. But you must tell *me* what's going on. I'll make it okay, but I *must know*."

"Sorry," said Blake. "I was worried you'd tell me not to."

"I would have told you not to, sir, but then once I realized you were going do it, I would have made it so it went right. That is my job. Anyway, lawsuit averted: apparently the parents signed some waiver. However, you will be leaving out of that window, and the bus will pull up in fifteen minutes."

"Out of a window?" asked Curtis.

"Like Bing and Danny in *White Christmas*!" said Blake cheerfully.

Andy closed the door behind him, puffing his cheeks in relief: "We're alright! But there's a lot of press by the stage door, and they're going to run with it: this is going to have one of two results. It's either going to catapult us into the stratosphere or it's going to set us back. That's in the hands of God. We can do nothing about it. Onwards and upwards."

"Any publicity is good publicity?" asked Jack, somewhat more tentatively than usual.

"That's a point of view, and it may be true where you come from," said the Damager, "but these are the United States of America. And you ain't from round these parts."

By the time the headlines appeared in the tour bus, we'd already seen the whole thing on CNN, watched in amazement at the blurry circled bubble where one of the kids' heads smashed down, then cracked back. You could actually see, with CNN's helpful televi-sual enhancement, the teeth fly through the air, the trajectory of the blood; one of the kids went down like a prizefighter, the other merely looked dazed and continued his feather dance. It'd be a YouTube sensation nowadays, or a GIF, viral in seconds, but in those days, you just saw that stuff once, for a day or two, and that was that. All you could do was talk about it; and everyone did.

The newspapers had run with it, everything from "GIMME SOME TOOTH!" and "GOING DENTAL!" to "WONDER-SKID!" Blake, with the label's approval, declined to give interviews, opt-ing instead to play an impromptu busking set next day at the hos-pital sickbed. A television crew was waiting, by arrangement, and Blake finally agreed to talk: dignified, contrite, slightly cheeky, very charming.

"The record is zooming up the charts and your performances are sold out coast to coast. What's next for the Wonderkids?"

"Well," said Blake. "We're going to do some free gigs at chil-dren's homes. I have an adopted child myself. *And* we're plan-ning to turn our life into a cartoon. We're going to market a brand of Wonderkids peanut butter. And then we thought we'd open an amusement park."

As with many things in Blake's life, this too started as a joke.

We sat in the back of the bus, Blake's arm around me as we watched a black-and-white comedy on the VHS.

"That could have gone really, really wrong, couldn't it?" I asked.

Blake laughed indignantly. "NO!"

"Yes, it could."

"No, it couldn't."

"But there's a lesson there isn't there?" I said, trying the role on for size.

"Alright, *Mitchell*," he said with an amused sneer. "What's the lesson? Why does there have to be a lesson? The lesson is: everything's fine, and it worked out very well for us." Inasmuch as a shrug can be triumphant, his was.

"But it could have . . ."

"Could; if; would; might . . ." He waved all the conditionals away and paused the video for emphasis, leaving some old character actor frozen mid-antic gesture, his eyes bulging behind a pince-nez as though he were just about to sneeze. "WAS! DID! We got on TV!" There was no arguing with him; it was slightly infuriating, but ever so lovable. And, besides, he was right.

"You're just making this up as you go along, aren't you?" I asked.

"Nonsense resists plot," he said and jabbed at the remote control, freeing the screwball actor from suspended animation. The movie was about a huge inheritance, which finally fell to the poor orphan, who also got the girl.

"Will I ever find out who my dad is?" I asked casually, after the little fanfare that accompanied "The End." Blake reached over for a mess of papers from which, to my surprise, he pulled out my birth certificate with the bloke's name on it: Simon Traherne. Sweet was my mother's maiden name. I turned it over—nothing— and handed it back. "Hmm. Have you cooked this all up, and I'm going to find out that my father is someone really interesting?"

"That only happens in old-fashioned novels and silly comedies. I'm your dad, right?"

"Yes, Blake."

He put his arms around me.

"And Daddy needs a nap."

Back in the front, Mitchell called me over to his "office." "Hey, scissor boy," he whispered confidentially. "Help me out. Be on my side, too."

Almost nothing but good came from what might otherwise have been an epic banana skin. The upcoming shows were bumped up to larger venues, and the furor sent "Rock Around the Bed" over the edge. It was time to think about another single ("The Story of Dan, Beth, Chris and Blank") and accompanying video. The record company wanted to get the Wonderkids into the studio as soon as possible, but that meant going back to LA for more than a night, the last thing our agent had on the band's agenda. Andy was thrilled.

Almost nothing bad happened, but there was something. One of the many ensuing articles contained the following revelation: "Becca Fonseca, the band's bass player and daughter of long-time children's favorite, Simeon, has been on tour with the Wonderkids since the band first arrived in America. But she hasn't seen her son once. Sam, six years old, lives with his father in San Francisco, while Becca entertains other people's children around the country."

It was our publicist, the friendliest woman in the world, Jennifer Armstrong of Strongarm Publicity, who reluctantly, but immediately, brought this to the band's attention. A news clipping service had turned it up in a tabloid that had never previously bothered to cover the band before. This aspect pleased Jennifer greatly.

At the band meeting, as the WonderBus hurtled through Nebraska, Andy chewed the inside of his mouth and spoke of "damage control." Becca sat quietly in the corner; I felt like reaching out for *her* hand, but I didn't. We called Becca Mum, but it hadn't occurred to us that she had a child of her own. Perhaps when she held my hand, she was thinking of him.

"Time to see your son, Becca," said Andy.

"Let's get him on the bus," said Blake merrily. "Suffer the little children! Your father's house has many coffins!"

"Blake!" said Andy, as though Blake wasn't serious. But I knew he was, and he was right. It was a *family* show.

Friendly Jenny had good news too: our first truly magisterial press hit. An article in *Time*. It wasn't quite "I've seen the future of rock 'n' roll," but nonetheless, even I'd heard of *Time*, and it was a glossy step up. The photo shoot in Northern California was exciting, but when the issue finally turned up, everyone had tired of the anticipation. We all read it, and perhaps some secretly sent a copy home or instructed their parents to buy it, but no one got too excited. Jack was grumpiest: "I don't play a Les Paul. They always get the important stuff wrong. They wouldn't make that mistake in *Rolling Stone*. And that's where they should be writing about us."

"*Time* is way more important than *Rolling Stone*," said Mitchell.

"Not to me it isn't. It isn't more important than the *NME* either."

That's the trouble with benchmarks: there's always a higher mark to be made, and everyone has different priorities. But Blake loved the interviews—it was always a chance to wheel out some good gags.

Touring is tiring, however you slice it. As my sixteenth birthday approached, I found myself itching spectacularly, deep red blotches that floated beneath the palms of my hands. Mitchell asked if I'd been in a hotel hot tub—notorious, noxious purveyor of skin disease. I hadn't. The only relief was Jack's Benadryl, and I got used to getting on the bus in the morning, if we hadn't slept there, making myself comfy on one of the parlor benches, popping a Benadryl, and floating slowly away. Somewhere in Washington state, a doctor prescribed me a triangular blue pill, which stopped the itching but didn't send me to sleep as effectively. So Benadryl and the triangular blue pill: the happy cocktail. Others were doing worse. Everyone found his own way to relax. Pot stayed with the cigarettes in the back.

Becca had blisters; Curtis had drummer's wrist. Blake's problems were vocal-related, and, perhaps more accurately, vocal-anxiety related. Days became an obsessive quest for Throat Coat tea, Slippery Elm, and those particular Halls lozenges that squirt honey in your mouth. Some mornings he'd wake up sounding as though he wouldn't even survive the day, but by showtime he was miraculously fine: "The body knows." He even started to complain of a click when he swallowed, as though his throat was out of joint.

"That'll be cancer, mate," was Jack's standard, unsympathetic diagnosis.

The blotches on my hands came and went, depending how run down I was. Days off were spent in hotels, watching TV. You try to get up and about, maybe go out for a walk, see a sight, but all you want is to sink down into a chair and ring room service for some French onion soup. You try to pretend you're in the same place every day—only that makes it tolerable. Becca and I watched cooking shows; she was trying to keep a low profile, and I was about the quietest company you could keep.

Jack, on the other hand, had joint problems—a bad knee, a dickey shoulder—but he'd never have dreamed of toning down his act, now that he finally had one. He loved the twirling, the kicking right leg, the silly Chuck Berry duckwalk, the leap and land. He occasionally even smiled, but more in the manner of a Chinese gymnast who has just dismounted from the uneven bars and landed with a maneuver of the highest level of difficulty. It was all in a day's work. A smile just didn't come naturally to Jack: he only delivered what the world required.

My problems were far more insidious; Jack's were relatively easily solved, and I remember his moment of inspiration. We went to visit a big act backstage—we were on the same benefit. The star received us graciously and threw open his dressing room, welcoming us, his Boston accent all misplaced Rs and unnaturally elongated vowels. But what struck me, rather than his aura, his surprisingly diminutive size, and the fact that I hadn't realized he was more or less albino, was the table full of neoprene: two knee supporters, a thigh strap, stretchy greaves for the lower legs, one for the ankle, a fuzzy corset, a back-plate, various bandages. He was a medieval knight going into battle in the name of rock, and he was only playing six songs. The only thing missing was neoprene gauntlets and a horse he'd be winched upon. Soon, Jack, too, was laying out the stretchy armor. Mitchell suggested an all-in-one neoprene body suit: one-stop shopping.

What the audience sees is show business, the glow of health and rebellion. The reality is that rock hurts: your knees, your ankles, your voice, your well-being. You rarely hear people complain, because it isn't very rock 'n' roll. Rock has been rebranded—successfully—as an acceptable job for old men, and though there's no reason old men should give up, they have to rethink the act: it's harder the older you get. Dylan rarely, if ever, plays guitar and harmonica together anymore—which I'm guessing isn't only an aesthetic decision. I have a feeling that the combination of guitar strap, harmonica holder, and the neck contortion necessary to play the two simultaneously might have taken its toll; that, if he persisted, he might need an *actual* cervical collar. Barry Gibb went through the biggest Bee Gees tour ever barely able to move. If you look at videos, he's standing stiff as a poker, corset (I assume) squeezing him half to death, fixed grin on his face in an attempt to summon the immortal falsetto one last time. And now he doesn't have any brothers left to harmonize with. Poor Barry. And you'd be surprised, when musicians meet musicians, how quickly it all comes back to Pepto Bismol, Neti Pots, health insurance, and hernia operations. One particular legend talked to Blake for two hours solid about stomach ailments. They didn't touch on the NYC underground art scene in the sixties, the meaning of his greatest lyrics, electro-shock therapy, or amplifiers: they talked runny tummies.

With my blotches came itchy head, which was really bad. Life became an ecstasy of irritation unless I washed my hair every morning, and perhaps again after the show. Blake pictured a Dr. Seuss microscope world, where a thousand fleas had set up a five-ring circus around the edge of my scalp. Becca suggested a couple of shampoos you could buy over the counter, both dingily medicinal. There wasn't a shower on the bus, and there were times it was so bad that Becca would hold me over the sink and shampoo me there and then, then dry me with a towel just like she really was my mother. The menthol tingled like tiger balm. Seb Derm, the doctor called it, presenting itself in the usual ways. It was so bad, I sometimes felt like going the full Sinead.

Plus, I hadn't even turned sixteen: I was going through all the normal stuff—raging hormones, uncooperative skin—too. How do the Biebers do it these days? They're more cosseted, of course, but then I never had the emotional pay-off of getting on-stage. Not that I wanted it.

Physical health was one thing; emotional health another. Jack had already found his addiction, and he needed his fix increasingly often.

He liked the mothers; the mothers liked him. They perhaps liked Blake more, but didn't Ringo get the most fan mail of all the Beatles? (Of course, that might have been something the Fan Club dreamed up, so that it wasn't all John and Paul, but that's another matter entirely.) Blake was all about the kids; he'd already seen the darker side of mothers. Jack had never had an experience like that, but he longed for one. He'd never really met girls who did what he wanted, and that was what he wanted.

After the shows, Jack had time to do a little window-shopping while the kids occupied themselves with the main attraction. He was a willing consolation prize. He'd long bored of the hotel porn (heavily censored in those days) about which he was quite vocal: "I'm not paying good money to watch a man's sweaty, hairy, heaving buttocks." Nowadays the hotel porn channels are uncensored—you have to go to Japan if you're nostalgic for sterilized porn—and they don't bring in the money they used to because everyone's hopping on the complimentary Wi-Fi. Back then it was Jack's only choice. So he had to turn his attention elsewhere—unfortunately, there was much to distract him.

We all know about MILFs now. Back then, MILFs hadn't earned their acronym, and cougars were something you saw on *The Wonderful World of Disney*. MILFs were just older women or, as Ray Davies calls them in his autobiography, "a nice bit of old"; in our world, "the mums." And they weren't that old. And they looked good. Jack was always scribbling his hotel number down on a CD cover, just in case anyone fancied a drink. Becca turned a blind eye, but nothing got by Blake: "Two cups of coffee tomorrow, ey, Jackie?" His brother would smile sheepishly and we wouldn't see him after the show.

I was first in line on the way back into the dressing room one night, and I opened the door to find a woman, topless, artfully posed on the sofa. I froze. The parade behind ploughed into me like the elephants in *The Jungle Book*.

"No parking on the dance floor," Mitchell called from behind.

I pulled Becca forward. Mum would handle it. She weighed the situation, turned to the elephants and said: "Dressing room off limits momentarily. Everyone into Mitchell's office."

Blake asked what was up.

"Naked female, actually." She closed the door.

"What a conundrum," mused Mitchell, all sarcasm. "Why on earth would there be a naked female in our dressing room?"

Jack looked the other way: "I'll be out on the, er, bus," he said and made his getaway. And there he'd sit, fiddling with his video camera.

It was around this time that backstage started to get weird. It became a bit of a freak scene, particularly when Becca was doing tai chi in one corner with the incense on smelly and some freaky yoga drone playing. It seemed like everyone was on drugs, even when there weren't any. There'd be a little gaggle of mothers, mostly flirting with Jack or, if their fantasies ran that way, Curtis. Sometimes they had the nerve to approach Blake, but the mothers weren't his favorite part of his job, and once he'd dealt with their kids, he'd slip back onto the bus. For a little while, he took to wearing a Baby-Björn with a doll in it, which he'd bounce up and down and occasionally shush, thinking it would put the mothers off, but it just gave them an opening line, an excuse to compare notes. Though useless as a deterrent, it wasn't a bad briefcase, and he kept sporting it; the mothers were surprised to find, wedged beside the doll, a fifth of booze, a packet of cigarettes, and a paperback. Sometimes it seemed like he'd stepped out of one of his own songs.

No children backstage was a rule Mitchell strictly enforced, and eventually it struck me: maybe the husbands of all those mothers, like groupies' parents in the sixties, were waiting in the parking lot, looking at their watches tetchily while a kid snoozed in the car seat. Or maybe the mothers hadn't even brought their kids; they'd just come to see the show, and now here they were, hanging out with the boys in the band, like they used to: a Wonderkids show was an excuse to either relive reckless youth or sample it for the first time. Then I noticed that some of the women with backstage passes were closer to my age: they had no kids; they weren't babysitters. They just liked the band. It really was Everyone Music, after all. From time to time, there was too much drinking; occasionally there were unnecessary tears upon departure, or a furtive glance between Jack and a female autographee.

But, despite the wear and tear, sprits remained high. Jokes helped.

Supposedly it's the one good pedophile joke: a kid's just been bought a welder's helmet for his birthday and he's walking down the road, and a guy drives up, opens his car door, and asks the kid if he needs a lift. And when the kid's in, the guy asks him if he's ever seen a man naked and the kid says "no"; and he asks the kid if he's ever been to the men's bathroom and the kid says "no"; then he asks if the kid's ever touched a man's penis, and the kid replies: "Look, mister, I want to make something quite clear. I'm not a real welder."

Blake hated that joke. It was Jack's. Jack once told this one in the parlor—you might have heard it before: a guy's leading a little girl through a field towards some woods, and she looks up at him and says "I'm scared." And he looks down at her, takes her by the hand, and says "You're scared? I've got to come back alone." Blake didn't speak to him for twenty-four hours after that.

Blake liked jokes that made no sense. "Mad!" was his greatest compliment. His repertoire was massive, and many of the jokes ended with the punch line "Chicken DAT!" This was from Blake's time teaching preschoolers, long before the band took off. This three-year-old knock-knocked him: "House," "House Who?" "House DAT!" And Blake wondered if the kid had made it up himself; it was a good joke for a two-year-old. So he asked him to tell another, and the kid, who hadn't understood which bit of the joke was funny, but realized where the laugh was, came up with: "Knock Knock," "Who's there?" "Chicken," "Chicken Who?" "Chicken DAT!"

And "Chicken DAT!" it was for the rest of time. Blake would send me a picture, say, of a homemade loaf of bread with the accompanying text: "Chicken DAT!" It came to mean PUNCHLINE!, SUCCESS!, or even simply FINISHED! Every kid on earth laughs, whatever the setup, if the punchline, delivered with a modicum of gusto, is "Chicken DAT!"

And "DAT!" sent Blake off on a course that lasted the entire career of the Wonderkids. He liked to hear children's versions of jokes; he'd retell their version rather than the technically correct one. Sometimes, that was his entire stage banter: jokes gone wrong.

Once, at a signing at a record store in Hershey, Pennsylvania—I always remember that place; it's where the crappy chocolate comes from—just after we'd played some local amusement park, he heard a kid, egged on by his mother, tell a pirate joke. (Why are pirates called pirates? Because they arrrrrr. You know the genre.) She was standing over him, like he's auditioning for *Pop Idol*, and the kid goes "Okay, mom. So a pirate goes into a bar, and he has a ship's wheel around his tummy"—his mom's standing over him, encouraging her kid with a fixed grin, poking him in the arm when his pacing lags—"and the barman says to him 'Why do you have a ship's wheel round your middle?' And the pirate says 'Arrrrr! It's steering me balls!'" And the kid bursts out into hysterical laughter, but the horrified mother shouts: "Noooo! *It's driving me nuts*!" Blake told that joke a million times, always with the wrong punch line. He never even considered whether "balls" was an appropriate word to say in front of children.

There was another kid called Liam, one of the playgroupies, a little titch who came to loads of gigs, always with an uncle, always in California, and he told us the following joke. Loudly: "My dad went into a shop and asked for some fish 'n' chips," followed by a whispered "and then he asked for them quietly." Liam thought that was the best joke in the world. He could barely get to the end without laughing. His contortions in trying to tell the joke without cracking up made the joke, in itself incomprehensible, hilarious. Even that short edit took about three minutes. Blake loved the whole shtick. It turned out that the actual joke was: "A guy goes up to a counter and says: 'Can I have some fish 'n' chips please?' and the woman says, 'Sir, this is a library,' and he says 'Oh, I'm so terribly sorry,' and then he *whispers:* 'Can I have some fish 'n' chips please?'" A great joke, but Liam thought his version was equally funny, if not funnier, because what was really funny about it was that the person who told it SAID SOMETHING LOUD and then said the same thing quietly. And that's basically what Blake thought was funny about it, too, because what made children laugh made him laugh.

Jokes were our lives, and some of our best times were spent sitting around a diner table late at night, some way past our bedtime, others just getting going, maybe after a show. I remember one classic night, July 4, 1990, at a Denny's. In this most ridiculous of venues, we never felt more like a family. Mitchell, of course, had procured fireworks for later. The major offenders were always Blake, Jack, and Mitchell—in that order—then Curtis and me. No lightbulb went unchanged, no door unknocked, no road uncrossed, no drummer uninsulted. When they got onto musicians, you knew it was going to be a long night.

"I want to be a musician when I grow up, Mum."

"Well, son, you can't do both."

Jack would tell that joke. And I'd tell the one about God having a girlfriend. Then he'd tell the one about the kid who goes to a singing teacher and says: "I want to sing real bad" and the teacher says: "You do." (His jokes were much shorter than mine.) And then I'd tell him the one about the superstar band up in Heaven; the punch line of which was "Yes, the *real* Jerry Garcia"—harsh but fair.

Drummers, in jokes, are stupid. Curtis wasn't the greatest joke teller in the world, but he was an encyclopedia of drummer jokes. His natural voice, a sweet but uneventful drawl, wasn't the best medium, but when it was as short and punchy as "How do you get a drummer off your porch? You pay him for the pizza," he could get a laugh (even though he never actually asked a question and waited for an answer, he just said them all at once as though it was one sentence). In Curtis's Joke City, drummers went into a fish 'n' chip shop to buy drums and tattooed L and R on their legs, but the wrong way round. They drooled out of both sides of their mouth (if the drum riser was level), and you could always tell it was a drummer knocking at the door, because he didn't know when to come in. The point was: he knew them.

My best musician joke is this. I know that's death to a joke, but given that reading is the least preferred joke delivery system, I've got nothing to lose. A record producer arrives in purgatory, and a saint greets him and says, "Okay, so you were a record producer, I have two tapes to play you . . ."—Tapes! That's how old this joke is!—". . . and you can choose one and that'll be your destiny." So he plays him the first tape, and the record producer hears lambs bleating and birds singing their melodious song and perhaps the sound of bacon crackling in the frying pan and children playing on their bikes in the front garden, that kind of thing, and he's looking a bit bored and the saint says, "Well, here's the other tape, maybe you'll like this more."

And the record producer hears the sound of people humping each other, bodies grinding together, cocaine snorted, champagne corks popping and pinging about, someone's groaning "oh yeah, lay a line on her back while I fuck her from behind," etc. And when the tape is done, the record producer, over whose face has spread a silly grin, says: "Well, yeah, that sounds good. Sounds kinda like my life. *That's* my choice." And the saint reveals an elevator and presses the down button and before they get out, he says "Welcome to your choice. For all eternity." The doors open and all the record producer can see is flayed figures, once-human, screaming in agony, neck deep in shit and piss and blood, open sores oozing puss, while weird monsters torment them with lashes of whips.

And, in horror, the record producer screams: "What about the tape? What about the tape?"

And the saint says: "The tape? Oh, that was a *demo*."

Blake often set me up so *that* was the best joke of the night. (He'd told it to me in the first place.) And sometimes when I got to the punch line he didn't even shout "Chicken DAT!" at the top of his lungs. But it was such a good joke that it could handle even that intrusion. As they say about a good song: it can survive any mauling.

When these epic sessions took off, it was a ride that ended with everyone weaving their way down the pavement back to the hotel, me full of whatever awful sweetness I'd eaten for dinner. That was always the trouble: everyone else used to get quietly loaded as the evenings gathered momentum, but I never really liked alcohol, or anything that altered my head at all, so I just kept nibbling cookies. I don't even like coffee, or really *any* hot beverages (except hot chocolate).

I never worried about the inequity of a restaurant check, even though I didn't drink any of their booze. You can tell everything you need to know about a person when it's time to split the check. And on tour, there are a lot of checks that need splitting. Yes, some people are poorer than others, and they eat within their means, and shouldn't have to subsidize the overindulgence of their bandmate, but there are ways to handle this well, and ways to handle it badly. And the truth is, on a tour, you're all living large on your per diems, and there's really no need to scrutinize a check for your portion. (Latin's attempt to become the official language of rock 'n' roll never got much further than "per diem" and "Status Quo." That's about it. Procol Harum isn't real Latin.) And those who divvy up checks so they end up paying the smallest possible amount are always, without fail, the ones who short you on the tip. That was when Blake always threw down another $40. He knew the culprit. When he started making money, Blake laid down the law at the beginning of every meal: "We're either going Dutch or I'm paying for the whole thing, but I'm not haggling over who had what starter."

I did sometimes make up for it with dessert, though. I'd have two or three. Well, people have two starters instead of one main course. Why not one starter and two desserts? Or no starters or main courses and *three* desserts? I should say that I'm over that now. I knew a guitarist who used to drink, literally, seven quadruple cappuccinos a day. That in itself is disgusting, but he used to put four spoonfuls of sugar in each one, which I really admired. A girlfriend once said to me: "Oh, my family *really* likes sugar. No one likes sugar more than my family." And after about two days, when she broke up with me, she said: "And I take back that thing I said about sugar and my family. You're way worse."

Though I spent nearly all of my time with the band, every now and then, encouraged by Jack's sashays in that direction, and by Jack himself, I'd talk to someone nearer my own age—an older sister, perhaps, or a babysitter enjoying the show more than she thought she would.

One girl, Jennifer, came up to me by the booth: "Is he really your dad?" I wondered how she knew until Vern, my comrade-in-merch, winked. She asked me out after the matinee; she was tall, too, with long straight brown hair, maybe half-Mexican, sixteen. I told her I was eighteen. We went to a movie, *Total Recall*: "get ready for the ride of your life," promised the poster. I was horribly aware of her arm's proximity to mine but decided against radical action. Afterwards, we ate ice cream in what was meant to be a park, but seemed like a Lego facsimile, blown up to full size. We sat on a bench where, little by little, we edged closer until it was unavoidably time to kiss. My heart was beating fast, she tasted like chocolate sprinkles, and she gave me a lift back to the hotel where I slept alone.

The next afternoon—it was a two-day stand in Atlanta: you get really attached to your hotel room if you stay that long—she returned, this time flanked by a couple of guys. She seemed less than happy, and it dawned on me that I should linger at the merch table as long as possible. But they wouldn't go away, and I exhausted my ways to look busy.

"There's your girl," said Vern.

"She's brought the cavalry."

"Should I get Mitchell?"

I groaned. I couldn't avoid them any longer, but calling in Mitchell seemed boy-who-cried-wolfish; plus there was the possibility that she was in distress, that she needed a white knight. They drove me to some creek where they cracked beers. I started to drink, which made me feel awful.

Their forced good spirits made it all the more sinister. Jennifer only had a chance to say one thing, an instruction quickly whispered in my ear: "Nothing happened." I was in their clutches now, in their car, and they drove me back to the kitchen of a house that, thank God, didn't seem far from the hotel. Jennifer smiled helplessly and was led away: we'd been separated for interrogation. I denied everything, per her instruction, and finally, after much "tea bag" and "limey," they ran out of questions and insults, and just when things seemed bound to escalate, showed me the door.

"Can I say goodbye to Jennifer?"

"No," said the first. "You can just go."

"Can you call me a cab?"

"No."

"Can you tell me the way to my hotel?"

"No."

It was a long, dark walk home, a long, hard look at myself.

• • •

After that, I decided never to stray too far from the bus. It was like we were too weird for the outside world.

This was one of those secrets that make you feel like you have to tell someone or you'll explode, and Becca winkled it out of me. It wasn't hard. She'd just dried my hair, and we were sitting on our own at the front of the bus watching another cooking show. I even admitted that my bright idea had been to tell them that Becca was my girlfriend.

"Did they believe you?" She was loving every moment of it. I was, officially, "sweet."

"Yeah, I guess so."

"I can be your beard."

"You're old enough to be my mother!" I said.

"No, I'm not," she said tartly. "Nowhere near it, thank you very much." And then she said, with a smile, "but you really should eat more savory food."

After that, she started giving me bass lessons.

"If some of you girls want to get yourself KISSed, meet us in the Ladies Room."

MY SIXTEENTH BIRTHDAY IN AUGUST, MUCH ANTICIPATED, WAS sensational. Blake gave me a card that contained a fake itinerary, a schedule of events for the celebration, complete with laminate. The card itself said only "Happy Birthday, mother-fucker," the phrase that accompanied any birthday gift in sacred memory of that flying cake.

Blake and Andy, using up which favors I can hardly imagine, had half of Disneyland opened to us after hours, Michael Jackson style. No lines, no crying kids, no one but us—bliss. I didn't know it, but this was also a reconnaissance mission of sorts; the pair were researching the viability of one of Andy's more ambitious propositions for "the diversification of the band's brand." The two of them, deep in discussion, hardly seemed to notice what ride we were on.

So, much of my birthday I shared with Becca. It was beginning to feel weird calling her Mum, especially when someone else had a prior claim. Sam was a natural comedian, she told me, full of goofy expressions and funny walks: Charlie Chaplin, John Cleese, even the moonwalk—the whole collection. The father didn't let her see him as often as she wanted and was now using the newspapers as his mouthpiece. "He should come on the Wonder-Bus!" I said, echoing Blake. He really did sound like a perfect candidate.

"What's the similarity between the Yardbirds and Khrushchev?" Jack shouted over. "They were both banned from Disneyland!" He'd sneaked in alcohol, and, though I never do, again I did, what with it being my birthday and all. Everything got giggly. We went faster and slower and splashed and laughed. We screamed. We went round and round and up and down and round and round again. I liked being wedged in tight with Mum, the warmth of her thigh against me. She was especially playful as the rides got more reckless, and, in one of the darker corners of the Haunted House, she took my hand and placed it on her leg; her knee felt soft above the bone, her inner thigh softer. She whispered ghostly in my ear: "Wanna do me a favor?"

"Probably," was all I could manage.

"Fulfill a fantasy?" As she turned to check no one could see us, the car turned sharply, and we were confronted with our own reflection in a mirror, my hand on her leg. I panicked, but only we'd seen—everyone else was involved in his own spinning, jolting journey through the singing ghosts.

"A fantasy?" I asked. She took it as a *yes*.

"Not now. A particular ride."

Look, I wasn't stupid. And I wasn't even naive. I just ate a lot of sugar. It hadn't occurred to me that Mum thought of me that way. But she wasn't my mother, I wasn't Blake's son, and she was only ten years my senior. And I was a pretty tall, normally developed, sixteen-year-old, if inexperienced, particularly in fulfilling people's fantasies, which seemed as alien a concept as you can possibly imagine. *My* sexual fantasy, as I once heard a comedian say, was . . . to have sex. My body conducted the warmth of Becca's inner thigh, and I found myself with an erection that tried to bayonet the safety bar, a standoff in which there could only be one winner.

And as the Haunted House trundled to a squeaking stop, I reluctantly removed my hand, asking myself whether all the hair-washing and drying, the menu of cookery shows, the bass lessons, had been in the service of a seduction of which I had been completely unaware. As we headed to the pitch-black Outer Space ride, Blake and Andy still deep in discussion, Jack sipping from a flask and having a cheeky cigarette, Becca took my hand and swung it from side to side in the friendliest way. What this meant was: we're sitting together on this ride, and there is no way anyone else is sitting next to me, because I have had a drink or two and this is what I have planned. And what it looked like to everyone else was: Mum's a sport.

The rides lose a little atmosphere if you get on too quickly, a nuance that probably always eluded the King of Pop. Disney does a good job of ramping up the excitement, stoking the narrative, while you idle your engine in the long line. But I couldn't have cared less. All I wanted was to get in that front car with Mum (birthday boys always get the front car), plunge into darkness and see what fantasy we were fulfilling.

It was already the most thrilling ride of my life, and the safety bar hadn't even come down. As we ascended into the helter-skelter blackness, she placed my hand on the inside of her leg again, and opened her thighs. I knew what to do—we'd had a trial run—but there was one thing that needed clearing up.

"Did Blake put you up to this?" He was always putting people up to things. I didn't want her to have been put up.

She laughed in my ear. "Oh no, kid," she said, "This is all mine," and encouraged my progress into the unknown, shivering as my hand traced up the inside of her thigh. She seemed to be hurrying me towards my destination. And then . . . I'd been with girls, while unwillingly retaining my virginity, but this was new. Becca's hair was orderly, trimmed in fact, into a straight line, soft soft skin either side.

"Why me and not . . . them?"

"Because I was sixteen once too. Concentrate. Time is tight. Get this right, and I'll be very grateful later on."

Oh shit. I wasn't actually sure how to get it right, let alone within the constraints of a time trial, so as we flew around corners, I made sure my hand cupped and rubbed as much of her as possible, and let her, and the lurching of the car, do most of the work. I tried to right myself, which she took as a signal that I was enjoying myself. She started to move determinedly against me, reaching over briefly to show her appreciation, succeeding only in squeezing the safety bar. The ride started a slow climb before we got to a peak from which we hurtled down at top speed, Jack and Curtis actually screaming a car or two behind us. She groaned, lifted her shirt up, started to play with her breasts, and had what I took to be an orgasm. At the precise moment I pushed my fingers inside her, there was a flash of light that brightly illuminated everyone and everything for a stroboscopic second; my hand was right up her skirt. Becca screamed for real. I pulled myself away, taking the opportunity to prop my cock into a more tolerable position. She couldn't stop laughing, as though her orgasm wouldn't quit, and let out a whoop of exhilaration, perfectly appropriate for public consumption, given the situation.

"Hey," she said. "Thank you. A lifetime went into that. And you know what the flash was? That was a photo. They took a fucking photo of us!"

"They what?" We were slowly coming to a standstill but my heart hadn't realized.

"You buy it as a memento. A photo of the scariest moment of the ride."

"They what? They took a photo?" I looked around. "Did you know they were going to take a photo?"

"No. No. It wasn't part of my fantasy if that's what you're asking." She couldn't stop laughing.

"What are you going to do?"

The ride stopped with a shudder. Everyone phewed enthusiastic relief.

"I'm going to be first out of this car, and then I'm going to go and buy it, if necessary; and make sure nobody else sees it."

"Aren't you worried?" I asked. She was being so practical, which I loved, though I remained horrified.

"What about? Maybe I'll give it to you as a birthday gift . . ." and she whispered: "That's up to you."

As we left the park, an employee handed me an envelope emblazoned with the Disney logo: the photo, I assumed, by the knowing look on his face. But when I opened it in my bunk on the bus, I found nothing more than a certificate commemorating the fact that the park had been opened specifically for me on my sixteenth birthday. Maybe they didn't take a photo at all. Maybe it was just a flash, like when a speed camera fakes you out.

That night, birthday karaoke concluded, I heard a tap-tap on my door. Unmistakably, Mum.

There followed the longest, most clandestine game of footsie ever played.

Nobody could know. That was absolutely the most important thing. We never even discussed the alternative. But when you think about it: why not? Did we get off on the deception? Did the sharing of our little secret make us feel slightly superior? Did it make the long months of touring more bearable, more interesting, worth getting up for? Was it amazing? Yes, yes, yes, and mostly.

I'd be innocently reading in the darkness of the front of the bus at the lone table, and she'd sit opposite me, snaking her toe up the inside of my leg. Or she'd be reading too, or listening to her Walkman—that same yoga music—and her hand would casually alight on my thigh and rub me through my pants. Or she'd be sitting next to me and, her attention supposedly on someone further forward, leave her left arm trailing, loitering, teasing.

We never had sex on the bus, though once, as I lay in my coffin, head flaring, wondering how I could ever get to sleep again without washing my hair, a hand reached in, burrowed under the covers and offered a different type of relief entirely. I lay there, imagining her in the passage, standing with her back to Blake's empire (her own bunk was on the same level as mine, opposite), knowing how relatively easy it would be, in the hallway gloom, for her to withdraw her hand if someone happened by. This was not the moment to reach out to her. It was the moment to let her have her way, let her soothe her patient with a sedative orgasm considerably more powerful than Benadryl. Another time, she reached across the divide and parted my curtain. I could just see her naked in her coffin, a pale corpse in the half-light. She looked at me. We didn't touch each other.

Outside the bus, things were more brazen. One night, at one of the many random stops offered by the American Interstate system, we all found ourselves eating fried chicken—or, more precisely, chicken that had once been fried, but was now served frozen in the middle. As we waited for the meal to be re-presented, I went for a pee, only to leave the toilet to find her blocking the way back to the dining room. She dropped to one knee, left foot jammed against the door, unzipped my pants and took my cock in her mouth. Sure, we'd been idly footsieing in the bus, but nothing that had unavoidably led to this. Maybe the undefrosted poultry had caused her to overheat. If one of our gang had needed to use the bathroom themselves at that moment . . . that's all she wrote. Time did not allow this act to reach any specific climax, but it's always been one of the highlights of a spotty sexual career. I've teased myself with the image many times (though her messy blonde hair censored any specific view of the action), often conclusively, often even as others did precisely the same kind of thing. The crucial difference was that, with those other women, I was not inches from my family—my closest friends—as they waited for unfrozen chicken in a roadside diner, looking down on a woman ten years older, on one knee, with her foot blocking the door. Oh, Mum. We went back to the table separately, of course.

What was she thinking? What I mean is: I'm not putting it down to my own irresistible charm. I'm infinitely resistible. She must have liked educating me. Or maybe I was a bit of Blake, and maybe she loved him a little. Things get weird in the bubble. It was born of our close quarters and close friendship. She wanted it, and I could provide it. There was never any talk of "love." The relationship, the affair—what was it?—seemed to have no downside. It became a habit; then an addiction. "This can't last forever," she said once, and she was right, but it didn't fizzle. There was no reason for us not to. Neither of us had anyone else; I wasn't even in the band; she had a child; she was ten years older than me. So what?

Only once were we caught. There I was in the drink and ice room on the seventh floor of the wherever Holiday Inn, lying on the ground, eyes closed, pants open, illuminated by the televisual glare of the vending machine; and there too, hair over her face, was Becca, half way down my body. And there too, though I didn't register him at first, Mitchell, stepping over whatever obstacle we presented, dropping quarters into the machine. His purchase clunked its clumsy descent into the delivery tray, and my eyes opened for a second. Becca froze; nothing improper was on display; neither of us moved; perhaps he didn't know it was us. Of course he knew it was us. He probably knew we were in there before he'd even gone to get his water. But it was Mitchell. Mitchell wouldn't say anything.

He delivered a breezy "See you in the bus, guys!" as he left, stepping right over my head, his tone so friendly that I couldn't deny him a polite "Good night." I think even Becca mumbled something.

When he'd left, I buttoned myself. "What are we doing in the ice room anyway? Can I come to your room?" I wanted to be somewhere private, where it was only her and me. There was no reason to be lit by vending machines.

"Better go back to yours and Blake's," she said. I watched her disappear down the corridor, then bought a can of Pepsi. My head began to itch. I thought of my bed, next to Blake, who'd be snoring or maybe he wouldn't be there at all, out on a midnight stroll. Sometimes I yearned for privacy, though I loved sharing a room with him. Whether he was there now or not, he'd be back. However late Blake was out, he *always* ended up in his room. Just when everybody else was converging, yawning, on the elevator, he'd go for a late-night amble, but he always made it back and—however wasted he was when he got to the hotel, however little he'd paid attention at check-in, rolling out of the back of the bus where he'd been doing heaven knows what, however much this hotel was an exact carbon copy of the previous hotel and all hotels before it (as though the same hotel was being transported from city to city, narrowly beating us there)—he always found his way to his room. Nothing kept him from his bed. How do I know? Because I, in the adjacent bed, was invariably woken from my slumber when he stumbled back in, whacked his shin on the luggage rack and swore. He'd come over, reeking of his night out, kiss me on the forehead, and say "Goodnight, Sweet." And I'd pretend to sleep.

He wasn't back, so, taking advantage of this solitude, I masturbated, the smell of Becca's hair product still on my hands.

• • •

Fearing a lesson the next morning, I made a halfhearted attempt to avoid Mitchell, but he invited me to sit at his desk.

"Everything good?" he asked, absentmindedly shuffling papers.

"Sure."

"You're all my children, you know," he said. "I have no favorites, and I just like to know that all my children are happy."

"Very happy," I said, getting up. He took hold of my wrist firmly.

"Good," he smiled. "Because sometimes you need a Dad who you actually get to call Dad." My impulse was to shake him off. At this precise moment, Blake yelled my name from the back. Mitchell let go, rather theatrically, raised both eyebrows and, with a little bow, ushered me beyond into the bowels of the bus: "Here when you need me," he said. "At your cervix."

I had a mind to tell Blake, but that would require over-explanation. And anyway, maybe Mitchell was just doing his job. Still, my wrist smarted like he'd given me an Indian burn.

By the time I had traveled the short distance down the corridor, Blake was already off on a classic tangent: "Listen to this! Listen to this! It's from *Alice*. '"Here, you may nurse it a bit if you like!" The Duchess said to Alice, flinging the baby at her as she spoke,' . . . *blah blah* . . . 'Alice caught the baby with some difficulty.' How about . . . now how *about* . . . and picture this . . . tell me what you think . . . Middle of our show: a little toddler comes on, dressed to specification, walks towards me and goes behind the dressing-up box, and while he's hidden behind there (unbeknownst to the audience) . . . I pick up a replica toddler, a doll, and fling it out into the audience. And they either catch it or they don't, but everyone screams. Great, right?"

I looked at him in awe. "Are you serious?"

That he was seemed to be confirmed by the fact that he immediately burst out laughing. "Quack!" And I started laughing too. In fact, I laughed so hard I collapsed on the other bench.

"Chicken DAT!" he yelled. "Chicken fucking DAT!"

• • •

Since Altamont, there'd been regular children's home and hospital visits to demonstrate that the Wonderheart was in the right place. The label was ruthless in its exploitation of such opportunities. In California, we played some place in the Valley. I don't know whether the facility was coincidentally full of Asian kids, or whether they threw all the Asian kids together—that doesn't seem very American—or whether we were just in a very Asian area.

Whatever the venue, the Wonderkids' busking set was always a good time. Jack played his acoustic; Curtis banged on a couple of boxes with some brushes, sometimes just smacked his knees; Becca had a little acoustic bass that didn't even need to plug in, though it clicked more than it sounded a note; and Blake hammed it up as the room allowed. They played different tunes, and I remember Blake singing a Randy Newman song, something about a yellow woman and a yellow man, which seemed an odd choice; all these Asian kids seemed to enjoy it anyway.

There was a wide range of ages, including one girl, Chinese I thought, who sat close to the stage. She looked sad, as though nothing would ever cheer her up, but as the band got going, she loosened up a bit. I could hardly keep my eyes off her. It wasn't that I fancied her—and anyway it was hard to judge her age—but she was intriguing. Her expression, which at first read as sadness, was merely impassive, and when she smiled, she beamed. She smiled, however, only at Curtis. On a whim, he handed her the brushes, and then it was her banging the box on the two and four as the band played on. After the show, we mingled. Curtis was deep in conversation with the girl.

For some reason, it was thought appropriate to eat Japanese that night in a mini-mall. It was the first time I'd ever had it. While others laid into great pink and red strips of raw fish, as if this could ever be normal, Jack and I tiptoed around big bowls of bland soup and battered prawns, after which I ordered a dollop of profoundly disappointing green tea ice cream. No one with a sweet tooth wants green tea or red bean. (This was years before mochi came along and saved the day.)

"Great girl, that Mei-Xing," said Curtis. "Terrible life story. Sold, you know."

"Sold?" I asked. "For, er . . ."

"Yeah." He was playing with his dreads, twirling them round in his fingers, which I'd never seen him do before. It was like he was untangling them, tangling them and then ironing them out all in one movement. "When she was six."

"Poor little girl," said Becca. "How old is she?"

"Fourteen. Anyway, I thought I'd invite her to the show tomorrow: spread the love."

I tried to remember what I, another orphan, was doing when I was six. I was safe in the orphanage, playing Ping-Pong, occasionally getting into scraps, dressing up when people came to take a look at us. It wasn't much fun, but that's all it wasn't and all it was. I wasn't *sold*. I was fiddled with once when I was eleven, but it hadn't stayed with me like it does with some other kids. I just thought the bloke was pathetic and I told him I'd tell his wife. That scared him off. (I mean, I don't mean to be a dick, but these days you could base a whole literary career on that kind of thing.)

The next day at the gig, Mei-Xing gravitated towards me at the back of the hall, recognizing a friendly face, someone in the clique. Did we seem the same age? She looked like a child in her off-white smock, except for the surprising brown wisps peeking from her underarms; it was like she was keeping a pet vole warm. From her neck hung a little red purse, decorated with yellow flowers. She played with that thing constantly, running its string through her fingers, buttoning and unbuttoning it. She seemed happy to be standing near me—but she didn't say hello. She didn't demand much of a room, and only ever spoke to one person at a time (mostly Curtis), and then quietly. She hardly said *anything*. You kinda forgot she was there.

Curtis reintroduced us backstage as though we hadn't been standing next to each other for the last half hour. But then you always felt you were meeting her for the first time, even later when we were . . . well, anyway . . .—she was always constantly reintroducing herself or being reintroduced.

"Let's go for a drive," Curtis said, only to her. "Let's go and look at something. What's there to look at?"

She whispered something in his ear, and they went out, leaving Jack, Becca, Blake, and I in a dressing room that smelled like burned plastic. On arrival, someone (I) had rested an open guitar case against the many-bulbed mirror, and someone else (Jack) had, unsuspectingly, turned the lights on. There was an enormous blister in the outer casing of the guitar case. It didn't look melted, however, so I'd poked it, leaving a fingerprint that lasts to this day.

"Strange one," said Jack, not quite to himself, as if writing Mei-Xing's epitaph.

"Strange situation, you mean? It's sweet," said Blake.

"It's sweet and a bit strange," said Jack, flicking through the Guitar Center catalog like a man pretending he isn't titillated by, or even interested in, the copy of *Hustler* that's somehow found its way before him.

"There's nothing strange about it," said Blake dismissively.

"Grown man like that? Young girl?" asked Jack, still refusing to look up. Blake and Mum couldn't suppress a giggle.

"I don't think she has anything to worry about with Curtis," said Becca.

"Well, he's a *gentleman*," said Jack, defensively. "Course he's a *gentleman*. But it's who he chooses to spend his time with."

"Yeah, Jack," said Blake, winking at me. "But he's a . . . he's a *gentleman's gentleman*." Jack looked up; his smile melted away. "You actually didn't know, did you?"

"Yeah, yeah," said Jack unpersuasively, "I knew. Course I knew . . ." His tone changed to exasperation. "NO, I didn't know. I try not to think about *any* of your private lives."

"And we try really hard, really really hard, not to think about yours," said Becca. "You didn't know?"

The truth was, Jack had a slightly hard spot for gays. He wasn't anti-, exactly; he just didn't like it. He once drunkenly confessed that he'd agreed to a threesome with some woman and her deaf husband, but changed his mind because he couldn't tell if the husband would touch him or not. Blake said he should have made the deaf bloke sign something. Jack concluded that anyone who wanted to have a threesome involving a preponderance of men was gay. "But you *wanted* to have a threesome," said Blake.

"But I didn't," said Jack, "so that proves I'm not." The argument was destined to run and run.

"Sweet," said Jack, canvassing support. "Did you know Curtis was . . ." He actually couldn't bring himself to say it.

"Erm. No."

"Oh, don't try to make him feel better!" said Blake. "You knew."

"I wasn't sure," I said honestly. "How would I know? He never tried it on with me."

"That's not how you tell if someone's gay!" Blake said. He couldn't stop laughing. "Maybe he just doesn't fancy you! Becca hasn't tried it on with you; doesn't mean she doesn't like blokes."

No comment. Jack was delighted.

"Right, so neither Sweet nor I knew. Are we so stupid?"

"Two against two," said Blake. "The casting vote therefore goes to Mitchell," who materialized in the dressing room at that moment. "Mitchell, is Curtis, once Kurt Zero of punk band the Hard Cocks, gay?"

Mitchell stroked a non-existent beard. "Is this a trick question?" We shook our heads, all at once, like the Monkees. "When was the last time you saw a straight black man with dreadlocks like that?"

Jack shook his head. "Okay. 3-2 to the clever ones."

"Put it this way, Jack," said Mitchell. "If I were black, that's how I'd wear my dreadlocks."

Jack nodded, deep in his own thoughts, his face impassive. He was almost surrounded by them. (I'd had no idea.)

"Anyway, Jack," said Blake, "no need to worry about Curtis's ulterior motives with regard to the orphan. I think there's a bigger issue. I'd say that the Wonderfamily may be expanding. Just a hunch."

However much red tape there was I have no idea, and I don't know whether it was cut, crossed, or followed to the letter, but within the week, Mei-Xing was on the bus, traveling with the family. Blake was totally behind it. And if Blake wanted it, I wanted it. She barely spoke, and she certainly didn't get in the way, I'll say that for her. She made the tea for everyone: it just came very naturally to her, and Becca was happy for someone else to be Mum for a while. We started drinking a lot more tea. Green tea. A few spoonfuls of sugar in there and . . . well, not the same of course, and it isn't strong enough to defend itself against milk, but . . . bingo.

The only downside was that I was evacuated from my coffin, the consensus being that Mei-Xing should be opposite Becca. I found myself below Blake and Curtis, though Blake generally sacked out in the back room anyway among his secondhand books, dusty vinyl, hangings, and hookahs.

Curtis had his project: a fourteen-year-old Mei-Xing who made tea and said very little. I didn't want to take an uncharitable view—wasn't I Blake's project too?—but it seemed like she was his doll. He loved to take her clothes shopping. Soon she was out of those loose white smocks and wearing much more modern, less attractive clothing. Who's to judge? Nevertheless, his sweet little dolly.

And there we were in the bus: growing in number by the day. It was around this time that Sam, Mum's actual son, joined us for the odd trip—that was when the fun really began: Hide and Seek, Tickle Monster, Dinosaur Races ("Pterodactylus vs. the Edmontosaurus")—and there I was, back to reading to the "little ones" again, organizing pre-bedtime Olympiads. What a funny kid he was: he'd wait until he was sure you were watching and then make you laugh with some quick eye movement, just to show you he could. And his walks were good too.

When Sam was around, Becca and I took a break. Everyone loved having Sam on the bus, but sometimes I counted the days till he was gone. Jack bore it without grinning. It wasn't quite his idea of touring in a rock band, having all these children underfoot, but, then, what about the Wonderkids was normal?

Blake sat in the back and wrote songs. One began:

> We might indeed be out of tea
> Out of tea we might well be
> Who will make the tea for we
> Mei-Xing! Mei-Xing!

And we all called back, because that's how the song went: "She's from Beijing, and she's Mei-Xing!" The next verse was about Sam; and the last one was about me.

Cartoons are not drawn overnight, nor theme parks built in a day, and plans were already afoot for both *Wonderkids to the Rescue!* and Wonderland itself. The TV show I could just get my head around; but the theme park? Ludicrous, and yet it was all part of WBA's plan: make your own audience, blaze a trail, "*if you build it they will come.*" Storyboards with amusing caricatures of the band dressed as superheroes vied for the band's attention with designs for bizarre fairground rides. These were ideal projects for Blake and Jack: things at which you could simultaneously laugh and stare in awe.

The Wonderland engineers—"imagineers" in Disney terms —arrived with cute scale models that they placed carefully on the table, prior to a demonstration involving little hand-painted carriages and toy humans. Blake would sit back, the picture of contemplation, and consider the miniature WonderWaltzer, the WonderKinderGarten play area for tots, or the WonderWander nature ramble. Our park was never going to compete with the big boys, but the money behind it had staked out some land in the southern valley, and the whole thing seemed like it was veering towards reality.

First things first: it's every performer's fantasy to be able to play concerts and not travel, to stay in one place; that's why all those country guys open their own theaters: let the mountain come to Missouri. With the WonderTheater, we would now have our own venue. Sure, the band could go play wherever they liked, whenever they liked, but this would be home base: a gig with some rides attached. And if the band wasn't around: no problem. Some excited youngsters with Equity cards would be the Wonderkids, and mime to the backing tracks. The intention wasn't to fool people, just to let them enjoy a reasonable facsimile: The WonderKindas. Maybe that's who'd play all the time. I could be in them, Blake suggested—he was always trying to push me in that direction. I already subbed for him at soundcheck when he couldn't be bothered. I didn't do a bad impression either; at least enough to make Becca laugh.

Blake's only, but overwhelming, objection to the theme park was its lack of a magical theme. There was the band, and their characters, and their songs, but beyond that, no particular narrative. Blake suggested Edward Lear. Disney probably had some proprietary claim over Lewis Carroll, after that psychedelic cartoon of *Alice In Wonderland*, and obviously no one wants to mess with a Disney lawyer. But Lear—he was still up for grabs, until such time as Disney decided to sink its money into a full length feature of "the Dong with a Luminous Nose" with the very amusing voice of Robin Williams in the title role and "Julia Roberts *is* the Jumbly girl." It wasn't going to happen. "The Owl and the Pussycat"? Surely it was made for a ride lasting "a year and a day" in a beautiful pea green boat over an expanse of sea that ends with a dance by the light of the moon. They could have a couple of thrill rides, small ones, to keep the imagineers happy, but what Blake wanted was the nonsense come to life: Gromboolian plains, slices of quince.

And with their new instructions, these purposeful men-children went back to the drawing boards in their imagineeria. Clearly, they were happiest designing the big room with all the feathers floating around, and the one really fast ride that wasn't appropriate to children under 42" tall, but they'd put their all into the quainter rides too. Though demographic research did not point to the popularity of a theme park based on the poetry of Edward Lear, the band's own brand was somehow considered sturdy enough to incorporate Blake's whimsy. And so those rides, those stately, beautiful, old-fashioned rides were imagineered. And within a few weeks, the imagineers were back, and Blake was as happy as I'd ever seen him. He'd taken a lot from nonsense and now he was giving a little back.

Life was a series of meetings on the bus. The next set featured a new breed: the record producer. This was Jack's department; Blake merely reported his intuitions about the applicants. One by one, confident, mostly tanned men, climbed aboard to hear new songs, see a show, get the feel of the band, *make sure everyone is on the same page*, each introduced by Andy as though he had all the answers. Some producers, slightly older and with shorter hair, seemed ready to throw a good party. Others, longer hair, sometimes bald on top, talked technical, how easily, how updated, how automated, how fast the faders flew; others just wanted to make a good impression, hardly mentioning the music. Jack asked the technical questions; every now and then Blake asked for their star sign as though this might affect a decision, or their opinion of Jonathan Richman's new record.

"If the label's happy, I'm happy," said Andy, who was himself *to all intensive purposes* (oh, how we missed Greg) the label. WBA had put these producers forward, so why wouldn't they be happy when one of their puppets was finally on the throne? Jack had suggestions of his own—but such producers, we were told, weren't really interested in the Wonderkids . . . *yet*. That was always the word. *Yet*. But people invariably go where the money is, so what was the problem with the Wonderkids' money, the Wonderkids' points?

"Daniel Lanois is just not about to make a kid's record," said Andy, assuming this was whom Jack wanted; though Jack of course knew this. He was just making a point. "Mutt Lange is not about to make a kids' record." They would these days, of course. They wouldn't even think twice about it. Hell, they've probably done it.

"George Martin made hundreds of kids' records," argued Jack. "Listen to 'Nellie the Elephant,' pristine Ron Goodwin arrangement, and who else but George Martin?"

"Let's ask George Martin," said Andy.

"Too tall," said Blake. "Who's next?"

Next was Denny, who had a Grammy under his belt, corkscrew curls, dark glasses, and drawled as though he'd had a minor stroke or his teeth were in funny. He was perfectly nice, very boring. It was all work to him, but he and Jack bonded and he uttered a few magic words as though primed by Andy: "It doesn't really sound like kids' music to me; it's all just *music*, isn't it?" I never saw him without the glasses on. "It reminds me of the Kinks. And that's what it should sound like." When he name-dropped George Martin, I wondered whether the fix was in. The procedure had been lengthy, a decision had to be made, and Denny was the least bad option.

"I like a lot of focus in the studio," he said. "I have some of my own guys who can help out, but they'll never get in the way of your band, and if you're uncomfortable with anything, you tell me. I'm here to make you happy."

No one who says that is telling the truth, but he did give them a hit record. I never liked him.

The tour ended at just the right time; there was an "end of term" feeling around the bus, but everyone was too knackered for practical jokes. You know you've been playing too much Gameboy when you get close to a city, see the skyline, and wonder between which buildings the next Tetris block will neatly drop. I no longer wanted to be reminded daily, when brushing my teeth, that I had forgotten or was in need of essential toiletries. Becca and I had stayed our course with ferocious focus, but even we were flagging.

Also, Curtis's obsession with Mei-Xing had become a little unnerving. At one point, I was eavesdropping on them in the dressing room. I didn't mean to be, and, to be fair, she was technically too quiet to eavesdrop on.

"You're going out wearing that?" It was a tone I'd never heard from him. Her reply was inaudible. "Turn around," he said. I was painting a surrealist picture in my mind. "Bend over . . ." Slight pause. "No, you're not."

"Curtis!" I heard *that*. It was whiney.

"Did I buy you that?"

Another inaudible reply.

"Well, put on whatever you changed out of. I love you."

"I love you too, Curtis."

"Now change."

She emerged in blue jeans and smock top over a T-shirt, always that little purse dangling around her neck, and waved at me as she disappeared.

He didn't like smoke anywhere near her. Before Mei-Xing appeared, he hadn't loved the backstage routine, which involved a little weed when possible, or the back of the bus routine, which involved a lot of weed more or less all the time; now he didn't like it at all. He started to get quite verbal, and it got a bit awkward—it seemed like Jack and Blake (which basically meant Jack) might have to remind him that it wasn't his band. But just as things seemed to be reaching a head, the tour was done and there was nothing to complain about. We all looked forward to glimpsing real life again—even the thing that passed for it in that Hitchcock house at the top of the canyon. Perhaps our blotches might disappear, our wrists recover, our skin stop flaking.

Becca and me, Curtis and Mei-Xing, Jack's nightly excursions around the MILF bars—it was hard to tell where everyone was headed. Only Blake seemed constant. He was working on his songs for the second record; he was daydreaming about the theme park; every late afternoon, and sometimes even into the evening, he put on an amazing show, as did the whole band. Yes, he smoked; yes, he drank; and yes, he got stoned. But he never let the crowd down. The records were selling; his eye was on the ball. Jack was the businessman, but Blake was the captain of the ship, the leader of the gang. The only trouble was: I wasn't sure he was really enjoying himself much. Perhaps we were all just tired.

One of the turning points, as I look back, was on the way home at the Burbank airport. We'd flown separately from the rest of the band, and it felt good to be on our own.

"Good ride idea for the theme park," Blake said. "A baggage carousel. Everyone travels round and round in their parents' luggage. It's a ride, with bonus metaphor."

And that was when we saw a very famous rock star, someone he really admired, a hero—I just can't even write down which one he was, but think of the two biggest bands in the sixties, okay, not them, but then think of the other one, and it was him— bearded, scruffy looking, stoopingly tall, epic nose, definitely him, with an obtrusive entourage

Blake walked up and said, quite casually, "Hi, I'm a big fan and I'm in the band the Wonderkids." This, mind you, when the Wonderkids were officially a huge success. He didn't ask for the bloke's autograph or a photo or anything like that; nor did he get in his face. He was just friendly and efficiently fanlike; he even made it clear that that was as far as he wanted the conversation to go. He knew how to handle that stuff, being the victim of so much silliness himself.

And the rock star stopped, looked Blake straight in the face and said with a smirk, taking care also to address his coterie: "Congratulations! You're in the worst fucking band in the whole universe!"

Then he walked on.

Blake's mouth fell open, and he looked at me and let out a little laugh of disbelief, shaking his head. We made no mention of it until we got in the limo.

"Am I in the worst fucking band in the whole universe?" I didn't answer, since he seemed to be asking the window or the passing scenery. "It doesn't matter," he said, confirming how much it did. Then he turned to me: "If you ever tell Jack . . ."

"Mum's the word," I said.

Coincidence or not, that's when it started to fall apart.

"Does anyone remember laughter?"

BECCA, CURTIS, AND MEI-XING WENT INTO THEIR RESPECTIVE hibernations. It may have been time to get out of each other's pockets, but going cold turkey after such an intense period together makes you feel like you're missing key teeth. And you can't stop your tongue checking.

As Blake readied the songs for the new album—the nonsense tumbled out of him quite naturally, but he liked to tinker—Jack and I spent a lot of time hanging out, watching TV; he even started teaching me guitar. You have a lot of great notions of how you'll spend your time on the road—ambitious sightseeing, reading improving literature, Spanish in thirty days—but the hours aren't conducive to anything much except playing gigs, flipping through magazines and chatting. The bigger projects never quite get off the ground. Learning the guitar: that's a commitment—one we now had time to make.

Jack took me to one of the old hair farmer places on the strip where every employee was dreaming either of a gig at Gazzarri's or an appointment at Hair Guitar, and the soundtrack is a cacophony of metal riffs. Among the transparent flying Vs and the flame-colored right-angle-necked ESPs, which Jack roundly mocked, he found an off-white 1978 Telecaster that he carried as though he was my roadie. When we got home, he sat me down and placed it in my arms gently, a sleeping baby.

"Nice, right?" He smiled. "How does she feel?"

Right, it's female. I balanced the guitar, using my thigh as a fulcrum, thinking that that might be the right thing to do, like when you taste a glass of wine that's more or less the same as any other and pretend to notice a big difference. I considered her curve, the way she fit under my ribcage. I had no idea.

"First I'm going to teach you how sound works. Then I'm going to explain why a guitar has six strings. Then I'm going to tell you how to tune it and why it's tuned that way. And then I'm going to relate it to the wider world."

"Can you just teach me some chords?"

"This is how I work. Now the bottom string," he twanged it, "is an E. Why?"

"First letter of the alphabet?"

"Don't be like Blake. Wrong. And stand up. Let's get this strap the right length."

The goal was that I'd play one rhythm guitar part at the next recording session. Unrealistic. I could hardly make a barre chord—it's a tricky thing to do—and he wouldn't let me pop my thumb over the top as Blake did. No. Bad habit, best avoided.

Bass lessons with Becca had quickly become an excuse to loll around. She taught me stuff, mostly about fingering (that was her big joke), but I did know where all the frets were and where you pressed the string down. With Jack, all that had to be unlearned, because I was going to do it his way or not at all. To my great surprise, there turned out to be a touch of the Barry about him.

The problem with being an expert at nothing is that you're always at the mercy of the teacher. This can also be a good thing too—see above—but it was time for me to work out what I actually wanted to master, what would be mine. It wasn't going to be the guitar, but for now, that seemed as good as anything.

Off the road, with no merch to inventory, hawk, or reorder, my status was unclear.

When recording began, I was hardly required at the studio.

They didn't even need anybody to get food; you just ordered from a flip file full of menus and lo, it was delivered. I couldn't drive anyway, so my orbit was limited to where I could walk, which was, basically, nowhere. Besides, it took half an hour—slight exaggeration—to cross the road. It was too hot to bother walking half a long block to the crosswalk, and a policeman stopped me for jaywalking: I hadn't even known it was a crime. He heard my accent, didn't like the thought of the paperwork, and let me off with a warning, before offering me a lift to the other side of the street, and asking me to elucidate the rules of cricket.

Inside the studio, beyond the front desk, there was an annex of sofas, a TV that showed nothing but baseball, a pinball machine, and a kitchenette with a library of tea bags. Beyond this comfortable holding cell was the recording studio itself, where, though officially welcome, I wasn't made to feel at home. Once, I made the mistake of complimenting Jack on a guitar part, to which Denny replied: "You a producer now, kid?" I would have expected Blake to leap to my defense, take Denny down a peg or two, but he hadn't heard: he was scratching down lyrics on a piece of paper and decorating them with elaborate doodles. I kept quiet after that and stuck to the decompression chamber, into which the band emerged only occasionally to get, or to pass, water. Only when they'd finished a basic was there any fun to be had.

At first, it was good to see Curtis and Becca again. Mei-Xing was around as well. She and I kept each other company, not having much to say, occasionally sitting side by side on the couch and playing Super Mario, where the little guy jumps around, avoids the forces of Bowser and liberates Princess Toadstool. One afternoon a few days in, I glimpsed some nasty scars up the inside of her left arm, bared by the maneuvering of her joystick.

"Hey," I said. "What happened?"

"I cut myself," she said.

"Oh," I said, because I'm a fool, "that's terrible. How did you cut yourself?"

And she said, all the time boinging that stupid little guy up and down to get the magical coins, "No, I cut myself. I mean, I like to cut myself."

"Oh, right," I said, understanding and not quite understanding, wishing I could slide down the side of the sofa so all that was left to show of me was the lead from the Super Mario console. Just enough that they could reel me back up when she'd left.

Curtis was the first to leave the sessions, depriving me of my Super Mario opponent. The drummer's usually the first to go when his parts are done, popping back only to rattle a tambourine when everyone else is having dinner. But no sooner was he out the door than more drums appeared, along with another drummer to whom I was never properly introduced, and the same tracks ran once more.

Becca and I hardly exchanged two words. After she'd made her bass fixes, she was heading back north to Sam. We found ourselves standing together in the annex ("and it's a two-run homer, McLeod standing at fourth bass"), and she said very softly: "I'm just trying to keep a very low profile right now, bury myself in cement." Weird image.

"Okay," I said, trying to let her know . . . I wasn't sure what I was trying to let her know. Perhaps that it would be fine if we had a bit more sex.

"Are *you* okay?" she asked, though she didn't want me to answer in the negative, let alone say I missed her or anything like that.

"Sure," I said. It was true, though it was weird being off the road. I couldn't read her, and I wondered whether she was somehow jealous of Mei-Xing. But, you know, it isn't all about you. You just sometimes wish it was.

"I'm pissed at Blake too," she added, slinging her jacket over her arm. Too? In addition to how she was pissed off with me? Or "I'm pissed at Blake just like you are"? I wasn't pissed off. Or "I'm as pissed at Blake just like all the other people who are pissed at him"? I didn't like any of these alternatives, but I couldn't ask her to clarify. She continued: "We were going to duet "Noon In June," but they've talked him into doing it with somebody else. He just *happened* to mention that. And he wouldn't even tell me who." Made sense. I'd heard Denny dropping a couple of famous names, but I hadn't put two and two together.

"Oh, is that all?" I asked, then reconsidered. "I mean, is that all there is . . . er . . . to it?"

"That isn't all," she said.

That was all. She'd be back in a few days to do her harmonies; that was the plan. She never came.

I found myself inventing projects to keep myself occupied—a video diary for the label with Jack's camera, some other rubbish. Denny ran a tight ship—office hours, more or less—and the ringers he brought in were not in the business of having fun; they were in the business of running from session to session, too grand to carry their own gear. The music sounded, y'know, great—but it got to the point where I was so bored of Denny instructing Blake to sing a line infinitesimally differently that I feared I'd never be able to listen to the finished thing with any pleasure. And so, when it all changed to Jack overdubbing endless guitars, I decided to stay at home. They left early and got back tired. I practiced the guitar, and got so bored that I took to turning on the baseball. I was even happy to see the cleaners. There was a chauffeured town car at my disposal, but I somehow couldn't be bothered. It seemed better to be forever traveling on the tour bus, in motion, where boredom can't catch up with you.

Blake was gone all day and some evenings; Jack went out on the prowl at night. On my own, it was easy not to do very much, but the guitar rarely left my hands. It felt like convalescence, watching the sun creep shadows across the walls, wondering how to divide my time between pool, hammock, and AC. I mastered Jack's geometric dance patterns up and down the fingerboard. Scales were no more interesting than the ones I'd rejected on the piano years before, but my fingers felt sprier on the guitar, and they got to actually interact with a bending string rather than just plunk a dead key. It was easier to practice lying on a hammock, than sitting on a threadbare piano stool at Clements, watching the rain.

Jack would grab my left hand on his return and inspect it, like a parent checking for evidence of bitten nails or Terry making sure you'd washed before dinner.

"Nice calluses," he'd say in admiration. "Dip your fingers in a glass of your own piss. Seriously."

• • •

Lazy spring dragged on, though you couldn't tell it wasn't summer. Seasons aren't really relevant in Los Angeles: it's a whole metaphor out the window. The album—tentatively titled *Number Two*—was close to completion. Blake's bit—writing and singing the songs—was done, and now Jack got to enjoy the bits Blake couldn't stand: editing, mixing, mastering. The songs, which I'd heard in various states of undress, were great. "Time to Sing a Song" was the heir apparent to "Rock Around the Bed." Some of Blake's greatest nonsense was on there too: "The Color of the Crocodile," "Noon in June," "The Second Pear Tree," the song about Mei-Xing, now called "She May Sing."

I once heard a famous musician say that it's a musician's job only to make the best record he or she can, and to convince the label to release it. Then it's the record company's job to do the rest. But it's more complicated than that. First, you have to convince everyone else, your fellow musicians, that your vision is worth pursuing—and if you have a weird vision, a vision that doesn't fit into a vision pigeonhole, then that's all the more difficult. Next, you have to convince the record company; but then you have to be willing to work with them, and keep producing your very best. And that's what Blake had done. It was easy to forget that this hadn't even been his original vision, so easily had he rolled with the punches.

We had a listening party at the house, speakers up to eleven, after which we all dived in the pool with our clothes on. Denny was happy; the record company was happy; Andy was happy: "The ironically titled *Number Two*," he called it, meaning I suppose that it would actually go to number one. Though of course he could equally have meant that it wasn't shit.

Theme park blueprints on the wall; second album about to drop; a five-minute pilot for the cartoon series; TV knocking; an agent with no consideration for our mental or physical wellbeing—everything was perfect.

But then one night, Andy showed up unexpectedly wearing the look of a man without good news. He threw an open newspaper on the table. When I saw the full-page photo, the hairs on the back of my neck vibrated like antennae and my scalp started to itch ferociously.

The banner headline: "**CK AROUND THE BED!"

Beneath that: "Simeon's Shame".

The picture: Mum and I on the ride at Disneyland, though the publishers had been so demure as to put a black CENSORED sign across her front.

"Whoa!" said Jack with misplaced enthusiasm. Blake nodded and pushed his lower jaw forward, giving himself a Springsteen underbite. It was a difficult expression to interpret.

"Well, *I'm* not in that picture," said Andy. "I'm sitting three cars behind."

"I am!" said Jack, pointing where no one would ever look. All eyes turned to me.

"Sorry," I said. "God, I'm so sorry. What paper is that?"

Andy raised his eyebrows; Blake and Jack said nothing.

"We have a problem," said Andy. "It's this, and it's a problem that mercifully goes unmentioned in the article: what is depicted in this photo is, in the state of California, statutory rape."

"But I'm sixteen!" It just fell out of my mouth.

"In Connecticut, this would be entirely legal, unless the female in question was the male's guardian or athletic coach. But Disneyland is not in Connecticut. Disneyland is in California. And in California, this is illegal. And someone could go to jail; someone from a band that entertains children for a living. As I say: it goes unmentioned in the article. So our entire legal strategy depends on the fact that no one notices."

"Is that a good legal strategy?" I asked.

"It's not a legal strategy at all. It's a hope-against-hope."

I could hear only the ceiling fan and my own pulse. Blake got up, opened the freezer, and lobbed a choc ice at me.

"Look at it this way," Blake said. "There's nothing illegal happening. To start with, you can see Mum, and the shape of someone sitting beside her, and maybe the hands a bit down there. Nothing illegal."

"You're wrong, Blake. Aside from anything else—how could you let it happen? You're in charge out there. It's your ship."

"How could I let it happen?" Blake smiled. He raised both

of his hands, conducting a lengthy pause. "I let it happen, because I liked her; because I'm a man and she's a woman; because we're in each other's company a lot; because it just kinda happened."

I looked at the photo again. My face, my entire body except the white of one of my arms, was in the shadows. You couldn't see me at all. *We* all knew who it was, but no one else would have the faintest idea. And you couldn't see Blake either. You could only just see Becca and her redacted tits. I computed the collateral damage: Blake now knew about Mum and me. Deal with that later.

"I get it, Blake," said Andy. "I see what you're doing. But we have the band to think of as well."

"Firstly," said Blake, "nothing is going to happen. It's a black mark, sure, but it'll just blow over. We're Teflon; nothing sticks. If anyone says anything, then between us all here and one quick phone call to Lady Godiva, it was me in the front seat of that car, and that's what we say. Not that we'll ever have to say anything. Right, Sweet?" I nodded. "It'll never come to that. People are just excited to know there were some boobs flying around. She's Simeon's daughter. She's in a kids' band. Boobs! We see them at our shows the whole time. Does nothing for me."

"Can't you guys just keep out of fucking trouble?" said Andy, but I could tell he was relieved. I'd never heard him swear. "I mean, for fuck's sake: you're a kids' band, whether you like it or not."

"We like it!" said Blake.

"Then behave like a kids' band!"

"You mean behave like adults," said Blake. "Look at the photo! We're in fucking Disneyland! How much more like a kids' band can we behave? We've chosen to spend our day off at an amusement park! Besides, how do kids' bands behave? Give us a role model. The Muppets? Andy, they're being moved by other people; they have hands up their bums; they don't have bodily functions and they don't need to get laid. They're not real. The Monkees? That was a TV show. You know what was happening in real life: a lot of pussy and drugs. The Wombles? You may not know the Wombles, but that was Chris Spedding in a big rat suit eyeing up birds in the front row. The Beatles? Pot and the Maharishi. We're people. We have feelings. Prick us; do we not pop?"

"Okay. I get it." Andy sat back down. "But now I get to the bad news."

"What happened to the good news?" asked Jack sarcastically.

"There is good news, but this isn't it. Listen. The record company won't have it. They could rip up the contract over less. The press already got Becca for ignoring her only child; now she's flashing on a ride in Disneyland and every reader of this rag gets to see her. The kids get to see her."

"That's all she's doing, flashing," said Blake. "That's it. Calm down. It's California. Everyone goes topless these days. I egged her on. We'd been entertaining kids. We were letting our hair down. I'll speak to her."

"They want her out. She's tarnished the brand; she's damaged goods. Take action now. You have a great album in the can. They want to get behind it. They want to send it to number one. But I am not looking forward to my meeting tomorrow, unless you tell me what you have to tell me. And I expect to hear from you either tonight or tomorrow morning. You, Jack,"—somehow Jack was the only one Andy really trusted—"take some responsibility—get your head up from the magazines and out from behind that video camera! Blake, you're supposedly in charge. Act like it. And as for you . . ." He turned the daggers on me for the first time. "Sell some merch."

"Andy!" said Blake. He rarely got annoyed.

"I'll be cleaning this shit up."

"Before you go," said Blake, "do you know that joke about the guy, the lowest guy on the totem pole at the circus, who gives the elephant its enema and then has to clean up all its shit, and the doctor looks at the ulcerous running sores on his arm, and tells him he has to give up the job immediately, and the bloke says, incredulous: 'What? *And leave show-business*?' Andy, sorry. Thank you."

The Damager left without a word.

I puffed out my cheeks, expecting silence.

"Shall we order food?" asked Blake.

"We could go for a drive," said Jack.

"It's so far," said Blake. It's true. It sometimes felt far enough just walking to the car. We ordered Chinese and waited.

The paper lay between us, photo pulsating grainily. Blake chucked it over his shoulder: out of sight, out of mind. Jack raised an eyebrow: "Nice work, son. Honestly. Got to hand it to you." I didn't want to say anything until Blake spoke. Jack didn't care. He shrugged. "It's only natural. She's the perfect age for you. I would've. Anyone would've. Photo, though!" he pursed his lips and inhaled: "Nasty." It was a little code word with Jack and he always said it "narrrsty" like Kenneth Williams in a Carry On film. It was "nasty" if it was a personal problem, and "tedious" if it was professional. Blake kicked his legs over the back of the sofa so he was upside down.

"You didn't know, did you, Jack?" he asked. Had Blake known?

"Look. Don't start. I told you. I try not to pay attention to your private lives. I'm scared what I'll find."

"Well, of course you have your own to deal with." The tone was conciliatory, the remark anything but.

"Yes, maybe, but it's not splashed all over the papers, is it? It's still a *private* life. And what do you do, Blake?"

"Aside from having an affair with Mum, you mean? Well, I'm at the helm; I make sure everything is shipshape; I'm the cap'n. I have no time for a personal life. Aside from Mum, obviously. So," Blake turned his upside-down attention to me. He was upside-down fairly often, like he'd fallen through the center of the earth and come out the other side by mistake. "When did you find out about me and Becca, Sweet?"

I answered slowly, wondering when he had first known. "I guess it just became evident while the tour was going on." Noncommittal.

"Hmm," said Blake. "We tried to keep it a secret, but I guess it was always going to come out."

"Well, you notice little things," I said, warming up. Seemed kind of a fun game.

"What like?"

"Oh, you know, lingering hands, smeared lipstick, slightly too long spent drying hair, extended TV watching; sometimes the opposite—a lack of fondness when there should be more, and you think: weird."

"You guys are hilarious," said Jack without humor, as he got up.

"And yet one thinks one's being so clever," said Blake. His leg was playing an imaginary bass drum above his head like Tommy Lee.

"Why were you trying to keep it a secret, then?"

"Well," he said, reading my mind, "because it's exciting to keep something to yourself. And we're all cooped up in that bus and it's good to have something that's yours and no one else's. Isn't that right?"

"Yes, that's right."

"And I suppose the trouble is that sometimes, if you keep things a secret, it's fine when things are going well, but not so fine when things aren't going so well and you don't understand them, because then you've got no one to talk to. And you feel like you have to deal with everything yourself, when you could just be talking to someone who loves you."

"Yeah," I said.

And I started to cry.

Blake beckoned me over—he was still upside down—and wrapped his arms around me. That's how we stayed for a little while.

"I couldn't believe you guys did that in the coffins though," I said, slightly recovered.

"What?" asked Blake.

"Oh no," said Jack, shaking his head. "Not the coffins. Not necrophilia in the coffins. Just don't."

"Really?" asked Blake. "In the coffins?"

"No, no, no." I said. "Of course not. Never." I mean, technically it was trueish, though the distinction was Clintonian at best. Food honked from the driveway.

"It's up to you, Sweet," said Blake. "How would it be without Mum on the road? It's your call."

"That's unfair on the boy, Jimmy," said Jack.

"Is that unfair on you?" asked Blake.

"No. It's alright."

"But don't say anything you think you *should* say, because there is nothing you should say. Just answer: would you mind it if Becca wasn't there? Cos that's all I care about, whether you'd be unhappy."

"No," I said. "That'd be okay."

"Okay," said Blake. "Okay."

Blake made the call straightaway, while I unpacked the food; he then stretched out on the big sofa and said in his I-am-quoting-Alice-In-Wonderland voice: "They're dreadfully fond of beheading people here: the great wonder is there's anyone left."

Becca wasn't proud of herself, but, although I'd signed her death warrant, there was no need to fire her—no need for bad blood, or guilt. Her father had got to her: it was bad for the family business. He wanted her out, soon. She sought a graceful exit; she had a son to look after, a tricky family situation. It was all too intense.

And Mum was sacrificed: an offering that appeased all the gods.

Blake and Jack briefly pondered yesterday's model, the return of a twin, but it was agreed that only a woman could occupy the bass berth. I had expected a little more solidarity from Curtis, but he had Mei-Xing now, which trumped Becca. In fact, Curtis had a suggestion—a friend of his, Camille, whom he escorted to the house to say hi. It happened that I was the only one there.

The three of us sat by the pool.

She was a rangy, elegant black woman, self-contained and confident (not the full Grace Jones, but on the scale), her slinky panther body, emphasized by a shimmery dress, rippling to in-finity. If she was as good as Curtis said, there was absolutely no way Blake and Jack wouldn't want her in the band, but I couldn't see that dress jammed and feathered out on the road: she was too elegant. Bizarrely, she seemed not only to know what was re-quired, but happy to take it on the chin or wherever else it splashed.

"And Blake's your father?" A dazzling smile accompanied everything. I explained. "Ah," she continued, "I have a child of my own: Aslan."

"Oh, the more the merrier," I said. It's what Blake would

have said. Aslan: unexpected. "And where's Mister . . . er . . . Aslan's father." She'd said her last name but I didn't catch it.

"Aslan is a miracle," said Camille with rapturous joy. Okay: friend of Curtis's. *Aslan has two mummies.* I was getting good at this stuff. "I don't eat meat," she announced. She wanted all her cards on the table.

"Oh, that won't be a problem; catering is always very helpful. Mitchell sorts all that out."

"And you don't travel with any animals, do you?"

"Only Jack."

"I don't like animals." She'd named her son after one though.

"Oh, he's not that bad."

"I honor them, but I don't like them. I don't like to pet them and I don't want them inside my body. That's why I'm a vegetarian. The human being is a natural vegetarian, based on her anatomy and physiology."

"Well, we all eat meat like crazy, I'm afraid."

"I respect everyone's right to choose their own vitals. God said, 'Behold, I have given you every herb bearing seed, which is upon the face of all the earth, and every tree, in the which is the fruit of a tree yielding seed; to you it shall be for meat . . .'"

"Did He?"

"Genesis 1:29. Rastafarians use this as a justification for smoking marijuana."

"Oh well . . ."

"Of which I don't approve."

This was a possible obstacle. At no point did I have any idea which way the conversation was headed. She kept entertaining me for the next half-hour or so. Curtis hardly said a word.

Blake and Jack's car bumped into the driveway, and I headed them off at the front door: "Your new bass player is sitting outside with Curtis."

"And?" asked Blake.

"Shoo-in," I said. "Black, very beautiful, quite serious, slightly eccentric, possibly gay, definitely vegetarian, and Christian."

"Don't knock it," said Jack.

They played together the next day back on Gower, where

they'd first met Mum. Blake returned with a big smile: "And now we are four!"

Curtis had found us a new bass player with the minimum of fuss; perhaps he felt he was owed a favor. He wondered if we could split into two buses. Maybe he, Mei-Xing, and Camille could travel in one, nothing fancy; and Jack, Blake, Mitchell, and I—the family, he called us—in the other. Blake nodded. "Like, we'll have the Animal House party bus and you can have rainbow meditation and prayer meetings in yours?"

"Well, it's just that the smoking . . ." said Curtis. "And the staying up late . . ." He looked over at Mei-Xing who, very deliberately, finished his thought.

"We have been talking to Camille," she said, enunciating very clearly, "and she wants to bring Aslan with her. And we think of having school lessons on the bus too." It was the longest sentence we'd ever heard from her.

"The family expands!" said Blake. He loved it.

"Wow," said Jack. "Good work with the English." He meant the talking, rather than the English.

"All down to her new surroundings. You guys are to thank, too," said Curtis. That was generous.

"Thank you," said Mei-Xing with a bow. "And now, teatime."

"It's also Camille," said Curtis, keen to keep the buses on the agenda. "She's used to . . ." He paused. "You know she was on tour with Sting."

"Say no more," said Blake.

"Well, she's got to muck in," said Jack. "She's in a band."

"Onstage, of course," said Curtis. "But offstage . . ."

"I don't mind it," said Blake. "Jack?"

"Can we afford it?" Jack asked.

"Course we can," said Blake. "And even if we can't, we have a record label who'll charge it back to us later. Who's paying rent on this house?"

"Most bands break up when they start traveling separately," said Jack. "You know, singer goes first class, band in steerage."

"Yeah, but this isn't that, is it, Curtis? You've come to us. It's an upgrade. We're not relegating you."

"Besides," said Curtis as Mei-Xing returned with a tray, "it's your band, guys. We're just the in-laws. No need to make a big deal of it. I think it makes sense."

"Well, you'll have Mei-Xing; Camille has Aslan—that's one bus," said Blake, doing the math. "I'll have Sweet, and Jack has Randy. And Mitchell can play with himself."

"Narsty," said Jack.

"Mei-Xing's been drumming too," said Curtis.

"And Sweet has been playing the guitar," said Blake. "If Camille teaches her boy the bass, we can start a kind of replacement band. Genius."

As we ramped up to the release, events previously penciled were inked, and the calendar filled with o'clocks. The record company were appeased by Becca's exit, and the cartoonists considered the new latitudes Camille afforded them; Andy took Blake off to meet this radio programmer, that music supervisor; Jack and I went for drives up and down the coast, never very far.

There was one problem trying to get our attention from the sidelines. We shouldn't have ignored it.

The Parent Music Resource Center, aka the PMRC, was still causing trouble. It had been a few years since Tipper Gore first heard the lyrics to Prince's "Darling Nikki." 1985, the PMRC's Annus Mirabilis, had seen Tipper release her Filthy Fifteen, a list of the foulest songs ever written, including some really naughty ones by famously anti-establishment rabble-rousers like Cyndi Lauper and Sheena Easton. The list came with a dinky rating system (V for violence, O for occult, D/A for drugs and alcohol and X for sex), along with an accompanying series of "demands"—*Warning: Parental Advisory* stickers and so on—that the record companies, fearing a drop in sales, willingly caved to. The next year came the hearings, seen around the world on MTV, for which musicians like Jello Biafra, Frank Zappa, and John Denver came out against censorship (even though the PMRC thought Denver was going to speak in its favor; turned out he was actually more interested in becoming a spaceman). You'd have thought the whole thing would have died a death, but apparently the good state of Pennsylvania had only recently passed a bill requiring a warning label on any album with explicit lyrics. The argument rumbled on.

So much for rock music; how about music aimed directly at children? How extra-vigilant would the organization have to be with this new genre: rock music for kids? How much more pernicious was music without any adult constituency at all, which aimed to corrupt children directly? The truth is that no one, until now, had said anything remotely dodgy in a piece of music for children—oh, sure, "Puff the Magic Dragon," but I mean not *really*. Now the Wonderkids—causing riots, baring breasts, and singing songs that said . . . well, what exactly? Clearly, the Wonderkids were a special case.

Why did these society matrons start picking on us? Three things: one of them saw Altamont on TV, another heard Blake say "balls" at a live show (in the context of the pirate joke), and they all got an eyeful of the Disneyland photo. Perhaps initial fears were confirmed by the discovery that these Wonderkids had once been Wünderkinds, occasionally flaunting their evil with an umlaut, suspiciously reminiscent of the two floating about in Mötley Crüe.

The Wonderkids earned itself a case file larger than any other group. And, in a way, the PMRC was right, but for the wrong reasons. What the Wonderkids were doing was much more subversive than anything W.A.S.P. or Twisted Sister would ever manage. Those jokers were about as threatening as a Benny Hill sketch; they were merely being saucy. The Wonderkids were changing children forever. You still see it in their grown-up eyes. They look at you slightly *Midwich Cuckoo* or *Children of the Corn* when they talk about their early experiences of the band; you know they were taken young. One quick story: a guy came up to me recently—a music supervisor who later did the band an incredible service—and told me that he and his father got lost in the crowd once at a Wonderkids gig: "It was the first and last time that ever happened. I was five or so, and we went with my best friend and his dad. I was on my dad's shoulders and my friend was on his dad's shoulders, and our dads couldn't find each other, but we, the kids, thought it was so funny because we could see each other clearly above the crowd. And our dads were looking for each other for ages, but we never told them we could see each other; we were laughing so hard. It was my first experience of rock 'n' roll *and* my earliest memory of disobedience—at that show." You can only imagine what went down in the mosh pit.

Scrape the surface of any lyric; you can pretty much find whatever you want. When it came to the Wonderkids, there was certainly subterranean activity: the subconscious is an ugly thing, and Blake mined his without remorse. They were playing "Rock Around the Bed" when one Jacquelyn Belmer, our nemesis-to-be, had first seen them. Forget the girl who pushes Blake back on the kitchen table, what about the innocent little boy in verse one who's "got a rocket and knows how to fire it"? She didn't like the sound of that very much. And then, within minutes, blood and teeth flying on live television: what clearer sign of the cause and effect of the group's moral corruption?

And so the PMRC suggested a "break the ice" meeting with the Wonderkids, an invitation the Wonderkids respectfully declined. Then the PMRC asked for a sneak preview of the lyrics to the new album (surely even they couldn't object to an album called *Number Two*?) to predetermine the nature of its "concerns," a request the Wonderkids did not dignify with a response. And then, much to WBA's disquiet, the PMRC, feeling rebuffed, sent out a press release stating that they had "earmarked" the Wonderkids. They had nothing on the band for the time being, but the lyrics had to be submitted ("voluntarily") and a judgment would be made. A sticker would cause problems. Blake refused: "It's the stupidest thing I've ever heard. They can listen to the lyrics when the record comes out. Like everyone else."

When Norm Bloch himself turned up at Lookout, we knew it was trouble. It was the only time I saw him in the fleshy flesh. I observed proceedings from the kitchen.

"You need some art on the walls," he said, trailing Andy behind him. "We put you in here?"

"Yes," said Blake. "Thank you."

"No problem. Enjoy. Now about these Washington Wives," he said. "What they're doing is a disgrace. It's un-American. It's an affront to free speech. Chuck Berry wouldn't have got one song past them."

"Absolutely," said Blake. Norm didn't like interruption.

"But the fact is, they're real, they're here, they're now and we need you to give them your lyrics. We can't have a sticker on a kids' record."

"They can't sticker a record they haven't seen the lyrics to."

"I think what Norm is trying to say . . ." said Andy the diplomat.

"What Norm is trying to say," said Norm, "is you should *give* them the lyrics so we don't get a sticker."

"They'll be no sticker," said Blake. "There's nothing remotely offensive on the record—no swearing; no reference to drugs or alcohol; no sex, well, not that anyone but I would know about, and certainly no reference to the occult."

"Then hand the lyrics over," said Norm with an amused shrug. "Who cares?"

"It's the principle of the thing."

Norm went from benign to beetroot red fury in a second: "THERE ARE NO FUCKING PRINCIPLES IN ROCK 'N' ROLL! DO YOU WANNA SELL RECORDS OR NOT? GIVE THEM THE FUCKING LYRICS!"

Andy, in desperation, started managing. "We'll get you the lyrics, Norm." He gestured Blake to be quiet. "Maybe the label could transcribe the lyrics and hand them over and Blake wouldn't feel like he . . ."

"I might feel that way," said Blake.

Norm looked at him and shook his head. "I thought you were smart," he said and as he walked, "I thought you wanted to teach the world to sing." His car revved in the driveway while Andy attempted unsuccessful peace talks through the window.

"Jeez, Blake," Andy said on his return. "That's Norm. Norm Bloch."

"Is that who that was? He should watch out for his heart."

"He's not used to people saying no."

"Then he shouldn't put people in a situation where they have no choice."

"Why am I always having to clear up after you guys? I haven't even got a car now to drive me back to the office. You know, Blake, you just said no; you may never have the chance to say yes again."

"Well, you can't say Norm without saying 'No.'" Blake was just trying that one out, but even he wasn't convinced by his timing.

"Guys," said Andy. "Don't come over here behaving like the Sex Pistols. It wasn't the Pistols who broke; it was the Police and Duran Duran. You don't stand for anything. You're a kids' band."

The label handed over the lyrics. Andy told Norm that Blake had seen sense, but it was too little, too late. *Number Two* went unstickered. But Blake had won the wrong battle.

The PMRC's problem was that they couldn't quantify the corruptive potential of music itself. They could only run the rule over naughty words, saucy record covers, and what-the-butler-saw videos, and as the Wonderkids had none of these, they slipped through the net. But PMRC couldn't accept that there was a realm over which they had no claim—no good fascist ever does—so they invented a "Mini Me" version of themselves, to keep an eye on the new genre of music known as Kiddie Rock. This new pressure group called themselves MOMs—Morality Over Music—and they were even more vindictive than their progenitors.

The innocence of America's children was at stake.

And the Wonderkids were Public Enemy Number One.

We first saw Jacquelyn, the MOM-in-chief, on television, in her pearls and her red business suit—a proto-Palin without the ammo. Jack remarked without irony: "Now, her; her, I could go for. Look at the rack on that."

"Go on, Jackie Boy," said Blake. "Give her a ring. Sort her out."

12

"Ever get the feeling you've been cheated?"

THE MOMENT WE HIT THE ROAD AGAIN, THINGS GOT WORSE.

On the very first day, Blake and I found ourselves in a cab to a radio show. He was tetchy. He'd just had twelve sorts of trouble wrangling his new guitar case into the vastly empty trunk. Mitchell, who'd been off with some band supporting Pearl Jam in his "spare time" (his verdict: "The kids at our shows are way more unruly") wouldn't join the tour until the opening night. I was filling in.

Blake hated even *carrying* a guitar. Hard cases were designed to be unwieldy. They didn't fit where they should; they hit the person standing behind you; they fell where you leaned them; they bruised the side of your knee; their buckles buckled; their handles broke.

Next problem: the driver. All cab drivers want to be able to say they had that [*insert name here*] in the back of their cab once, so they see the guitar, and they get nosey. Blake had always been good at this stuff. The guy behind the wheel would say: "So, who do you play with?" and Blake would tell him and then he'd say "Oh, yeah?"—which conversation leads nowhere—or "Oh, never heard of you." Rude. Inevitably the cabbies *hadn't* heard of the band, because they only listened to the classic rock station, the rabble-rousing right-wing talk show, or the news. Even then, Blake would take it all in good turn.

But here we were in Boston, and the cab driver says: "So we're going over to WFNX; you a musician, huh?" And Blake just said: "No." Killed it. And the driver said: "Oh, I thought maybe the guitar . . ." And Blake said: "No." And the guy said: "Oh, maybe it's a favor for a friend, huh?" And Blake said: "Do you know where we can get any prostitutes round here?" The cab driver laughed awkwardly.

Something was weighing Blake down. The absence of Mum? The spat with MOMs? Norm? Misgivings about Camille? Perhaps just the long tour ahead. When we finally got to the station, after an aggressive silence that ended only when the cabbie turned on the radio which continually announced the imminent presence of Blake Lear of the Wonderkids, the cabbie said: "So you're Blake Lear, huh?" And Blake, without confirming it, asked the cabbie for a receipt, and the guy said, which they always say: "Is a blank one okay?" and Blake said: "No, write me one out please." He didn't even want the receipt. He was just wasting the man's time.

"Everything okay?" I asked as we stood in the radio station foyer, call letters above us like the Hollywood sign.

"Yeah. A whole tour of explaining myself suddenly doesn't seem so appealing."

And I said, all child-is-the-father-to-the-man: "Well, it's not maybe so good for you to go around being rude, so how about you let me do the talking from now on? And you can just sit back and relax, and I'll be friendly. Chicken DAT!"

He ruffled my hair: "Okay, sport," he said. "Sorry. You take over."

"And I'll carry the guitar too."

Blake took to wearing a Walkman, though quite often there wasn't any music playing; it just kept idiots away. I did the talking, following scripts he'd unconsciously written for me. I'd so admired the way he handled everything that I just let myself kind of become him. It was much easier on me, summoning this recent memory of him. Greg would have assumed this role in the old days. That's kind of how I saw myself.

• • •

Separate buses made sense. There was no point in Blake's increasingly hectic promotional schedule inconveniencing everyone.
Curtis, Mei-Xing, Camille, and Aslan had the "school bus": lessons, organized games, bedtime stories. All the kid's videos graduated there. Needless to say, there was no smoking, not even in
the back, which had been designated the meditation room, tai chi,
et cetera. The food was healthy—always a nice pile of trail mix
and yogurt-covered pretzels in neat, color-coded snack cups—and
the drinks non-alcoholic. One of the coffins was converted into a
makeshift library; in another, bungee cords secured a collection
of board games. I mean: it was cool in its way, for sure. It also
seemed a little like an alien universe.

"Their own nuclear family," I said.

"Nuclear? *Un*clear," Jack answered. "Weird."

"Uncle Arly," said Blake. "Unclearly."

During soundcheck and gig, Mei-Xing played nanny, but the
rest of the day Camille was actively mother-henning. There'd
been no honeymoon period. Camille was no sooner in the band,
and playing well, than she started to get under Blake's skin. Part
of it was Aslan. Sure the kid was quiet, but he hid behind her
knees and you could never get a feel for him. There were games
to play, jokes to make, fun to be had with this six-year-old addition to the family; it was as if the boy had been expressly instructed to stay away from Blake, from us. When Blake referred
to them as "the Lion, the Witch, and her Wardrobe," I knew things
were going askew. We needed Mum.

In our WonderBus, the sieve we'd gone to sea on, things
went on as usual, but with greater latitude. With no Becca and no
Curtis to ensure best behavior, the merry prankster atmosphere
no longer confined itself to the back of the bus. Blake slept there,
rarely changing out of his pajamas. It was his nest. He called it
China. When he got out of the bus, even at the beginning of the
tour, he looked scruffier than before.

Because Blake was emperor of China, Jack had the front to
himself, and he spread out as never before. Sure, there was
Mitchell and me, but all Mitchell required was the Captain's chair
beside Randy and a small berth at the table where he could finesse
the ever-evolving itinerary. I, on the other hand, had the run of the

bus. I even had my own special seat on the front sofa. I didn't ask for it—it became mine, and Jack sat anywhere but there. I was the glue that held the bus together. Jack only went back if he wanted to get stoned, so I'd pass messages back and forth: what Blake had in mind for the gig, when we were going to eat. Mitchell didn't like the fumes, though it wasn't in his road-managerial nature to complain: we moved coffins as far from China as possible.

In the outside world, despite the fall-out with Norm, it was onwards and upwards. The tour was sold out, the second record was climbing the charts—the real charts, this time. But in the undergrowth of WonderWorld, there was a rustling. There was little enmity among the troops, but there were different needs. When we drew up somewhere, it was Mitchell and I who made a point of heading over to the other bus, just to be friendly. The two factions now met only backstage and at soundcheck, and increasingly Blake took a separate dressing room, at first with Jack, then on his own. Only I was allowed free access between the different parties.

"Oh," I heard Mitchell tell Camille. "He's just got a mild case of LSD."

"Blake's on acid?" she asked, aghast.

"No. Lead Singer Disease. I've seen worse."

Perhaps Camille assumed this was what it had always been like, but of course it had been *nothing* like this. Curtis seemed to prefer it. Perhaps he'd only managed to survive the WonderBus with gritted teeth and an ever tenser jaw.

It got to the point where the two factions seemed surprised to bump into each other offstage, as though one bus had forgotten the other existed. The drivers, however, carried on regardless. Randy and his counterpart, who was called Beau but was known only as Randy 2, coordinated their movements via CB radio, even the synchronized circling of a Walmart parking lot in the middle of the night for a pee-dump.

It started with the most innocuous thing.

A support act had been thrust upon us. Having an opener at all went against Blake's wishes, but he gave in to Andy, heaven knows why—perhaps it was an apology. A solo acoustic act was the compromise. The first lasted one night: his name was Jeff Trap, playing under the name Mr. Guitar. He was unnaturally shaggy and Blake christened him the Young Bob Dylan. His less-than-twenty-four-hour career as our support act is indicative of where things now stood.

The Young Bob Dylan shuffled from foot to foot as he introduced himself in the dressing room. He made the tactical error of taking one of Jack's special beers out of the fridge, then asked all the wrong questions—was Aslan Curtis's son? Was Mei-Xing my girlfriend? It couldn't have gone much worse, his wholesome folksiness notwithstanding.

"Thanks for letting me travel on your bus, by the way," he said enthusiastically.

"I beg your pardon?" asked Mitchell, otherwise involved with a fax machine.

"Letting me travel on your bus. Thanks."

"Have a good show, Mr. Guitar," said Mitchell. And out went the Young Bob Dylan to play to a crowd who had never heard of him, didn't want its time wasted before the headline act, and wouldn't be won over. In fact, all they'd get was bored, thus making the Wonderkids' job more difficult. That was why the whole support act idea had been nixed in the first place.

The moment he left the room, Curtis offered a tentative: "Mmm. Mitchell?"

"Everything okay, Mr. K.O.?"

"Is he traveling with you guys?"

"Not that I know of."

"Only we never heard anything about him traveling on ours."

"No," said Camille, too promptly.

"Though he seems like a nice guy," added Curtis.

"Is this one of Blake's faits accomplis?" asked Camille, as though it was only the most recent in a long list of insults.

"Ladies and gentlemen," said Mitchell. "Calm. Kid seems under the impression that's what's happening; perhaps he's been misinformed. I'll talk to Blake. Perhaps he intends Mr. Guitar to travel in our bus. You heard anything about it, Sweet?"

I shook my head. It seemed unlikely. Things on our bus didn't bear too much scrutiny.

As Mitchell left, Curtis and Camille turned to each other in stage whisper. It was as if they'd been waiting for just such a slight, some real indignity. That's what happens when you split people up. The focus goes. It's a bit less of the all-for-one and a bit more of the every-bus-for-itself. I mean, each bus had eight coffins: four spare—we were living like kings. Even so, I wouldn't have let the Young Bob Dylan on the bus for all the tea in China.

Mitchell returned. "No cause for alarm. It's a miscommunication." Mr. Guitar had just started his strumming. Mitchell climbed up to turn off the tannoy. We didn't need the added guilt of having to listen to the guy's performance hissing through. "Blake hadn't heard a thing about it." Camille didn't believe a word. "A promise has been made by someone, not us, and this isn't our responsibility. I'll sort it out. Carry on as usual."

The next day in the parking lot, we were ready to roll, when out of the hotel, axe slung over back campus-style, saunters Mr. Guitar, just about to board one or another of these huge, luxurious tour buses, then set out on the trip of a lifetime, a trip he could possibly only afford (given how little he'd be making) because the Wonderkids, those good old Wonderkids, had generously offered the guy (or reluctantly agreed, those amusing old curmudgeons, to offer the guy) a ride. And he'd probably never been on a bus before. He was looking forward to it, the space, the luxury, ignoring America as it rolled by. He probably felt like a million dollars as he strolled out of that lobby.

Mitchell positioned himself at the top of the steps and Mr. Guitar found his way blocked. Randy fixed his gaze straight ahead, hands on the wheel.

"Hi," said Mr. Guitar, all friendly.

"Good morning," said Mitchell, without moving.

"Can I, er . . .?" asked Mr. Guitar.

"No," said Mitchell. "Sorry."

"Oh, okay. Am I on the other, er . . ." He looked to his right. Mitchell shook his head. His body language told Jeff all he needed to know. "Oh, my manager said that he'd arranged that I could go on the bus."

"No one asked us," said Mitchell.

"Oh," said Mr. Guitar. "Isn't there room?" Bit naive.

"We can't take you."

"Well, there's no need to be a dick about it," said The Young Bob Dylan. Mitchell *was* being a dick about it, and it pained him. He knew he was in the wrong.

"Sorry. No one asked us."

"Can you at least give me a lift to the next venue? I don't know how I'm going to get there otherwise."

"Rent a car?" said Mitchell, then over his shoulder. "Randy, let's do it."

"Leaving the flop box," Randy rasped into his CB, and the buses pulled out, leaving a forlorn Mr. Guitar with his tote bag in one hand and his guitar slung over his back. We never saw him again. Either he was pissed off, or he literally couldn't afford to make the gigs. Whichever, he was never to be heard of again.

Mitchell scowled and took his place at the desk. Then as an afterthought, he shouted down to Blake:

"Fuck you very much, Blake!"

"Fuck you too," shouted Blake. "Hey, Sweet!"

Mitchell shook his head and sighed as he flipped through the itinerary. I sat next to him. That wasn't the way you did business. It wasn't kind. Blake shouted my name from the back once more. Then the moment I finally got up, as though he'd known, he yelled: "Doesn't matter!"

An acoustic support act was bad enough; one who expected to travel with us worse; but worst of all would be the support act who stayed the course. It was as if Norm insisted on the Kidders, another of his signings, as a punishment. The fact is: at this precise moment, in this small world, a warm-up slot for the Wonderkids was like opening for U2. Money may have exchanged hands. I have no idea if you paid to play back then.

After the mistreatment meted out to the Wonderkids by bigger acts in their fledgling Wunderkind years, you'd have thought that Blake and Jack would be extra vigilant when it came to their own support acts. But that's the cycle of abuse, isn't it? You promise yourself you won't do to your kids what your parents did to you, and then you do.

I actually liked the Kidders. They put on a good show, with none of the Wonderkids' special sauce: just songs and vibrant personalities. Offstage they were hardly less dynamic, and they gravitated towards Curtis and Camille's dressing room, where they continued playing to an even smaller audience. The show never stopped; the bonhomie was unceasing and a little tiring, but they meant well, and a little friendly enthusiasm, even a cheery "good morning," goes a long way. Sure it was cramped, and their gestures were extravagant, but they didn't clock on and off like Blake in his new mode. He didn't seem to pay them any attention; I'm sure he said hello, but he didn't want his schedule tampered with or affected in any way. He didn't want them hanging around at soundcheck; he didn't want them in the dressing rooms; life was the way he liked it, and he was just stoned enough not to realize it was all a bit selfish. The shows—and I know I say this a lot—never suffered.

"Give 'em a year," Jack said.

The Kidders traveled in a beat-up van that looked like they'd been following the Dead since 1969. The four of them, without road manager or roadie, piled into it at the end of every night and drove off: where? To sleep by the roadside? A cheap motel? Crash with friends? None of them drank. None of them smoked. They knew what they were doing.

One night, both bands done, I didn't feel so great, and I feared a repeat of the Seuss incident. Blake stayed at the booth—it astounded me that his good cheer in the melee never wavered—as did Vern, who was starting to stash the merch. My stomach felt funny, so I went out to get some air, a can of Coke in my hand. (I used to think the fizz helped.) I decided to head to the bus, maybe even have a lie down. It was curtained as usual, locked I assumed. But when I stretched out the lanyard from which my key dangled, the door opened with the merest pull.

I had hardly turned down the aisle when I realized I was not alone. Far from it. In the dim light, all I could see were the great cratered moons of Jack's buttocks as he ploughed in and out of a woman—unknown, unknowable, given that all I could see were high heels either side of Jack's ears. Neither Jack nor his partner knew I'd come in. My initial reaction, jaded in the extreme, was: "I can't believe they're using *my* place on the bus." This would have been my opening verbal gambit, but I just stood there, not knowing whether to clear my throat, or walk past to my bunk, where it had been my intention to lie down, or just leave. The door fell closed behind me, and Jack looked around, noting my presence, frowning, then turning back again without missing a stroke. I have no idea if the woman knew I was there. I left, slamming the door. She knew now.

I was more annoyed than upset. You get inured to these kinds of things, and though I'd never been exposed to anyone's shunting arse before, I wasn't shocked. But I guess I was shocked that I wasn't shocked; shocked that it hadn't happened earlier. And I wanted to lie down. I shouldn't have had to run that gauntlet just to lie down in my own fucking bed.

My next thought was the other bus. I was welcome there, despite the decontaminated atmosphere. And so I knocked and gamely skipped on, trying to leave my recent shitty experience on the asphalt of the parking lot. I even made a polite attempt to wipe my feet: their bus had that effect.

"Come in," said Camille.

Everything was a picture. Camille was applying some preparation to Curtis's dreadlocks and Mei-Xing seemed to be teaching Aslan to read. I mean, it was truly picturesque, very Happy Valley. There were fresh cut flowers on the central table, and the whole place smelled like a girl's bedroom, pink and cleansed. Music was playing: something very tasty, maybe even Sting playing some kind of lute. On the sideboard sat a basket of bananas, grapes, and apples, just next to a blender so pristine it looked mint. It was all lovely, and completely uninviting. I felt like a cancerous leper. It was too much; it was the Stepford bus. It had the astonishing effect of making me feel even worse. It was like they were all members of a religious cult. And as it happens, they were mostly wearing white.

"Hey," said Camille with a huge smile, extending an arm of invitation as if from Heaven. "Would you like a smoothie?"

"Oh," I said, as my nausea returned with a vengeance. I was sullying the place, bringing it down to my level. I was crapping all over their nice carpet then stepping in it and walking all over the rugs, smearing it on their pillows for good measure. "Any sign of, er, Jack?"

"Jack?" asked Mei-Xing.

"No Jack," said Curtis. "Anybody seen Jack?"

Nobody had.

"Right," I said, "Okay. Thanks. I'll be off then."

"You can stay if you like," said Camille. "We've got all the drinks you like." That wasn't true: it would all be diet this and no-fructose-corn-syrup that. She was going to offer to teach me macramé or finger knitting.

"And," Curtis said, "Mei-Xing wondered if you wanted to . . ."

"Yeah, I'd love to, but I have to go now."

I honestly felt like vomiting.

Standing outside, I took one look back at the gig, then one look at my bus, then one look at the bus behind me, and I felt like weeping in frustration. I just wanted to be alone—without anyone—and there was nowhere. Perhaps Blake hit the same wall every now and then. The only possible refuge was the Kidders' van, dwarfed in the shadows of the two tour buses. It was unlocked—typical: hippies—and I laid myself out on one of the seats, closed my eyes and tried to zone out.

Finally, I was joined by a couple of Kidders.

"Hey, man," the girl said, Regina was her name. She called herself Reggie "like Audrey Hepburn in *Charade*." Cute. "Did we leave the van open?"

"Yeah," I said wisely. "Thought I'd just lie here and keep an eye on it for you."

"Thanks, man," she said. "Good show, tonight, huh? Your guys were on fire." They were? Good.

"So what's your story?" she said, handing me a bottle of backstage Coke. "Is he really your father?"

• • •

The wheels kept rolling, but something was missing. Fortunately, the audience had no idea. Blake could always get lost in the performance, and he was still writing new songs, but it wasn't the same. It had been a perfectly amicable separation, tarnished only by small moments of distrust, but no infidelity; the band's dealings were now purely professional.

The unspoken truth was that there was every reason, commercially, to keep going. The Wonderkids were still a winning formula. They'd found a way to coexist fairly peacefully, and, with a packed calendar, the new single riding high, invitations to go on TV rolling in by the day, it seemed like the road could go on forever. A dysfunctional family band: go figure—it wasn't the first time.

The first invitation from a major late night talk show was cause for celebration. The Wonderkids were known primarily as children's artists, so this was a real accolade: no children are up at 11 p.m. (East Coast), let alone midnight (West Coast and Central). This was for the parents, because the band had a hit and made great music. No other reason. Blake and Jack were thrilled. Andy was suddenly everywhere: "Okay. You should do the single."

"Agreed," said Blake.

"We want this to present the seriously fun side of the band, and we want the network on our side. Let them know exactly what we're going to do."

"Okay. So you basically want us to plan something like exactly what caused us so much trouble last time, but tell people in advance."

"Look, Blake," said Andy. "We don't want to give MOMs cause for complaint."

"Leave it with us," said Mitchell. "Blake, let's talk."

It's a wonder people took MOMs seriously, but their PMRC affiliation got column inches, and Jacquelyn Belmer's proto-MILF act didn't hurt. She called the Wonderkids "one of the greatest evils facing America today." Like Communism? Like the Beatles when John said they were bigger than God? Jesus Christ.

"They're afraid of rock 'n' roll," said Blake. "And they're afraid of us. So we should give them more rock 'n' roll. The whole history of rock 'n' roll."

He laughed MOMs off, but it was an irritant. He didn't seem to understand that there was cause for concern; the members of the band were not ideal children's entertainers. Two of them were fine—the two that didn't matter. But the other two . . .

That night we were on the road, and I picked up some random video I found in the front: *Laura*, scribbled in capital letters on the spine in Sharpie. Jack had already gone to bed.

"Oh yeah," said Blake, who was making snacks. "Great flick. Clifton Webb. Gene Tierney. You'll love it."

"Shall we watch up here, Mitchell?"

"Throw that classy entertainment on, sir."

I slotted in the VHS, and sat back in my usual place, recently shifted a few feet to the right of a stain that I feared was the legacy of Jack's humping. Before I'd made myself comfortable, a stereophonic groaning indicated that this wasn't the black-and-white classic Blake and Mitchell had imagined. Mitchell looked up. Blake turned from the kitchenette. We were confronted with a close-up of a screaming woman in the middle of shuddering sex. All you could see was her face. The moaning was earsplittingly loud.

"What the bejeesus is that?" A rare communication from Good Buddy.

"Yeah, yeah, sorry," said Blake nonchalantly, as corn popped in the microwave.

Mitchell had the presence of mind to reach for the remote control, mute the sound, then turn off the television. It's a funny thing to admit, but I'd never seen pornography (though I'd heard Jack talk about it enough), and it genuinely shocked me. At first I'd thought someone was killing her. If this was pornography, rather than, like, a slasher movie, was it always so amateur-looking?

"That was yours?" I asked Blake.

"Yeah, yeah."

Mitchell laughed: "What's it doing spilling out here? Keep it back in your lair. We'd only need the presence of a young child and a representative from MOMS for the moment to be complete."

"Well, thank the Lord that the Happy Campers weren't here," said Blake, as he ejected the tape. He winked at me.

Subject broached, I said, "Yeah, it's a bit like a religious cult on that bus. Like they're all going to be wearing purple raiment soon. It's all a bit Heaven, you know, where nothing ever happens."

"Hmmm." Mitchell declined to commit himself. I remembered what he'd said: all the children were under his wing.

"Well, maybe we'll just put HELL on the front of this bus, and HEAVEN on the front of theirs. Can you do that, Randy?"

"If you want it to say HELL on the front of the bus, then that's what it'll say."

Turning to China, Blake said to Mitchell: "Get us that hair dryer, man, will you?"

"I'm not going to get you a hair dryer that you never use."

"Just please get me the hair dryer. Good night."

After the door closed, Mitchell casually remarked: "Wasn't his tape."

"Doesn't seem like his kind of thing." Mitchell didn't answer, just shrugged without looking at me. "Wasn't mine," I added, unnecessarily defensively.

"Wasn't mine either," said Mitchell. "And we know who carries the video camera. Things are bubbling."

Once, around this time, Blake and I were walking down a hotel corridor, ready for "the out," rolling our suitcases, me carrying his uke. As usual he was a pace or two behind. We had left the room talking about some or other trivia, nothing of importance at all. And after about fifteen paces, maybe a quarter of the way to the elevator, Blake faded out absentmindedly mid-sentence, and I took up the conversation, finishing up with a "Right? Right, Blake?" He didn't answer. I eventually looked behind me to find him half a corridor away, standing propped on his rollie, staring at the wall, in tears.

"Blake? Blake? What's wrong?"

He awoke as if from a trance.

"Nothing," he said, surprised to find himself crying.

"Nothing?" I asked.

"Nothing," he said again, and shook his head, as if to shake away the tears. "Really. I don't know what happened. Just, nothing."

"Everything?" I asked, encouraging him towards the elevator, wondering whether it might be better to go back to the room.

"No," he laughed. "Nothing. C'mon, let's go."

Heaven thought Hell was out of control. Hell thought Heaven holier-than-thou. News of the pristine blender and the proffered smoothie was further evidence of sanctimoniousness.

Jack hung a doctored dartboard on the inside door of the toilet; he'd assigned a quadrant of the board to each member of the school bus, just like the one Blake had seen at school. With the door open, he could play darts pretty successfully without putting anyone's eye out.

"It's mean," said Mitchell. "Take it down. Or put my name on there as well."

"It's only a bit of fun," said Jack.

"Oh let him play darts. Can you get me a pig's head?" asked Blake.

"No, I cannot get you a pig's head."

"I thought you said if I asked you for something then you'd make sure I got it."

"I did say that, Blake, but I then said, very quietly, under my breath, 'unless it's a pig head.' Because that's where I draw the line."

Blake and Jack were asking Mitchell to take sides, and this he could not do. Every now and then, they'd ask me to swing a vote this way or that, but Mitchell wouldn't be drawn. At one point there was a "clear the air" band meeting. Blake showed up wearing comically aggressive war paint.

"What do you think?" he said. Camille tutted. "Thought I might put it on for the show. Also, Mitchell, we should have face painting at the gigs. Kids love face painting." It was a great idea.

"My children," said Mitchell. "You need some guidance from the adult world. I am from that world. Let me be your guide." Blake only wanted to talk about further plans for the

show, and Camille and Curtis kept their counsel. It never de-
volved into a slanging match; better if it had. Such meetings only
polluted the air further. Blake and Jack were getting a kick out of
the tension: they were the bad boys, onstage and off. Back on the
bus, Blake even went so far as to say: "I know it's a bit awkward,
but it makes for a good show. We're still playing really well. And
the kids know what they want to see."

"Blake," said Mitchell. "Don't do it this way. You could just
ask them to be like that onstage. They're good. They can do it.
You're getting off on this. That's the problem."

"How about that hair dryer?"

"You know what, Blake? You're losing the plot."

"Who needs a plot?" Blake asked as he headed back and
then, over his shoulder, as I knew he would: "Nonsense resists
plot."

Mitchell closed the door firmly and invited me to sit opposite him: "I'll tell you, and you only, who needs a plot, my friend:
Blake, this band, this tour. It needs a plot and it needs a structure,
and I, the road manager, am the one who provides it, because
without me this would spin out of control. Blake can only do
what he does—lovable, laughable Blake—because of the structure, because of me, and because of you: he needs us. Trouble is:
he doesn't know it."

"No, I . . ." but I couldn't even finish the sentence.

"Don't," he said. "Don't try. And besides we need him too.
There's no show without the singer."

Mitchell and I were the intermediate beings, licensed to float
freely between Heaven and Hell.

The stage was a safe haven—the show was sacrosanct; to
admit any more mayhem would have been suicidal—but backstage was a no-man's-land with endless potential for practical
jokes and small indignities. Most of it was harmless; all of it was
childish; some of it was funny (spurious announcements delivering misinformation only to Heaven's dressing room, that kind
of thing). Heaven remained aloof. Besides, it was mostly just
Blake doing what he did onstage, being Blake. In Heaven itself,

the angels thought themselves safe, so it was always likely that their bus would be the scene of the worst outrage.

"Curtis seemed to be enjoying his smoothie tonight," Jack remarked out of nowhere, flicking absentmindedly through a catalog of guitar cables. The smoothie had become symbolic of all that was precious about Heaven. Mitchell had recently stepped off our bus, so Hell could talk freely. The voice of reason had come to be associated with the forces of good purely because he refused to align himself with "us": he had to be doubly fair, doubly annoying.

"Yeah, it was kind of a luminous green. Looked a bit spooky," I said. "Full of vitamins."

"Spirulina, probably," said Blake pointedly.

"Wheatgrass."

"Bee pollen." Blake over-enunciated every syllable.

"And pee," said Jack.

"Pee pollen?" asked Blake, interest piqued. "Don't tell me he's fucking drinking his own pee. My friend had a boyfriend who used to. Didn't Roger Daltrey? Anyway, don't tell me Curtis's drinking his own pee."

"Much better than that," Jack said. "He's drinking mine."

Silence. Blake started to giggle: "No, no, no, no, no."

"Yes, yes, yes, yes, yes. I was caught a bit short and someone was in the toilet, so I nipped on their bus, and the blender was right there with this green concoction in it and . . ."

"Need you say more?" asked Blake. They were two brothers in the playground.

"I needn't, but I could."

"Guys," I said. "That is debased." They looked at me, giggling. "You pissed in a man's smoothie, Jack. They're drinking your urine." They couldn't stop laughing.

"I'm going to get a big conch," said Blake, apropos of nothing it seemed to me.

"Nasty!" said Jack.

"Blow it at the beginning of the show . . ."

"And then smash it at the end!"

I looked at them nonplussed.

"*Lord of the Flies*," they said at the same moment.

I should have told Mitchell.

13

"The brown acid that is circulating around us is not specifically too good."

THE SMOOTHIE WAS THE ABSOLUTE NADIR, BUT ONLY THE THREE OF us knew about it. Thus, the official nadir was not the urine (which, had anyone else known, would have led to the band's immediate demise) but the gun. "Mitchell," Blake had asked at some point. "Can you pick me up a vaguely realistic toy gun? Second thought, it doesn't have to be that realistic."

"No one will stand for a gun onstage," said Mitchell.

"Of course not. Just for me."

That forgotten, and after enough time had elapsed to serve his purposes, Blake made an unexpected cameo in the other dressing room. He was in a bad mood. MOMs had started picketing the gigs—I still have some of the pamphlets—and a guy, not realizing who Blake was, had tried to force some propaganda on him as he went backstage from the bus. There had been a minor scuffle.

"Hey, Mitch," asked Blake, "do you have that fake gun?"

"Yes, hold on. I was wondering when you'd ask. A couple of options . . ." He delved inside a plastic bag with a big red logo.

"I don't want toy guns around Aslan," said Camille.

"Oh," said Blake. "It's just a silly thing."

From the bag, Mitchell pulled out a gun. But it was not a toy

gun. It was his gun; his real gun. He looked at it, initially horrified, then guilty, like Cary Grant at the UN in *North by Northwest*.
Immediately, Blake took unnecessary control of a nonexistent
hostage crisis: "Mitchell, now calm down! Take it easy, man!
Think of the children!"

Without a word, Mitchell placed the gun down, barrel carefully pointed at the wall, dialed the combination on his case,
opened it, removing the toy gun Blake had somehow snuck inside,
which he pocketed, put the real gun back in its rightful place, and
locked the case again: "Blake, in the bus now."

"Just a bit of fun," said Blake, daring anyone else to laugh,
adding in mitigation: "It didn't go off." I calculated the lengths
Blake had gone to: learning the combination, substituting the
guns, patiently waiting for the perfect moment. It was an impressive amount of work for a bizarre payoff.

"IN THE BUS!" shouted Mitchell, face red, veins bulging up
his neck. It was the only time I ever heard him shout.

"Unbelievable," said Curtis, after they left, Mitchell's anger
still echoing around the room. "Unbelievable."

"Is everything okay?" Camille asked me, genuinely concerned.

"Yes," I said, thinking of the urine they'd been drinking, the
dartboard, Camille's horror at the very possibility of a *toy* gun.

"Was that a real gun?" asked Aslan with reverence.

"No," said Camille, at the exact moment Mei-Xing said
"Yes."

Nobody moved. I sat.

"Are you worried about him?" asked Curtis. "Seriously."

I mean, I *was* worried about him, but, curiously, I wasn't
worried about the gun gag. Could it be that the whole prank was
revenge for the hair dryer? It was harmless enough. No one was
"waving a gun around," whatever they said later.

"A little, I guess."

"Do you want to come and hang out on our bus more often?
Travel with us?"

"We can play Monopoly," said Mei-Xing with a kind of smile.

It actually sounded appealing: Monopoly and a smoothie.
Of course, I'd blend it myself.

• • •

Though Mei-Xing and I, victims of backstage apartheid, rarely spoke, she hovered near the booth, and I got the feeling that, despite the differences between our buses, she wanted to hang out. Besides, if there was mayhem on the floor, the booth was a sanctuary. Curtis knew she was there and she'd wave. I'd wave back. We all waved.

Once in DC, the second of a two-afternoon-stand, she unexpectedly asked if I'd take her to a disco, a pre-birthday treat. She was a little dressier than usual, wearing a noticeably shorter skirt than Curtis generally allowed.

"Should we ask Curtis?"

"He told me about a place," she said. "He'll arrange for us so we get in."

Backstage, I felt like I was being set up, introduced to my girlfriend's father for the first time.

"So, Sweet, are you up to the job?" asked Curtis. Maybe this was part of my indoctrination into their happy cult, a strategy to save my soul.

"Well, I hope so, sir," I said. Mei-Xing laughed. "Wouldn't you rather take her yourself?"

"No, no; she doesn't need old Curtis hanging around her the whole time, do you, little miss?"

"Well," I said. "I'll do the best I can, to, you know, chaperone."

He scribbled an address. "It's a teenage disco, no alcohol. I know you're not interested in that stuff anyway."

"Is it . . . churchy?" I asked, fearing the absolute worst.

"No, no," he said, surreptitiously slipping five $20s into my hand. "It starts at five. Cabs everywhere. Go get a burger. Then straight back to the hotel. No later than nine."

A disco wasn't my preferred evening off—a bit of a busman's holiday—but it had got to the point where I could do without the sometimes tense atmosphere, and if Mei-Xing needed an accomplice, I was happy to be one. We barely spoke in the cab, but after what appeared lengthy private debate, she said: "You can pretend to be my boyfriend, right? No one will bother me that way. We'll just dance."

We gave our names at the door—some kind of VIP deal. The doorman seemed listless, spared even the checking of IDs, the bouncers likewise in the grip of mild existential crisis. There may have been no alcohol—though little huddles of teenagers were scattered about the club, up to no good—but everything else was a perfect facsimile of the real thing: the smell, the bodies, the pounding bass of "Shiny Happy People" vibrating through the dance floor, the themed rooms. Mei-Xing chose which mirror-ball to dance beneath. I've never been much of a mover, so I was content to stand back and watch this mysterious almost-fifteen-year-old, lost in music, but she finally roped me in with that invisible lasso mime native to all of the world's dance floors. She was making fun of an adjacent group who demonstrated all the old favorites without irony: the nose-dive snorkel, the two-finger cats-eye, the iconic *Saturday Night Fever* teapot.

At one moment, eyes closed, she rubbed her leg—actually, the bit between her legs—up and down my knee. I was an innocent bystander, a prop, but I wondered whether, as her "boyfriend," I shouldn't evince a bit more enthusiasm. The other boys were very aware of her. What she really wanted was a bodyguard. I am no one's ideal bodyguard.

"Dance like nobody's watching," she shouted over the music. Conversation was, happily, impossible.

"I'll go and get a drink," I yelled, accompanying it with a Greg-ish mime.

"Okay. Coke," she said. At least she had good taste.

Holding both our cokes, I watched from the side of the room. She was oblivious, surrounded now by a throbbing group of teens. A kid approached me, fifteen, dressed like this was the big night of his life.

"Hot stuff!" he said.

"Hot stuff?"

"Yeah, bro. Your girlfriend."

This was exactly what I was here for. "Yep. That's her."

"Kudos, my man." He seemed just a middle class kid, living out a weird fifteen-year-old *Saturday Night Fever* fantasy. Sometimes it was like I didn't speak American.

"My friends over there. We have some coke too," he said.

"Right," I said.

"The other kind of coke." I nodded. Something about coke, uniquely among drugs, appealed to me, perhaps just the name. "Would you and your lady friend like to . . . indulge?" *Indulge. Lady friend.* He had it down.

"She just wants to dance, I think."

"Well, maybe I should ask her."

"She's really just here to dance."

"Well, maybe I should ask her."

"She doesn't speak English."

And so on. By the end of this stand off, which had involved a lot of dorky encouragement from a small scrum of friends furtively smoking over by the side wall, nothing was resolved. There wasn't anything remotely threatening about them, despite their drugs. I'd been more scared of five-year-olds. Often.

At that moment, Mei-Xing ran from the dance-floor. "My purse," she said. "It's gone."

We swept the floor in the unlikely event that it had flown off her neck, but, even given the difficulty of searching in the black light, the purse was nowhere to be seen. The coke kids looked on in amusement as we searched with ever-diminishing hope.

"Someone stole it," she said, distraught. "Someone stole my purse." And then, after an awful pause, with all eyes upon us: "YOU stole it!" She started beating my chest with her fists. I was tall enough to restrain her by enveloping her in my arms. One of the group laughed in contempt.

"Mei-Xing. Stop. You know I didn't. Did you have it when you started to dance?"

"Yes." She was crying now.

"Okay. Then let's be calm and look around."

Almost incredibly, she found it stuffed behind the back of a cistern in the ladies. Only the cash was gone. She brought it back to me, shamefaced. You could see where someone had cut the string. The group was deriving maximum enjoyment from our discomfort. It was time to leave.

"Go over there by the bar," I said, seeing the original kid come over again. "We'll get a cab."

"Hey, man," he said, watching her leave. "You were going to introduce me."

"I'm afraid we have to go," I said.

"Well, maybe I should ask her."

We were back to that again, so I said: "No," and put my hand on his shoulder. Without warning, he lifted his cigarette and, with a swift jab, extinguished it on my forehead right between my eyebrows. I felt, and smelled, my skin burning and pushed him back, more out of surprise than pain. I put two of my fingers up to cover the area and winced.

"What the fuck did you do that for? Ouch! Fuck!"

But he was gone already, strutting back to high fives from his little gaggle. Luckily the incident was spotted by a bouncer bored enough to take it quite seriously.

"You alright?" he asked, shepherding me towards some ice at the bar where Mei-Xing was waiting. Radioing another employee, the bouncer set off towards the would-be hoodlums. At the moment of confrontation, Mei-Xing was dabbing my forehead with ice wrapped in a towel. After a scuffle and some shoulder jabbing, the whole group was led away, and I noticed the guy who'd just used my forehead as an ashtray ditch a couple of items, perhaps mindful of an imminent requirement to turn out his pockets; two tiny handmade white envelopes. Only I'd seen, and since they still lay unnoticed on the floor as we left, destined to remain there until the cleaners came the next day, I thought it best to take them myself. Blake might like it. You never know.

Mei-Xing, at least, had got what she'd come for, but the combination of the purse incident, her accusation, and the occasionally searing pain on my forehead left the evening in need of a little salvation.

"Thank you for defending my honor," said Mei-Xing over a chocolate milkshake. "My hero."

"Guy was a dick," I said. The memory made me scrunch my eyes as if in preparation for another attack, which served only to irritate whatever pitiful scab was trying to form. I also had a vicious headache.

"Poor boy," she said tenderly, squeezing my hand. It was an apology. I wasn't at my most entertaining, and she showed me the pictures of her parents from her purse, the reason she'd been so upset. There was one of Curtis as well.

"All my parents . . . Curtis's music is so beautiful."

"Great drummer."

"No, his own music that he makes at home and on the bus. It's so beautiful. I tell him he shouldn't be the drummer in someone else's band; he should be the singer in his own band. Maybe he's wasting his time."

It didn't occur to her to sugarcoat this remark, and for a moment I got a feel for the way the angels spoke in Heaven. It was a wonder that Curtis allowed her to fraternize with me. I suppose I was handy: the right age; I didn't drink; I didn't do drugs. Perhaps they saw some salvageable good.

I escorted her to her room, keen not to see anyone else until I'd iced and camouflaged my wound as best I could. Who was I kidding? Blake was up and strumming, of course, and I told him the whole story. He called Jack, and I had to tell it again. Jack didn't make it any better.

"You look like an Indian with a fucking bindi!" he said.

"Thanks, Jack. Thank you."

"Nasty," he said, sympathetically squinting at the perfectly circular burn. "You want a Band-Aid on that."

"And some Savlon," said Blake, cradling my head between his hands, as he applied cream to the trouble spot. "And a good night's sleep."

I felt I had to tell them what Mei-Xing had said about Curtis, even though I knew it was a bad idea. I just couldn't help myself.

"What's he gonna do? Ask for some songwriting credits?" asked Blake. "His *invaluable contribution?*"

"And who the fuck does she think she is?" asked Jack. There was an edge to his laughter: "Yoko fuckin' Ono?"

"She's *Chinese*," I said, but I laughed, more out of obligation than anything else, hoping it wasn't a nickname that stuck.

Our relationship was probably a bad idea, a potential disaster, but looking back, it's possible that Mei-Xing and I kept the band together for a while beyond its natural lifespan. Just the fact of our friendship made for a better atmosphere; everyone was less tense around one another on our behalf. I should have told Blake the truth, but yet again I didn't. It started out as a kind of extended apology on her behalf. She somewhat offered herself to me, and I somewhat didn't refuse.

Having said that, she played by my rules, and my rules were strict, if unspoken. She was too young, now just fifteen; it was technically illegal, and that was a book I didn't need to reopen, if only out of loyalty to the band. It was also partly because of her history; I didn't want to be one of those men, like those other men. So we never had actual sex, at least in the beginning. What we did have, because we could have it, was a form of parallel play. We'd lie next to each other, without touching, and we'd make ourselves have orgasms, and then we'd cuddle. That was it. And it was perfect. We also played a lot of Monopoly.

"Was that nice?" I'd ask. We kissed occasionally. I used to lick the scars on her wrist, then blow on them to make them go away. We didn't speak very much, sometimes at all. One night our entire conversation consisted of "Rent" and "Will you trade Park Place for Atlantic Avenue?"

"We are like brother and sister," she said.

"Possibly," I said without conviction.

"Cousins?" She suggested. "Kissing cousins?"

"Maybe Romeo and Juliet."

Our mostly chaste misdeeds took place only in her hotel room, never on a bus and never, needless to say, backstage, where Monopoly represented the sublimation of our "desires."

That was how it began and how it continued and how it was going to stay. But you make these rules only for them to be broken, and I now realize that it was nailed on from the moment we began. My reluctance to go any further became a course of frustration; she even accused me of withholding something "special," as though I considered her unworthy of it. This was far from the truth. She was totally worthy. And I was soon to be seventeen (though my seventeenth birthday would pass much less eventfully than my sixteenth—almost unnoticed, in fact). One night, after she tried to convince me it wasn't that big a deal, I told her why: her backstory and her age.

"Is that all?" she asked. "I thought you were just being care-ful. You're a virgin, right?" I wasn't sure what she wanted to hear, so I let her assume what she liked from my silence: an embar-rassed admission, perhaps. "You don't have to worry about my age," she said, taking her clothes off. "I'm eighteen."

"You were fifteen two months ago."

"No." She was completely, impressively naked now. "My old passport is right. Everybody thinks I'm younger."

"Get your passport," I said.

"You're actually going to make me show you my passport?"

"Definitely." I perused the documentary evidence.

"Why?" I asked.

"And the story about me being sold: not true either. I'll tell you afterwards."

Her guardians had managed to get her to America by over-amplifying her history and faking her age. The children's home required her to be younger than she was: they hadn't known. Cur-tis didn't know. He liked her fifteen. But I knew. In the darkness, on all fours, she was a pony with a long black mane.

The late-night talk show appearance was finally upon us. New York City, as Blake said, was our Oyster Bar.

For once, there would be no deviation from the perfect plan: Blake was going to set fire to a ukulele during "Time to Sing a Song," the new single, for which a video already existed, the song intercut with snippets of the pre-teen comedy (directed by a John Hughes protégé, produced by the man himself, and starring a very young Phoenix family member) for which it was now the theme. All negotiated with the network. Great.

Within the band, there was a general burying of hatchets, the game face that accompanied any excursion into the upper eche-lons of show business—TVs, bigger gigs, award shows, anywhere the audience couldn't jump onstage.

The younger generation stood among the wires at the side of the set and clapped along. It was a killer performance—the best this version of the band ever was—and at the end, as arranged, Blake torched his ukulele and encouraged it voodoo-style, just like Hendrix. It was a magical, shamanic moment, in response to which the host unexpectedly invited Blake to join him at his desk. (Perhaps there was time to kill before the next block of ads.)

"Well, we're lucky none of our other guests is playing the ukulele tonight," said the host, then to an imaginary producer off-camera: "Do we have any ukulele players on the show tonight? No? Tiny Tim here? No? . . ." Back to Blake: "Because they'd be hard-pressed to follow that."

"Well, they could eat it maybe; play tennis with it," said Blake, clapping his hands together boyishly.

"Top Ten Things to do with a ukulele except play it," said the host. "Eat it. Hmm." He licked the lead of his pencil, then ticked his notecard. "Your band's a sensation. So tell me: what's it like playing to all those kids?"

"Well," said Blake, "it's great to know that at any given moment during a show one of them is innocently relieving themselves without repercussion."

The host tapped his mug with the pencil and looked out at his audience: "Don't get any ideas, people. So tell us about the Wonderkids."

"Okay. We're trying to give kids the real rock 'n' roll experience for the first time in their lives. Kids love mayhem and that's what rock 'n' roll is all about. Kids aren't self-conscious about the subconscious, like grown-ups. They're natural anarchists. And we're giving them real rock 'n' roll."

"Aren't you worried about dumbing down?" asked the host mock-seriously. It was a good line.

"Nooooo! If I were, would I have set a ukulele on fire?"

Uproarious laughter.

"That thing will *never* be played again. Look at this footage," said the host, banging his cue cards on the table. "What the heck is happening here?" It was film I'd never seen, shot recently, of Blake, almost entirely covered in peanut butter, doing what came naturally.

"I ran out of bread," Blake said.

"Could Iggy Pop sue you for that?"

"We, the kids, are going to sue him! He stole his whole act from naughty children!"

"But do you see yourself as role models for the kids? Aren't you being a little . . . *bad* yourself? Shouldn't you *behave*?"

"Absolutely not. That's why grown-ups are scared of us. We're the 'id' in 'kids.'"

"Well, I'm scared of you. And you're a great band, whoever you're for." The host caught sight of an anxious producer, who was trying to attract his attention by means of a raised finger. "Okay, then. Have you got another song for us after the commercial break?" This was unexpected. "How about 'Rock Around the Bed'?"

"Yes, sir!"

"Then we'll be right back, folks, with, once more, the Wonderkids."

Applause. The host turned away for an urgent conference with the producer, who explained that the next guest was incapacitated at her hotel. It was all hands on deck to get the next song ready, but the Wonderkids were troopers. They'd worked in the deadliest trenches of show business; this was nothing to them. No one needed to change instruments, or reprogram a synth, or put new cheat sheets up on the monitors—these were hardened live musicians, doing the corporation a favor. Blake asked for a second ukulele, which Mitchell had on hand. All was ready well before the ads had even finished.

"Welcome back. Let's hear it once more for the Wonderkids."

And then, "Rock Around the Bed." No messing around; just the song—the hit. And, since there was no time constraint, and we were on adult television, late-night television no less, Blake was always going to sing his favorite verse. Then he went ballistic, climbing up on one of the gantries, then beating the crap out of another ukulele. Everyone was having a ball, even the host. Mei-Xing dragged me on the set with Aslan. We threw confetti. They danced. It was stupendous.

"I can't thank those guys enough," announced the host. "They're playing Westchester tomorrow. Go and see their show. A wonderful band! The Wonderkids! Good night, folks. See you tomorrow night, *unless you see us first*!"

It was the zenith of their fame. It didn't have to be; from there, they could have gone anywhere. But they went down.

My fault.

• • •

After the show, the record company took us all out to eat, and we wound up back in someone's room, where we put dance music on the little Walkman speakers. Mei-Xing waltzed with Jack; Blake did the lambada with Camille; Curtis and I did the limbo. It was just like old times. But parents needed to get kids to bed and, rather than wait up for the broadcast, some drifted away, and the focus was lost. By the end of the night, it was, as usual, Jack, Blake, Mitchell, and me, and Jack had a phone call he had to make—other fish to fry. Blake wanted to get something off the bus, and thought he might just watch the show on there, and Mitchell was bored. I walked down with Blake. The bus was impudently parked on the street. Inside, he turned music up full blast—one of the limitless supply of live albums we were always listening to—and ricocheted off the coffins on his way back: "Let's have some fun," he shouted over his shoulder as I threw my jacket down.

The music from the front was cranking, but we couldn't be bothered to walk forward to turn it down, so we shut the door on it instead. Blake rolled a joint and breathed a sigh of relief. "What a day. Magic."

He never required praise, or fished for it, but he deserved it: "You were so good on that sofa."

"Well, he made me look good."

"You were great."

Blake lost himself in a reverie, a poignant remix of the old dream: how the Wonderkids, given a few opportunities like that, could come to be seen as more than a children's band. It wasn't that it wasn't true; it was just that it meant so much to him. I became aware that the music down the other end had been turned off. Probably Mitchell. I opened the door a crack and put my finger up to hush Blake. I saw, quite clearly illuminated, two of New York City's finest; between them and us, the lone figure of Mitchell in his smart tan suit. I closed the door as quietly as I could: "Blake," I said. "There's policemen on the bus. Mitchell's stalling them."

Without panic, Blake opened all windows, gathering various pieces of paraphernalia into a Tupperware box; this wasn't the first time he'd cleaned up. "Sweet," he said. "They probably only care how we're parked. Can you get out of that window?" I reckoned I could. "Okay. Take this up to the hotel room. Then come back, walk in the front and say you're looking for me, then knock, and I'll come out. Okay? Unless it's all died down."

I nodded and did exactly what I was told, walking round the entire block just to avoid the front of the bus, carrying the Tupperware like it was sandwiches for my night shift.

When I returned, only Mitchell was there, on the phone: "Yes, Precinct 35. That's where they took him. I know. I know. Andy, Andy. I know. I'm doing my best here. Get a lawyer soon." Mitchell looked at me: "Don't tell me. I know exactly what you were doing. He's been arrested."

"But I had all the gear."

"Amazing. But he wasn't arrested for pot."

"For what? Parking a bus illegally? Playing music too loud? Being annoying?"

"Save that laugh, funny man," said Mitchell. "Possession of cocaine."

"But Blake doesn't . . ."

I looked over where I'd thrown my jacket. There it was, pockets emptied, contents strewn.

"When I happened by," he continued, "the door was wide open, and there were two cops on the bus."

"Oh, God." I actually put my head in my hands. I hadn't even locked the door. Rule One: nothing good happens when you leave the door open.

"And after you'd done your Midnight Express flit, they wanted to search the back and Blake emerges, and there's nothing back there, but they've got the scent and there's that jacket and guess what they find in there. What was it doing there?"

"Oh God," I said. "I've never even done cocaine."

"Well, Blake's taken the fall. And he really has. And guess who has to deal with it?"

"Can I . . .?"

"You've done enough. Go to bed."

I didn't have the stomach to turn on the talk show. The high, when everything had felt possible—even the marriage of Heaven and Hell—had lasted such a relatively brief time. I couldn't sleep, thinking of Blake in his cell.

In fact, his jail experience went okay, primarily because of the dented, ancient TV bracketed to the wall outside the holding cell. When the show came on, his cellmates—no one too terrifying but nevertheless, large men who knew the score—put two and two together, mainly because the newest arrival, wearing the same clothes as the guy on TV, stood directly beneath the screen, sang along and did the same moves. At least, that's how Blake told it. When his TV doppelgänger sat down to chat with the host, Blake's stock rose further.

"What you here for, rock 'n' roller?" asked a Mexican guy. It was one of the most exciting questions Blake was ever asked. He quoted it a million times.

"Drugs, my friend. Category A drugs."

"Celebrating your TV appearance, *ese*?"

"Got out of hand."

"Didn't expect to be watching it down here, though, didja?" asked another man, laughing.

"No, I didn't." "Rock Around the Bed" began. "My name is Blake Lear and I'm fairly happy to meet you all."

The lawyer had Blake out next morning, though he'd have to return for a hearing: it was unlikely to result in anything but a hefty fine.

We picked him up at the precinct. It was hardly a hero's welcome, though Randy applauded. (One could only imagine the curled lip of Heaven's disgust.) Blake launched straight into anecdote, as though the whole thing had revitalized him: "Okay, here's the key detail. Best image of the night. We're all given these little peanut butter sandwiches in plastic Ziploc bags, and no one eats them, because they're disgusting. No. What they do is, whoever wants them most trades them for whatever they've got, and then they use them as pillows. Peanut butter sandwich pillows. You can't make that shit up."

As the bus moved, Mitchell announced from his desk-office, very matter-of-fact: "Andy is going to meet us in Westchester, and I guess there'll be some kind of band meeting. Blake will be lying low. Sweet will be thanking his lucky stars."

"Hey, come in the back with me," Blake said to me. "Let's finish that conversation."

When we were settled, I thanked him.

"Better me than you," he said.

"Why are you always taking the blame for things you didn't do?"

"Because I never do anything except onstage. And it's all allowed up there. I'm very lucky, right? Even this. There's an opportunity for a song here. Where's the Tupperware?"

"Don't you think you should . . ."

"Don't *you* think you should absolutely never tell me what to do?"

"It's in my coffin."

"Good lad. So, blow, then, now is it? Good high? Missed out pot? Moving straight to heroin? Injecting it in your dick? Giving it the old Dusty Miller?"

"I've never even tried it." I told him the story: I'd seen the kid drop it on the floor, and I thought Blake might want it. And then I'd just forgotten it.

"That would have to be the unluckiest bust in the history of drugs. And totally deserved. But look," he was crumbling some rather dry, smelly grass into a small pipe, "whether I want cocaine or not—and thanks for thinking of me, but I don't—you are not my drug runner. I must set a horrible example, but be a teenager. You wanna do some coke? We'll do some coke together."

"I don't want to do coke." And I didn't want to do it with Groovy Dad either. Where was the middle ground? In fact, I just wanted him to tell me off. But he wasn't thinking of discipline; he was inhaling deeply.

"The lesson here is, don't pick up packages that don't belong to you just because they're there and you can. And if you do, take the drugs as soon as possible: everything's got a moral, if only you can find it. Here's a story. Once, at university, I was going to a demo, which turned out to be the one demo in the history of our many demos where everybody was arrested, taken to the cells and searched. And that would have been me. But, strangely, my father called that day—he happened to be in town, it was the only time ever—and I reluctantly met him in some quaint little tea shop. I totally missed the demo and the arrest because I was eating scones and clotted cream: that's how committed to class warfare I was. Anyway, I was kind of annoyed about it, until a few days later, when I found three tiny blue tabs of acid in my pocket, which someone had given me at a party a few days before, and I'd completely forgotten about. And that would have been the end of my university career right there, finished, sent down. You gotta keep your nose clean and know what's in your wallet." He put his arm around me. "I know it's a little weird round here, but everything will be okay. It's not your fault."

"It is."

"A little drug bust can't stop this juggernaut."

"Blake," I said, since we were being honest, "I'm sleeping with Mei-Xing. She's actually eighteen, even though everyone thinks she's fifteen. I'm the only person who knows. Even Curtis doesn't know."

"Which bit?"

"All the bits."

"What is it with the older women? Do you wish you had a mother?"

"Do they count as older women if you think they're younger?"

"Are we using protection?"

It was then Jack joined us in the back. He was white as a sheet.

"Bad night for all us," he said, collapsing onto the remaining seat.

"Possibly worse for Blake?" I suggested. But there was a look in Jack's eyes, and I realized that, during all that morning's excitement, he'd been completely quiet, expressing no opinions whatsoever, not even "nasty" or "tedious." He hadn't said a single word when his brother got on the bus, let alone made the usual snarky jokes about Blake's cellmates' sexual preferences. In fact, there hadn't been a word since he'd left us the previous evening.

"What is it, mate?" asked Blake, handing Jack the spliff, which his brother rejected.

"Look, there might be cops waiting when we arrive."

"No, it's sorted. We're all done with cops for today."

"For me." Blake looked up. Then Jack told us.

The previous night, he'd phoned up this woman, and she'd invited him out for a drink somewhere they could see the band on TV, then taken him back to her anonymous tenement building. (It was at this point that, without looking at us, Jack began to rub at an imaginary mark on his right palm with his left thumb. "Never tell anyone, not even Mitchell.") It turned out she liked a bit of *the rough stuff*—he said the phrase in inverted commas with a pained smile, but there were so many elements of this story upon which one might judge him that there didn't seem any point pussyfooting around this aspect; the whole thing was coming as quite a shock to me. She'd asked him to tie her up, not to the four corners of the bed, which request he was never cruel enough to deny a willing participant, but from this hook in the middle of the room, from which her feet just touched the ground. She knew precisely what she was doing; the hook wasn't there by chance.

At first, Jack felt a little out of his depth. He was no stranger to silken sashes, but the meat hook was a little more torture chamber than slap and tickle. He didn't want to disappoint the nice lady, however, so he got into it. He gagged and bound her semi-clad body, dangling her from the meat hook as requested. Things were going swimmingly. On an inspiration, Jack decided to heighten the suspense by going out for a packet of cigarettes. He told her what he was going to do, and not to do anything he wouldn't do, got her front-door key and took the elevator to the ground floor.

His quest for smokes took him slightly further afield than he intended, and in his slightly drunk, somewhat high state, as he sucked on a welcome Camel Light back on the street, he realized he couldn't remember the number of her apartment, and it wasn't written on the key. At first, this struck him as funny, because he pictured himself having to try the key in every apartment door in the building. But then . . . he looked around him, not quite sure which way he'd even walked. Forget the number of the apartment; he didn't even remember what building it was.

"So how did you find her?" I asked.

Jack put his hand in his pocket and ruefully showed us her key, letting it dangle from his finger a little too graphically. He groaned.

"Well, call her," said Blake in exasperation. Jack looked up and sighed. She wouldn't be picking up the phone. "For Christ's sake! How long ago was this?"

"A few hours."

"You've slept?"

"No," said Jack. "I don't even remember what building it was."

"You looked everywhere?"

"YES!"

"Have you got the receipt for the fags? Check."

Miraculously, he fished it from the depths of his coat pocket. That was the starting point.

"Okay, Jack. You and me, right now. We're going to put that key in every keyhole around that cornershop until we find the right one."

"She's going to be livid," said Jack.

"She's going to be pleased to have the chance to be livid. I'm livid! Anyway, maybe you gave her the night of her life, you prick."

Blake opened the door and in a completely different tone of voice, ordered: "MITCHELL! Turn the bus around. 14th Street and 7th Avenue, please, now, before we leave town. Jack and I have some work to do." He turned back. "Jack, we'll sort this out. We're going to be very calm, and you're going to give me every ounce of help. Sweet, you too. First, we're going to get three keys cut. Then, we're going to spread out.

I'd never had a handle on Jack's sex life, the true Gothic horror of which was revealing itself in a slow striptease. I'd tried to suppress all memory of that video, and I can't claim to have known much about the further reaches of sex—the Marquis of This, and Whiplash Girlchild von That, all that Velvet Underground stuff. You try not to judge, but what on earth was he doing in his spare time?

Back at the bus, Jack wore the smile of a man recently spared the gallows. She'd picked up finally, after he'd left his fifteenth message from a pay phone.

"But how did she . . .?"

All he said, once we were safely behind the Great Wall of China, was: "She wasn't best pleased. Seems like the cleaner found her. But she told me to be in touch."

The band meeting took place in a conference room at the hotel the next morning. Everyone apart from Blake was on time: Andy, John from WBA, Curtis, Camille, Mei-Xing, Mitchell, even Aslan, who was laying out a Thomas the Tank Engine track in the middle of the floor. There was a decanter of water and some freshly cut flowers.

"Good morrow," said Blake. "Who's got the *good* news?" He clapped his hands as though he'd been relishing this little get-together. Backstage the previous night had been like a morgue. The other Wonderkids had found out then; the world at large this morning.

Curtis shook his head, sadly. "Blake, what were you thinking?" he asked. Before I had a chance to clarify, which I intended to because it was my fault, Blake hushed me. Mei-Xing rolled her eyes. It was hard to imagine what they'd have made of Jack's little adventure.

"Blake," said Andy. "There actually is good news. But, first, can I just say, and I'll take a vote on it, but wouldn't it be better if we restricted this meeting to band members?"

"Is it getting a little too *Let It Be* for you, Andy?" asked Blake. It wasn't even a jab at Yoko, just a reference to the fracturing of a band, the opposing points of view around the table. It was a harsh reminder of a time when we had all been singing from the same songbook, just like the Beatles when they were happy boys with matching mop tops.

"Just so we can focus."

"He might have a point," said Jack. It was true; Camille was looking at Aslan; Mei-Xing, my beautiful little pony, was sitting quietly next to Curtis, holding his hand, as if offering moral support. And what about me? Who was I?

"Meh," said Blake. "Take us as you find us. So, good news then."

"Orders have gone through the roof since the TV appearance. The single will chart. The band is in great shape. The band's image, however . . ."

"Tarnished," said John who seemed more executive than ever.

"Would this," Blake asked, "be the ideal time, strategically, to morph from a children's band into an Everyone Music type band?"

"Are you being facetious or amusing?" asked Andy, politely.

"No," said John. "We've identified a market. We are the number one brand in that market. What we want to do is stay number one. Do we diversify? Yes, we diversify. Do we increase productivity? Yes, we increase productivity. But we don't ditch a marketing plan just because . . ."

"Alright. Alright," said Blake. "Jesus. Just throwing it out there." Camille, serene and interior, was paying no attention at all. She smiled encouragement at Aslan every now and then.

"The main problem right now is this." John opened a newspaper to a picture of Jacquelyn Belmer; she was brandishing a copy of *Number Two*. "We won't go into the history of this antipathy, the rights and the wrongs, but this kind of behavior—a drug bust—is grist to her mill."

"This is literally insane," said Blake. "Rutles arrested! Nude girl and teapot!"

"It's not insane," said Andy. "You're the lead singer of a band for kids. Parents don't want their children entertained by junkies. Four upcoming promoters have pulled out, dropped us. We're not playing those shows. We are losing money. Contractually, in fact, they can't, but they have and you can see their point. The pith of this *particular* article, however, is that you legally cannot now play your upcoming show in the District of Columbia. You are banned from playing there."

"Can we actually go into the District of Columbia, but not play a show?" asked Jack, as though this were salient. Perhaps he had a date there. "Or can we just not go there at all?"

"We're banned from DC?" asked Blake.

"So we're free the Friday of next week?" asked Camille.

"*So we're free the Friday of next fucking week?*" repeated Blake. Camille immediately started crying, which he ignored. "You want a night off? Take a night off! We've been BANNED in DC. We can't play there. What court granted that injunction or whatever you call it?"

"The lawyers are dealing with it. They're appealing," said John, adjusting his Lennon glasses. "The trouble is that this isn't one of those PMRC things where everyone gets to expatiate over whether the lyrics are subversive or not. It's a drug bust; it's against the law; it's real bad behavior." I looked at Blake shamefaced. "And there's this other issue of "incitement to riot" she keeps banging on about. Everyone saw what happened at that other show. You're like the Jesus and Mary Chain of the pre-teens. People are scared of you."

"You seem quite excited by it," said Blake.

"Well, it's a unique opportunity for moving product," said John. "But it has to be handled carefully. Apparently you're pushing all the right buttons; just don't push any more. And obviously, no more drugs. And some anti-drug public service announcements. Believe me, WBA has been here before."

"It wasn't his cocaine," I said.

"Yes, it was," said Blake.

"The thing is," said Andy hastily, "it doesn't actually matter whose it was, because it is now officially Blake's. Or he gets in even deeper shit for lying. We know Blake's a kind, generous, occasionally overly flamboyant man. That's not the issue. The issue is public perception of a band who are primarily entertaining children, and who shouldn't really be seen taking a sip of beer or smoking a cigarette in public, much less flashing at Disneyland or being arrested for hard drugs." There was silence. "We're shelving the theme park for the time-being," said Andy, making it clear that this punishment was Blake's uniquely. "The money's vanished. We're concentrating on meat and potatoes: live performances, records in the charts, staying out of trouble. No grand statements. Contrition."

"Hey," said Blake, who'd been cooking something up during the lecture. "DC gig. Okay, we can't play DC, so we play right on the edge of Maryland or Virginia, as near DC as we can possibly be, and we make it a free gig and we do the best show ever, and we get the ACLU to help us put it on. The Pack 'n' Play Festival."

"Is that exactly the kind of grand statement I just mentioned?" asked a weary Andy.

"No, I like it," said John. "It's great. It'll take planning."

"Well, we can all have the Friday of next week off," said Blake pointedly, "but let's get the date for this festival and advertise it before next Friday. Let's not let the kids down."

"Okay," said Andy. "There's more." And there *was* more: there had been threats. "We're putting a stop to the autograph sessions after the shows. Now most *artistes* would be absolutely delighted by this but . . ."

"That's half of the show," pleaded Blake. "That's what they come for."

"We won't shift so many units," I said.

"Even so," said John.

Wow.

"Look, I'm not afraid of threats," said Blake. "What are they gonna do? Shoot me? No, they're gonna spit on me or egg me or give me a damned good talking to. I'm not scared. We shouldn't give in to them. We should just carry on . . ." He'd said just about everything he could say, but he was fighting a losing battle. "What? What?"

"Well . . ." said Andy.

"Have there been actual threats?" asked Blake. Andy nodded. "But you're more worried about the threat I might offer."

"I wouldn't put it that way, at all," said Andy. "But I'd say now was a good time to lie low, play shows, sell records, and get ourselves together: contrition." Blake sniffed. "And one other thing: don't think you stand for anything. That's dangerous. You're not Lenny Bruce. You're not a martyr. You're a guy with a drug bust."

"Well," said Curtis, prodded by Mei-Xing as the meeting was

coming to a close, "since we're all sharing, I have an announce-ment: I'll be leaving the band at the end of the tour. It's been a wonderful ride, and I thank you for the opportunity, but I want to pursue other ambitions."

"The solo record?" asked Jack. "*Man And His Cymbals*?" Mei-Xing looked at me again. I tried out a smile.

"Okay," said Andy. No one was shocked—we'd grow an-other Wonderkid. "Well, that's a shame. But if that's how you really feel."

"Yes," said Mei-Xing, mostly to me. "Curtis wants to make his own music now."

"Curtis," said Jack, raising an eyebrow. "She's fourteen years old." *She's not.* "You're taking advice on your musical career from a fourteen-year-old?"

"She's fifteen. You forgot her birthday," said Curtis. Jack had, but I hadn't. It was her eighteenth, and I was the only one who knew. I'd let her win at Monopoly. There had been forfeits.

"Right," said Jack. "Well, happy birthday, Mei-Xing. Con-gratulations on breaking up the band."

Please don't call her Yoko.

Blake was being unusually grown-up about the whole thing. As far as he was concerned, it was a minor wrinkle on the ironing board: "Till the end of the tour, then, you say?"

"Yes, absolutely. I'd never leave you in the lurch."

"Well, then, let's have a word with the agent and see if he can have the tour go on forever. I don't want to see you go, Curtis. I'm going to make you see sense over the next few weeks."

"Okay," said Curtis. "I appreciate your attitude."

"And Jack agrees with me," said Blake.

Jack nodded. "Sorry. Bit of a shock, you know, what with everything else."

"Well, it's partly the *everything else*," said Curtis.

"And I'll be leaving too," said Camille, attempting a laugh, "so you'll need another chick as well as a black guy." No one spoke. "This situation is too stressful, and I can't give Aslan the care he needs. This is no way to bring him up. I don't know what I was thinking."

"I'll tell you where you're wrong though," said Blake, looking at Aslan. Kid was so happy, playing with the trains on his track, making them endlessly crash off the wibbly-wobbly bridge. "This is the best place to bring a kid up. This is it." It was? Did he believe that?

"Drug busts, buses, guns backstage?" asked Camille. "Sound-checks, naked mothers, and playgroupies?"

"Life! As it is lived!" said Blake, voice raised. "Life! *Live a little*!"

"Oh," said Andy, hoping to draw the meeting to a close before it fell apart, "and the record label want you in one bus. They feel that two draw unnecessary attention. And it's an extravagance."

"Why?" asked Blake, full of indignation. Camille and Curtis would walk out right now rather than travel on one bus. "Who cut the tour support?"

Andy didn't know how to answer, then said quietly: "I told you he wasn't used to people saying 'no.'"

"Okay," said Blake. "We keep the two buses. I'll pay for the other one. Who do I make the check out to, Mitchell?"

"I'll get you that information," said Mitchell, who hadn't said a word. "But if it's cards on the table time, I'll add this." His final words, spoken with great dignity, as befitted a man who wore Brooks Brothers coats, a raffish scarf, and carried a gun, were: "Gentlemen, Ladies, there is only so much I can do to help you, and I have reached the limits of my patience. My work on your planet is done. I wish you well. I am returning to sanity."

He took off his laminate, let it hang from his finger until it dropped, then left. I watched him. We all did. No one could believe it.

I'd been Mitchell's go-between, his protégé. I understood his frustration, and no one understood more than I how difficult his job had become, but even I was surprised he left in the middle of a tour like that. He didn't even turn to say goodbye.

"You wouldn't want my trousers to fall down."

ONCE READ A REVIEW OF A LOUIS XV BIOGRAPHY IN WHICH THE author marveled that bystanders were actually instructed not to look at the King. But isn't that standard practice for folk music's Bob Dylan? Or is it Diana Ross? Well, regardless—Blake wasn't *that* bad.

But looking back at Mitchell's departure—so ill-timed, such a disaster—it's possible that it all started with the request for a hair dryer, a hair dryer that Blake would never use. It was a senseless imposition—difficulty for its own sake—yet Blake kept on about it, even though he knew that Mitchell knew that there was no good reason for it. Mitchell just couldn't stand it anymore—it was the gun, the drugs, the atmosphere. He said more than once, in that paternal, *everything's under control* way, that he'd never had such trouble from any of the hardcore bands he'd toured with. And nor did I, in the years that followed. I was surprised by his timing though. Even Curtis, even *Camille*—who felt no great tie to the band—knew you didn't just pick up sticks. I asked him about it later, and he said: "I'm a road manager, not a road sweeper." The left hand must know what the right is doing.

The tour couldn't function without a road manager, but the unspoken question was whether the band could function without

Mitchell. It would have been the last thing Andy and the record label wanted. I alone seemed to understand that he was leaving because he knew I could take over, so I suggested myself. Three people said "no" at once, the firmest of which was Blake's.

"You should be having fun, Sweet."

"I'm not sure anyone's having fun, are they? Anyway, that's why he left, because he knew I could do it."

"You think that's why he left?"

"Besides I'd like to. I know what to do. Mitchell taught me."

"Over my dead body."

Andy took the reins for the next few dates until we were entrusted to a hardy, pockmarked survivor named Adam. There was no time for an audition, no bedding-in period. It was Adam or nothing.

"Randy!" He high-fived the driver, boarding as though he owned the bus. "My man!" Oh joy.

With him arrived a portable fax machine, an impressively small mobile phone, and a massive collection of laminates, all of which hung from his neck as though he might at any moment require Cheap Trick credentials from 1981. I expected him to gather us, sit us down, tell us a bit about himself, but there was no ceremony. He spread himself thickly around the parlor and perused the itinerary, evaluating its success: "Seattle to San Fran, *then* back to Portland. Jesus. What joker came up with that bullshit?"

Adam was supposedly in the same line of work as Mitchell, but there the similarity ended. Adam set himself up as everyone's adversary: the agent, the promoters, the label, even the band. Everything had to suit him and his schedule. He was the king of the ulterior motive. He liked to hold the cards and deal at his leisure. He withheld information, regardless even of a "need to know." This had the function, first, of putting everybody on edge and, second, of reducing people to a state of dependency upon him, which, though he invited it, he seemed to resent. He wasn't officially the band's adversary, of course, that was just his personal style. He was pleased to mock everyone on the tour for his own amusement, and this had the effect of uniting the Wonderkids, if only in their dislike of him. It was like we'd been sent a Boot Camp road manager "for our own good." Who knows? If Mitchell couldn't bring us into line, maybe Adam was exactly what we needed. It was hard to like him; he didn't care. It wasn't his job to be liked. Though it *was* apparently his job to say that it wasn't his job to be liked, because he said it very often.

"I'll get you there on time, and I'll check you into the hotels," he said, "and if you do your jobs, which I hear you do, the shows will go like clockwork. And I'll pick up your money. But I'm not wiping your asses."

"Good to know," said Blake.

"Did the other guy wipe your asses?"

"It's a metaphor, right?"

Blake and I watched *Fanny and Alexander* in the back of the bus one night. The kids have an idyllic, noisy childhood until their father dies, and their mother remarries a bishop into whose cold, wretched house they are moved. And thus was pockmarked Adam rechristened the Bishop, the least likely nickname of all.

"Just get him out of the bus, Jimmy," said Jack wearily. "Where's Mitchell when you need him?"

After three more days of torture, Blake said: "Hey, Adam, do you mind traveling in a separate car or with the road crew? I don't think this is working. We need some space."

"If that's what you want," said the Bishop. "Your money."

"God be with you."

The Pack 'n' Play Festival was confirmed. The record company agreed to rush release the new single: "Life, As It Is Lived," classic Blake. The lyrics somehow managed to be flippant, yet they took in all the recent mistakes and revelations, especially the breaking up of the band. Roll with the punches, was the idea, and everything will be okay. It might have been a recipe for *depressing*, but the chorus was infectious and the hook moreish, with the band at their joyful sloppiest—they'd recorded on the hoof in a couple of studios along the way. It certainly spilled out of Blake, something he had to say, all delivered in glorious nonsense—we all make mistakes, we're all human, life throws some funny things in your path, let's keep having fun. It was one of those songs he had to get out of his system—his "Give Peace a Chance," except he actually bothered to get out of bed to record it. The single was on the radio within a week of its recording. A scandal, MOMs' disapproval, a TV appearance: the perfect hothouse atmosphere for the cultivation of a hit.

The big Maryland show was hastily expanded into a pay-per-view event, affording the Bishop many opportunities to paint himself as greatly put-upon and massively overworked. In the run up, Blake dabbled with a few experimental changes to the old routine: yes, peanut butter; yes, feathers. He watched a few Alice Cooper videos. A guillotine was too heavy, biting the head off a plushie toy not quite enough. He tried putting red ribbons inside one, so they left a trail of "blood" behind, but that wasn't doing it: too visceral and not funny enough. Rod Stewart kicking footballs out into the audience seemed promising, but how: ping-pong balls? Bouncy balls? They'd all get thrown back anyway, as Mitchell had suggested years ago—kids give as good as they get. Jack suggested dressing kids up in Hells Angel gear and having them pretend to do security at the outdoor concert. Altamont reference: tasteless. The trouble was: though these ideas were all ripe for parody, and good fodder for an amusing parlor game, they were, as far as Blake was concerned, self-parody. He needed that one real coup de théâtre for the pay-per-view; the bit of rock 'n' roll that outdid all that went before. The rest of the show wrote itself. This was where we really lacked Mitchell. No one was overseeing Blake now, encouraging him in the right direction, while simultaneously restraining him, and he wouldn't let me do the job. Adam had been employed to keep a firm hand, but he wasn't on the bus anymore. Blake's imagination was free to roam, but it roamed without focus.

As the date came closer, the general mood improved. Blake never tired of doing shows or meeting his audience, on the rare occasion this was now allowed, and he was genuinely excited about what the band was doing, particularly the fact that the Wonderkids had sparked a little debate about censorship and the role of art. I didn't think for a moment that Blake was planning to go out with a bang. I just thought he was looking for a good show.

Some people can't stand reading about themselves or seeing

reviews of their shows. Certain highlights passed before our eyes: a lengthy editorial in *Billboard* that sheepishly supported the band, citing some pretty astonishing sales, without excusing their personal habits; Kurt Loder came out as a fan with a series of hastily-assembled pieces for MTV News. But for the most part, and though I was curious, we didn't pay attention. Now with the Internet, you have to make a conscious attempt not to know things, but back then, if one didn't read papers or watch much TV, it was easy—and none of us, not even Jack, was aware of quite how the Maryland concert had mushroomed into an *event*. Andy had issued an edict that Blake shouldn't be put in front of the cameras before the show, which meant no press to talk to, and the Bishop had a strict policy of hoarding and withholding information: he told us nothing. "It's going to be a circus," was all he could spare. "The equipment will meet us there." Most of what I knew, I found out from the Kidders, who hung on for dear life, cheerfully doing as many shows as still remained on our itinerary. With all the cancellations, we had an unusual amount of time on our hands, but Blake and Jack hardly got out of the bus, except when their requirements exceeded the capacity of the toilet.

Mei-Xing and I didn't see each other as often as I would have liked. I once bumped into her in the aisle of a CVS. She smiled like a long-lost friend.

"Wanna play Monopoly?" I asked. The contents of her trolley looked outlandishly large, family-value this and that. My purchases were all travel-sized, rattling round the bottom of my basket; minuscule shaving foam, ten-squeeze toothpaste, a shot glassful of mouthwash.

"No," she said. Her refusal seemed to upset her.

"What's wrong?"

"It's emotional to say no when I don't want to say no and you know that I don't want to say no. Do you know what I mean?"

"Yes."

As we drove towards the festival park, passing the first battalion of television cameras, I wondered what was going on. Then I realized: what was going on was us.

Progress to the backstage area was majestically slow. There were protests, and people protesting the protests, and other people drawn simply by the fact that a crowd represented as good a reason as any to dust off a placard that proclaimed WHALES AREN'T ENDANGERED: YOU ARE! or IT'S BETTER TO BE RACIST AT NIGHT! or whatever bizarre thing they happened to believe.

The police were out in force, wearing shorts on a hot afternoon. A cop always seems less threatening when you can see his knees. The park was packed, full of happy picnicking families, many in Wonderkids T-shirts. Police later estimated the crowd at four thousand, which meant eight to ten. There was even a video screen to the right of the stage for those too far away to see the details. It was a beautiful scene. There'd be no Altamont action here. This was a bright, shining celebration of youth and music— two fingers at the moral majority. The ACLU had a big booth; there were food vendors everywhere, some offering PB&J sandwiches (Andy had probably negotiated 5 percent of every sale). Blake, Jack, and I looked out of the bus window like children misting up the outside of a toy store. It really did seem like the pinnacle of everything, as though this was precisely what the band had been invented for.

Backstage was mayhem. Some band, not the Kidders, was already playing, and music was swirling around this way and that. There were plenty of microphones pointing in our direction, and Andy and his worker bees were buzzing everywhere, trying to save Blake from this, steer him towards that. We found our way to an air-conditioned Winnebago, where the rest of the band was waiting. Curtis and Camille's departures hadn't been further discussed, even between Jack and Blake, and now wasn't the time. Everyone was ready to forgive and forget, because this was clearly as good as it got: headlining your own free festival.

"Wow!" said Curtis. "What a party!" Mei-Xing gave me a peck on the side of the cheek and whispered in my ear: "rent." Camille too was happy. The sylvan vibrations had rose-tinted everyone's spectacles.

"Okay. People," Blake said. "This is it. Sit back and enjoy the ride."

"Anything special planned?" I asked. I'd be Mitchell if I had to be, whether he liked it or not. I'd even pretend to be annoyed at the late warning if the answer was "yes".

"Look," said Blake. "We're doing it all. Nothing crazy new. It's live on TV; people are paying to see us all over America; let's give them the best show we've got; the one we do so well; the one the kids love. We always get it right onstage, so we're not going to get it wrong tonight."

I couldn't wait for showtime, but, as the Kidders went on, there was a lot of fun to be had in the fenced off backstage. Mei-Xing and I played Ping-Pong, Blake got a massage, and Jack sat down with some mums to sample catering—there was even a paddling pool in which Aslan performed some kind of water ballet under a sprinkler. Blake was itching to get in: he loved a paddle. It was all, literally, too good to be true. Maybe this would all prove so seductive that Curtis wouldn't ditch the band. I was so excited I got wired on Coke. You'd think I was too jaded for a sugar rush, but no. And then I ate some Ben & Jerry's and got that terrible frozen face where you can't do anything but pinch the bridge of your nose, and people ask you if you're okay, but you can't even look up to let them know you're not choking. In my excitement, I'd forgotten how to eat ice cream.

It was wondrous to behold the sea of humanity before them as the Wonderkids hit the stage. TV cameras danced around Blake, movements he incorporated into his usual pogoings. The dressing-up box came out earlier than usual. It was great, and it didn't really matter what music the band was playing—everybody loved it: the kids were dancing, the grown-ups were dancing, everyone was screaming and singing along. Aslan, Mei-Xing, and I watched from a VIP area at the side of the stage: a perfect view of both the audience and the band. I always loved it when Blake, knowing where I was, winked. Is there anything better than when a performer singles you out for special, perhaps private, attention? And best of all, Mei-Xing was drawing a secret line down my back with her index finger.

Along the edge of the crowd, at the very perimeter, there was some unrest. This was where MOMs and their various acolytes had gathered and, at any lull in the set, they booed loudly, boos almost immediately drowned out by cheers.

"I guess there's a little boo in everyone," said Blake, before the band hurtled into "Dan, Beth, Chris, and Blank."

As the show stormed to its finale, however, I could tell that Blake was reaching for something he couldn't quite grasp, but it didn't seem out of the ordinary when he introduced the penultimate song: "You know, sometimes you make mistakes, and the world gets at you, but when you make a mistake, your family forgives you, and that's when you know you're at home!" And everybody applauded. "To people who can only see the bad in things, I say, that's sad. And for everybody here, and watching on TV, I want to say, thank you. This song is called 'Life, As It Is Lived.'" As he sang, I realized it was actually all about me. And then I wondered if everybody listening was feeling that at the same moment. It was magical.

Somehow during Blake's wild pogo and ludicrous scissor kick at the climax of the song, he ripped his pants, and when the song finished, he noticed that the right pocket was flopping about. It looked like it was inside out. I watched him as he tried to sort out exactly what had happened, but he was in that onstage space where sometimes you can't figure out the simplest thing.

"Blimey," he said, "I've ripped my pants. We've got one more song to play for you; I hope they stay up!" Everybody cheered. And then he said in his trademark terrible Mockney: "I think I popped a button on my trousers. I hope they don't fall down. You wouldn't want my trousers to fall down now, would you?" It was Mick Jagger on that live album. We'd seen the film on the bus. I'd heard Blake say it a million times in so many different contexts that it hardly seemed like the beginning of the end.

The protestors took this as a provocation. For a relatively small group, they were very spirited, like the away fans at a football match. The rest of the crowd, the families, had never been up for a serious fight over civil liberty issues, and they'd been baking in the sun for a long while now. Children were getting fractious; ice creams had melted; diapers were full; real food had not been consumed in some time. It was a tinderbox.

Blake seemed somewhat put out by the fuss. He'd given his

all in the heat. But the fact remained that he'd been striving for a moment of artistic nirvana that had eluded him, and this was his opportunity. Does a switch flip? Does a light go on? I've no idea. But it was now too late. The Eureka moment had happened.

"Oh, you guys, stop ruining everybody else's fun. We're going to play 'Rock Around the Bed'"—great cheering—"Ready, band? Not yet! First, I've got to look in here to find something to cover myself up. This rip isn't getting any smaller." The band was enjoying the teasing, ready for the count, when Blake shouted: "Love me. I can't take it no more without no good love. I want some lovin'. Ain't nobody gonna love my ass?"

I had no idea what he was going on about, nor why he was suddenly talking about "ass," nor that he had transported us, unwitting victims, to the Dinner Key Auditorium in Coconut Grove, Miami, to a 1969 Doors concert in a packed hangar. It was the night Jim Morrison tried to start a riot and ended up getting done for indecent exposure.

"This is the end," he said, looking through the dressing-up box, and then, when nothing came to hand, removing his shirt. "This is the end. One more song. The blue bus is callin' us." Then he started reciting lines ending up with "Father, I want to kiss you. Mother, I want to—" He interrupted himself. "Hey, you at the back!" He gesticulated at the protestors. "Hey, you at the back! You! Idiots! You wanna see a little skin? Shall we get naked? All the kids! Take your shirts off and wave them around!"

Blake kind of waved his shirt in front of the crotch of his pants like he was going to do some magic trick, make a rabbit appear or something. Certainly, he made some suggestive movements, but at this point fathers were more worried about how long it would take to get to, then exit, the parking lot; they just wanted the last song to start. There was no way the kids were leaving before the last song: they wanted glorious memories of "Rock Around the Bed" rather than the small satisfaction of having beaten traffic.

"You wanna see it?" Blake asked. That was the turning point. Laughter was one thing; entertainment was one thing; even saying "ass" was one thing; but the Wonderkids had form when it came to flashing, and nobody wanted the expense of sending their children through therapy. "You wanna see it?" He asked again, all confrontation. Cameras froze around him—this wasn't what they'd come to film, but if this was what was happening, they'd film it. "Come on. You're so scared of it. But you wanna see it. You don't like it. But you wanna see it." He turned to the band. "'Rock Around the Bed'? 'Rock Around the Bed'! 1,2,3,4!"

And at that precise moment, as the band kicked into the song, Blake whipped the scarf away in front of every single member of the audience to reveal for a horrific moment, his penis, hanging limply, and slimly, out of his trousers.

People started to scream, like, *really* scream, like they do in horror films and when the Beatles arrive. But, hang on, I'd seen his actual cock a million times—as one does—though not up close of course—and this didn't look much like it. And Blake was still standing there with this thing hanging from his fly and a great big smile on his face, because the thing hanging from his fly was his finger: classic kid's playground gag. Classic Blake. He was so pleased with himself, the quality of the gag, that he just stood there with his hand down the front of his pants and his index finger waggling away. The kids would love it!

All I could see were people's backs as they packed away hampers and headed for the parking lots with their disappointed, uncomprehending offspring. There were still people watching, but rather in the manner of rubberneckers on the freeway. There were also people throwing stuff. The MOMs and their various affiliates were incandescent, lathered into a frenzy at what they thought they'd seen. Or at what they had seen: they'd seen what they wanted to see. And suddenly there was Jacquelyn Belmer herself, large as life, all in white like a violent Gandhi, with a fucking megaphone. A megaphone! Which air-conditioned trailer had she been hunkering down in, putting on her makeup, fussing with her pearls, waiting for this precise moment to make herself known to the cameras?

By halfway through the song, police had gathered at the side of the stage, blocking the exits, and it was becoming the least joyful version of "Rock Around the Bed" of all time. Blake went over to the side of the stage and shouted at one of the cops: "It was my finger, right? Did you get that?" The policeman made a ludicrous

"Why I oughta!" gesture, and Blake took refuge at the central microphone, like a kid shouting "this is base!" to his friends while he gets his breath back.

There were those in the crowd who hadn't noticed what had happened at all—you'd be amazed how much people miss at events they're actually attending—but even they now knew, and they didn't want to miss out on the outrage. Word was spreading. Had he done it? Either he had or he pretended he had, but he shouldn't have done either. The stage was now the only place Blake was safe. He was completely surrounded. The band played manfully on as the Titanic went under, and the MOMs groups worked their way to the front. Blake couldn't stop laughing. It may well have been helpless, nervous laughter, but there was something remarkably surreal about the whole thing. One playground sight gag!

And then, with the song about to end, Blake turned, caught my eye, and gave me a look I knew well, the one that preceded mayhem. What he was communicating, I had absolutely no idea, but I was ready. Mei-Xing saw it too and grabbed my hand: "Be careful," she said. "Stay here with me."

And as the band continued, the police looking on from the side of the stage, Blake sprinted towards me, grabbed my hand, and we ran to the back of the stage, past Camille and Curtis, where we took a flying leap, Butch and Sundance style, to the ground and legged it to the bus. The police were slow to realize what had happened and, by the time they got anywhere near the door, we were safely locked inside. How much time did we have? However long it took for the Bishop to hand over his key. He wouldn't last as long as Mitchell, if he bothered to last at all.

"It was my finger!" said Blake. "They think it was my . . ."

"Everyone thought that."

"Oh god!" He was ecstatic, frightened, running on empty. "Now would be a really bad time to smoke a joint."

"Have a drink. Have a cigarette."

He opened the window a crack and dangled the very same offending finger outside, waggling it, in case anyone noticed.

"Okay. Sweet, I have to sort a couple of things. I want you to stay here. Do not, under any circumstances, open the door."

It was now that they started banging: "This is the Maryland police, Mr. Lear. Please open the door."

It was amazing. It really was like Butch and Sundance. Did they have a last stand? Maybe it was more like Custer, circling the wagons, or *High Noon*: definitely some Western, anyway. I had no idea what to do.

"Open up," shouted the Bishop, suddenly the loud voice of reason as he ran down the side of the bus banging on windows. "Don't make this worse, Blake." He was loving it.

"Okay," said Blake, when he reappeared, sweaty. "There's a box in the front coffin, up top, and a folder. Never look in them. Do not let the police find them. You have to get them off the bus and back to me."

"How on earth am I going to do that?

"Try."

"Okay, Blake."

"Okay?" He fixed me with a stare.

"Okay."

"Good boy. Well, I said we'd have fun. Well . . . bits of it were fun, weren't they?"

I buried my head in his chest. "Is it over?"

"No. Never," he said. "Well, temporarily. They can't stand nonsense. Time to face the music."

He detached himself from me, put on a clean shirt, looked in the mirror and said: "Now's when I wish I had that hair dryer. Fucking Mitchell."

He walked to the front of the bus, turned around and said: "It's gonna get ugly and then I'm going to disappear. I love you, Sweet."

"I love you too, Blake."

We'd all gone a bit American.

As he opened the door, I heard the rattle of camera shutters. Standing on the steps of the bus in front of the assembled crowd, Blake started to recite poetry. And there I was, with a load of weed in the back of our bus.

Jim Morrison got six months for "indecent exposure and open profanity" with a recommendation of hard labor. The judge said he had "utter contempt for our institutions and heritage." Morrison appealed and was bailed for $50,000. He never served time, dying before the lawsuit was resolved. At some point he was offered a plea bargain, if that's the right phrase: all charges would be dropped if he played a free concert for the people of Miami. He refused. He was a spent force anyway. At that late date, you didn't get the boyish Love God Lizard King; you got a fat, beardy, mumbler.

Years later—last year or something—Morrison was pardoned by the Florida Clemency Board. Nowadays, it'd just be a *wardrobe malfunction*, exploited by the label, a breast milked for profits.

Jack and I watched it all on CNN the next morning—everything was there in hideous detail: the glorious day, the gig, the climax, the flying leap off the back of the stage, the stand-off, even that little detail of Blake appearing to give the police "the finger" out of the bus window. No, you fools! You can't tell a finger from a penis, sure, but can't you tell *a* finger from *the* finger?

Best of all—and there was a lot of competition—was Blake standing at the top of the steps of the bus, blinking in the light in his fresh shirt, reciting to the camera:

> How pleasant to know Mr. Lear!
> Who has written such volumes of stuff!
> Some think him ill-tempered and queer,
> But a few find him pleasant enough.
>
> He has ears, and two eyes, and ten fingers,
> Leastways if you reckon two thumbs;
> He used to be one of the singers,
> But now he is one of the dumbs.

It was a final short turn for the kids before they went to bed. "Good night little ones," he said as he finished. "Time to go home, Blake is waving goodbye, goodbye. Blake is going home now. Goodbye." Then, offering his wrists for handcuffs that were not forthcoming, he descended into a sea of policemen in which his head bobbed like flotsam.

We were magicked back to the studio where the anchor concluded: "Mr. Lear, recently bailed on a charge of cocaine possession in New York City, was found in possession of marijuana. All this on top of his remarkable performance at the pay-per-view concert." A caption flashed up: OUT OF CONTROL.

"Not the kind of person we want entertaining our children. We spoke to the legendary Simeon, father of Becca Fonseca, the band's previous bass player." And, yes, to cap it all, there was an interview with Simeon, in front of a heartwarming fire, his guitar purring cozily on his lap.

"Do you think," asked the interviewer, "that we ask too much of our performers?"

"Well, I'm okay," said Simeon, giving a less sympathetic response than the talking head had perhaps hoped. "If you can't stand the heat, get out of the kitchen. I don't know if anyone really knows Blake Lear. Certainly, my daughter left the band to get away from him. And her replacement felt almost a hostage in the band, had already announced her departure and traveled separately by her own choice, fearing Lear's influence on her child."

This was followed by an interview with a cheerful, possibly post-orgasmic, Jacquelyn Belmer, above the caption VINDICATED. She was happy to plug a book, shortly to be published, called *American Quilt: Sewing the Moral Fabric of America*, in which there would be a whole chapter on the threat of the Wonderkids. With the band getting her such good publicity, it was almost certain to hit the bestseller list.

Footage of the festival ran yet again, and there was Blake once more on the steps. Back in the studio, the anchor concluded: "Blake Lear of the Wonderkids: we'll be keeping a close eye on this story as it develops. Weather."

The court dates were set: two separate trials in different states. Bail looked unlikely. Sadly, he was not to be tried for incitement to riot, or revealing himself on stage. Those "crimes" just annoyed everyone.

The bus was searched and impounded. I wasn't even allowed to remove personal possessions, including, though I knew I was letting Blake down, the box he'd wanted me to take. It wasn't my fault: I'm not a magician. I couldn't just disappear it, spirit it away. The authorities weren't letting anything off until they were good and ready. I was, however, able to sneak his folder out, stuffed down the front of my shirt, though I can't imagine they'd have been greatly interested in this selection of indecipherable rambling. All that was written on the front: "Clock," with a classic Blake doodle of the forces of evil looming over some innocent child. But the box was staying. I couldn't do a thing about it, whatever it was: with any luck, not that we'd had any luck recently, there was nothing too incriminating back there.

As they made their first sweep of the bus, I was sitting outside with Jack. A cop emerged with a little metal contraption. I'd never seen it before; it was some part of an engine. The cop confided: "We know this is what you use to cook your coke." I could barely muster a laugh.

"What?" said Jack. "There's no drugs on that. Test it. It's a spigot, something from the engine. Ask the driver."

"We're clean," I said, speaking a language the cop would understand. He cackled and disappeared back on the bus.

"Don't say *we're clean*," said Jack. "That's not the way you normally talk. It's drug language. It makes us sound guilty." He went quiet for a moment, watching a sniffer dog wag its happy tail as it clambered aboard. "And we *are* guilty. This is gonna be bad. I've gotta make some calls."

The Bishop left the sinking ship. The band played on no longer. We waited for final news about Blake's bail. If there had been gigs, there would have been no one left to play them.

Camille, Curtis, Mei-Xing, and Aslan flew back to California so, with Hell in custody, we requisitioned Heaven, taking Randy with us. He felt as out of place in their sweet-smelling bus as we did.

"See you soon," Mei-Xing had said as we lay in our last hotel bedroom. "We'll both be eighteen next time we see each other."

"God, I hope not. Maybe we'll be even older," I said, my head resting on her thigh. She smelled bready. "When are you nineteen?"

"Same day I'm sixteen. When are you eighteen?"

"August."

"I'll see you before then."

That was our last time together.

Jack and I lived on the bus, aimlessly, watching movies—the ones the police hadn't impounded. It's tedious enough living life on the road when there are gigs; when there aren't, you're just going around in circles. Randy was sinking into depression, muttering grim phrases like, "Give me a destination, man, further the better."

"Sorry," I'd say. "We just have to hang tight. Keep close until Blake needs us."

None of us had a cellphone; so we kept up with Blake via the television. Whenever we stopped, we threw in a random call to his lawyer, to keep the man on his toes. It was therefore horrible news, and a complete surprise to me, when we heard on CNN that "compromising material" including "pornography" had been found in the impounded bus. It fit the bill perfectly—drugs, crazy man, too close to the children, temptation—but there was not an ounce of truth in any of the grimmer of the associations, as the police finally—and belatedly—confirmed. It wasn't even primarily the contents of that fucking box: though they were nothing to be proud of.

The contents were Jack's, of course, a fairly comprehensive video library of his sexual encounters since his arrival in America. His particular predilection, what he liked to film, we all now knew, was women's faces. He hardly ever filmed them entirely naked, though there was a bit of everything in there, but thankfully none of the "rough stuff," all neatly labeled: Laura, Annie, Katherine, and occasionally, Mrs. Stanley, or one that just said "Kelly's Mom." Some touring musicians keep a box of Polaroids or a discreetly named iPhoto folder. Jack had videos of women's faces while they were having orgasms. That's what he filmed and what he liked. Beautiful? Sick? I think we know how he met his subjects, but had I too met them backstage? I assume he watched this collection over and over again—was that what he was doing peering into his viewfinder on the bus?—but fetishes are funny things; perhaps he never watched them. Perhaps the videos just sat there in his suitcase searing a hole in his memory. Perhaps he showed them to other women. I honestly don't know. But Blake knew. I wish I had managed to get that box off the bus, if only so I could have handed each video back to its star with an apology, and perhaps advised them not to do it again.

The bigger problem was *Blake*'s library. All those second-hand art books he kept back there: Robert Mapplethorpe, Lewis Carroll photographs, Andres Serrano, Charles Gatewood, some strange arty nudist books of kids gamboling outside quite happily in the heather. I'd seen them all and hadn't thought a thing about it. Except for one specific image. There was a paperback art book called *Temptation*, a very seventies artifact, full of paintings illustrating the subject from Bosch onwards. One by Delvaux, called *The Visit* from 1939, showed a young naked boy with a small limp penis, walking into a room in which a naked older woman, seated, waits for him. She is cupping her breasts, looking directly at his cock. It's one of the most arousing and disturbing images I've ever seen; you feel like you could get into trouble just by looking at it. Blake liked some weird stuff, sure, but possession of controversial photos and paintings isn't a crime, unless they're illegal. And none of them were. The most dubious stuff Blake possessed was some Victorian images of childhood. But all those kids were clothed, and they were in nice paintings, so those weren't even discussed.

The books and the videos added up to a nice little story. America likes a tale of redemption, but two and two makes four; you float this kind of suspicion, and all bets are off. Nothing ever made it to court, of course; it was just mentioned. I'll admit that I've removed the accusation from the Wikipedia page myself on a couple of occasions. Blake loved kids. He was Jarvis Cocker protecting the kids from the weirdo; he wasn't Michael Jackson.

"Life, As It Is Lived" had been climbing the charts: it would have been number one, for sure, but the record company, under massive pressure from MOMs, pulled the plug. Norm couldn't give a damn. There'd be another one round the corner. The thing is, if Blake had handed over those lyrics willingly, Norm probably would have taken the Wonderkids' case all the way to the Supreme Court in the name of freedom of speech and the interest of publicity. As it was, he probably just muttered "Oh, please. I don't want to hear any more about 'em" down a phone line, and that was that. He was the only person Blake never endowed with a nickname. He was always just Norm.

Blake was granted bail—generous, since he'd just violated the terms of his previous bail—and even allowed to leave the state, though in truth there was no reason for him to be out. There were no more shows. It was just nice to have him back.

"Hello ladies," he said as he entered, sniffing Heaven's air. "Nice in here. Only girls can keep a bus this clean."

He sat down. "Okay. Bonnie and Clyde time? Leg it back to England?" We both looked at him. "Randy? California!"

"Yessir!" said Randy. At last, a destination.

Blake put on a brave face, but a lot of the zip was missing. Jack could never be relied upon (besides, the word was out on him and he was lying low, too) so it was left to me to keep things bubbling. The saddest moment was when Blake started to consider replacement members for the band: maybe we could get Becca back? Somewhere, Andy was shaking his head in amazement.

There was no official statement from either the Wonderkids or the record label. Andy had said it himself: he wasn't one of those "down in the foxhole" managers. He'd told them plainly: "let's not go there." Well, we were there and he wasn't. Blake would have happily fought that Jim Morrison trial, or even the *Ulysses* trial. He would have willingly been one of the Chicago Eight, trading Wildean one-liners with an irate Judge Hoffman. He would have even loved to be involved in the "is it art or is it pornography?" debate. He would have happily read the court transcripts at gigs like Lenny Bruce, and he would have been a martyr for any one of these causes. None of these options was on offer. And the drug busts were so dull. That's what he was really facing: a bail violation and two drug busts, one on my behalf, because I was a fool. It was very likely that Blake would go to jail because of me. As we drove across the country, he seemed resigned to this, and when we finally arrived back in California, we found the house on Lookout locked to us, and Randy due out on another job.

Of course.

We were homeless.

Blake, Jack, and I moved into a motel somewhere in Toluca Lake. We had managed to be off the radar for as long as we drove across America, but now we could be found. And we were. And not by any of the people we might have wanted to find us

These were grim days, in a state that didn't want us, shortly to fly back East to face two different trials.

You knew when things were bad with Blake, because he lost his fight; his mantra became "it doesn't matter." He couldn't afford to be caught doing wrong, he was too ashamed to have fun, and without stimulation he dulled. He even stopped jiggling, his leg no longer vibrating like a tuning fork. He wrote lonely songs on a tiny uke in the corner of the room. They didn't sound like anything I'd ever heard from him before. Maybe they'd be released from his prison cell, like those Charlie Manson albums.

When you thought about it . . . all he'd done was smoke weed and, being the front man, the wild man, the face of the band, taken the fall. Yet he never asked for our apologies, rarely got our thanks, and took what was coming his way. That's what a dad does, right?

And a dad also offers a press release, like one of those family news Christmas cards. He faxed it to the record company from the shabby motel lobby: "The Wonderkids are breaking up because it's time to sing a new song. With apologies and love from Blake Lear and the Wonderkids. P.S. And, in our absence, don't forget to grow up! Or grow down! One way or the other! It's fun either way!!"

It was a relief to go to trial.

The lawyer had been in touch with the British Embassy, which dispatched a rather harried Mr. Bean character. There was a lot of waffle about "internationally accepted standards" and "prisoner's rights," but on no account could he get a British National out of prison or detention, or assure him special treatment. It seemed certain, however, that Blake would be able to serve whatever sentence he was handed at the British taxpayer's expense, due to a prison transfer deal that was part of the "special relationship." This was the best news we'd had in ages: we just wanted to go home.

After that, nothing seemed very important, and I realized that what I had feared most was simply the foreignness of the situation. All we had to do was get him back to England, then it'd be like *Porridge* or one of those groovy open prisons, something we understood.

As for the trial itself, I'd been fantasizing along the lines of "Is this all some kind of a *joke* to you, Mr. Lear?" but this was bureaucracy at its most tedious. Blake was tried in Maryland on all counts and given, coincidentally just like Jim Morrison, a six-month sentence, in this case not suspended, to be served in full. I assume he would have jumped at an offer similar to that which Morrison received—the opportunity to trade it all in for a free concert—but this was never mooted.

In an interview room afterwards, I asked whether he'd like me to stay somewhere close by until we traveled back to Britain.

"I'm not on death row," he said with something approaching a smile. "They're just holding me here for a couple of days until the transfer."

"No, but . . . I can come by whenever you like."

"You both go back home. I'll see you there. I'm sure I'll be in one of those prisons my dad is always complaining about."

"More Butlins than Broadmoor," Jack quoted.

"Blake Lear in Folsom Prison?" I suggested.

"Exactly. I'll see you there. Dad has the key to my apartment. Look after it for me."

"Home." What was home except a tour bus?

How was I equipped to deal with that?

I'd been away nearly two years.

15

"Thirty-six dollars for picking flowers and a night in jail. Goddamn. You can't hardly win, can you?"

BLAKE WAS "IN TROUBLE" FOR SIX MONTHS. THAT'S WHAT HE CALLED it. There was no chance of parole due to the complicated nature of his transfer. Six months in trouble; six months *off*.

I visited at the end of the first week, as soon as I was allowed. Blake and I faced each other across an empty table, as though we were about pit our wits in a game of Racing Demon. It was one of those situations where it's tough to be natural because you've only ever seen it on TV, and you wonder whether that's how people really behave. I felt like I might have forgotten to learn some lines; it was all a bit of a bad dream. Blake was trying, failing, to be chipper. I desperately wanted to avoid all the dumb jokes we would naturally have made on the subject—the file in the birthday cake, the soap in the shower—but this self-censorship, in which we were both complicit, served only to make the conversation more stilted.

"Everything okay?" I asked only unavoidable questions.

"Yeah. Time to think, you know. How's the old flat?" At his suggestion, I'd moved in. Rent was paid; the gas was on. But I'd forgotten how to sit still, and I was already feeling claustrophobic. "Give it a good spring clean? Time for a new start. Oh and I'm going to ask one favor. It's this: don't visit. It's great to see you, and I can't wait to get out, but . . . I think that's best." He wasn't looking at me. "Anyway, plenty to do in here. The library's pretty great, if you don't want a book written in the last fifty years."

"You don't have to pretend you're enjoying yourself."

"In a funny way, I am. I'm writing new songs. I'm reading. I'm taking a breather." I caught his eye; even he didn't believe him. I wanted him to wink, but the wink was gone.

"Right," I said. "Better than being a rock star."

"Look. This isn't perfect." To avoid my gaze, he was reduced to checking out one of my fellow visitors who was in the middle of a hissed argument with her husband. "I'm not happy to be here, but I might as well make what I can of it. And to that end, I think it would be better if you didn't come."

"Why?"

"Because it'll make the time go slower. And because I don't want to have to pull a long face even longer than yours. I don't want sympathy. I don't want to be reminded of the real world. I just want to get on and get out of here." He promptly changed the subject. "Some people actually get to work out in the community a bit; come home by curfew."

"Bit of a holiday camp, is it?"

"That's what Dad would say."

"Will he come?"

"I didn't have to tell *him* not to. He's under the impression that the punishment is mostly his. I told Jack the same as you. It'll be gone in a flash. I'll write. Often."

I watched my breath mist the window of the little bus that ferried the prison visitors back to the train station.

"What's wrong, love?" asked a woman whom I'd seen inside growling at her husband. "Your mate'll be okay."

"He's my . . ." I was going to say "dad" but it suddenly seemed a ludicrous thing to say. He didn't look old enough to be my dad; I didn't look anything like him or behave like his son. I mean, all children finally get to know their parents as real people—don't they?—but I'd never really had the previous bit with

Blake, the absolute trust, the unconditional blind love, despite his countless kindnesses to me, his wish to protect me. He said a few times that I'd missed out on a childhood, but he couldn't do anything about it despite his best intentions. I mean, not criticizing me for eating sugar wasn't going to do it. I remembered I was in the middle of a conversation: "Yeah, he's my mate."

"Well, he'll be fine, love. My Bob's got three more. Won't hardly know Sharon. I'd take her in to visit, but I don't want her to see him like that." She dismissed the thought with a swat of her hand. "Next week? Same time, same place?"

"I'm done," I said. For some reason, she took my hand and squeezed, reminding me of Becca.

The majority of my knowledge of Normanside Prison, which wasn't quite as open as I'd imagined, comes from Blake's letters, rather than that sole visit, for which I was muddled, annoyed, and finally a little teary-eyed, though I didn't let Blake see.

At first, the letters were merely descriptive of the daily routine, the lack of privacy, the small acts of kindness. It was easy to read between the lines but clear that Blake was doing his very best not to communicate any negativity about his experience. Anger and resentment were notable by their absence. The letters were controlled, documentarian. They implicitly begged me to adopt the same tone in reply. I wasn't as good at disguising my own feelings.

"Why doesn't he want us to visit?" I asked Jack.

"Spoils the rhythm," he replied. Blake had sold him on that story too. I wasn't buying.

"How's Barry taking it?"

"Doesn't want to know. Hasn't told the neighbors. Lucky no one's heard of the Wonderkids over here. I knew failure would pay off." Jack laughed. Scandal or no scandal, he wouldn't need to work for a while (even though the money was mysteriously held up mid-Atlantic). Nor would I. What with my rent-free apartment and Blake's cashpoint card, it was like I was still on per diems. But I was already antsy. Blake cooped up made me want to keep moving.

"Bit of bother of my own, actually," said Jack. "Lucky it's not muddled up in all this." He flicked imaginary fluff from his sleeve. "Remember how we really thought we'd arrived when that first paternity suit popped up? Well, we can't laugh this one away. I haven't got such a good excuse."

"Oh." I raised my can. "Congratulations? Further icing on the WonderCake?" Maybe it was that woman on the front seat of our tour bus, heels to the ceiling. That was a mental image I could do without. Why is it that all the horrible stuff stays with you and the nice stuff disappears? And why, for that matter, hadn't Mei-Xing called me back?

"But the thing is . . . my girlfriend is coming over and I don't know what to tell her."

"I didn't know you had a girlfriend." This seemed far more significant than a stray baby.

"Well I didn't, and I do, and we're going to give it a go."

"Did I meet her?"

"You heard about her. Rita."

"Oh," The penny dropped. "Is she the one who . . .?" I put one wrist over the other in an x, palms up. He nodded. "Right. Not the . . . not the kid type then? But . . ." I didn't know quite how to put it. "Sane?"

"Oh yeah. Sanest woman I ever met."

"Then tell her the truth. Jack Lewis, father, boyfriend: what next?"

"Guitar God would be nice."

I wanted to organize something but couldn't seem to start with myself. I shuffled papers around my desk, jiggling with impatience, fingers itching to get working on a project, an itinerary, a chart. Greg was my one distraction. I always felt at home in his flat, that rundown, dusty museum of rock 'n' roll of which he was the laziest curator in the world. Barry was in denial, Jack otherwise occupied, but Greg was thoroughly put out by the *No Visitors* rule.

"I could help," he said. "I was in as a lad. I know the drill, the language."

"That's the last thing Blake wants. Says he just wants to learn from it and move on."

"But I've always wanted to see one of those new prisons."

"Well, perhaps it's time to cool the tourist impulse and consider the needs of the prisoner."

"Spoken word," said Greg. "I sent him a postcard of Strangeways with *Wish You Were Here* written on it."

"Nice," I said. It's the most versatile word ever, "nice." I can inflect it to mean almost anything. In this case it meant: "Not very nice, and not at all considerate." The whole idea of incarceration made him misty-eyed. He imagined prison a pleasant existence, like working at a record label in the seventies but without the bother of compulsory late night gigs. Life was too many choices; prison would simplify things.

"He'll be out in a couple of weeks with good behavior," was his wistful conclusion.

"It doesn't work like that. He stays for the entire time. And then if he ever gets caught with drugs again, he's in big trouble."

"Wanna cuppa?" Greg shuffled into the kitchen, asking over his shoulder: "What do the letters say?"

"Well, they've changed a bit actually. At first, he just told me what was going on; and then he started to tell me more about his feelings about stuff." Greg groaned at what he interpreted as a negative development. "No, it's good. He was ashamed but he wouldn't admit it. Now he's over it, over trying to rise above it; it's his punishment and he should accept it, or he might as well not have been punished at all. Have a look. It ends: 'I'm going to come out of this a better person. I'm just looking for a little humility.'"

"Yeah, well, he'd probably like a holiday somewhere warm," Greg remarked from the kitchen.

"What?"

He popped his head round the corner: "Humidity?"

"*Humility.*"

"Read that bit again." I did. "Bit *Jesus-y*, isn't it? *Humility.*" He didn't like the taste of the word.

"He's looking for a little meaning."

"That's how it starts," said Greg.

"He's probably joking."

• • •

The next time I saw Greg was over snooker at Framed on the Uxbridge Road. It was one of those places he went to keep in touch with whatever cartoon version of the underworld he liked to feel himself familiar; the place scared the crap out of me. I'd seen a cue or two broken there before, in one case *wrapped* around an opponent. It was, he thought, a haunt for *villains*. Greg loved villains, though they existed only in his imagination—old-fashioned gentlemen gangsters who loved their mums, wouldn't hurt a child, wore sharp suits, and occasionally maimed people. In fact, Framed was racked with louts.

As I bent over to play a shot, I happened to scratch my behind. A heavy bloke announced to Greg in a thick Ulster accent: "I didn't know your mate . . ."—he said it "meat," if "meat" had two syllables—". . . was getting married!" I assumed it was the overture to trouble.

"He's what, mate?" asked Greg politely but with an atypically working-class accent, quite the reverse of Mrs. Terry's approach to the word "duvet."

"I said," the man repeated aggressively, "I didn't know your *meat* was getting married." He addressed me directly. "Son! Are you getting married?

"No," I answered.

"Oh, only I just saw you *pickin' your ring.*"

The assembled company nodded and laughed mirthlessly, in considered appreciation of this line rather than specifically at me. Greg, however, nearly cried with laughter. "Pickin' your ring!" He took to repeating it in a variety of accents and deliveries, chuckling after each reinterpretation. We finally got back to our game, which, as usual, he was winning. He could be mystically calm around a snooker table. I preferred pool.

"So I've had a chat with Blake. He's called me in for a meeting." Greg loved meetings; they were the high point of existence, reason to get up in the morning. And a meeting in a prison: too perfect. Meetings, I told myself, didn't count as *visits*; that's the only way I could keep from being upset. "He's got an album of material ready to go, acoustic."

"Is Mr. Hedges interested?" Maybe I'd tag along. No.

"Nick?" He polished off the blue ball, lined up the pink, and set his sights on the black. "Not at all interested, though I think he'd be quite interested in never hearing from me again. Wanted are in though, and I'm taking William in to meet with Blake. They've got American distribution."

Greg had the phenomenally annoying habit of, after he'd lined up the winning ball, looking directly at, and talking to, you while he nonchalantly potted it. I bet he got it from Blake.

The letters took a sharp left turn.

We'd gone through resentment, shame, Blake feeling sorry for himself. Now he wanted a new life. He had a guitar with him, he was playing pretty much all the time: new stuff, all true, about his life, the band, this and that girlfriend, the one who left him when she was pregnant. "Twilight in My Cell, Twilight in My Heart" was one title he mentioned; "The Devil's Daughter" another. "The thing is," he wrote, "I don't find myself worthy of any of this yet. I mean *trouble*. I didn't do anything to really deserve it, so I should do something that makes it all worthwhile."

It was a bit over the top. When did a drug bust and subsequent imprisonment do anything but enhance the glamour of a musician's career? I mean, it gets a bit undignified on the David Crosby end of the spectrum, smoking crack under your jacket on an airplane, but the great coked-up walrus was still flying first class. For those in coach, the rest of rock 'n' roll, a drug bust's not really going to do any damage.

"I can't write the nonsense anymore," was perhaps Blake's saddest pronouncement. "It was perfect then, but now I need a new way. Start making sense. But it's still a battle against the Philistines! Against Respectability! Against Self-Importance! Against Orthodoxy!"

What on earth was he reading in that library full of out-of-date books? I assumed it was the Bible. (I mean, you would, wouldn't you?) Or maybe Karl Marx. But it wasn't the Bible; it was Oscar Wilde. And a Wilde Complex is just as bad as a Messiah Complex. The Gods gave Oscar everything, but from the disgrace of his prison cell, he saw that he had allowed himself to be lured over to squander his talents over on the dark side. It was perfect for Blake.

And now these songs, these new true no-nonsense songs about his life, the ones he'd started writing on our shiftless trip across America. What on Earth were those going to be like?

Blake was released in February 1993, his new album the following month. He didn't let us know exactly when he was coming home, but he made it clear that there was to be no celebration: no champagne, no bunting. Barry in particular was not to be told.

The first I knew was the surprise turn of a key in my own front door. There he stood with his guitar and a bag of possessions. I hugged him: "Welcome home. Thank God that's over."

"It isn't," he said, surveying the recently "spring-cleaned" apartment. "It's just starting. But, hey, it's good to be here."

"Right," I said. "Well, I'd better give you some space."

"You stay here, no problem. I've got another place lined up. There'll be some gigs for the album. I've got to stick around for a bit on curfew and take a job. In fact, I'm going back to The Regal. And then I'm going to dust off the old passport."

"Well, you've been inside a lot." It was precisely what he would have said. He didn't crack a smile.

"I'm going to write a book, or read some good books; one or the other. They both sound nice."

"About your experiences at the prison? About the band?"

"No. Wanna hear a record?"

An Act of His Own, the first Blake Lear solo album, bore two quotations on the back cover: Emerson—"Nothing is more rare in any man than an act of his own"—and Oscar Wilde—"Most people are other people."

I don't know what he hoped for from its release, how he imagined the best-case scenario. Certainly, the songs meant a lot to him. They passed his ultimate test, remembered from university: the unity of a thing with itself, the outward rendered expressive of the inner. But hadn't the nonsense songs that brought him such unexpected success passed exactly the same test? That was the sadness: he was unable, consciously, to do the thing that he had been able to do so easily unconsciously. Like the owl and the pussycat, the sublime and the ridiculous danced hand in hand on the edge of the sand by the light of the moon. Blake was at his best, his sandiest, when he was at his most trivial. And he couldn't, or didn't want to, access that side of his brain. What was he now afraid of? Did he feel a need to keep a tighter rein on his subconscious? I'd always thought that the nonsense was a kind of safety valve for him. So what would happen now that he couldn't let off steam?

The new songs were a perfect marriage of form and content, truly expressive of the new Blake Lear; judged by those standards they were entirely successful. Judged by any other, the album was a bit of a nightmare. I'm not saying for a second that I didn't like it. But anybody else who bothered to judge said precisely that.

Unfortunately, whatever he hoped for from the release eluded him entirely. The worst-case scenario played out tediously. The album, about which he was initially enthusiastic, albeit with an air of slight resignation, should perhaps have been presented with a bit more pizzazz: "Welcome to My New Direction!" But that wasn't the new Blake Lear. Why he even kept the name I'll never know. The spirit of Blake Lear, and his component parts, Blake and Lear, were nowhere to be found, unless you went back to the "Little Lamb, who made thee?" stuff. There was a bit of that, but without the childish wonder that had always been his strong suit. The whole thing seemed weary. You longed for the old Blake, "Lord High Bosh and Nonsense Producer," amusing himself for his own diversion.

He rented a rather characterless apartment, to which he never specifically invited me, two streets down. Two streets down! And he was working at the Regal again. It was as though he wanted all the same things, the same haunts, but didn't actually want to be the same person. His new place seemed more of a prison than the relatively spacious Normanside. There was a kettle, a bed, a guitar, no TV, and lots of books. I was in the habit of knocking on his door every now and then, just to check up on him. (He was always in.)

Once I was sitting on the only comfortable chair when Greg

rang, instructing Blake not to buy the *NME*. Blake immediately told me to pop out and buy the *NME*, which I did, assuming there was finally a good review to be had. When I returned, he tossed it on to the sofa nonchalantly. It sat there, waiting to be read, but Blake wouldn't pick it up. Finally, I did.

"Oh leave that till later," he said, dunking a tea bag like he was ducking a witch.

"Well, presumably there's a review if Greg told you to buy it."

"Well actually he told me not to, so it probably isn't a very good one."

It wasn't.

At a time when so many of this country's Britpop heavy-weights are almost self-consciously rejecting transatlantic influences in a bid to throw off grunge's post-colonial yoke, the despairing pursuit of 'Stateside' success of which Blake Lear's press-release misguidedly boasts might at least have the whiff of a heroic failure about it. Unfortunately, it doesn't. Taking H. L. Mencken's famous maxim that "Nobody ever went broke underestimating the taste of the American public" as its gospel, Lear's band—fancifully named the Wonderkids, after a failed UK launch under the name the Wunderkinds: remember them? No—pursued a demographic of cloth-eared mall-rats and Walmart-weaned teenage shut-ins with suffi-cient principle-free relentlessness to eventually earn them-selves a small piece of the MTV major label pie.

And how did Lear celebrate this triumph of musical bad faith? He immediately got himself thrown in jail by means of an embarrassing drugs bust, that's how. Sadly, mak-ing yourself a walking rock 'n' roll cliché does not carry a mandatory life-sentence in the Land of the Free (otherwise half the current Billboard top 10 would be languishing be-hind bars). But Lear's next move was calculated to take even the most hardened cynic's breath away. After sucking Satan's cock in pursuit of airbrushed corporate pop success for the previous few years, he decided to reinvent himself overnight as a tortured artist. And if you think that what the world really needs is another depressed Oscar Wilde–quoting Oxbridge graduate strumming an acoustic guitar, his new album might just take your breath away. —Tom Benson

And on.

"Could it be worse?" asked Blake as though he didn't care.

"Not really," I said.

"Should I read it?"

"If you weren't going to, you wouldn't have bought it."

"That's the thing, see?" said Blake. "There's no pigeonhole for me now. You go through that and there's no way back; you go to prison, and when you get out that's when you're abandoned, just when you need the help most."

"Blake, are you actually okay?"

He didn't answer. He was staring at the kettle flex, which looked like the curly lead taut between the young Dave Davies's Epiphone and his amp. Not to Blake, it didn't. He was looking right through it. After an interminable pause, he said: "The trouble is: you get punished for the good you do as well as the bad you do. That's what happened in America. And yes," he said. "I'm fine. I half-expected it. I knew I was going out on a limb."

"Is the album coming out in America?" If there was a silver lining, I'd find it. "Seems like the notoriety might give it some profile."

"I'm pulling it."

"Since when?"

"Since now. I don't want to thrive on notoriety. I want people to hear it for what it is, and obviously the time isn't yet." I'd never seen him so still.

"So what next?"

"I'm going to get some money together and travel."

"Do you want some company?" I was worried about him on his own. It was that bad.

"No thanks. I'm going take a breather from London, and from music, and from society, and I'm going to put my trust in nature."

"You're going to be a tramp?" I couldn't see him sleeping rough.

"Far from it. I'm going to Italy. San Remo."

"San Remo? Isn't that on the Riviera?" It was the last place I would have predicted. I just didn't see him swapping the city for a casino holiday.

"Yeah, Edward Lear spent his last twenty years there. That's where he's buried. Lived there with his cat Foss. I'm going to write a novel about him. At the age of forty or so, he grew two new teeth that he'd never had before. Weird, right? So, it's back to nonsense for me."

This actually sounded not horrible, the least worst alternative. I imagined the old Blake peeking out.

Apparently, there was a serious problem extricating the money from the accountants in Los Angeles; there were bills to be paid, royalties owing, contractual disputes. The money would come, but not yet. Blake put in extra hours at the Regal until he had just enough to leave with. And he was gone.

Greg didn't complain about the abject failure of *An Act of His Own*. It seemed to give him perverse pleasure, as though its pitiful showing and disastrous reception made it more memorable, more successful even, than albums that had merely done okay, got a few good reviews. Its immediate consignment to the dustbin gave the record a kind of mythical status, perfect future anecdote material, another story over a pint of beer: Blake Lear's solo record. Remember that one?

"I mean, seriously, man," Greg said with a kind of awe as we stood with Jack at the Coachy. "It's a real achievement. Anyone can have a record out, anyone can have a hit if they've got enough dough behind them, but it's a one in a million record that does that badly. I don't think it's sold twenty-five copies. And the reviews were amazing."

"They were *terrible*," said Jack.

"Yeah, but amazing. I mean, it's much easier not to get reviews at all. A record's got to be seriously great or earth-shatteringly crap to get that much bad ink. That's something you really have to earn."

Jack also derived pleasure from the album's self-immolation, but his reasons were less bizarrely poetic, more self-interested: "The band was always a band. Jimmy should've had me put together a combo for him. I should have written the tunes."

"When's he back?" asked Greg.

"Dunno," I said. "Expect azure blue postcards from San Remo. He's writing a book."

"Licking his wounds," said Jack, real older brother stuff. He blamed Blake entirely for the demise of their band, the canceled endorsements, the lack of a free lunch. "Oh, I have to duck out. I'm meeting Rita at the flicks, though she'll probably be late."

"Maybe she's tied up," I said. It was certainly what Blake would have said.

"Who needs Blake when you're around?" asked Jack. We watched him go, an unusual bounce in his step: Blake's failure, Rita's submissiveness.

"Greg," I said. "I'm so bored. I don't like sitting around. Can you get me on the road? I know what to do. I'd be good at it."

"Merch? Roadie?"

"Road manager, Greg."

"You're very young."

"I'd be a very good, very young road manager."

Greg liked the smell of it. Another tale to tell.

"I'll ask around, mate. I'll ask around."

"What's Blake going to do for money?" I asked. "When's that all gonna clear up?"

"Oh, he'll be okay. He's sold a lot of those old posters and the rest are on consignment."

"Posters?" I just didn't put two and two together; besides, Greg often misremembered.

"Yeah, those old posters from the Regal. He's been getting them out on the sly, a few every night."

"Ernie's posters."

"Dunno. Yeah. He got, like, a grand for a *Citizen Kane* poster or something. A grand! For a piece of paper!"

I said nothing; I couldn't believe it, but there was no point talking to Greg. I later found out that the widow was dead, and that there were no children, but somehow that didn't make it any better.

"So, a road manager," said Greg. "Lemme think."

I've plied my trade as a gentleman of the road ever since.

I'll save those stories for another book, one I'll never write. You don't need to know that I am familiar with every motorway service station in Britain; with every promoter who promises cash then pays by check; with the rainy festivals of Europe and the third-floor clubs of Japan where shows start at dusk; with the backstage toilets in which not even GG Allin would take a dump. I learned many years ago that "the phones have been ringing off the hook" means that there will be no walk-up whatsoever. And of course, the rules of the tour bus are exactly the same as they always were—still sleep feet first, still no shitting, and, most of all, don't get left behind. As tour manager, this has only happened on my watch once: Joan Baez.

None of it would I describe as glamorous, even the bits that others do. Sometimes it's a bit like getting married every day, eating the finest food, drinking bubbly, being showered with gifts; eventually, you just want a day off. (Ian Hunter said that.) Other times, it's just like you're never going to stop getting divorced from the same person.

In fact, long before I began my career as a road manager, before I was even eighteen, I'd reached the point most people hit in their thirties, when travel stops broadening the mind, when a day off no longer represents a chance to explore a city or even go to the gym, when you can't even be bothered to leave your mark on another dressing-room wall. And that point is when, frankly, you should stop. But I didn't because it was where I felt at home; and somehow I pushed through it, broke on through to the other side, and got better. And it was all because of the Wonderkids: I knew exactly what not to do. It's not only about how many clicks you are from your destination, or being on time; it's about living a proper life while you're doing it; it's about caring about where you are on the map. And reading. And learning. And it was only when I realized this that I became really good at my job. And I am good, as good as Mitchell in his prime. Being on the road is a beautiful thing if you're not on the run. It's just that every now and then I'd like to settle down; run the company and have other people do the whizzing about for a while.

And one thing I'll say for the job: it's kept me in cufflinks even through the recessions—my price has never gone down. And it's kept me moving. You should have seen my apartment when I was ever there; worse than Blake's post-prison cell. But it all becomes a blur. Funny, isn't it? Touring with the Wonderkids is as clear as day, fresh as bread. And everything I do now, I remember because I write most of it up for my blog. But the middle years? Sixteen or seventeen of them! I mean, I remember the bands, I've moved with the technology, but they're not in the hard drive.

I saw the Terrys recently. Old Terry can't remember if he's had dinner, can't follow the plot of the TV show he's watching (unless she continually reminds him), can't even remember if he's turned the radio down or not, but he can talk about his childhood as though it happened yesterday. Though of course, that's a bad simile, because if it had happened yesterday, he wouldn't remember anything about it at all.

"Don't you have anything you could be reading?"

BLAKE LIVED NEAR THE VILLA TENNYSON, LEAR'S HOUSE IN SAN Remo. At first, there were postcards. The entirety of one early arrival was "Hello!" but the signature encouraged me: "Chakonoton the Cozovex Dossi Fossi Sini Tomentilla Coronilla Polentilla Battledore & Shuttlecock Derry down Derry Dumps." Communication was patchy. Perhaps he was gambling away his ill-gotten gains at the Casino: unlikely. No more the long letters, the Ballad of Normanside Prison, soul-searching from his cell. I mean, it was a breakdown, wasn't it? He'd probably grown a beard. The postcards became more occasional, hastily scratched, often showing the same stretch of San Remo beach, as if he'd bought a job lot, generally consisting of only one word: "writing" said one; "breathing" another. Then finally, almost a year later, he really let the ink run free: "Coming home."

Blake looked healthy, tanned, shaved, surprisingly slim with his shirt tucked in. He did a good impression of being happy to be back, but was no more forthcoming about his missing year than he had been by mail. There was a pile of pages to show for it however, and this continued to grow on the side of his desk. It was more or less the only thing that changed in his room, so you noticed.

He moved his old stuff into a new place, which emptied mine out though I was hardly ever there. He went out drinking with Greg—that was his one regular appointment—but the new focus was a book deal, for which he'd fly under his own flag: James Lewis. Greg had much advice on the subject, about which he knew as little as I did, including "Yeah, don't have it by Blake Lear, because it'll look like you're related."

Blake wanted to know how my new job was going, and why, of all things, I wanted to be a road manager: "Stop organizing other people. Do your own thing."

"I like doing something I'm good at. I like being in charge. I always admired Mitchell. I took notes."

At the mention of Mitchell's name, he looked up: "God, is this all my fault?"

"This suits me. I feel like I'm putting knowledge to good use."

He asked about girls, but I never had much to say. Despite my good albeit unconventional education, I was always a bit awkward that way, up to quite recently. Maybe I wanted it to be as easy as it had been, all Disneyland and Monopoly, and it wasn't. It was the initial bit I found difficult. The road isn't conducive to lengthy relationships, but it's good for one-night stands, which aren't conducive to lengthy relationships. Don't have sex with people you're on tour with. That's the basic rule. Don't even ask them on a date until the tour is over: so embarrassing if they say no.

As I was closing in on this girl's hometown once, I sent this text: "What you got on?" It's perfectly acceptable British *textage* for "What are you doing today?," a casual way of inviting her to the show. But she took it the wrong way, was in fact offended, because she was American and thought I was asking what she was wearing, assuming I expected the response "nothing but a smile" or "a nurse's uniform." She wasn't having any of my excuses and that was that. Another time, a woman replied to a casual text of mine with "I'm busty." Much as I wanted to take it literally, I knew it was a typo.

So back then, I didn't have a girlfriend. I didn't want a girlfriend. I was the most, least experienced twenty-year-old in the world. I asked Blake whether he had one. He answered obliquely: "Lear, you know, proposed twice to the same woman; she was nearly fifty years younger than he was. She refused twice and that was that. None of his friends came to his funeral, not one. I don't want to end up like that."

How Pleasant to Know Mr. Lear, Blake's novel, was finally finished. He handed over the manuscript, an imposing overly thick, single-spaced doorstop, with the sole remark: "Well, it isn't nonsense."

I am not a literary critic. I do a bit of paid writing occasionally for those who ask, generally friends or acquaintances or those who have read my blog (*gentlemanoftheroad.com*), and I read a lot, but I assumed a lot of it was over my head; Blake was the expert. I told him I enjoyed it, but I can't say I did. I remember a sinking feeling when I looked at the pile of read pages and realized it was still smaller than the pile of unread pages. When they reached equality, I was ready to be done, and there was still a long way to go; well, halfway I guess, but a long half.

Besides the fact that the book wasn't terribly exciting, it was hard to tell whether it was a novel or a biography (I'm pontificating; that was one agent's criticism, verbatim). Most depressing of all was that Blake sought to explain away all of Lear's nonsense. None of it was allowed to be simply nonsense. Lear was gay but couldn't face it, therefore his work is full of images of impossible relationships (owls and pussycats, nutcrackers and sugar tongs, etc.). Lear's health was bad—he was an epileptic; he had bronchitis and chronic asthma; he was a depressive; later he was partially blind—hence those quarantined freaks, the Pobble, the Dong, the Quangle Wangle. His lack of money explained one poem; his fear of matrimony another; his antipathy to noise, perhaps due to tinnitus, another. I'm not saying that biography can't or shouldn't inform literature; I'm just saying that the book actually ruined Edward Lear for me forever. That can't be good.

Perhaps *How Pleasant to Know Mr. Lear* is just what his college Monsignor wanted all those years ago when Blake instead chose to hand in his own nonsense. Perhaps Blake finally wanted his First from Cambridge. As Blake explained away Lear's nonsense, so Blake explained himself away. He wasn't putting his own nonsense down to illness or unresolved sexuality; he was saying that nonsense couldn't just be nonsense, perhaps thereby challenging anyone interested to discover the reasons behind his own. Well, I wasn't going there. He couldn't have children, therefore he chose to entertain other people's: that's pretty obvious. So, it wasn't just that the book wasn't objectively good—though nicely written, even I could tell that—it was that he'd spent almost three years on a project that was, more or less, the burial of the Blake Lear I, *we*, loved.

There were interesting bits, but mainly for what they told me about the author rather than his subject. Edward Lear too found himself successful, almost overnight, in a field far from the one he had originally envisioned. He had intended to make his money as an ornithological illustrator, but ended up a famous Nonsense writer, rather as Blake, too, had ended up a children's entertainer by mistake. There was Lear's childishness, what one critic called his "Peterpantheism," his fear of "the demon boredom," his travel fetish. I bet he was a fidgeter, too. Though I'd never associated Blake with the feelings of manly inadequacy to which Lear was prey, it made you wonder about his lack of permanent girlfriends, his scant interest in the peripatetic art of the one-night stand. I remember once looking at an oil painting with him in the Philadelphia Museum of Art, an amazing Eastern landscape called *Mahabalipuram*; tall elegant green trees either side of a ruined temple. Blake asked me the painter, and I read the little plaque: "Edward Lear. Is that the same Edward Lear? Can't be, right?" He didn't answer. When I looked, he was crying. I guess there was a period when he cried a lot, and I should have paid more attention.

If his book had been a success, if he'd ended up chatting on *The Book Show*, and been asked to write a Top Ten List of Nonsense Poetry for the *Guardian* website or whatever you did back then, perhaps this would be a different story with a different ending. But the book wasn't published. And when the wearying, slow-motion process of rejection was complete, when the cycle of phone calls to people who don't call you back, so you call them again but they don't take your call and you instead talk to their brusque assistant (who is polite but firm and to whom you realize you may sound a little desperate), when you realize you're hurrying them to say "no" and that no amount of phone calls will elicit an enthusiastic "yes," and may in fact ensure a hastening of the final, regretful "no," when all these things were done and the last name on the list had been crossed out, Blake gave up.

He was afraid where nonsense would lead him; but sense wasn't doing anything for him either. He couldn't record under the name Blake Lear; he couldn't write under the name James Lewis; he couldn't teach because of his flirtation with the dark side. And because he couldn't do any of those things, he became a ghost. Blake Lear only haunted us from hereon. He was there; he was around; he floated about in our orbit; he occasionally clanked his chains. He had to find something else, but what can a ghost do? He is insubstantial, not of this world. Society, as Blake once said, it seemed to me rather dramatically, had no place for him. It was right around now that his shirt untucked itself again. He "went floaty," is, I think, the phrase. His waistline expanded. The adrenaline was no longer keeping him slim. In what I can only assume was some kind of drunken stupor, he decided to put the band back together. About this futile reunion, the less said the better, beyond the fact that it wasted two years.

What can ghosts do? They can ghostwrite.

Jack and Rita had their first child, Charles, aka, to Barry's disquiet, Chuck. (No one mentioned the paternity suit kid, apparently female, though she exerted a financial toll on Jack that spoke for almost all of his American royalties, siphoned in her direction before they had a chance to cross the Atlantic. In fact, for various reasons, no one made a lot of money from the Wonderkids except the record label, managers past and present, and lawyers; funny that.) Jack was a good dad to the kid in his own front room. He griped about it, but he was generally happy, even when Chuck squirted nappy rash cream into the sound-hole of an old Gibson. Suddenly all the amps were moved to some rehearsal studio and guitars hung out of reach. I helped his new band out every now and then, when I was free and couldn't be bothered to do nothing. His ultimate compliment: "Nice to work with a professional."

And then a year and a half later, there was another kid, Johnny, a dark-haired boy to match the earlier fair-haired model. I enjoyed being Uncle Sweet (technically Cousin Sweet, but we were and would remain an unconventional family). I'd been educated into the role, and I knew what to do, but Blake, the man who was born to it, got little out of the experience. Gone were all the games and the card tricks, as if he'd forgotten them. He didn't even get down on his hands and knees. It was Barry who surprised the family with his willingness to get his cuffs dirty. He also turned out to be a hysterical prognosticator of a child's future profession: "Perhaps he'll be a footballer," if the kid so much as swung a leg; "I wonder if he'll be a comedian," when the kid smiled. It was an obsession with Barry: "I think he'll be a musician, just like his dad."

Rita was great. Sure, she and Jack met in odd circumstances, but they're still married. She once told a joke: when the masochist says "beat me, beat me," the real sadist says "no." And Jack presumably never said no. So who's in charge? Their bedroom door was always firmly closed. Just as well. I wouldn't have wanted to discover any hooks and pulleys or nooks and crannies in the walls.

Jack remarked on the kids' development with grumpy wonder: "why does color matter so much? Chuck *has* to eat off a blue plate. If it's not blue he won't touch it. Maybe he's color autistic."

"Would you play a pink Stratocaster?" I asked.

"No, but that's totally different."

One Christmas, he was sifting through a set of twenty-six animals, the first letters of which corresponded to a letter on a particular play mat: "Urial and ibex, what are they? Are they new species? Can't they come up with something better? I mean, granted they're in trouble with *x*, and x-ray fish is the only option, but urial and ibex?"

"What's wrong with unicorn and imp?" asked Blake. "Like

in the old days." It was the funniest thing he'd said in about three years. At the pub, he was always happy to listen to Greg make the old gags.

"It was always iguana for *i*," said Barry, after consideration. "But I don't remember what *u* was. Certainly not Urial or Unicorn. It's political correctness gone mad."

Blake and he were uneasy together but nothing ever came of it. It simmered, a bit like me and the Terrys once upon a time.

"And how are you keeping yourself busy, Jimmy?" Barry would ask. "Idle hands, you know, idle hands."

How on earth *did* Blake fill his days? He'd got into electric trains, I knew that, inspired by Neil Young, who had used to inspire him in other ways. When Blake flipped the switch, his attic became a whirr of activity, scale models zipping around a labyrinthine layout to a futurist soundtrack of chuffing and puffing, perhaps reminding him of the distant days when he was planning his own theme park. Did he spend all his time up there? He took me up once or twice, to show off his new points or something, but never invited his nephews. It wasn't for kids.

As daft adult hobbies went, even therapeutic ones, one might have hoped for something a little steamier. I honestly had no idea what he was up to apart from perfecting his impression of the Fat Controller.

The first thing I knew about Judith Esther's *The Dark-Headed Clock Trilogy* was the first thing most people knew about it. It was everywhere.

You probably had a better idea if you were in primary school, chatting in the playground, or reading a trade journal. But for the rest of us, the ones without children, those outside the publishing industry, there was nothing, a vacuum. And then there was *The Dark-Headed Clock*.

At first, there were stacks of the first volume on the front tables of bookshops, cheeky Gothic cover luring you in; then its spine started appearing on the shelves you least expected, in friends' houses, on Greg's bedside cabinet, behind the prime minister's head in an interview on TV. Apparently, the first volume,

The Toll of the Dark-Headed Clock, was one of those books enjoyed by both children and their parents alike, similar to the Pullman books and the Harry Potter books, of which the Judith Esther book seemed to me—paying the scantest attention—a great rip-off (though I'd never read the Potters, and only seen two of the films, both as hotel pay-per-views, purely as a sleep aid).

Then there were posters in the Underground advertising the second in the trilogy, *The Shadow of the Dark-Headed Clock*, which morphed imperceptibly into posters advertising a movie of the first volume, featuring many stars, mainly British, directed by a recent Oscar-winning Yank. Waiting at a bus stop in autumn, one looked down to see a frantically ripped-open and then rapidly discarded wrapper from some *Dark-Headed Clock* trading cards. Christmas would bring *Dark-Headed Clock* sponsored Christmas decorations down Regent Street as surely as, beneath them, Hamley's window would bulge with fake snow and Dark Clocks of various shapes and sizes made in China.

In reality, this took a few years, I suppose, but in *life as it is lived* time, it happened overnight. It was like someone said "Let there be *Dark-Headed Clock*," and there was *Dark-Headed Clock*, twenty-four hours a day, seven days a week. It was one of those phenomena that is felt everywhere, in casual jokes on TV chat shows, in the pop charts, in Halloween costumes, in questions in the Houses of Parliament, and in comment, for and against, in the newspapers; some liked its message, some didn't.

The Dark-Headed Clock Trilogy consisted of the classic *Toll*, the superior sequel *Shadow*, and the climactic *Midnight in the Dark-Headed Clock*, the biggest seller of them all, whispered by some to be a disappointing finale, though the franchise had by now reached critical mass and couldn't possibly underperform. And I will also remind you that it was about twin boys, one with blonde hair, Bill, and one with dark, Ed, their father conspicuously absent in fine fairy story fashion, who discover (*Toll*), confront (*Shadow*), and battle (*Midnight*) a secret cadre of scientists perpetrating an enormous and terrifying fraud upon the general populace for their own selfish gain.

The trilogy was heavy on the Christian allegory (lauded by none other than the Archbishop of Canterbury, attacked by no less than Richard Dawkins), and even seemed to include—to the distress of rationalists everywhere—a subliminal course in self-realization, combining Christian philosophy with elements of those weird books like *The Secret*, which sell a million copies but no one really knows what they're about or why anyone is reading them. There was a whole lot of Lion, plenty of Witch, and shelf upon shelf of Wardrobe, and certainly no need for me to read them. You just picked up on them by osmosis.

I do remember thinking one specific thing however, one night on public transport going home. There were thirty people in the carriage, and six of them—20 percent!—were reading one or other volume of *The* fucking *Dark-Headed Clock*. And what I remember thinking, knowing whatever it was that I knew of these books: Blake would have absolutely hated them.

Well, of course, Blake did hate them. Unfortunate, really, since he wrote them.

I mean, that's a bush I can't beat about, and you've probably figured it out, if you didn't already know. By the time Blake did announce his authorship to the world at large, the moment had passed; the clock had tick-tocked its last and would never be wound again. There were six separate volumes by the end; Blake had made all the money there was to be made, and would be making that money for most of the rest of his life. I'd been wondering if he was skating by on whatever Wonderkids royalties trickled his way, along with the poster revenue, but no, he had another source of income we knew nothing about.

We knew nothing about it because he wasn't proud of it. He didn't like it. The books had hardly been his idea. They started life as a joke. Greg's mate, Kirk, the wordsmith behind many hastily-remaindered rock biographies, at whose house they occasionally gathered after last call to smoke pot and listen to Johnny Cash, had started, one stoned night, to muse aloud: "You know what someone should do? A Christian twist on those Harry Potter books. That would be huge."

It was one of those conversational gambits that open the door on many silly suggestions and puns. The books could have died then and there, stillborn, in a lengthy stoned sketch, but, it was agreed between toke and exhalation that such a series, if

written, would clean up. Blake stayed up that night and wrote
the synopsis for the first three—based on a silly idea he'd had
years before, a silly idea for which I had rescued the doodled
blueprints from the WonderBus—and, over a subsequent drink,
told Kirk he'd found a plot: it was something he could do, and
he needed something to do. Kirk, only mildly miffed (he didn't
envy Blake the epic task, though he would always take credit),
explained that he'd recently had a meeting with a children's
book editor who had expressed the desire for something to cap-
italize on Harry Potter, which had set him thinking in the first
place. Not his bag, obviously, kids and all that. Why didn't Blake
meet with the editor?

That is apparently how books are sold, not actually by writing them in dignified solitude at a distance: who knew? A three-
book deal was put into place by an agent delighted to oversee this
relatively sure thing (she hadn't remembered a rejection letter she
wrote Blake for *How Pleasant to Know Mr. Lear*: "the contemporary marketplace is not forgiving enough for this kind of book")
and Blake found himself with a signed contract, a decent advance
against a very good percentage, and some fairly tight deadlines.
He didn't want them under his own name, James Lewis, because
he wasn't sure of their merit; no one suggested the books be published under the name Blake Lear. Blake suggested a mysteriously
Christian looking pseudonym: a *Christian* name, as it were. *He*
didn't want to do any promotion for them at all, in the unlikely
event that any was required, and it was generally agreed that a
Pynchon-esque air of mystery with regards to the author would
be appropriate. "Judith Esther" it was: two consecutive books in
the Catholic Old Testament.

The first copy I ever saw, Blake finally reminded me, was on
one of my rare trips to his place.

"What's this bootleg-looking book?" I asked.

"Some crap someone sent me," he replied, shelving it. It was
the advance reading copy of the first volume. He cleaned his desk
up better after that. Certainly I never saw, as you do on authors'
shelves, the spines of every first edition, including translations
into various dialects of Chinese.

How did I finally find out?

Greg, of course. The man couldn't keep a secret. The publishers managed to keep the pseudonymous author's identity strictly under wraps—it was a contractual obligation on the part of both house and author—going so far as to put a picture of a middle-aged woman on the inside back cover, with a fake biography. She lived in Tuscany where she wrote in peace and seclusion. As the books got more traction, people presumably thought it peculiar that Ms. Esther didn't court the limelight at the Hay Festival, but I don't know that her identity was a mystery people were dying to solve. If anyone had been, all he would have to do was hang out at the Coachy and talk to Greg for five seconds. The man simply couldn't be quiet about knowing famous people, even fictional ones.

So we're at our table, just by the general knowledge machine, and in shambles Blake. I'm fresh off a big summer festival badly timed against the European Championships, there's conversation to be made, Greg is temporarily mute for some reason, and I remark, quite innocently, that there was a moment in the bus on my last tour with the Britpop band when every single person was reading one of the *Dark-Headed Clock*s. This was around the publication of the third volume, when all of London was bracing itself to queue at Tower Records at midnight to buy *Midnight in the Dark-Headed Clock*. At its mention, Greg looked particularly pleased with himself.

"Do you want to tell him or shall I?" he asked Blake.

"About the football tickets?" Blake answered vaguely.

"No. About the . . . you know . . ."

Blake sighed. "Greg, we love you because you're Greg, and you *are* Greg, but how can you be so unfailingly Greggy all the time? Doesn't it tire you, playing yourself?"

"I haven't told him anything, not a word," said Greg in his own defense. "He brought it up."

"So what?" said Blake.

"Well, then it's like lying and I never lie."

"We know you never lie."

"What?" I asked. "You've got to tell me now."

"Look," said Blake. "It has to be a secret, right?" I liked the sound of it, whatever it was.

"But Greg knows it," I pointed out. "It can't be a secret."

"Unfortunately," said Blake, "Greg was there when it happened. But he's sworn to secrecy, and so are you. I mean, you really are. Money depends on it."

"Mum's the word," said Greg.

"I'm Judith Esther," said Blake, under his breath.

"How do you mean?" I asked.

"I'm Judith Esther. Judith Esther am I."

"You wrote the *Dark-Headed Clock*?"

"Yes."

"Under the name Judith Esther?"

"Yes."

"And you've ghostwritten the books for a real person called Judith Esther. She makes all the money."

"No. Judith Esther doesn't exist. I make the dough."

"So you're rich."

"I stand to be."

"Right." I said. "Who knows?"

"Greg and everyone he's ever met, though somehow it's still under wraps, probably because no one believes him."

"Yeah, he did once say he knew Madonna."

"I didn't," said Greg. "I said I'd *met* Madonna."

"But you hadn't."

"Yes, but I only missed her by a few moments."

"Anyway," continued Blake, "apart from Greg, there are no other threats to my security apart from my agent, my publisher, Jack, my dad; oh and Kirk, who came up with the idea originally."

"And that old lady on the back cover of the book."

"That's my mum," said Greg.

"Mum's literally the word," Blake confirmed.

"She's no longer with us. Probably turning in her grave."

"Blake, you wrote this best-selling book?"

"I wrote that best-selling book."

"You couldn't get your last book published and you are now a best-selling author under the name Judith Esther."

"In one."

"Jesus Christ," said Greg in exasperation. "It's not rocket science."

"*I understand*, Greg," I said. "*I get it*! I'm just trying to take it in."

"Look," said Blake. "The books are what they are. There was a niche to be filled, and I filled it. I'm quite fond of Ed and Bill, and some of the baddies, but I'm not big on the overall message."

"Which is that Science is bad and Christianity is good."

"That," said Blake with a smile, "is a grotesque simplification of the *Dark-Headed Clock Trilogy*." There was an element of pride in his voice.

"Is that a yes?"

"Yes."

"And you don't believe that."

"Not at all. Which is why it's very important that no one knows anything about Judith Esther, because, basically, the books originated in a cynical marketing ploy."

"People think they're sincere, right? Everyone assumes Judith Esther is Christian. This isn't all part of some lengthy religious conversion you've had that started in jail?"

"Might be," said Blake, and he winked. "None of your business." He was joking, being serious, and joking. "But the important thing is: *no one ever knows*. The deal depends on it. My job depends on it. My pension depends on it. I was going to kill them off at the end of Volume Three but that became, literally, and contractually, impossible. They're bizarrely immortal. So we're going for three more."

"But the third one isn't even out yet."

"Sweet, I'm on the fifth."

"How's it going?"

"I cannot legally tell you."

"And isn't there a film of the first one about to come out?" He nodded. "All I can say, Blake, is congratulations."

"I'm really happy for their success. My bank manager is very happy. My father is for once proud of me, though he keeps on about whether I'll ever have success under my true colors, like he fears the name Lewis will disappear off the planet. It's lucky Jackie's got some kids. But please, please, just forget you ever knew it."

"It's not a joke, right, Judith?"

"I never lie," said Blake. "As sure as my name is Judith Esther. And Blake Lear."

He could still surprise you: perhaps there was life in the old dog yet.

Blake's circle of acquaintance was small, and he traveled often, always alone. His secret success was easily forgotten; he had everything he wanted, but he didn't want much. He bought a house, bequeathed me the apartment, went through a girlfriend here and there, sisterly figures with whom he shared space for a time, rode the *Dark-Headed Clock* wave as long as he was able and, as far as I knew, played no music at all. He didn't approve of my chosen profession, thought it a waste, and, as any father would, encouraged me to do anything but. He liked me to play the guitar for him, though—it was the only workout his old Takamine got.

There was another pseudonymous trilogy after the *Dark-Headed Clock*, but, because he couldn't legally write it under the same name, he was back to square one; it never caught on. Years passed. Middle-age spread. He went about his business and I went about mine—"Road Scholar Tour Management" (I know). I even persuaded Mitchell to start up the American chapter—now there was *always* a chart, a schedule, an itinerary. Without wishing to bore you, and believe me, Blake never wanted to know a thing about it, we were the first vertical touring company: we offered it all, from driver (of buses we owned), merch management, tour management, all the way to therapy and AA meetings. We got good. Our motto was: "Hands On! Hands Off!" You know, I'll even teach a band to take a look out of the window, go for a walk. I see Road Scholar like one of those universities that takes on promising athletes: you've got to educate them too. Every now and then I think of Clement's; we're *in loco parentis*. Mitchell was a bit that way for me. Blake was just *loco*.

"It's all one song."

AND THAT'S HOW THE STORY WOULD HAVE ENDED, WERE IT NOT FOR something called the Kidology Conference—or KidCon—at which I found myself one morning four years ago.

The venue was a grim, satanically black Brooklyn concert hall that reeked of beer and disinfectant. The stage was lit, an expectant crowd loitered, but there'd be no live music until the evening. The barman would have served you booze, but most of those milling around happily stuck to coffee. Not me, of course. I had a Diet Coke, like when I choose wheat over white, or low-fat cream cheese: very grown-up.

People were politely advertising their bands (in one case, by means of attention-grabbing propeller hats) and unself-consciously glad-handing sampler CDs and stickers. Others idly swung swag bags from their fingers as they took advantage of the "unique networking opportunities." I happened to be talking to a guy called Niall. He was in charge—I could tell by the two gold stars on his nametag.

KidCon existed, he explained, because there were now so many people making Family Music—that was the preferred designation—and such a bewildering array of outlets for its distribution that it was easy to get lost. At KidCon, registrants got a chance to hear from successful artists, publicists, agents, and other "industry insiders": the conference's mission, to embrace today's market in all its diversity, to offer a blueprint for success. "It's a place to see and be seen," Niall said. It was, in other words, South by Southwest for people who write *hello* songs, *goodbye* songs, and *when-do-we-get-there* songs.

My initial silent thought was "if only there'd been a blueprint for the Wonderkids . . . " swiftly followed by: "If only they'd had any guidance at all . . .." But, I equally swiftly concluded, even if both those things, the outcome wouldn't have been any different: they'd still have fucked it up. They'd have found a way.

"Are you making music yourself?" asked Niall, bracing himself to give the keynote.

"No," I said, hoping it hadn't come out dismissive.

"Oh, you have that look in your eye."

"I do? No, I'm behind-the-scenes. You don't want to let me too near a stage. Actually, I was asked to write about the conference."

"A journalist?" He sized up my usefulness.

"Not so much," I admitted. "Well, if you like. I mean, put it this way: I'm not about to write a song about socks."

Why had I agreed to write the stupid article? Mostly because a friend, drunk backstage, desperate for copy, offered money and a plane ticket after he read a thing I wrote about some of the weirder Wonderkids concerts. Blake's old apartment, which was still how everyone referred to it, was making me antsy. Might as well get back on the road.

The story of Family Music is basically this: the children of rock 'n' roll grew up, had their own children, and needed options other than crappy Raffi. They wanted their kids to listen to music they could stand to listen to themselves, because, unlike *their* parents, who thought it was all rubbish anyway, they actually liked pop music, and could tell the difference between good and bad. They didn't want to pollute their own kids' minds with crap and certainly didn't want to contaminate the stereos in their cars and kitchens. (I went to a three-year-old's party the other day—the bespoke mixtape was Pixies, the Clash, and Ramones. I was actually aching for someone to sing a song about going to a zoo, zoo, zoo, and I bet the kids were, too.)

Then some of these parents, musicians who were themselves in rock 'n' roll bands, found they couldn't make a living—it's not uncommon—and decided to take matters into their own hands, to provide music for their own kids, music that they, and other parents like them, wouldn't mind listening to: music that was anti-Raffi, anti-Barney, not the Wiggles. And this music, some of it, totally reinvigorated the children's music scene. Think punk, alternative comedy, that kind of thing.

Crucially, it was music for kids and adults alike—that was the trick—but when you sliced it right down, it had to be palatable to adults, at least initially, because they were the ones with the money. Disney worked this out years ago, but kindie (indie music for kids, right?) worked it out for rock 'n' rollers. The secret is that rock 'n' roll has always been for kids. A-wop-bop-a-loo-bop-a-wop-bam-boom. This music just made that slightly more explicit.

Now these guys had their own conference. And I was the ideal person to cover it.

Niall gave his introductory speech, the climax of which was the announcement of the first annual Jim-Jammies Awards, to be held later that year. It made sense: everyone's got his own awards show—why not these guys? Why not *us*? Children's literature, Kid Lit: the reverence with which memory turns those yellowed pages, the *Oxford Companion to Children's Literature*, with its hearty essays on Beatrix Potter, Lewis Carroll, and Dr. Seuss. Think of those bookshelves of hallowed first editions of J. K. Rowling, Joan Aiken, and even Judith Esther. But children's music? *Carnival of the Animals*, *Young Person's Guide to the Orchestra* or bust, innit?

And as for modern children's music, consider the Grammys—where and when are the Family Music awards in that overstuffed celebration of entropy? Long before you tune in, is the answer. They're somewhere between Best Historical Album, Worst Album Notes (Gospel), and whatever category it is in which

Aerosmith still triumph. Sure you wouldn't turn down a Grammy, but you'd be home in time to give Granny her medicine. The indie kids' musicians deserved their own awards show. Of course they did, and the conference crowd agreed. Wholeheartedly.

The name of the first panel was tailor-made for the article I was destined not to write: "How to Succeed While Really Really Trying" (others, later on, would be franker: "Money: Where Is It?"). The first moderator, perhaps a children's entertainer herself, could have done the panel all on her own; she opened by serenading the attendees to the tune of "Pop Goes the Weasel" (*Let's all get out of the lobby / And come on into the panel . . .* you've got three more minutes, then mercifully I'll stop singing") before coaxing answers from her panelists like a kindergarten teacher. Behind her, the KidCon banner peeled partway from the wall, an inexorable descent that looked likely to accelerate towards a tragic conclusion threatening to upstage the unwitting panelists, until Niall shuffled up to throw some gaffer tape about; everyone "Ah!"ed like when the couple kiss at the end of a romantic comedy.

I had wanted to explode the myth that family music was made by failed rock musicians. Sadly this would not be possible. It was the truth, confirmed by almost every speaker, the only exception to this being the family music made by already *successful* rock musicians, who had decided not only that the kids were alright, but that the toddlers were alright, too, a move known, among cynics, as "last chance for a Grammy." One notable success story summed it up on the second panel: "Well, I'm singing the same stuff I sang before when no one listened, except now the songs are accompanied by cartoons of a talking strip of bacon. Otherwise, no change." The differences between playing for kids and adults boiled down to a few good jokes: "you get a different sort of bottle thrown at you." Much of the overall message was: "Work every day, work really hard," and it all turned out to be very American—"This is a wonderful country," someone said, earning a round of applause, "You can fake your way through anything." There was no sign of modesty among the panelists, but they weren't here to hide their lights. They were here to blind you in their glare.

I felt sorry for the people with questions, but most of my sympathy was reserved for anyone trying to come up with a name for his kid-friendly band. Honestly, have a go. Then Google it: it's taken. As my mind wandered—it's hard to be in a rock club all day, and I should know; you become inured to the smell, but the chemicals in the cleaning fluids are working on you just the same—I toyed with the idea, a possible hook for the article, of making up a fake Kindie band. So I began to play a parlor game, and here's the list: the Cribs, Spitrag, the Blankies, TANTRUM, the Meltdowns, Booster Shot, the Swing Set, Potty Mouth, the Mad Hatters, the Magic Words, the Bad Words, the Balloons, the Pop-Tarts, the Pull-Ups, the Dr. Spocks—oh, there were hundreds more. My iPhone corroborated that every single one of them was taken. And not all by bands playing for kids, mind you.

By the next panel ("Social Networking and Fan Development When Your Audience Can't Type Yet"), my article had written itself, though I never bothered to transcribe it. In fact, I was about ready to call it a day when one of the moderators treated us to a bit of a history lesson, addressing the changes in the industry over the last twenty-five years. The smooth narrative laid before us told itself so neatly that it struck me something, *something*, must be missing: from Mister Rogers to Raffi, from Simeon to Sesame Street, and then to the alternative bands making their children's albums, and finally to the real stars of today, some of whom were in the house at that moment: Dan Zanes—who's really making "Everyone Music," these days if anybody is—and Laurie Berkner, "the Sheryl Crow of the diaper set," who once successfully rhymed "aunts" with "grandpar-ants." This story brought us up to date, but there was an absence that felt—to me—quite conspicuous. I'm not saying that it was a conscious whitewash, I'm just saying something was missing. I knew the reasons, and they offended me.

And I felt it well up inside me, like if I didn't ask the question, I'd explode or vomit: that huge Dr. Seuss print presented itself right in front of my eyes. It was all very unlike me, because I was never one to put my hand up at school and was criticized for hiding in the back row. But suddenly there it was, my arm, shooting up above me like a periscope, giving away my position in the anonymous sea of faces, waving, drawing attention to both of us. I felt immediate sympathy for those other people with their daft questions: they couldn't help themselves either. And when the charming moderator picked me out, I stood up and waited for the microphone to bob over.

"Yeah, thanks. Ed Sweet, er, writer. I heard what you said about Raffi all the way up to They Might Be Giants and Mr. Zanes, up there on the panel, and I just wondered . . ." A few people in front craned their necks to see. Other people were talking among themselves, but I seemed to have the undivided attention of the panelists, who nodded like dashboard dachshunds. ". . . Yeah, I just wondered if anyone remembered the Wonderkids and where they fit into all this."

For a millisecond, it was like that bit in the pub in *American Werewolf in London*. Then the moderator started to cough, as though to preempt choking, perhaps due to the unexpectedness of the reference; everybody else looked dumbfounded. And someone behind me started to giggle.

"The Wonderkids?" asked the moderator, clearing his throat, wearing the forlorn, pensive look of a baby taking a crap.

"Where are they now?" asked someone else on the panel.

"Anyone want to run with this? The Wonderkids—remember *those* guys?" I didn't like the stress on *those*. No one took up the moderator's baton, until Roger Wrong, a middle-aged, baseball-capped Midwesterner, the comedian on the panel, came to his rescue.

"I've got a Wonderkids story." It was going to be a good one; you could see it in his eyes. He considerately motioned for me to sit down. "I guess they were kinda inspiring to me, although I know that wasn't always a cool thing to say, but you know credit where it's due, and there was one time I went to see them in Boston, and it was just after that big hit they had . . . er . . ."

"Life, As It Is Lived," someone shouted out from the audience. Like the peeling banner, we were gathering momentum.

"No, no, maybe "Rock Around the Bed," and I guess I'd made my first demos right then, and someone showed me back into their dressing room, and I had this little cassette I was clutching, Maxwell ferric oxide C-30, of three demos . . ."—he was laughing just thinking about it—"and the first person I ran into was this kid who was running around like he was in charge, and I suddenly realized it was a kinda real weird, slightly heavy, scene; there was the girl from the band—Simeon's daughter—in a tie-dye leotard, doing tai chi, the guitar player looked like he was passed out on the couch, and a couple of mothers, not the Mothers of Invention or heavy mother you-know-whats, just actual mothers, who were back there, lots of cigarette smoke, definitely a bunch of bottles, I'd say some weed . . . yeah, weed . . . and you think about these days, I mean I wouldn't even carry my merch in a cardboard box with the name of a brewery on it, right? No one wants anyone putting that picture up online. Anyway, it was a weird scene, like a *real* band, and then the next thing I see is Blake Lear . . ."

At this point, the audience let out a collective "ooh!," like at one of Blake's beloved pantomimes. And then someone actually *hissed* in a kind of affectionate way, as though he was a cartoon villain you wanted to warn the hero about. It was a great moment, really.

". . . and, man, he's larger than life. And he'd just got off the stage, playing to, what, I don't know, maybe 600 kids between the ages of four and ten and he's sweating and he looks kinda like he might be dying. Like, if you saw him beforehand, he'd be all dandy and dapper but you see him afterwards and he's like a ghost, a little, and there's sweat running through his makeup on the side of his face, and he's got peanut butter smeared all over his jacket, and he looks at me and says: 'What do *you* want?' It wasn't unfriendly, but it was a little intense, at least I felt that way until he 'Quack!'s right in my face. And I remember he was waving around a bottle of bourbon. Anyway, so I say, 'cause I was just a young kid come to give the great man some of my songs—this was before they got into any big trouble—and so I say: 'Well, Mr. Lear, I don't want to bother you, but I made some demos and I thought you might like to hear them.' And I handed him this cassette and, man, I'd slaved over that thing, great artwork, 'cause first impressions are everything, all that bullshit . . ." And that was the first time anyone had sworn onstage all day, as though the spirit of the Wonderkids had suddenly possessed KidCon.

"And, long story short, Blake Lear takes it off me real friendly, and smiles at me, and he doesn't take one look at it, not even a glance, and in the blink of an eye, he says 'thank you, thank you,' and he hurls that cassette over his shoulder."

He burst out laughing again, and, really, he's telling the story so well that everyone is laughing with him now.

"And that thing flew, it *flew* through the air—I mean . . ." he made the Superman flying gesture with both arms, "And Blake didn't even look around, but the cassette sailed straight through an open window. He couldn't have executed it any better if he'd tried. You could hear it skittering on some gravel outside, maybe along the road, and then hitting someone, and a polite little scream. And I just looked at him, and he looked at me. And he made this kinda funny cross-eyed face like Eddie Cantor or some-one, and he looks around and says 'Where the fuck did that go?' And I said 'Right out the window.' And we both just started laughing. And we couldn't stop.

"And the kid I saw first runs by me and before I know what's happened, he's gone outside and he's handing me back the cassette and says: 'Blake, you want to try that again?' And Blake says: 'I'll never get it through the window again!' and we're still laughing and the kid says 'No, receiving the cassette from the nice man.' And I say: 'Forget about the cassette, man, but I'll have some of that bourbon.'

"And Blake put his big arm around me and he said: 'You're alright, whatever-your-name-is,' and he empties out a plastic cup, rinses it in the sink, and pours me a drink.

"And that's my Wonderkids story."

And everybody applauded. But Mr. Wrong wasn't quite done, and he said: "You know sometimes when I tell that story, people think I'm telling it to say what a . . ."—now he'd closed the backstage door on the world of the Wonderkids, handed in his laminate, he couldn't quite utter the word, so he just left a blank for us to fill as we pleased—". . . Blake Lear was. But that's not the reason. That was a real funny thing to do, and I got it. And so if I do that to your CD, don't be offended."

And the moderator, trying to get everything back on track, as though the Wonderkids were outside the purview of KidCon, asked: "But you listen to everything, right—every single thing they send you?"

"Yessir!" said Roger Wrong. "But the thing with that band was, the music was great, no question, but there weren't any rules back then, and they were too crazy. Nowadays we know the boundaries, but the Wonderkids were making it up as they went along. I read an interview with someone about the Wiggles, maybe their manager or lawyer, and they asked him why the Wiggles always did the Wiggle dance with their hands in the air when they met the kids for photos. And he said, quite frankly I thought, that it protected them from possible litigation; he said something like 'that way you know where the hands are.' Smart, I *guess*. And, looking back, that was the thing with the Wonderkids: you never really knew where the hands were, and they wouldn't show you. I'm not talking about anything weird. I'm just saying that they could have made things less . . . well, maybe it didn't occur to them, but they paid for that, I think."

"Well," said the moderator, pointing at me, "I guess that didn't really answer your question. But it certainly got a good story. If you don't mind my asking, why did you think of the Wonderkids?"

I stood up again and addressed the microphone: "Well, I'm interested partly for personal reasons, because, for example, I actually remember that story very well. I was the kid who went to get the cassette, and Blake Lear was, and still is, my father."

There was silence, then a very strange thing happened: someone started to applaud. And the whole room began to applaud, as did the panelists. It certainly took the moderator by surprise: the band really didn't quite fit into The Gospel According to KidCon. But, you know, there are other Gospels too: they're real—they just didn't make the final edit. And that's what everyone was applauding: the Secret History of Kids' Music, the one where the Wonderkids weren't disgraced and forgotten.

"Man, nice to meet you again," said Mr. Wrong. "Did you ever listen to that cassette? We'll talk about it afterwards."

"The Wonderkids!" said the moderator. "And where is Blake Lear now? What's he doing?"

I was keen to relinquish the microphone.

"Oh," I said, "he's fine. He's fine. Still writing."

In the bar, two or three of the performers made a beeline, and I suddenly found myself the center of a little scrimmage. They were all full of praise for the band. Roger Wrong couldn't have been friendlier. I was able to bring them up to date about Becca, who I knew to be newly divorced and running a yoga retreat in Northern California (not ten miles from the nerve center of her father's Empowering the Child empire); and Curtis, who had gone back to acting and just landed a minor speaking role as an alien in the latest incarnation of *Star Trek*; and Jack, of course. But I managed to avoid talking about Blake, though it was all they wanted to know.

"Are you really his son?" asked one of the female performers, whose name I didn't catch. She was about my age, attractive; the kind of woman you see and immediately think: "I wish I was a little less like me and a bit more like whatever it is that she likes."

"Yeah, though I was actually only ten years younger than him."

She offered me beer—it was that time of day, and there weren't any cameras or kids around. I opted for a Sprite. There was an ice-cream van outside, and I asked her if she'd like anything: "You could make, like, a beer float, or something."

"Would that be good?" She was definitely flirting.

"*Maybe*?"

"As in 'maybe yes' or as in 'Hell, no?'"

"What's your name?" I asked. "In case I have to page you on the white courtesy phone."

She had a beer in one hand and a Sprite in the other, and she gesticulated at her right breast, where long brown hair obscured a nametag. It was left to me to brush her hair aside so I could read "Joni Johnson." Even I'd heard of her. I must have been the only one who didn't recognize her. That can be flattering, right?

"You're a journalist?" she asked.

"Not really. Well, more on the side." I leaned towards her as though it was a confidence: "I'm a road manager."

"A romancer?" She asked nonplussed, having totally misheard me. Perhaps my accent was the problem; perhaps the volume in the club. Under any circumstances, it was a great mishearing.

"No," I said, laughing, "a road manager."

She seemed suspicious. It was as much fun as I'd had in ages. "You don't seem like the type."

"I don't?" *It's because I'm urbane, isn't it? It's because I'm a bit of a gentleman.* I didn't say this out loud. I'd wait for her. She was going to like the name of my company too.

"You don't drink. You don't smoke. I bet you don't do drugs."

"All assets in a tour manager, I believe."

"You seem too baby-faced," she said. Hmm. "Do you win them over with your British accent? You're squeaky clean." I liked her honey voice. You just wanted it to drip all over you. "Do people take you seriously?"

"Yes!" I said, immediately regretting my defensive tone. "I was voted "Most Seriously Taken Road Manager" in *Touring Monthly* only last year."

"We need a new road manager," she said nonchalantly, as she fished in her inside pocket for a business card. I immediately began to reconsider my golden rule: never date someone you're looking after. Of course, the money would have to be right too. "Our last road manager left."

"Oh, why?" I asked, purely out of professional curiosity.

She laughed gaily: "Oh, I broke up with him! It got awkward."

Poor bastard. Lucky Bastard.

"Well, I'm in the book," I said casually.

"Hey," she put her hand on my arm as though I'd shown any sign of leaving. It was an exhilarating moment: she didn't want me to go. It was as though I was playing hard to get.

"How's Blake?" she asked. She had a look in her eye, and I didn't like it. I was really trying not to ask: "Oh, did you know him?" but I did anyway.

"Oh, no. I met him. I bought an LP at a gig once, and he signed it for me. I loved the Wonderkids." We'd met before! At the merch table! I'd leave that little gem in my back pocket. "I'd love to meet him again to thank him for the inspiration."

"I'm going to get some ice cream." I looked outside. The line of conference delegates was about twenty deep.

"Aren't you too old for ice cream, *road manager*?"

"Aren't we all just big kids? Isn't adulthood just a polite fiction?" I asked as I left, hoping these heavy thoughts did a bit of work in my absence.

She'd gone when I came back, and I found myself wondering why I hadn't gone, too. A band's soundcheck is not conducive to conversation. Niall materialized by my side.

"That was quite a revelation," he said in admiration. He had an ice cream too: dipped cherry, rich blood red.

"Are you going to ask if I'm really his son?"

"No, I checked online. So, Sweet," he'd done his research, calling me by my last name, "what do you think of our little shindig?" He'd been friendly before, and now I realized he wasn't being quite so friendly. The reason was obvious: we were doing business.

"Yeah . . ." I said, nodding my head.

"And you're sure you don't have any ambitions to . . . er . . ."

"Follow in the family business?" The ice cream was fine, though I wished I'd had the cherry. I'd forgotten how ridiculously good that color looked. I shook my head. "It's not really my scene. I'll stay for the show though."

"Well, I was wondering . . ." Here it came. "I was wondering if maybe next year—you know we do this big gig in Prospect Park every year. I was wondering if you thought that the Wonderkids would consider playing it. I mean, it'll be packed. Have they thought of getting back together?"

"Well, I . . ."

"You probably worry that there'd still be a residual Pee-wee Herman effect, but you know Pee-wee's having the last laugh now, right?" In his mind, the gig was already happening. I was witnessing a promoter promoting. I hadn't been thinking anything like that, although perhaps he was right. It was more that I was considering that in order for there to be a reunion, we'd need the lead singer. It's probably how the Pogues feel every time they play. "I think you'd be surprised," he continued. "Everyone's prepared to, well, forgive and forget. I mean, you saw the reaction in there. I think a lot of the parents would feel the same way."

"You make it sound a lot worse than it was. I love Pee-wee Herman, but he was actually guilty of a sexual offense."

"Well, the rumors about the Wonderkids were probably worse than the actual events."

"They were. Considerably." Niall was beginning to annoy me, but here I was: the band's representative.

"I mean Peter Yarrow's still performing to children," he said by way of comparison.

"I'm not sure that example is really working for you."

"And anyway," he was off again, promoting, trying to iron out problems as they presented themselves, "the thing with Peter Yarrow is that it was 1970 and things were very different then. Also Carter gave him a presidential pardon or something."

"I think this may not be your best argument, Niall, because, without being specific, the Wonderkids weren't actually or even technically pedophiles and if they were, you presumably wouldn't be asking them to perform, unless they were Peter Yarrow, with his presidential pardon."

"Well, sorry, no, perhaps I'm getting ahead of myself. But do you think there's any hope?"

"Of the Wonderkids reforming to play the KidCon Festival in Prospect Park?"

"Yes. A show where we re-present them to America. And we carry the can. And they get paid very well."

"No, Niall. No. There is absolutely no possibility whatsoever."

There was absolutely no possibility.

And yet, four years later, it happened.

I watched the show, looking around for Joni Johnson, nowhere to be seen, as I fielded this and that inquiry about the band for which I was now the known earthly representative. And always the same question, like he was a cross between the Waldo and the Thomas Pynchon of Kiddie Rock: "Where's Blake?"

"Rattle your jewelry."

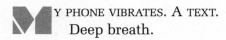Y PHONE VIBRATES. A TEXT.
Deep breath.

As I reach for my iPhone, the sound system explodes into volume. No one around the Wonderkids table misses my frantic lunge. It feels like if I don't read that text straightaway, it will self-delete, evaporate into the digital ether, lost forever, and with it, its author: "Can't find the stage door! Meet me outside the big windows. Come alone."

"It's Blake," I hiss across the table. "Everything's okay. He can't find the stage door. I'll go and get him."

There is a general sigh of relief. Greg, completely gray now, crew cut to disguise the lack of alternative, gives it the smug "*I knew he'd be here*" nod of his head, accompanied by an equally annoying two-handed "be calm." Perhaps he knows something: they're as thick as thieves. "Shall I go?" he asks.

"No, it's okay. Back in a tick." I don't mention Blake's instruction that I come alone. Why worry anyone unduly? I mean, it's probably nothing, right? The lights dim.

"It's time to turn off your cell phones," advises a voice over the PA, as I plot my exit. Squinting, I see a large series of plate-glass windows at the back of the room. "WELCOME TO THE FOURTH ANNUAL JIM-JAMMIES!"

Time to make my way. But "the fourth"? We're the *fourth* Hall of Fame inductees? Who were the other three? Pete Seeger? Peter, Paul & Mommy too? Who else? Simeon? It's fair to say that we may represent a fairly radical change of direction.

As I get up, the show begins. Why, if it isn't Star of Stage and Screen and Part-Time Children's Presenter . . . actually, I have absolutely no idea who it is, but it isn't Dan Zanes (hair), They Might Be Giants (glasses), a Wiggle (primary colors), Simeon (very old, asshole), Joni Johnson (extremely attractive), a character from Sesame Street (furry), and it certainly isn't 1-Z (black). But there's a house band, and this guy's behaving like the cameras are on.

My most direct route to the back of the hall involves a wayward meander through a maze of circular tables, a game where points are lost for failing to avoid obstacles, tripping over longer legs, kicking purses. I prepare the wording of inevitable apologies. There are these weird girls dotted around, arched eyebrows and short Betty Boop skirts. They look like they might be selling cigarettes but they're not; they're just stylish. Or perhaps they're a Kindie act: the Boops. Probably up for Best Newcomer (Group). I smile at one. She ignores me.

The chain of events that has led to the Kravitz Center flashes before my eyes, as though—well, as though I'm dying. The band may yet die here tonight, so it's quite appropriate. It's like *The Last Waltz* by the band the Band. They got back together to break up for the film. Maybe the Wonderkids are doing that too.

First there was the genius music supervisor who put "Rock Around the Bed" in a Judd Apatow movie a couple of years back. The Wonderkids were always ripe for rediscovery, but that rediscovery seemed impossible. It was always going to take someone with a little vision and a lot of enthusiasm to put the band back before the public eye. Turns out that this guy was at the Pack 'n' Play Festival and witnessed the rogue finger, aged eight. On the back of the movie, the original video was recut, premiered on Vimeo, went viral (however that magic happens), and suddenly this 1-Z kid starts talking about the Wonderkids, how their anarchy influenced his Gangsta Kindie. Blake was the nearest thing Family Music ever had to an outlaw.

And then Niall from KidCon started sniffing around again. I'd thought him rather ineffectual when we'd met, a bit of a standard poodle, but he was more like whatever dog it is whose jaws lock after he's sunk his teeth in. Anyway, Niall just wouldn't let go of our trouser leg. And finally, it was just like any band reunion: whatever the band says to the contrary, whatever the claims of "the time is right" or "we've all grown up and when we started playing together again, the bad vibes just melted away" and "sure we'll be doing the old songs, but we're debuting great new material as well," it's always all about the money.

If the idea had stayed with Andy and Blake, nothing would have happened. But Jack found out, and as much as Blake didn't need it, Jack and Rita did. And Blake, finally, couldn't refuse: his brother, his family, his nephews. Perhaps there was a (totally unacknowledged) sense of pride in the accomplishments of the Wonderkids, as well. Anyway, he gave in, though it was clear that it would be up to me to take care of everything. "I'll turn up" was about all he said. Things needed sorting out, but when you needed an answer, he wouldn't call back; he barely understood email. The promoters needed to know this or that, and I'd answer as best I could. Blake didn't seem to have any particular plans for the event, and I knew he wouldn't get back to me anyway. There was an increasing air of desperation when people asked me what the band was going to perform. You can only tell people everything's under control so many times.

It wasn't any trouble getting Curtis and Becca, though Curtis's filming schedule was a minor hiccup. It wasn't like anybody had been in touch much over the last few years—though Curtis was an inveterate Christmas card sender, always with those pictures of Mei-Xing and the last year's progress report—a bit ridiculous given that she was in her mid-thirties and on her second marriage. But the moment news got around (and I imagine Niall was behind a little of the rumormongering: he was dogged), it couldn't not happen.

And so here we are in Manhattan—a gig to follow at the KidCon Festival in Prospect Park and, icing on the cake, induction into the Jim-Jammies Hall of Fame: redemption. Niall pressed all the right buttons. I had to cancel the second half of a tour with some Scandinavian Goths—hard as fucking nails onstage, pussy-cats off, all vegan and organic underwear—just to get to grips with the logistics and visas. Blake hadn't made things any easier, but I wasn't complaining. It's what I do.

The Wonderkids' entourage has been carefully placed, like a re-cently soiled diaper, at some remove from the action. And not one person, not one single person, has come up to say hi. Actually, strike that. Two people: Niall (who doesn't count because he was paying his respects everywhere) and Simeon, but only to say hi to his daughter. Nice touch.

Andy, one-time manager, is with us but paying little atten-tion; ditto Nick Hedges. Andy seems far more interested in his wife, much younger and faker than the one before, though there remains the possibility that she *is* the one before, but with work. And what on earth has he been doing for the last eighteen years? I bet he moved with the industry, left the majors, went into con-sulting, got into digital distribution, licensed stuff online, devel-oped a very briefly top-selling app, rolled with the punches. Back in the day, nothing was too little trouble for him. The Wonderkids were his problem once, but not anymore, no sir.

Jack has been fidgeting like crazy, right hand twitching like Blake's used to. He's been drinking too quickly. "Tastes like piss" is the only non-Blake-related remark he's made so far, referring to the wine, winking for my benefit only; oh, the secrets we share, the jokes only we can make, the smoothies we defiled. There's nothing wrong with the wine, but he wouldn't let that stand in the way of the joke that only I understood. All these years on, the same stimuli provoking the same reactions from Pavlov's Wonder-Dogs. Rita is wearing the largest pair of silver cuff bracelets; they'll steal the show, clinking in toast and clattering in applause. Becca, more hippieish than she used to be, is with Sam. I met him when he was six, and now he's twenty-five, a stand-up comedian. It always seems like that would be the punch line. In truth, every-one seemed on edge except Andy.

Of course we are: the Wonderkids are going to play live for the first time in, let's be precise, eighteen years, and there's no sign of the lead singer. The last I saw Blake was the night before, when we gathered at the hotel bar. When I turned in, he was unsuccessfully trying to swivel round on his stool, yelling "Quack!" in Greg's ear. Curtis then witnessed his departure for a "midnight creep"; I could confirm his return because I woke him with a phone call around lunchtime to go over the schedule. He subsequently didn't turn up to soundcheck; no surprise there. He hasn't shown up to any of the rehearsals either. I stood in for him. Like I always used to, while we wondered where he was.

On top of the fact that there's no Blake, there's a weird energy in the room. Granted, it's an awards show: *everyone's* edgy. There will be winners and losers; some of the bigger names, confident of a good showing, speeches prepared in their back pocket, feel comfortable in their finery. Others haven't bothered to dress up at all. They'll grin and bear it, assuming failure while secretly hoping for the success that would make a monkey suit worth the expense. The good news: the Wonderkids will be spared the more competitive aspects of the evening. We are being honored, Hall-of-Famed, inducted, whatever the exact phrase is: *the band has won just by having existed.*

The Jim-Jammies is, by its nature, a family event. Not in the sense that there are any kids in evidence. Oh, maybe there are a couple: one male nominee is sporting a BabyBjörn (full of wriggling baby, unlike the one Blake used to sport), but you get the feeling that the contraption and its contents are fashion accessories, part of his brand. It isn't like the dude's babysitter fell through or his kid desperately needed an evening out suspended across his father's stomach. It's a bold move by dad; luckily the ergonomic Björn leaves his hands free to pick up possible awards later on.

The irony is, I would have been invited to the Jim-Jammies anyway, since it's Joni's world; she's sitting with her manager at a different table. I would have been there as her guest, her date, rather than as her tour manager, so I'd have been dressed rather smarter. I'd stuck to my policy of never dating someone you're working with, but she can barely have got her key in the last hotel door before I texted her to ask her out. There'd been a bit of flirt-ing—she used to call me "Sir"; I once said she looked so good she'd make her teenie audience come of age (she acted shocked but I could tell she liked it)—but I wasn't positive she'd say yes. She did.

I push hopefully at a glass door that turns out to be a window. An usher, seeing my mistake, holds the actual door open for me.

There's no sign of Blake outside but there's a fountain, bathed in a white watery light, and that's where he'll be. He has a soft spot for fountains: a chance to throw in a coin, make a wish. I half-expect to see him paddling—bedraggled, shivering, laugh-ing—but he emerges, dry as a bone, from behind the central spout, obscured by spray, calling my name. The first thing to say: he looks fantastic, in white suit, white shirt, and white tie. He's spared us the halo, but he still appears saintly, angelic.

"Where on earth did you get that?"

"Garment district today. That old boy's still there. I couldn't believe it. He measured me up. Too much?"

I remember the guy. We'd stopped there the day before Blake spent the night in jail. "Perfect."

He takes me in his arms, kisses my cheek.

"Is it time yet? How's it going in there?" He takes a brand new pack of cigarettes out of his pocket and, in one deft sequence of movements, removes the cellophane, bangs the pack hard on his hand, opens it, whips out the silver protective wrapper, and rifles through his pockets for a lighter. He doesn't have one, but I do: it's just the kind of thing you get used to carrying. You become other people's pockets. I also have a church-key bottle opener on my keychain. And a Leatherman.

"Well, it's quite ritzy. Everyone's going to be relieved that you're here. Jack's on edge."

"Yeah, yeah, sorry . . . the suit took time, and I actually wrote a little speech . . . So this isn't too much?" he asks, drawing at-tention to the suit once more.

"No, it's fine. But there's no alternative, right, so why are you asking? It's that or underwear, right?" It's unlike him to worry.

"There's another one inside. You're going to wear it."

"I'm what?"

He brushes away my concerns. "How about this?"

He produces a large silver cross on a necklace.

"Depends what you're going for," I say circumspectly.

"Gotcha. 'It' is what I'm going for. I'm *going for it*." He's sucking the life out of the cigarette. He still smokes twice as quick as everyone else; even an American Spirit doesn't slow him down. Smoking doesn't relax him; that isn't the point. "I couldn't find the stage door." He fiddles with the cross, trying to get it perfectly straight.

"I know that. Because when you text me, I'm the one who gets the text." He nods as though this is news. "I also know the location of this elusive door. Look, I'll text Greg, and let everyone know we'll see them backstage at the intermission."

The fountain abruptly changes color to red as the light show continues through its cycle.

"Well, hold on, before you do . . . Let's talk as we go."

I lead him in the direction of the backstage door. We could never go back through the audience with him in his stage clothes: I mean, rule number one. Unfortunately this involves our walking around the entire complex and in through the underground parking, the way we arrived this afternoon.

"Reminds me of that friend of Greg's who was tech-ing for Prince. Remember that one?" asks Blake. It's a story I know well, and one I'd just thought of when Blake mentioned my matching suit, but I think Blake might want the chance to tell it, settle the old nerves. It's from the days when Prince made his whole crew dress up wearing braids and bodysuits, identical to whatever the little genius was wearing for that particular tour. Halfway through the show, at some barn in Germany, Prince has a kind of freak-out, and the guitar tech, his boss's peace of mind paramount, escorts Prince from the stage, while the audience wonders what's going on, whether it's something serious or some kind of James Brown "I've given too much" piece of showbiz. The guitar tech bundles a hyperventilating Prince into a taxi and off to his hotel, and heads back into the gig to make his report on the situation to a none-too-pleased stage manager, who will have to explain to a none-too-pleased promoter, who will in his turn have to announce to an arena full of hostile punters that Prince has left the building. Furs will fly. Has the small star even played long enough to ensure ticket money doesn't have to be refunded? (That's the key thing: I once saw Bowie play in a monsoon at Jones Beach, just long enough to get past the "no refunds" watershed.)

However, the door through which the guitar tech has delivered Prince to safety has closed behind him without his knowledge. In fact, all the doors around the huge arena are closed, since the concert is supposedly in full purple swing. Further, Greg's mate realizes that he doesn't have any of his stage credentials with him, such had been his haste to leave, and that therefore his only option is to return through the main entrance, around which only a few increasingly desperate ticket touts linger, and that, to cap it all, he is a small, slightly pudgy, white New Yorker, in Germany, dressed as Prince.

We never knew how the story ended. Probably he got in okay and all was well, but we loved that image of the bloke wandering around outside the Stadion Halle, dressed as Prince, wondering how he was going to get back in, while 20,000 people inside bayed for blood as the band manfully vamped an instrumental version of "Housequake."

By the time Blake's done, we're in the underground car park, and he's enjoying one final cigarette before we enter his nicotine-free backstage nightmare. He looks very much as though he's going to face a firing squad.

"I should text," I say. "They'll be on tenterhooks."

"Look, Sweet," says Blake, finally reaching the point. "I'm not going to perform tonight. I'm just going to make a speech."

"The band isn't going to perform?" I could talk him out of this. I could and I would.

"The band will perform."

"But *you* won't? What are they going to perform without you? An instrumental version of 'Housequake'?"

"No, you can sing. That's why I bought you the jacket."

I laugh. "No."

"You will sing."

"You're joking, of course." He doesn't seem to be.

"Look, I can't do it. I don't even want to do it. I don't want to be Blake Lear . . ."

"Neither do I."

"I'm just going to explain to the audience how honored we are, and what happened, and what's happened in the meanwhile, and that it just isn't in me anymore. If I sang the songs, I'd probably end up having a funny five minutes like Prince, and you'd get locked out of the gig, wearing an identical white suit. You sing them. I'll dance across the stage or something."

"You're going to be Bez from the Happy Mondays while I pretend to be you?"

"Bez, *the Dance Instigator*!" says Blake as though this might persuade me.

"Hands down, your worst ever idea, Blake; second only to when you wanted to throw a fake toddler into a screaming audience."

This actually provokes a laugh. A large transit van honks at the two guys in the middle of the car park.

"Well, it's either that or nothing, because I'm not doing it. I promise it'll be great. You know the songs."

"Better than you, probably, at this point . . ." To which I hastily add, "Not that that's an argument for me doing it. Anyway, that's blackmail. I honestly don't want to. I'll be terrible. Also, what about the Prospect Park gig? It's thousands of dollars. It's Chuck and Johnny's college fund or something, isn't it?"

"I already put the money in Jack's account."

"You're just going to cancel the gig?"

"I'll go to the gig, mate, if you do the singing."

"What?" Ridiculous.

He fusses over the stupid cross again, then fixes me with a laser eye: "Trust me. Do this for me." He winks. That's all, just a wink—a minute flexing of a tiny muscle. "Please, Sweet." And now it really is like I'm dying or he's hypnotized me. I remember how he delivered me through that dressing-room window, saved me from the Terrys, took me off to join the circus. Everything comes at me vertically and I don't want to look down. "I'm your Dad, right?" I only realize there are tears in my eyes when I close them to stop the stinging. "Would I steer you wrong?"

"Not intentionally."

"Then do this for me. I promise it'll be great. It'll be so much better than if I sang."

"It's going to be terrible. I can't front a band. I don't even want to. I'm too old for this shit."

"No, I'm too old for this shit. You're the right age. You know what to do. Trust me."

It's like that TV magician/mesmerist guy, when he turned a woman into a concert pianist in one week, despite the fact that she couldn't play the piano at all; his entire method was to encourage her to waft her fingers over the keyboard in a vaguely classical way, and tell her that it would be okay, however nervous she felt. I mean, that was the set up. The trick, the viewer found out, was that she'd been a concert pianist all along, but he'd hypnotized her to forget it, so when it came time for the concert he dehypnotized her, and voilà: Rachmaninoff's Piano Concerto No. 3. Genius TV.

But I'm not the lead singer in a band, nor have I ever been. Nor am I really hypnotized, though I do feel a little fuzzy. My entire stage experience comes down to a few songs with Jack's cover band, including (I will admit) a storming version of "Burning Love" by Elvis Presley, the odd bit of "Testing One Two," which sometimes, due either to my boredom or the tardiness and overwhelming lack of interest of a lead singer, has turned me into a vocal surrogate at soundchecks. Those are my meager qualifications . . . oh, and a working knowledge of the Wonderkids set earned by rehearsing the songs as Blake's voice-double. Jesus.

"Do you trust me?" He's shaking my shoulders. I'm in a bit of a daze.

"No," I say.

"Fine," says Blake. "Now let's you-go-and-do-this-thing. And don't say a word to the band. They'll just refuse to play. It's better this way."

• • •

I deposit him in the dressing room and walk back to our table without relish, foreknowledge weighing heavily. Fuck knows which award they're up to.

"Everything okay?" asks everyone without the need for actual words. I feel bad that I haven't alerted them.

"Yeah." I can only manage a half-smile. I'm feeling nauseated. It's not like that nightmare where you're taking an exam you haven't revised for—I do at least know the songs—well, it's a bit like that. Blake's asked it of me—okay—but that doesn't stop the Kravitz Center from swaying.

"Man," says Greg. "You look like you've seen a ghost."

"The ghost looks fantastic," I say. "He's raring to go."

At intermission, the band, Greg and I leave the rest of our party at the table and head backstage to the dressing room. Blake has affixed a note on a paper napkin to the room-length mirror with a square inch of soap: "Having a massage." Fuck. Just like before the Pack 'n' Play Festival. And look what happened then. And there we sit, Blakeless once again, twiddling our thumbs; those people who smoke, thinking about smoking, those people who drink, drinking.

"Nice back here," says Greg. "I mean, you could move in, couldn't you? Put a little bed over there, TV over here, kettle— groovy. Bit of a drag getting in past security and that."

No one's nervous, but there's also no natural opportunity for regular conversation, and no one's willing to take that bull by the horns. The moment calls for Greg, a monologue on something irrelevant: "Did I ever tell you about that band Arab Spring? Well, their manager . . ." but Greg perhaps feels a little self-conscious, unnecessarily on best behavior, unusually reticent; he's never known Curtis or Becca that well. Just when we need him most, he goes quiet. In fact, he's doing the *Evening Standard* crossword. He's in Manhattan and he's going the *Evening Standard* crossword. Perky P.A.s and downtrodden gofers keep us apprised of the show's progress. This finally kickstarts Greg into some story that passes a little time.

And then there's Blake, vivid in his white suit, rotating his shoulders as though he really has been massaged. He greets the room with genuine enthusiasm, abject apology, and takes the note off the mirror, as though he doesn't want it to be unclear whether he's back or not. He throws open a wardrobe door and hands me the white suit identical to his: "Throw that on; we're all going to look great tonight, even the crew."

"Guy's just about to induct us," he says cheerily, as I emerge from the bathroom, gleaming, vastly self-conscious. Our favorite P.A. comes to lead us to the side of the stage for the grand entrance. The band is to set up behind the curtain while Blake gives his speech. Blake asked Jack earlier whether he'd like to say anything. Jack said: "I think I'll let the music speak for itself, man." Very wise.

"How about if you let me speak for ourselves?" asked Blake.

"Great, man," Jack said. "Our band," but he said it like he was saying "your band."

Roger Wrong takes the stage. It's a lovely introduction, appropriate to the climax of the evening; he talks about how everything's an opportunity to learn, and how great the Wonderkids were, and then goes on to tell a very brief version of his Blake anecdote.

"Did I do that?" Blake asks. I nod. He grimaces.

"It *was* funny."

"It's funny that I don't remember."

As Roger Wrong goes on, my mind wanders. I feel myself floating like the tiny, stray feather currently fluttering to the ground in the glare of the lighting on the Kravitz Center stage. The feather swishes this way, then that, before it lands, buffeted by otherwise imperceptible eddies and currents of draft at shoe level. I've almost forgotten that I'm going to play some songs; it seems so surreal. I hope my landing is as soft. I had a friend whose first published poem was in *The New Yorker*. My first live stage performance as a lead singer will be to a thousand people in New York City. I first gave a woman an orgasm on the space ride at Disneyland. She's standing behind me now. She squeezes my hand. It's just like the old days. No one else notices. How did we get away with that for so long? Why did we bother?

And then Roger Wrong announces Blake Lear of the Wonderkids, and on Blake walks to, I have to say, an ovation. I wasn't expecting anyone to boo—everyone here knows what's what and who's who and why—but there's genuine adoration, even perhaps a note of apology on behalf of America. Add a dash of redemption into the mix, and you have the cocktail for *a proper comeback*. If only he was actually going to sing . . . or come back . . . but there he is, large as life behind the see-through podium in his white suit, like Alec Guinness, Hopkirk Deceased and David Byrne all rolled into one, but with a cross on his chest.

We are escorted behind the curtain to gather our instruments, or rather for the band to gather their instruments, and me to fiddle with Blake's guitar and check the positioning of his microphone as though he, rather than I, is about to sing. So we can't really watch him. But we can hear.

"Do you ever get the feeling you've been *inducted*?" is Blake's opening sneer: Sex Pistols. Risky, but the audience gets it. "Hey, at last, we get an award. About bloody time! Firstly, I'd like to thank The Man for this." There isn't a monitor near, so I can't be sure, but I imagine him lifting the award skyward, brandishing it in a Heavenly direction. Very Blake. Whether he believes in God is irrelevant. It's just the kind of thing twats do when they get an award. "And I'd like to say this. The Wonderkids were the best band I ever played with; we weren't perfect, but we were a great little band. We tried to communicate directly with the kids, with you, without mediation. We tried to show the kids a little rock 'n' roll, when you lot . . ."—and perhaps he's indicating a few of the stars of the contemporary scene; perhaps he is indicating my girlfriend . . . oh, what is she about to witness . . .—"when you lot were a twinkle in your fathers' eyes." Laughter. Good. It's like listening to the Oscars on the radio.

"I tried to channel Edward Lear, William Blake, and all the poetry I loved into these songs, for which my brother Jack wrote fantastic tunes." His voice floats around us in the hall, disembodied, echoey. "Originally I meant those songs for adults, for everybody—*Everyone Music*—but Nick Hedges over there, who made it all happen, thought that possibly our best audience was children, and that made total sense to me. Kids dream without restraint. Your great Dr. Seuss said that. They don't know how to do it, they just do. And as we grow up, we forget; so my appeal was directly to the subconscious, and that's what they enjoyed. So I'm proud."

I strum the guitar once and check the monitor. I'd need a whole lot more guitar.

"But I feel humble, too, because we weren't ready. And I say that frankly: we made mistakes. We were in untested waters. *We* were the kids. The *kids* were more grown up than us! Maybe that's why they liked us. We didn't mean to, but we screwed up. And for that, we're sorry." There is respectful applause, but I don't want to hear him apologizing for the band, particularly if I am just about to be its lead singer. *One two*, I whisper, as the monitor guy gives me the thumbs up. "Well, we're not entirely sorry, because we enjoyed monkeying around, and we indulged ourselves to the full, and we enjoyed the mums' company, and we made no secret of that then, I guess, which was foolish, and we make no bones about it now because . . . why bother? It was my gang and I was in charge. But we were made an example of. And now the rest of you are all *very* well behaved. Because you worked it out. And I'm pleased we died for your sins.

"But just because you've worked it out, don't always be telling the kids what to do and what to think and how to behave. The environment's up the spout; all animals are endangered species now, including humans; but let the kids be kids. The kids are cool! Just entertain them. That's what we tried to do. You know what nonsense is to kids? It's mother's milk. If you want to send a message, use FedEx. Kids are people too! Free the kids, man!" He's laughing, but all I can think is: he's right about kids, so why is he always wrong about me? "And to anyone who followed us, who took that leap of faith, we love you more than you'll ever know. And if we let you down, we apologize. We've spent the rest of our lives trying to work out how to make that up to you. I tried to be a mate, and I should have tried harder to be a role-model."

And that's when I know he's talking to me. The room's quite silent now. A drumstick skitters away from Curtis across the floor. He winces.

"I have no words of wisdom for you, except don't do what we did. Or do it, and know you'll pay for it. I paid for it, and then I tried to write songs that made perfect sense and that didn't work; so I tried to write a novel that made perfect sense, and that didn't work; and I ended up writing a series of young-adult books under the name Judith Esther, *The Dark-Headed Clock Trilogy*, six of them." Perhaps some people assume he's joking; there's also, however, an audible gasp. He's never mentioned his authorship in public before, and though this comes years after the books' success, their moment in the sun has lingered. They're still in print, still sold in select airport bookstores. "I won't write another of those. It's weird, having success as another person, a person who doesn't exist, but no one really wanted to hear from me, and I'd said all I had to say as Blake Lear. In fact, my life has been one of meaning to do one thing and ending up doing another.

"Sorry, I've gone on. We're really very proud of this award and the band is looking forward to performing for you, but I want to finish with this: I can't stand before you, or even jump around before you, and play these songs. It isn't in me anymore and it just isn't me. I'm no fool. I know when I'm done.

"And now, ladies and gentleman," he adopts a rather stuffy American accent, his old Ed Sullivan routine: "Yesterday and today our theater's been jammed with newspapermen and hundreds of photographers from all over the nation, and these veterans agreed with me that this city never has witnessed the excitement stirred by these youngsters from London and Los Angeles who call themselves the Wonderkids. Now tonight, you're gonna twice be entertained by them. Right now, and again in the second half of our show. Ladies and gentlemen, the Wonderkids! Jack, Curtis, Sweet and Becca! Let's bring them on."

I pick up Blake's guitar. The curtain rises.

The band looks at me. I look at the band. We all heard the speech, but nobody, I think, has been looking at each other aside from the moment Curtis dropped his stick; certainly I haven't been trying to work out what anyone is up to. I've been too busy pretending to ready Blake's equipment, while secretly trying to remember whether we're going to play "Life, As It Is Lived" or "The Story of Dan, Beth, Chris, and Blank" first, before we bring the house down with "Rock Around the Bed." We rehearsed them all, but we decided on two, and my mind has gone . . . "Blank." That was it!

The man in the white suit wafts off to applause, taking the award with him, and glances once over his shoulder: "What are you waiting for?"

Curtis counts 1,2,3,4 and we're playing "Dan, Beth, Chris, and Blank." And suddenly I'm singing: "There once was a girl named Dan / Who loved to fix and loved to fan."

The singing bit is easy; the guitar playing is easy; playing with the band is easy; but the whole thing is very hard. Partly this is because searchlights are circling the audience, and I can see in every eye, including those front and center, that I am a great disappointment. They want Blake. They don't want me. I daren't even look where Joni is sitting. Heaven knows what she's thinking, but she knows it's complicated. And here I am, exactly as I'd expected, the turd in the Super Bowl. I'm not actually doing anything wrong; I'm just not right.

Blake is standing at the side of the stage, conferring with Greg and smiling broadly, despite the fact that this is already the massive anticlimax I'd predicted. The band, on the other hand, is motoring, not in the least bothered that Blake isn't singing and I am; perhaps, I reflect, because they knew. At Blake's right hand, Greg is organizing left and right, an atypical display of leadership. I just go on opening and closing my mouth singing, the band go on playing, about which Jack particularly seems enthused, and the audience goes on being disappointed. The song ends and there is applause—it would be mean to deny us that—but there is no standing ovation. It isn't a nightmare; it doesn't qualify. Perhaps I'd give it a little more wellie if we were going to bother to do the other.

Those Boop girls, the look-alike cigarette girls that I saw swanning about, are now standing in little battalions around the room, all holding silver salvers. I'd thought there were three or four but there seem to be about a hundred Kindie-music storm troopers. Curtis is turning a screw on his snare drum and doesn't seem ready to start the next song. I feel I should say something but all that comes out is: "Sorry I'm not Blake."

I look out into the hall. The cigarette girls now flank every table, large silver-domed serving plates on their arms. Probably dessert. As one, they put the silver salvers down on the tables and remove the tops with a flourish. It's perfectly choreographed, whatever it is they're doing. The serving of the lukewarm starter wasn't nearly this spectacular. I struggle to see what's on offer. I'm the one who should be sitting down there eating ice cream, maybe next to my girlfriend, not standing on the stage.

"Hold on," I ask the house. "What's that?"

"Peanut butter and jelly sandwiches!" someone shouts back. And just as he speaks, the first sandwich, lobbed by one of these agent provocateur Boops, flies towards me on the stage. I duck.

"Hey!" I say. I look over at Blake.

"Chuck it back!" he mimes, laughing. Of course. I should have known. But it's going to take more than an orchestrated food fight to sell the band without him on stage. I pick it up and throw it at him, missing by inches. Curtis counts us in, and we are suddenly Rocking Around the Bed:

"I got my pajamas on and I look like a pirate."

By the time we get to the first chorus, the food has really started to fly. No one wants to eat a PB&J sandwich at the end of a meal, but everyone wants to throw one, if only out of respect to the Wonderkids: behave like kids. It's slow to get going, but quick to escalate. These are little sandwiches, cut into many different geometrical shapes, crusts removed (I happen to note) as I peel half of one, jam side down, from Blake's guitar.

The guitar's owner is still in consultation with Greg. Catching my eye, he licks his index finger and chalks one up to himself in the air. I'm actually doing what comes fairly naturally onstage. I mean, I'm no Blake. I'm not going to pogo or anything, but I can put the song over okay, particularly if there are a few distractions. KISS had stage effects for a reason, right? They weren't that good. Same with me. If Blake provides the fireworks, I'll stand here and recite the lines, but it's just so silly that *he* isn't doing it.

It is now that whoever's in charge of the feathers pulls the switch. And down comes the down. Hundreds of thousands of feathers, every feather in the world, wafts down on us slowly. That first feather I saw while we were waiting at the side of the stage? I hadn't given it a second thought. As they gracefully descend, Greg, stage right, turns on one of those Neil Young industrial strength standing fans, a matching one starts up stage left, and the feathers billow out into the audience. They fired the first volley; here is our riposte. The front tables in particular are bombarded. It is an onslaught of plumage, designed to penetrate every orifice, get caught on any spot of moisture, in drinks, on lips. Meanwhile, the shit actually does hit the fan; the gooey shrapnel of a first macerated sandwich spews all around us, dispersed far and wide by the vicious rotation of the blades. It's like someone in a dunk tank. You just can't resist.

The song is reaching the bridge, the audience is in uproar, and I couldn't have seen Blake even if I was looking for him, let alone Joni. This is partly, I now realize, because huge inflatable pillows, silver like the ones I once saw in the Warhol Museum, are floating down from the ceiling, bouncing up and down in stately, ponderously elegant fashion, like chrome blimps, picking up feathers here, delivering them over there, in calm slow-motion amidst the disorientating anarchy. It's how they'd have done the video way back when if they'd thought of it.

As we reach the last chorus—and this I can see quite clearly—the Cigarette Girls, the Boops (there are about thirty of them) in those black bodices and pencil skirts, come up the stairs in single file and flank me. The band continues full steam ahead as the girls, in one gesture, like a well-drilled chorus line, which is precisely what they are, rip off their tops with the surgical precision of seasoned burlesque artistes to reveal borderline pornographic bras, upon which the tops of their boobs rest. There is no actual nipple on display, primarily through judicious use of flesh-colored Micropore.

I look down at Niall, tarred and feathered, at the front table, half-expecting to see regret, even anger, in his eyes, but he is pissing himself with laughter, clapping along, receiving plaudits from the rest of his party. He fucking knew about this. Everyone knew about it. Did the band know? By the expression on Jack's face, yes, and he can't believe his luck.

And as we hit the last chorus, the Boops, at Greg's signal, squeeze some contraption . . . well, to be honest, I don't precisely know what the hell they do, but huge arcs of white liquid (let's presume milk, mother's milk) spray over the audience. Have you ever seen that bloke who can throw cards miles into a theater? The milk goes further than that. And it keeps flying, cascading down on the audience in giant ribbons. The nearest Boop turns and lets me have it right in the face. What could I do but open my mouth?

The audience is pounding the floor. I mean, we are it, and it is now, and we are all in one room, and it isn't time to stop. So we just keep playing the chorus over and over until the feathers have finally fallen and the food has stopped flying. Blake dances across the stage, one movement from left to right, and the audience, those who weren't already on their feet, stand to applaud, and as he passes me, he winks again—*Trust your old Dad, mate*—but this time the wink hits me a different way, and he registers my reaction: I couldn't even manage a smile. He waltzes off stage right.

I've seen the Wonderkids whip a crowd up, but this is beyond beyond; it's the adult energy, the fact that the audience is full of performers willing to muck in, unleashed at the end of a long evening, sheer relief, nonsense. It's ordained mayhem—Niall was clearly in on it with Greg and Blake—but its effect is unconfined. Above all, it is Blake, stage-managing, instigating the whole thing.

When we finally finish, after a climactic chord that goes on for about a minute as we applaud one another with our strumming, surrounded by Boops, covered in food and feathers, slipping in milk, Curtis shouts: "One more?"

"You think we're topping that?" yells Jack. "Leave 'em wanting more. We're done. They'll have to come to the Festival." Then he points at me and gives me the thumbs up. It's just assumed that I'm going to do this. The Boops walk off without any acknowledgement at all. Their night's work is done. Niall bounces up on to the stage before the audience drifts away.

"Wow! The Wonderkids! Nothing's going to top that," he announces to an audience who know they've seen all they can see. "I promised I'd get you the Wonderkids and I got you the Wonderkids! They'll be playing the Prospect Park KidCon Festival on Saturday! See you at next year's Jim-Jammies!"

The house band is back in position and starts to play, instruments untarnished by fluff, preserve, or cream. They'd known to remove their instruments. Of course they'd known. Blake knew; Greg knew; Niall knew; everyone knew except the audience and me. Becca's arm slips around me and she hugs me, but I suddenly feel very self-conscious about Joni: where is she? There seems now to be no distinction between the audience and the stage. Where the fuck is health and safety? How was this even allowed? Security!

"Greg," I shout. He is in conference with Niall.

"Good job, mate," he yells, heading towards me.

"Prospect Park's going to be great," shouts Niall.

"I'm not doing it!" I shout back. They both nod, letting me know that I am. I meet them halfway. "Why can't Blake do it? He's the lead singer. It can be the last ever gig."

"Dunno," says Greg, "you ask him."

"Where is he?" I ask vaguely, surveying the wreckage. "You knew all about this, right?"

"Yeah, man. We were at this soundstage on 27th running the timings all afternoon."

"That's where Blake was?"

"Oh yeah. Of course."

"So you've known all day . . ."

"I've known for fucking weeks. And I've never worked so hard in my life." Greg is quite unperturbed. He is, in fact, acting like a manager. I can tell because it is so extremely unlike how he normally acts. "These things don't happen by magic."

"They certainly don't," confirms Niall, with a raised eyebrow implying that there has also been insane expense.

". . . And, Greg," I continue, "you sat there all evening pretending to be worried whether Blake would show up or not."

"Yeah. Blake told me to." He picks feathers from my shoulder, as though one or two will make a difference.

"You're such a liar."

"I know, mate." He laughs and shrugs. "I'm the best liar in

the world, always have been, because people like it when I do."

"Well, I fucking don't!" It just comes out of me that way, angry, brutal. I turn away, shouting over my shoulder: "I fucking don't like it at all."

"What's wrong?" He can't believe I'm upset. He thinks perhaps I'm joking. It's the only explanation. "Hey! What's wrong?"

This evening is done and there will be no repeat performance. Of course, Blake is nowhere to be seen. Greg is trying to calm me down.

"Where the fuck is Blake?" I shout at no one.

I text Joni to meet me at the soundboard. I haven't spent a moment with her the whole evening, hardly said "hello": bad boyfriend. The great thing is, she understands. I was working, entirely focused on my charges, on my lead singer's absence. She looks beautiful in her electric blue dress; she isn't even fiddling with her phone, just waiting for me with a smile.

"Hey," she says. "You almost pulled that off."

"Never again." I hug her.

"Dark horse. You never told me you were going to . . ."

"I'm not a dark horse. I only found out at the last minute. Same as usual."

"Poor baby." Her sympathy is genuine. She's heard the stories. "I'll never make you do that for me. I promise."

"I know. Thanks." Suddenly, I feel like crying. "Will you be here? I have to talk to Blake, tell him I won't sing at this stupid Festival. But I have no idea where he is."

"Oh, I know *precisely* . . ." She points behind her through the plate-glass windows to the fountain where Blake is wading underneath the central spray, still in the white suit that so perfectly matches mine. I turn to leave without so much as a word. She grabs my arm just as she did the very first time we met: "What about me?" We kiss; she tastes of . . . peanuts. "You really weren't bad, but stick to what you're good at."

She isn't even teasing. I like it. "Road managing?"

"And romancing," she whispers.

• • •

By the time I get to the fountain, Blake is sitting on the edge, soaked, paddling; he's taken his shoes off, as though that was plain common sense. His clothes remain defiantly on. He beckons me with a cheery wave, splashes me.

"Quack! Get in!" he says. "Water's lovely." He's made a little origami boat from a page of the program; it's bobbing across the water.

"Hey, what an ending!" he shouts. "What an ending! Amazing ending, right?"

"Yes." I can't help but smile. He looks so harmless with his hair plastered flat over his forehead. He spits water from his mouth and wipes his sleeve across his brow. "A great ending, Blake."

He wrinkles his nose and sniffs, skimming an imaginary stone across the surface: "But it's the wrong ending, isn't it?"

"Yes," I say.

"You did sing for me when I asked you, though. Thank you."

"Yes. And now you're going to sing for me."

"Right," he says. "I'll be singing at the Festival, then."

"It's what you're good at," I say. "What else you gonna do? Do what you're made to do, and I'll do what I do. And I'll help you do what you do. And that's how we'll work."

"It's that simple, isn't it? Sorry for failing to notice that you're not me. C'mon! Get in, Sweet! Get your feet wet."

"Blake, why on earth would I want to get in? I should be telling you to get out. I don't want to get wet."

"Well, at least you have a change of clothes backstage. I got nothing. Look, I'll sing at the Festival. Get in. Actually, I'll only sing at the Festival *if* you get in."

"You're so annoying."

I sit down beside him, and he puts his big arm around me, as the fountain continues its rainbow routine. The door from the auditorium opens and music spills out on to the plaza. Joni.

"Towel?" she shouts, then noticing the development. "Oh! *Towels*?"

"TWO!" I yell back.

I take Blake by the hand and pull him up so we're both standing. Drenched, in our matching white suits, we stand in the arc of the fountain, shivering, waiting for the towels to arrive.

Seven Songs

Rock Around the Bed

I've got my pajamas on, I look like a pirate
I got some knock-knock jokes in my back pocket
I've got a rocket and I know how to fire it
I'm full of desire

I got a tennis racket that looks like a guitar
And an actual facsimile of Noah's Ark
A safari park, full of zebras and swans
My trains are all gone

I'm gonna rock around the bed
Gonna rock around the bed
I got a song stuck in my head
I'm gonna rock around the bed
And you can keep your peanut butter and your sliced white bread
I got a song stuck in my head
I'm gonna rock around the bed

I've got my blazer on and I look like a moron
I got a satchel I dropped in a big old puddle
And it's all a muddle but I know the scores
The chart positions and the dates of wars

Since I heard the first chord of "Hard Day's Night"
My love of sport abated
Used to make me feel alright but now it seems so overrated
Just for lightweights

I'm gonna rock around the bed
Gonna rock around the bed
I got a song stuck in my head
I'm gonna rock around the bed
And you can keep your ham and cheese in your mini-baguette
I got a song stuck in my head
I'm gonna rock around the bed

I met a girl who was a little bit older
She smelled of Body Shop and instant coffee
I offered her a toffee and she told me where to go
Like I'd offered her a cold

Then I met a girl I couldn't label
With her long dark fringe, she looked like a painting
She pushed me back on the kitchen table and I nearly fainted
As we got acquainted

Dear diary
I will no longer keep you
I am inspired to write poetry
My notebooks will be spiral bound
And they will quite astound

I'm gonna rock around the bed
Gonna rock around the bed
I got a song stuck in my head
I'm gonna rock around the bed
And you can keep your panini and zucchini bread
I got a song stuck in my head
Gonna rock around the bed

Lucky Duck

Kiss a duck to change your luck
Lucky duck
Place a penny on a dump truck
Lucky duck
In your garden, plant a ball
If it ever grows at all
One day, you will find a buck
Lucky Duck
Lucky Duck

Kiss a duck to change your luck
Lucky Duck
See a flower grow from muck
Lucky Duck
Close your eyes and count to ten
Do not open them again
Until the midnight clock has struck
Lucky Duck
Lucky Duck

Kiss a duck to change your luck
Lucky Duck
Throw an oyster you have shucked
Lucky Duck
If you see a dragonfly
Whirring in the evening sky
One day you will run amuck
Lucky Duck

Kiss a duck to change your luck
Lucky Duck
Kiss a girl and be heart-struck
Lucky Duck
Kiss her ankles, kiss her eyes
Kiss hello and kiss goodbye
Kiss a duck to change your luck
Lucky Duck

The Story of Dan, Beth, Chris, and Blank

There once was a girl named Dan
Who loved to fix and loved to fan:
She blowed and blowed
And sewed and sewed
And needled and needled
And wheedled and seedled.
She loved to fix and loved to fan
And that's the story of Dan.

There once was a fella named Beth
Who loved to break and hold his breath.
Inhaled, inhaled
And sailed and sailed
Navigated, navigated.
Stavikated, avadrated.
She loved to break and hold his breath
And that's the story of Beth.

There once was a cat named Chris
Who loved to kill and loved to kiss
He washed and wished
And fussed and fished
And lettered and littered
And glittered and twittered
She loved to kill and loved to kiss
And that's the story of Chris.

There once was a what named Blank
Who loved to drink as it sat and thank
So sipped and sipped
and supped and supped
The opposite. So neither did—quite ill-fitted,
to say what's the wrong of the . . .
(Zank!)
It loved to drink as it sat and thank
And that's the Story of Blank.

Why I Cry

The shiny-coats are coming!
The hummingbirds aren't humming.
They're flittering, anxious, and asking why:
Why I cry—
Why I *cry*

The cardinals are meeting!
The little lambs aren't bleating.
They're sermonizing, theorizing why:
Why I cry—
Why I *cry*

The animals embarking!
But Noah isn't arking.
Dogfish chasing oysters asking why;
Why I cry—
Why I *cry*

And it's the kind of a question
That leads to suggestion
I'd like your discres-tion, my friends
The reason I'm crying
No question of lying
Is that this song has come to an end.

The Dog Mustn't Speak!

Action, action, action,
Said the dog unto his faction.
The squiggles, curves—the skunk—was set
And now on: to bigger fish, he bet.
I bet! Let's let the poodle's posture employ,
inform, destroy, each thing. Be coy.

The dog mustn't speak!
The dog mustn't speak!
Not out of his nozzle
Or his toothy smiling beak,
The dog mustn't speak!
His sweet slobber can clobber
As he spits and sparks
His sugared word-barks
Not a squeak!
The dog mustn't speak!

Quickly, quickly, quickly
The skunk is smelling rather sickly.
Of course he is! He's bad on purpose.
Uh-*huh:* his depth's below the surface.
Believe. New reasons have a queer sound;
Whatever do you ask (you don't) the deer hound.

Chorus

Should every single common ca*nine*
Have its precious special sun*shine*?

Stay back, stay back, stay back
The Pooch as bucks and bones distract,
(this to his own reflection, by the way)
though not a message, just a mess, to say—
(he reads) and just a second, at a glance—
It knows. I haven't hooves and I can't dance.

Chorus

The Second Pear Tree

Yes, come and climb the second pear tree.
Because it might in fact be where she
Has sat up high; she wandered clear once
Against the rain and rays. Appearance
Always suggests the way to go.
You think about it yes and no.
Determine whether acting won't—
Will make things worse and don't
Demand solutions drinkable:
Suppose a problem unthinkable.
Don't hide beneath the hackberry bush
And though it might seem scary, push
Yourself and climb the second pear tree.

Yes, come and climb the second pear tree.
Because it might exactly be where she
Lives to this day; she flew there once
And made a bed of branches. Existence
Offered her a place to stay
Among the hedgehogs and their hay.
Regardless of the emphasis
We feel we need to ask you this
The overpass is underwhelming, no?
There is so much to run from. Where to go?
Don't hide yourself inside the herd
And though it might seem scary, gird
Your loins and climb the second pear tree.

It could in fact
—it might—
Be where she isn't.

Noon in June

Summer can, in trying to please,
Unsettle you by subtle degrees,
Painting your problems blacker. Freeze!
A noon in June implodes. You're left,
You're spent, you're drained, gray matter bereft,
Perspective gone, horizon dimmed,
Your joie de vivre, stolen, skimmed
Summer will return so soon
One noon in June
One noon in June
Summer will return so soon
One noon in June

The spring she will, in different ways
Cost far more than kings can pay,
Their welcome on her throne outstayed
A day in May escapes. You're right,
You're up, you're scuppered, gone the light
Italics in, Italians out
Reigns of doubt and rainbow trout
Spring, she will come back this way
One day in May
One day in May
Spring, she will come back this way
One day in May

Winter does produce its blues,
Auburns also in the fall
(The autumn oughtn't call at all)
Seasons colder reason
Eggs us on to plots and treason
So let's stop there
Two seasons, surely more than fair

Summer will return so soon
One noon in June
One noon in June

Summer will return so soon
One noon in June

Spring, she will come back this way
One day in May
One day in May
Spring, she will come back this way
One day in May

Chapter Titles

1. Ravi Shankar, *The Concert for Bangladesh*, 1971
2. Foghat, The Backstage, Seattle, 1996
3. Lynyrd Skynyrd, *One More From The Road*, 1976
4. The Beatles' Rooftop Performance, London, 1969
5. Elvis Presley, *'68 Comeback Special*, 1968
6. Lou Reed, The Bottom Line, New York City, 1979
7. Cheap Trick, *Cheap Trick at Budokan*, 1978
8. Woodstock Stage Announcement, 1969
9. Thin Lizzy, *Live and Dangerous*, 1978
10. Kiss, *Alive II*, 1977
11. Led Zeppelin, Felt Forum, New York City, 1973
12. The Sex Pistols, Winterland Ballroom, San Francisco, 1978
13. Woodstock Stage Announcement, 1969
14. The Rolling Stones, *Get Yer Ya-Ya's Out,* 1970
15. Johnny Cash, *At San Quentin*, 1969
16. Bob Dylan, Olympia Theatre, Paris, 1966
17. Neil Young, *Year of the Horse*, 1996
18. The Beatles' Royal Variety Performance, London, 1963

Acknowledgments

Special thanks to Mark Krotov for a fantastic edit, and Jennifer Rudolph Walsh and Kirby Kim at WME.

Many thanks to Eleanor and Matthew Friedberger, who helped give the Wonderkids words and songs worth singing; and to Tom Benson for his review.

And thanks also to the following, who lived this novel with me in some or other way: Adam Barker, Peter Barnes, Patrick Berkery, Joel Bernstein, Kurt Bloch, Jeff Bogle, Lisa Brown, Peter Buck, Eddie Carlson, Rosanne Cash, Ed Chauncy, Bill Childs, Joe Cohen, Glen Colson, Rick Danko, Martin Deeson, Tom de Waal, Glenn Dicker, Adam Gold, David Grand, Daniel Handler, James Healey, Levon Helm, Dan Hicks, Mark Hoyt, Garth Hudson, Mike Leahy, David Lewis, Robert Lloyd, Mark Linington, Steve Martin, Billy Maupin, Eric Mayers, Scott McCaughey, Chris Mills, Eugene Mirman, Rick Moody, Mark Morris, David Nagler, Kathy O'Connell, Andy Paley, Joe Pernice, Dave Rave, Josh Ritter, Tom Robinson, John Roderick, Gabe Roth, Carla Sacks, Abbey Stace, Christopher Stace, Al Stewart, Duncan Thicket, Jeroen van der Meer, Chris von Sneidern, Loudon Wainwright III, Gustafer Yellowgold, and Dan Zanes.

The Songs and Lyrics

Rock Around the Bed (E. Friedberger/Stace), Lucky Duck (E. Friedberger/Stace), The Story of Dan, Beth, Chris, and Blank (M. Friedberger/Stace), Why I Cry (M. Friedberger/Stace), The Dog Mustn't Speak (M. Friedberger/Stace), The Second Pear Tree (M. Friedberger/Stace), Noon in June (M. Friedberger/Stace), Fresh Air for My Nose (Stace). All songs published either by EF Debris/Plangent Visions (ASCAP) or EF Debris/Friedberger/Friedberger/Plangent Visions (ASCAP).